Dark Places

Books by Reavis Z. Wortham

The Red River Mysteries

The Rock Hole

Burrows

The Right Side of Wrong

Vengeance is Mine

Dark Places

Dark Places

A Red River Mystery

Reavis Z. Wortham

Poisoned Pen Press

First Edition 2015

10 9 8 7 6 5 4 3 2 1

Library of Congress Catalog Card Number: 2014958040

ISBN: 9781464204227 Hardcover
9781464204241 Trade Paperback

Poisoned Pen Press
6962 E. First Ave., Ste. 103
Scottsdale, AZ 85251
www.poisonedpenpress.com
info@poisonedpenpress.com

Printed in the United States of America

This book is dedicated to my maternal grandparents,
Joe and Esther (Estelle Gentry) Armstrong,
the real Ned and Miss Becky Parker.
"Daddy Joe" and "Mama Esther" never realized
the impact they would have on my life.

Acknowledgments

Some folks say my second novel in the Red River series, *Burrows*, was dark. One review said it was Stephen King meets Harper Lee. I guess it was dramatically different than *The Rock Hole* and the books after that. In a sense, *Burrows* explored a darkness inside of me that manifested itself in nightmares. Once I wrote that book, the monthly nightmares of tunnels, burrows, and claustrophobic underground crawlspaces ended. I'm sure a psychiatrist would suggest it was a catharsis or cleansing through the written word, and maybe that's what happened. Who knows?

In this book, *Dark Places*, I felt the need to explore the darkness that surrounds us all. Most of us in this country are fortunate to live with a minimum of emotional trauma, though it's always an unfortunate part of life. But there is darkness all around us, even though we might not see it. Have you ever thought that you've probably been within reach of a murderer at some point in your life, or at the very least, passed one on the highway, on the street, or in a shopping mall? If you drive much, I know you've been close to a drunken driver who may someday cause someone's serious injury or death, if they haven't already. People are always out there who would love to hurt you for the sheer joy of it, or to steal your money, either at gunpoint, or by cyber theft. Have you ever wondered what kind of darkness your friends, and even family members, hold inside themselves? I've explored this world through my characters, but they speak to us with the assistance of many, and not just the fingertips that types these words.

As in the past, many people have supported my work by reading early manuscripts, offering suggestions, and spreading the word about my novels. I won't try to list the dozens of people who fit into the above categories, but a few have to appear, because they are as much a part of this new career as I am.

Thanks to my mentor John Gilstrap; Craig Johnson; Sandra Brannan; Jeffery Deaver; Joe Lansdale (for showing me the road many, many years ago); Ronda Wise (for her ongoing medical advice); Sharon Reynolds and Mike Miller (for reading those first manuscripts); my English teacher daughter Chelsea Wortham Hamilton (for reading and offering academic insights that I never considered); my agent Anne Hawkins (who still believes in me); Poisoned Pen Press editors Annette Rogers (who always brings out more even when I think I'm finished); and Barbara Peters (who suggested necessary improvements that this manuscript desperately needed); and of course, the love of my life, my wife Shana, (who is always at my side). You all offer more faith than I deserve.

And thanks to you, the readers out there who support my work. It is humbling.

Following, is the complete Navajo Prayer of Healing that Betty spoke to Ned here in *Dark Places*. She used part, but not all of it in the novel, and it is too beautiful to present only small bits.

Navajo Prayer of Healing

In the house made of dawn.
In the story made of dawn.
On the trail of dawn.
O, Talking God.
His feet, my feet, restore.
His limbs, my limbs, restore.
His body, my body, restore.
His mind, my mind, restore.
His voice, my voice, restore.
His plumes, my plumes, restore.
With beauty before
him, with beauty before me.
With beauty behind him, with beauty behind me.
With beauty above him, with beauty above me.
With beauty below him, with beauty below me.
With beauty around him, with beauty around me.
With pollen beautiful in his voice, with pollen
beautiful in my voice.
It is finished in beauty. It is finished in beauty.
In the house of every light.
From the story
made of evening light.
On the trail of evening light.

Chapter One

The oil road stretching into the darkness made me feel queasy, giving me a sense that I'd been there before. Some folks call it *déjà vu*, but in Lamar County, Texas, we call it swimmy-headed.

The dull, sick feeling came from dreams of a flat, empty highway disappearing into a dark fog. The problem was my dreams have a bad habit of coming true.

My grandmother, Miss Becky, says it's a Poisoned Gift, and she's right. I'm not the only one who has it. My Uncle Cody sometimes dreams of what's to come, and not too long ago, I found out my Grandpa Ned once had a vision that no one ever talks about.

That's another reason I's half-sick. We were close to that spooky old Ordway Place. I was as afraid of that house as I was of a *bear*, and it scared the peewaddlin' out of me to even ride past in the truck. I'd seen ghosts coming down the staircase when Pepper lived there, and then only a few months ago, it was a slaughterhouse when Grandpa, Uncle Cody, and Mr. John Washington had a bloody shootout with a bunch of Las Vegas gangsters.

And here we were within spittin' distance of it again.

It hadn't been dark long, and we were shining flashlights every which-a-way, up in trees, and on each other. I bet from a distance that night, the six of us kids looked like a search party coming down the road.

Pepper kept her light pointed at her feet in case there was a snake on the still-warm road. Lots of folks who don't know us think we're twins. They can tell right quick though, after they've been around us for a while, that we're nothing alike.

Pepper loved adventure, but I'd rather have been home with a book. Instead, I was out cattin' around with a bunch of fartknockers to keep her out of trouble.

The head fartknocker was Cale Westlake. He gave me that look that he thought was cool, but it only made me know for sure I still didn't like him worth a flip. He'd taken to keeping his long hair out of his eyes with a silly strip of leather, like an Indian.

I usually didn't want to have no part of Cale and his gang of jerks, but Pepper'd been acting like she didn't have good sense because she started liking him again. He found out right quick that Pepper wasn't going to sneak out of her daddy's house and go adventuring with him that Friday night without me.

The Toadies rolled their eyes and held flashlights under their chins, making spooky faces. I was already bored with that. "Let's go over to Mr. Sims' pool."

Cale shined his light in my face for pure-dee meanness, blinding me. When I closed my eyes, he grabbed me in a headlock. I tried to push away, but he squeezed tighter. "Holler calf rope."

"No!"

He twisted his arm, grinding my head. "Holler calf rope!"

I tried to play possum, but it hurt too bad. "Okay! Calf rope!"

He turned loose. "You don't get to talk out here, Mouse. Remember that. You're just along for the ride, so shut up." He'd taken to calling me that to get my goat. "Frankie here says ol' Doc Daingerfield bought the Ordway house and has a monkey chained to that big pear tree out back. That's where we're going."

I felt sick at my stomach again as I rubbed my tingling ears.

Frankie felt pretty important to have information we didn't know. "Daddy said Doc Daingerfield has more money than he has sense to sink all that cash in putting this house back into shape."

Cale worked the beam of his flashlight over Pepper while Frankie talked, like he was painting her with a brush. The yellow light went up from her belt, past the fringe vest and big-sleeved shirt, and then stopped on her chest. I don't think he realized he was a-doin' it, because when he glanced over and saw me watching, he shined it back on Frankie. "I don't give a shit about that. Tell them about the monkey."

"Oh." Frankie stopped to regain his thought. "Uh, well, him and Daddy were talking about Daingerfield retiring from his vet'nary practice and moving here from town. That's when I saw the monkey climb out of the tree and pick up something off the ground. Then he shinnied back up there quick as you please. They got a harness on 'im and a long dog chain, so he won't go nowhere."

Pepper stuffed her fingers in the pocket of her jeans. "So what difference does it make?"

"We're gonna steal that monkey."

To tell the truth, the idea of a monkey was intriguing. "What are you gonna do with a stole monkey?"

My question threw Cale off. "Well…"

The idea popped out of my mouth before I realized it. "Hey, how about letting it loose in the Baptist church on Sunday morning?"

For the first time since I'd come to live in Center Springs a little over three years earlier, the kids looked at me with some respect. Even Pepper was shocked. "Shit! That's brilliant, but why the *Baptist* church?"

"Because I don't want to scare Miss Becky at the Assembly of God, and yours is the biggest one we have, next to the Presbyterians, so there'll be more people."

"That's it, then." Cale waved his hand, as if he was blessing the idea. His daddy was the Baptist preacher, and he didn't have much use for any of the other churches. He led off, with the rest of us lined up like baby ducks. "Lights out."

We used the silvery light of the three-quarter moon to cross the pasture toward the road. Bringing up the rear, Pepper whispered in my ear. "It's a good idea for *these* dumbasses, but what'n hell are you doing?"

I realized that I was tired of being by myself all the time with only Pepper to hang out with, and lately, she was being a horses' ass about anything and everything if it didn't have to do with them hippies and California.

"Hey, it sounded like a good idea to me."

"Well, it ain't smart."

Her sudden turnabout had me off balance. I never did understand how her mind worked. "None of this is smart, but we're out here 'cause you been making goo-goo eyes at that fool up there in the lead."

"They're not goo-goo eyes. He's not so bad to hang out with now that he's let his hair grow out, and besides, he hates Center Springs as much as I do. I'm scared to death I'll never get anywhere other'n where I'm from."

She'd been complaining about our community for quite a while, mostly after she started listening to that new kind of rock 'n' roll music and watching them hippie kids talk about peace and love and the new generation.

"You're only going to get in trouble hanging around with him." I sounded like Grandpa.

A ball of fear caught up with me again when that big ol' spooky house full of bloody murder and ghosts came into view. It rose above the trees like a nightmare and it took everything I had to get moving. Stomach clenched like a condemned man walking to the gallows, and shivering like a Chihuahua, I crossed the road.

We stopped beside the tired old garage. I'd already spotted the chain wrapped around the pear tree. Pepper leaned around me and then ducked back against the peeling boards. Her whisper wasn't much more quiet than her everyday voice. "Shit! That chain's on there with a bolt. We don't have any tools with us."

"No problem." Cale unfolded a sharp pocketknife. "Frankie says Cheeta there is wearing a harness. Rex, we'll cut it off and use your belt as a collar until we find some rope."

"It won't fit around a monkey's neck, it'll be too big."

"We'll poke another hole in it."

"Nope, it's new and Mama will kill me if she found out."

Cale glared like Rex owed him money. "All right, then. We can wrap it around his chest a couple of times and pull it tight like a girth."

I wanted to tell him that I doubted the monkey would sit still while strangers hacked at his harness with a pocketknife and then strapped him tight with a belt, but I decided not to open my mouth.

Goosebumps rose as I snuck up to that gnarly pear tree. The chain disappeared into the darkness. I shuddered, staring upward, every muscle in my body twitching like I'd stuck my finger in a light socket.

Cale and the others strolled right up to it like they were supposed to be there. Frankie grabbed the chain and gave it a tug. He must have felt that since he'd been the first one to see the monkey, he knew all about them.

He gave it a second yank, harder, like pulling on a vine. I guess he thought the monkey might just fall out, or come down like a puppy. "It's tight up there. You think it's wrapped around a limb or something?"

Cale studied on it like he was doing an arithmetic problem, but I knew his grades and there wasn't any hope he could figure it out. "Swing on it and see."

Before Rex could bear down on the chain, I aimed my light up in the tree and the whole world went to pieces. Two dogs came roaring at us from under the porch. I guess they were sound asleep and woke up when we started yammering at one another. We were lucky they were chained to the porch or I believe they'd have eaten us alive. Instead of trying to bite us, they got tangled up and went to fighting.

I wanted to scream, but nothing worked right. Pepper grabbed my arm and for a moment, I couldn't breathe. That's when I thought I was gonna die.

I guess that old monkey didn't like for anyone to shine a light on him in the middle of the night, or maybe he was laying asleep on a limb and the barking dogs startled him. He fell.

I've been scared before, but nothing like the horror I felt when that chain-rattling creature suddenly dropped on me and grabbed aholt with *hands*. The monkey clawed at me and I went to squalling and a-running. It was screaming in my ear and all I could see were lips pulled back to show a mouth full of man-eating teeth.

If I'd been one of them dope-smoking hippies, I would have probably understood strange sensations on and in my head, but it was the monkey's tail wrapped around my throat that sealed the deal. That kind of thing is *unnatural*.

Pepper dropped her light and fled the scene, running across the yard, thinking there might be another killer monkey about to attack *her*. Racing through the darkness, she was short enough to run under the empty, sagging clothesline. Cale wasn't so lucky and dang near throttled himself.

While they went one way, I skinned off away from the Death House. Despite the monkey, I was making a pretty clean getaway too and had a good head of steam when I hit the end of that chain. The monkey had such a tight grip on my head that when we ran out of slack it yanked me right off my feet.

The last thing I saw was my P.F. Flyers rising in the moonlight. I slammed to the ground like a poleaxed steer and lay there with the wind knocked out of me, which is probably what saved me from further monkey molestations. Cheeta didn't like being on the ground, so he bit my ear for good measure and scampered back up his tree to sit there, jabbering and throwing rotten pears at anything that moved.

Somebody picked me up and set me on my feet. "You all right, son?" My head spun for a second until I could focus on Doc Daingerfield. His white head almost glowed in the moonlight. "I said you all right?"

I nodded.

"You're Top Parker, right?"

"Yessir."

"C'mon in the house. Let's doctor that bite on your ear."

I didn't answer, because there was nothing *to* say.

Once on the porch, Doc Daingerfield held the door. I stopped in the spill of yellow light. Cale, Pepper, and the Toadies were long gone.

He gave me a little nudge into the foyer. "Did you learn anything tonight?"

"Yessir. Don't mess with a monkey in a pear tree."

Chapter Two

The warm nighttime breeze carried a blend of fresh popcorn, cigarettes, and the smoke from burning mosquito repellant coils into the crowded '51 Dodge truck. Marty Smallwood rested his left elbow next to the silver cast-metal speaker hanging in the open window, a can of warm Miller High Life dangling loose between his fingertips. John T. West, celebrating his recently regained freedom, mirrored Marty's position from the shotgun seat. He'd only been out of the Fort Worth jail for a month, and still had the stink of the place in his nostrils.

Freddy Vines was, as usual, the baloney in the sandwich, trying to watch the picture around the windshield's center dividing post.

On the only drive-in movie screen in Chisum, Texas, Warren Beatty stuck a cigar in his mouth and hefted two pistols in *Bonnie and Clyde*.

Marty wished he was alone in the truck with his ex-girlfriend, Shirley Fields. He'd-a lot rather have his hand under her sweater and thinking of Faye Dunaway than sit with the same two boneheads he'd been running with since they were all knee-high to a grasshopper.

"Watch this." He pulled the headlights on, lighting the car ahead, and the startled couple snuggled up in the seat. A horn honked as the couple flipped them off in the glare. Other horns answered from across the drive-in.

Marty laughed and slapped the lights off.

"That wathn't burry funny." Freddy's lisp had been a lifetime embarrassment. He was careful to disagree with anything Marty and John T. said or did, because they might not let him hang out with them anymore. Sometimes they made fun of his speech impediment, but neither one ever turned down his offer to pay for food, gas, or beer.

"Who's that?" John T. squinted through the smoke rising from a cigarette in the corner of his mouth. Right hand occupied with the beer can, he pointed with his little finger. He always moved with a minimum of effort.

The well-dressed man in question threaded his way through the rows of cars, balancing a cardboard tray full of popcorn and watered-down soft drinks. He was obviously a stranger to Chisum, because no one wore suits to a drive-in on Friday nights in northeast Texas. He stopped at a 1964 Impala parked ahead and to the right.

Marty barely took his eyes off the gigantic screen. He fancied himself as cool as Beatty. "I dunno. Some guy I saw in front of the courthouse a couple of days ago, hanging around with another guy, taking pictures in front of the statue and hammin' it up."

The man passed drinks through the open window. Marty twisted the speaker dial and lowered the tinny volume. "Guy dressed like that needs somebody to bring them down a peg or two."

"I can do it." John T. drained his rodeo-cool beer and pulled another from the cardboard box under his feet. He levered a triangular hole in the top with a church key hanging on a string around his neck and cut a vent hole on the opposite side.

"Whath the matter with you guys? It cost uth a dollar and a half to get in here and you're talking over the movie. We're gettin' to the beth part."

"Thut up, Freddy." Marty's response was without emphasis or expression. "I bet they're rich."

"What makes you say that?"

"They're driving a brand new car and wearing suits to the drive-in. Only rich people would do that."

The man opened the driver's door, but the dome light only allowed a glimpse of dark suits and oily hair slicked back and smooth. When he slid into the seat and slammed the door, the metal speaker jumped off the window.

"Dumb bastards." John T. lit snapped his Zippo alight with a practiced flip the girls always liked, and blew smoke into the night air. "You can break the glass that a-way."

"Rich people don't care."

Marty studied the car before turning his attention to the sedan beside them. He could only see a girl's leg, since she was sitting under the driver's arm. He tried to peek under the roofline, but with no luck. "Why do you think them rich guys came here tonight?"

John T. shrugged and watched two giggling teenage girls pass on their way to the concession stand. He unconsciously pulled the short sleeve of his tight tee-shirt higher over his bicep.

Marty reached past Freddy and flipped the pack of Camels from John T.'s other sleeve. He shook one out, lipped it, and scratched a kitchen match to light. "Let's have some fun with those city fellers."

"Like what?"

Marty blew a thick stream of smoke through both nostrils. "Like take 'em on a snipe hunt."

The cruel Southern rite of passage involved taking an unsuspecting victim into the dark woods and leaving them there with the empty promise that a fictional bird would run into a bag.

John T. cut his eyes through the smoke. "Strangers won't go with you. That sounds like something Knothead here would say."

Freddy wished they could get back to the movie. "How about thome popcorn? I'll buy."

In the Impala's front passenger seat, the passenger opened his door and headed toward the concession stand.

Marty lifted the speaker off the window and hung it on the post. "This cheap-ass Oklahoma beer is running straight through me." He yanked on the stubborn handle and the door creaked loudly as it swung open.

"Hey, get thome popcorn."

"Shut up, Freddy."

Bustling with activity, the concession stand was an oasis of light. A line of chattering teenagers stretched back to the screen door, waiting their turn to order refreshments. Marty scanned the customers' faces and not seeing Suit Number Two, he rounded the building.

A couple of fourteen-year-old boys with hair over their collars loafed outside the doorless restroom, sharing a stolen cigarette. He shouldered past them, knocking one off balance.

"Hey!"

Marty shot the youngster a look. The kid immediately broke eye contact and toed the ground. Inside, Suit Two was washing his hands when Marty caught the man's eye in the mirror. "You don't buy beer, you just rent it."

The comment earned him a brief smile and a nod in response.

His opening gambit failed, Marty tried again. "I don't believe I've seen you in town before."

Suit Two drug a pocket comb through short, thick hair. "Here on business is all."

"What brings you to a one-horse town like Chisum?"

The guy replaced the comb in an inside coat pocket, clearly ready to leave. A bulge in his coat convinced Marty the man carried a thick wallet. "Like I said, business."

"What kind of..."

Suit Two left, disappearing through the open door and leaving Marty hanging.

Heat rose in his face from the brush-off and embarrassment. "Unfriendly son of a bitch." He checked for feet under the stall, hoping no one had heard the exchange. The kids were gone when he was back outside.

John T. was working on a fresh beer when Marty returned to the truck. He slammed the door and hung the speaker back on the window. "I was right. That guy's wallet is fat with money."

Inspired by the shootout on the huge screen and his recent vacation with some of Fort Worth's toughest criminals, John T. had an idea. "Then let's rob 'em."

"Hey!" Freddy started.

Marty grinned. It was the perfect suggestion to pay the stranger back for ignoring him. "Check in the pigeon hole, there."

John T. punched the glove box open and felt inside. He withdrew a worn snub-nose .38 revolver. "Where'd you get this?"

"It belonged to my real dad. Don't cock it. That little bastard has a hair trigger."

John T. hefted the gun and Freddy's face flushed in fear. John T. handed it to him. Familiar with guns, Freddy still held it like it was a live snake and passed it back as quickly as he could.

The cherry on John T.'s cigarette brightened. "We'll take 'em. It'll be easy money. I need some cash to blow this burg anyway."

Freddy shook his head and fretted. John T. always scared him a little, because he had a reputation as one of the toughest and meanest young men in Lamar County, but he also loved their dangerous association. "Naw. Thomebody'll recognize uth or thomething."

Through the windshield, Bonne and Clyde fell in a spectacular slow-motion hail of bullets.

The movie ended and the credits rolled. Freddy was relieved. "Let's go out to the lake and finish the beer." He reached into his back pocket and pulled out a pint of J.T.S. Brown. "We can have ourthelves a party." Since Marty started working at the construction site, they'd taken to driving out to the unfinished lake to drink.

John T. kept weighing the pistol in his hand and Freddy felt his stomach sink. "We don't know nothin' about robbing people. You thaw what happened up there to Bonnie and Clyde."

Marty thumped the butt out the window. "Good idea, Freddy. We'll take 'em off down to the lake and do it."

"Hey, no, I didn't mean that!?"

John T. stuck his cigarette in the corner of his mouth, flipped out the cylinder, and checked the loads. He squinted past the smoke and flicked the cylinder closed.

The lights over the screen snapped on, flooding the cars with harsh light. Engines roared to life and vehicles crept toward the theater's only exit. Marty pulled behind the Impala.

Freddy had a bad feeling. "Why don't y'all drop me off at the house? I ain't feelin' too good."

John T. cut a glance to the left. "You're fine."

The doors on a Pontiac in front of the Impala flew open and a covey of shrieking kids boiled out in a Chinese fire drill. A second carload of youngsters behind their truck did the same, some switching vehicles and doubling the frenzy.

"Hot damn! Let's go!" John T. bailed out and jogged through the kids. As everyone jumped back into their cars, he jerked the door open and dropped into the Impala's backseat.

Paralyzed with fear, Freddy could only suck air. "I can't believe he'th doing that."

They watched John T. lean forward and rest his left hand on the passenger's shoulder. Sure the pistol in his other hand was against the man's head, Freddy mumbled to himself. "Oh, pleathe don't be cocked."

After only a moment's hesitation, the startled men slowly turn back around and the Impala inched forward. Marty finally elbowed him in the ribs. "Move over, dumbass. Folks'll think we're homos or something."

The Impala finally passed through the only exit beside the towering screen and steered onto North Main Street, heading north toward the Red River. They quickly left Chisum behind. Marty stuck tight to the Impala as they passed harvested fields and pastures full of dozy cattle in the cold light of the three-quarter moon.

Far off across the river, the first flicker of lightning signaled an approaching storm. The wind whipping through their open windows smelled of dust, moldy leaves, and fresh cut alfalfa.

In Arthur City they followed a farm-to-market road that soon crossed the Sanders Creek Bridge. Constable Ned Parker's sedan was parked in front of his house on the hill overlooking the bottoms. Despite the hour, a light was on in the kitchen and a dog's frantic bark filled the night.

Marty grinned. "We won't have to worry about that old fart this late."

"Where'th he going, anyhow?" Freddy checked over his shoulder to see if anyone following.

"To the lake, like we said." Marty slowed at the crossroads intersection in front of the closed general store washed in the harsh glare of a solitary pole light. Another left turn led to a dirt road. Bare tree limbs intersected overhead in a thick autumn canopy, creating a tunnel lit only by their headlights. The last leaves of the season caked the shallow ditch as they snaked deeper into the Sanders Creek bottoms.

Then suddenly they were in the open, overlooking a gigantic fire-and-smoke-filled bowl. Below, the moonlit landscape seemed to be the site of a recent artillery battle. Not a tree stood anywhere within view, and smoking piles of logs were scattered as far as their headlights reached.

Five years of construction had destroyed the once-pristine creek bottom for a mile across and two miles upstream as the Corps of Engineers built a dam and cleared the hardwoods in preparation of closing Lake Lamar's floodgates.

Marty thought it was the perfect place for a little thievery.

Chapter Three

Grandpa gave me a good, old-fashioned butt-whoopin' that stung like the dickins, but I knew I deserved it. I took it best I could, and then we drove home…slowly, so he could talk.

"I'm more disappointed in you than anything else."

"Yessir."

"You need to learn to make good choices, son. We're all trying to raise you right, and you need to think before you do. Hell, even Mr. Tom Bell believed in you and Pepper so much that he sent me papers that said he'd already paid for y'all's college. Think about it, boy, a dead man believed in you that much and here you are, getting into nonsense like that."

I knew Grandpa got a packet from Mexico, and it was a mystery to us all. Mr. Tom moved to Center Springs and tried to settle in, but he got caught up in some problems Grandpa had with bad folks who were moving marijuana into Texas. When it all came to a head, we found out Mr. Tom was a retired Texas Ranger who still had enough lead in his pencil to take on half the crooked Mexicans south of the border. We all thought Mr. Tom died down there in the jail shootout, but here we were, getting mail from a dead man.

"I miss Mr. Tom."

"That why you're acting out?" He rubbed his stomach where he'd been shot a few months before by some crooked Mexican police.

"Nossir. But I miss him all the same."

"Well, I do too, but don't get off on that. You need to straighten up and fly right."

I wanted to kick Pepper's butt, but I wasn't going to rat her out, neither. "I will."

"Good. Now, we'll keep this between ourselves. Doc said he wouldn't talk about it no more, so it's done."

One thing about Grandpa, once we got to the house, it was over. I guess it's like when someone goes to jail and pays their debt to society, they were back on level ground. He must have felt the same about kids.

My grandmother, Miss Becky, gave me the hairy eyeball when we came through the kitchen, but didn't do much more than shake her head. "Go to bed."

I tried not to rub my butt as I went past. I'd barely dozed off when my dog, Hootie, tuned up outside. Grandpa knew what was going on the minute he opened his eyes. "Get up, Top! Something's after the chickens."

Shirtless, he'd already pulled on his overalls and brogans before I could get into my jeans and tee-shirt. Miss Becky threw an old green army shirt over her nightgown and we rushed across the yard.

The chickens were carrying on something fierce in the brooder house, but Hootie circled it twice, and then shot off toward the oak tree behind the hay barn, trying his best to climb up the trunk. Me and Grandpa Ned hurried up the hill while Miss Becky stayed for a minute to check the damage.

I saw a coon's eyes reflected in my flashlight beam and had to holler over Hootie's barks. "Here he is, Grandpa, and he's a big 'un!"

Grandpa came around to my side and Miss Becky joined us. I could see chicken blood on the big boar's mouth when Grandpa added his beam to mine. He reached into the pocket of his overalls and pulled out the 32.20 revolver he carried as constable. He called it his Sunday Gun, and only carried the lighter pistol on the weekends.

He handed it to me. "Think you can hit him?"

It was the first time he'd ever offered to let me shoot at something other than a target, so I took him up on it. "Sure 'nough."

"Don't miss." Miss Becky added her own flashlight beam. "I don't want to lose no more fryers. He's done killed half a dozen tonight for meanness."

I thumb-cocked the pistol. Grandpa didn't say anything as I aimed. The barrel wandered around some, so I added my other hand to hold it tight. When I pulled the trigger, the muzzle flash blinded me, but I heard the coon thud on the ground at our feet.

Hootie charged in and I hardly knew when Grandpa took the pistol from my hand. "Good shot, Davy Crockett."

"Back!" Miss Becky hollered at Hootie. He turned a-loose and backed up, still barking. She used both hands to pick the coon up by the tail. "My lands, this is the biggest ol' bandit I've ever seen."

Hootie had it in his head that there was another one up there, so we left him barking at the empty limbs and walked back in the moonlight. He was still tellin' it when we went through the gate into the yard. Grandpa pitched the coon into his truck bed and led us up on the dark porch.

A car hissed past on the two-lane highway down the hill. Grandpa stopped, squinting. "Who's running the highway this time of the morning?"

A truck followed. Grandpa shook his head. "I swear, folks ought to be at home in bed at this time of night." He gave me the eye. "They're probably up to something. Don't be where trouble starts, and you won't get into trouble."

Miss Becky went in the house. I waited at screen door and hollered toward the barn. "Hootie! Get in here!"

He must have remembered what happened a few months earlier when a pack of wild dogs nearly killed him. He quit barking like I'd thrown a switch and high-tailed it to the house.

I held the door open for him and heard Grandpa talking to himself like he does.

"Folks out this time of night are up to no good. No good a'tall."

Chapter Four

When the monkey dropped onto Top's head, Pepper's sheer panic took her through the backyard and around the Ordway house. Cale and the Toadies' footsteps faded into the darkness. She made it back to the front in time to see Doc Daingerfield set Top on his feet and dust him off.

She waited in the shadows, thinking her heart was going to beat out of her chest when the doctor gripped Top by the shoulder and escorted him into the house. They were talking as they went in, but she was sure it wouldn't be long before her Granddaddy showed up with a belt.

When the door closed, she cut across the yard and headed down the highway, jittery with adrenaline. She'd barely reached the highway when Cale stepped out from behind a cedar. "I thought you'd got caught."

She recoiled and slapped him on the shoulder hard enough to sting. "Shit, you scared me! No thanks to you, Mr. Cale Westlake. Doc Daingerfield got Top, though."

"Well, he can have the little pipsqueak."

Pepper thought about slugging him, then she grinned. Nothing worse than a butt-whoopin was going to happen, so she didn't feel *too* bad about Top getting caught. "That's the most exciting thing that's happened in a while, and it wasn't even *dangerous*."

Cale walked beside her, staying on the hardtop. "Where are you going? Your house is the other way."

She jabbed him in the ribs with an elbow. "I know which way my own house is, idiot. I'm not the least bit interested in going home. We're out, so let's do something."

"You don't think Top'll rat us out?"

"Nope. He won't say a word." High on adrenaline, she stopped to think. "Let's do something *bad*."

"Like what?"

"Well, I don't know."

"You ever want to break into something?"

"No way! Folks around here'll shoot you if you try to get in their house or barn."

"I know where Old Man Peterson keeps his money."

"At his house?"

"No, in the store."

"His register'll be empty."

"No it won't. I snuck around behind the counter one day when he was in the post office. That blind old fool didn't have any idea I was there, and I snitched a twenty from a cigar box where he keeps his big bills."

"I'm not breaking into a store. Shit-fire, did you forget who my granddaddy is?"

"You said…"

"I said I wanted to do something bad, not *stupid*."

"Well, what then?"

"Let's run off."

"To where?"

"San Francisco." She dug her little transistor radio from her back pocket and spun the dial with a thumb. "Good Lovin'" by the Young Rascals filled the damp night air.

Full of youth and still bubbling excitement, they ran down the dark highway. Hair flying, she twisted to shout over her shoulder. "You can have me if you catch me!"

Cale tried, but she was fast as a deer and there was no way he could catch up. She quickly pulled away and he slowed to a trot, following the sound of her radio through the darkness.

When he came over a hill, Pepper was standing in the middle of the two-lane road with her head tilted back and both eyes closed.

"Now what are you doing?"

"Diggin' this music." The Stones had given way to the Mamas and the Papas. "They're in California. I mean it. Let's go there."

"Tonight?"

"Why not?"

While he mulled the idea over, he heard a car in the distance. At night, sounds travel. He figured it was still at least a mile away, but coming fast. "We need to get out of the highway."

"No. I'm going to stand right here. Whoever it is can go around."

"C'mon." Cale reached for her hand, but Pepper jerked it away, staying in the same position. "You're gonna get run over."

"I'm gonna *live* some."

"You're gonna get *killed*." The car was closer, and he heard the hiss of tires on the road.

"That's what I'm talking about." She used her thumb to turn up the volume. "It's this place that's killing me, from boredom. Say we can go to California and I'll move."

"Someday."

"No." She cranked the volume higher, distorting the sound.

Close to panic, Cale reached for her hand again. There was no way the driver would see them in time, standing below the hill.

"Stop!" Pepper drew a deep breath. "Feel it?"

Cale saw the glow over the hill, but he could no longer hear the tires over the loud music. "Please?"

"Titty baby!"

The lights grew brighter. Cale danced in terror. "Pepper!"

"I think I'll lay down." She dropped to the ground and threw her arms wide.

"No!"

"Promise me we'll go to California."

"I promise!"

"When?"

"Shit. I don't know!"

The lights intensified and it was only a matter of seconds before the car crested the hill.

"Then I'll die here, because this place is killing me already."

"Fine. When I get some money."

He saw her open one eye in the moonlight. "When?"

"In a few days."

"Promise?"

Panicked, he grabbed her hand. "Promise!"

Simon and Garfunkel came on, and she switched the radio off. "I hate that shit."

She lost her balance as he pulled, falling and cracking her elbow on the concrete. "Shit!" The radio flew from her hand, and with a jolt of fear, she suddenly realized she might have waited too long. Cale jerked her upright and her sneakers found a grip. They shot off the highway only moments before the lights crested the hill.

An Impala sedan flashed by, followed closely by a truck.

Both kids saw the passenger's head in back of the sedan jerk to the side as he caught sight of the kids lit by the truck's headlights. They recognized the local bad boy, John T. West, and the expression on his face scared them as bad as if they'd caught sight of the old Devil himself.

The moment the truck passed, Pepper and Cale ran across the highway and into the thick stand of trees dividing two pastures.

Chapter Five

Ned was barely back in bed when the phone rang. The late night calls weren't as aggravating when he was younger, because they were part of being constable in Precinct 3, but once Top came to live with them after his parents died, it worried him that the fourteen-year-old wouldn't get his rest.

"I'god, what *now!*" Wearing nothing but his boxer shorts, he padded across the linoleum into the living room and settled onto the telephone table's seat. "What?"

"Ned?" Isaac Reader's reedy voice on the other end sapped what little energy he had left. "What is it, Ike?"

The jerky little farmer began with his usual pre-conversational quirk. "Listen, listen. Leland Hale's cows are out on the road here, not far from his house."

"How many, you reckon?"

Ike paused. "All of 'em. That ain't it, though. You better get on out here, 'cause I done plowed into 'em and there's dead cows scattered all to hell and gone."

Ned glanced at the dark window, knowing he wasn't going to get any sleep that night. "All right, then. Are you hurt?"

"Naw."

"Good." Ned recalled the vehicles he'd seen on the highway less than a half hour earlier. "Why don't you go on and wave a flashlight around to keep anybody else from hittin' em. There's fools running the roads when they should be in bed asleep."

"All right, I hope none of 'em run over *me*."

"They won't, if you stay on the side and shine your light at 'em. I'll be there directly."

"More trouble?" Miss Becky asked when he returned to the dark bedroom to dress.

"Mostly with Ike Reader. Leland Hale's cows are out and Ike's done run over some of 'em."

"Oh, Lord. How does he know they're Leland's cows?"

Ned paused to think, then clipped the gallus of his overalls into place and grunted into his brogans. "That's a good question. I should have asked him." He dropped the bigger .38 Colt into the front pocket of his overalls and pinned the badge to his shirt pocket. "I'll be home after while."

When he stepped out on the porch, he chuckled. "A monkey. A damn monkey. Who'd-a had any idea a country kid would get in trouble with a monkey."

The engine of his new, used 1965 Plymouth Fury rumbled to life. He pulled the headlights on when he hit the highway, and accelerated. The cool night air flowed through the open windows. A four-point buck raised his head from a patch of grass beside the road and watched him pass. Two more eyes shined in the lights as a doe paused, then went back to grazing.

He plucked the Motorola's microphone from the dash bracket and pressed the key. "Who's working tonight?"

A strange voice squawked through the speaker. "This is Lizzie. Who's this?"

"Lizzie, this is Ned Parker. Sorry you have to work the late shift. I wanted somebody to know I'm heading out toward Isaac Reader's house because some cows are out and one or two are down."

"Mornin', Mr. Ned. All right. Call when you know something. I don't want to have to send the National Guard after you."

He grinned. "I'll do it, gal."

Minutes later, Ned slowed at the sight of Ike Reader's flashlight and half a dozen white-face heifers standing on the road. Twice as many were grazing on the thick grass in the bar ditches. One lay on the side of the road, bellowing and struggling to get up. A second stood on three legs with her head hanging low in pain.

Ike hurried toward the car as Ned pulled onto the shoulder and left the engine running. He hoped the bright headlights and emergency blinkers would slow anyone coming along the two-lane. He twisted the handle of the red spotlight mounted on the doorpost in the direction of oncoming traffic.

Setting the felt Stetson firmly on his bald head, Ned grunted his way out of the car. "You reckon this is all of 'em?"

Ike shrugged. Even that late at night, he wore his shirt buttoned at the neck under faded overalls. "Listen, listen, I don't have any idy." He paused to think. "You know, I didn't mean to hit 'em."

"I know it. Where'd they get out?"

"I cain't say."

Ned played his beam over the heifer on the ground. She groaned and scraped at the highway with her front hooves. "Thissun been up at all?"

"Naw. I believe her back's broke." Ike pointed with his beam. "Leg's broke on that'un, too."

Before Ned could comment that he could see the obvious, a glow through the trees warned of a vehicle heading their way from Direct. "Damn it. Somebody's comin'." They watched the headlights come around a sharp bend. Luckily the truck was moving slow, making Ned wonder if they were spotlighting for deer.

He crossed to the oncoming side of the road, waving his flashlight. Ike did the same, and Ned relaxed when he recognized the short-circuiting headlights of the Wilson boys' truck. Though Ty Cobb and Jimmy Foxx owned a farm and rented several sections of land to raise crops, Ned often wondered how they could work all day, yet hunt all night and throughout the weekends.

The truck crept to a halt and Ty Cobb stuck his head out the passenger window. "Ned? Y'all moving cows at this time of the night?" Coon dogs riding in the bed set up a racket so loud Ned couldn't hardly hear what the man had to say.

Ike always wanted to be first with any information even though he was farthest from the truck. "Naw! These is Leland Hale's cows, they got out...."

The dogs drowned out Ike's explanation. Jimmy Foxx got out. "Shut up!"

Ike froze in shock before he realized Jimmy Foxx was yelling at the dogs. They settled down, but hung over the side of the truck, tongues lolling.

"You boys having any luck?" Ned reached the window.

"Couple of coons and a possum. It's a slow night."

"Well, you should have been at my house a while ago. Why don't y'all help us round up these cows before somebody runs in the middle of 'em again."

"Sure thing." Ty Cobb stepped out.

Jimmy Foxx jerked a thumb over his shoulder. "We saw the fence was down back there."

"Want me to shoot that'un?" Ty Cobb pointed at the heifer lying in the road.

Ned shook his head. "Naw. Let's ease the rest of 'em back in the pasture before we handle these two."

Jimmy Foxx shifted into reverse and backed up to park the truck as a temporary block when the cows came down the road. He dug a hammer out of the cluttered floorboard and scooped a handful of staples from the bed full of dogs, hay, wire, and farm tools.

The others rounded up the scattered survivors and pushed them toward the gap. With Jimmy Foxx blocking their way, the cattle turned back into their own pasture. Jimmy Foxx tucked his light under one arm and pulled one of the loose wires back into place. Ty Cobb joined him and pounded new staples into the post.

They jumped at a sudden shot, then realizing what Ned was doing, went back to working on the fence. The second shot put down the cow with the broken leg. He slipped the .38 back into his pocket and joined them, waiting on the edge of the highway.

"That'll do for now, boys. I'll run over to the house and wake Leland up, if he ain't awake after all this shootin'. He can come out in the morning with a wire stretcher and tighten 'er up."

Jimmy Foxx saw a heifer in the pasture sniff at a thick stand of broom weed and jump to the side. "Ty Cobb, hold this fence."

He opened a gap in the wires and Jimmy Foxx stepped through. Seeing him in the pasture, the dogs leaped from the truck bed and joined him. They sniffed for only a moment until the pointer sat down, lifted his nose to the sky, and howled.

The mournful sound made Ned shiver. "What's wrong with him?"

Ty Cobb straddled the fence and when he was on the other side, added his own beam to the scene. "Ike, you might want to help Ned get through. He's gonna need to see this."

"What?" Ned didn't particularly want to fight the loose fence if he didn't have to.

A breeze flicked Ty Cobb's shaggy hair. "Leland Hale's layin' here dead."

Chapter Six

In the moonlit bottoms, Marty's headlights revealed bare tree trunks stacked like jackstraws in great piles. Splintered stumps lay on their sides, long roots like stiffened octopus legs splayed in irregular circles. Shallow pools of water reflected the brightest stars above.

Some of the stacks smoldered, red coals glowing in their depths. Others had burned down to huge circular piles of gray ash swirling in the random breezes. Smoke lay thick and heavy in the lowest levels, filling the truck cab. Occasional gusts kicked up sparks that flickered like fireflies. The eerie glow made Freddy think this was what Hell looked like when the old Devil wasn't home.

Or maybe he was.

Lightning flashed above the treetops like distant cannonade in the northwest. The wind freshened, whipping the smoke from one direction to the other.

Marty laughed and slapped the steering wheel. "Hot damn! Ain't this somethin'?" It was the meanest version of a snipe hunt he'd ever been on and that tickled him to death. He planned to play along with John T.'s deal for a while, but instead of robbing them like he wanted, Marty figured they'd take their keys and leave the strangers to walk out and find their car parked at the new overlook east of the dam.

It'd be a good joke on the city slickers and even if the laws found out, they wouldn't really care. Hell, they'd probably laugh, too.

They passed two quiet draglines, their enormous booms stretched high overhead. Tire tracks mixed with the prints of wide, heavy equipment treads fanned out in a tangle of trails.

"There she is." Marty pointed toward one of the largest bulldozers in Lamar County. The giant machine dwarfed their approaching vehicles. "There's my girl." The Caterpillar was his while he worked as contracted service to clear the future lake bottom. They circled a huge pile of timber waiting for a match.

He hit the gas to come up behind the slow-moving Impala and leaned on the horn, repeatedly stomping the dimmer switch to cause as much reaction as possible. In the backseat, John T. raised the pistol and gave the driver an order. He slammed the brakes.

Marty waved out of the truck window. "Stop! Stop! Get out quick!" With a harsh laugh, he jumped out of the truck with a two-foot pipe wrench from the floorboard, waving it like a tomahawk. He rushed to the driver's door and yanked on the handle, screaming all the while. "Get out! Get out now!"

In shock, the driver stumbled out from under the wheel with both hands in the air. "We'll do what you say!"

"Easy!" Freddy's voice quavered in dread. He followed, but much more slowly, first to keep his stomach from flipping over, and second, to maintain control of his suddenly loose bowels.

His heart beating fast, Marty grabbed the man's shirt and slung him to the ground, enjoying the power in his hands. This was *better* than a snipe hunt! Damn, that Bonnie and Clyde movie got him to going!

John T. came around the car, pushing the passenger ahead. "Keep your hands up, boys. This is a robbery!"

The frightened men did as they were ordered. John T. kept plenty of space between them and waved the barrel toward Marty and his shocked captives. "The driver's name is Harry Clay, and his friend here is Mason. We had a nice little chat on the way out here, didn't we boys?"

Freddy hung back. His voice trembled. "Easy guys, we have them now."

"That's right!" Running fast and hot on adrenaline, Marty strong-armed Harry Clay against the car. "Don't move!"

John T. aimed the pistol from one man to the other. Mason frowned and pled with his hands. "Hey, take our money. Take it all."

"That's what we're gonna do," Marty said, remembering a scene in the movie. "'cause we rob banks."

From beside the truck, Freddy spoke up with a nervous, high-pitched, voice. "Thith ain't no bank robbery. Let'th justh get their money and go."

Harry Clay agreed. "That's right. Take our money. We won't say a thing."

Marty snickered, enjoying the men's fear. He'd never felt such *power* before.

"Let's have it." John T. raised the pistol and pointed the muzzle at Mason's forehead. He thumbed back the hammer. His finger barely touched the trigger.

The muzzle flash illuminated the scene like a flashbulb. Mason's head snapped back and he collapsed in a heap. Freddy, Marty, and Harry Clay screamed in shock.

"Shit!" John T. froze.

The world stopped for a moment. "Damn, son!" Marty realized they'd crossed a line in the dark, savage landscape. He hadn't intended to *kill* anyone.

Now, all thoughts of the money were suddenly gone.

John T. swallowed, aimed the pistol at Harry Clay, and thought fast. "He was going for a gun!"

"Don't." Freddy stepped forward and tentatively reached for John T.'s free arm. "What are you *doing*?"

The situation was already beyond their control. John T. was no angel. He'd done a lot of things in the past, but murder was a whole 'nother game. He had to maintain their loose grasp of the situation, and the only thing to do was to keep up his bluff until Marty figured out their next step. Marty might be a mama's boy, but he had good ideas.

Harry Clay held out a hand. "He didn't have a *gun!*"

"Bullshit." John T.'s voice was louder but he was quickly losing steam. Already a two-time loser, he knew the next stay in jail would last for years. The muzzle lowered toward the man's knees, then the ground.

Marty jiggled the large wrench in his hand, uncertain.

Harry Clay's eyes flicked from one of his captors to the other. "There's money in my briefcase. Just take it and go." His voice was weak and hollow.

Freddy whispered. "Marty, let him go and let'th get out of here."

"Back off, Freddy."

Harry Clay's face became a mask of fury as his terror evaporated at the realization that his brother lay dead at their feet. "This is not *right!*"

"Back off, boy." John T. found himself admiring the man for his backbone.

Behind him, Freddy moaned. "Jesuth Christh. Y'all thop it."

"You're a *murderer!*" A gust of wind momentarily wrapped them in thick smoke. Seeing no other option and knowing they'd have to kill him because he could identify them all, Harry Clay seized the opportunity and lunged.

John T.'s pistol cracked again and red bloomed on Harry Clay's white shirt. The dying man grabbed the pistol and pushed the muzzle down. His nerveless fingers relaxed their grip and the body landed at John T.'s feet.

For the first time in his life, John T. was rattled. The local bad boy had crossed the mother of all lines not once, but twice.

Chapter Seven

Sheriff Cody Parker and Constable Ned Parker waited beside the crowded highway while Buck Johnson, the county justice of the peace, pronounced Leland Hale dead in the beams of half a dozen headlights.

Buck stepped to the fence, which was once again down, this time to allow access to the body. "Ned, you have any idea why Leland's shirt sleeve is yellow?"

"One of the Wilson brother's dogs histed his leg on him before we could call them off."

"Helluva way to treat a dead man."

"Leland don't know it."

"I'god, that's the truth. He's dead sure enough, and has been for a while."

Hands in the pockets of his overalls, Ned watched two ambulance attendants struggle with Leland's body. It was obvious the man's twisted corpse was broken, bones shattered by the impact of a vehicle.

"See them big cut marks on him?"

Buck studied Leland's face and the deep lacerations on his body. "Yep."

"I imagine somebody hit him so hard it knocked him through the wires."

"Well, we'll find out sure enough when we take him in for the autopsy."

Cody lit a cigarette. He'd once again taken up the habit. "You reckon he was out here trying to get his cows up?"

"That'd be my guess." Ned rubbed the back of his neck. "I doubt he wanted to be out for much else. Leland ain't been feeling good lately. The last time I saw him up at the store, he'd lost weight and his color was bad."

Isaac Reader joined them. "Listen, I didn't hit him."

"Didn't say you did, Ike." Ned took off his Stetson and rubbed his bald head, a sure sign of frustration sparked by his childhood friend. He felt a raindrop and replaced his hat. "Buck's done said he's been dead awhile."

Cody worried at an idea and waved at the distant farmhouse. "I wonder why he was out here at night to begin with." He exhaled cigarette smoke through his nose. "I wonder if he was trying to push 'em back in. Had to been, and man, whoever hit him must have been a-flyin'."

"That's what I've been studying on." Ned stared into the night. "They came off the road to knock him thata way. I 'magine we'll see the marks here in the grass when it gets light, what we ain't scuffed out already."

"None of this makes any sense." Cody adjusted the weight of the 1911 Colt .45 on his hip. "A feller fixin' a fence usually has his truck close by, and he for sure wasn't standing in the middle of the road in the dark."

"We'll find out when it gets light," Ned said. "After everything that's happened tonight, I can't wait to see the sun."

Chapter Eight

They stood in silence for a long moment, gulping the smoky air.

Mouth dry, John T. unrolled the crumpled pack of Camels from his shirtsleeve. He pulled one free with his teeth and held the pack out. "What are we gonna do now?"

Marty drew a deep breath, and with a shaking hand, he took one to calm his jangling nerves. They smoked in silence for a moment while Freddy stared at the corpses at their feet. Marty reached a decision and dug a set of keys out of his pocket.

"I'll make this all go away. Y'all put everything back in the car and then throw them in, too. I'll be right back."

Freddy knelt beside the bodies as Marty disappeared into the darkness. "Thith ith murder."

"Mason there was reaching for his gun."

Freddy patted the corpse, feeling his pockets for the familiar feel of a pistol. "He don't *have* a gun."

John T. reached into the open back door and withdrew a briefcase. He slapped it on the turtle hull and flicked the latches. It was filled with aerial photographs and map. "There's nothing in here but papers."

Freddy found a thick envelope in Harry Clay's coat pocket. He rose and seeing John T.'s back to him, stuck the packet under his shirt. "I hope nobody findth out what you did."

John T. paused for a long moment. "You meant to say what *we* did. You know, your fingerprints and Marty's are on this gun, too."

Freddy's breath caught and he stopped himself. "Yeah, thath what I meant."

They stopped talking when a huge diesel engine whined for a moment before rumbling to life with a hammering roar. Marty flicked on the dozer's headlights and accelerated. With a squeal of treads, it clattered and squawked loud enough to wake the dead. He piloted the big CAT in front of the Impala and lowered the blade. The engine changed pitch as the smooth steel dug into the ground. He pushed a bucket full of dirt forward, emptied it, and backed up for another load.

John T. immediately realized what Marty had in mind. He started the motor and added the Impala's headlights to the job. "Help me here, hoss." Without a word, Freddy gathered the papers and pitched them into the car. With the diesel growling in their ears, they wrestled the limp bodies into the backseat, John T. grunting and cursing at their dead weight.

Marty widened and deepened the excavation until it was big enough to swallow the sedan. Satisfied with the results, he drove the dozer out of the pit on the opposite side.

John T. crossed his arms. "All right, take and pull the car down in there."

Freddy's stomach rolled. "Why me?"

"That'll be your part."

Wiping the cold sweat on his face, Freddy was afraid he was going to puke. "But I helped you load the bodieth. That thould be enough."

The sounds of shrieking treads and the throbbing engine filled the bottoms as Marty steered the enormous machine in a circle.

John T. took another sip of beer, his eyes never leaving his skinny boyhood friend. Freddy's throat ached and he wanted to cry. He swallowed the lump and moved on numb legs toward the car.

"Hey!"

Freddy flinched, anticipating a bullet.

John T. grinned at him. "How about some of that J.T.S. Brown you got in your back pocket?"

Giving John T. the whiskey and shaking from relief, Freddy settled into the seat and shifted into drive. The Impala's fouled interior smelled thick and coppery from the congealing blood, making Freddy gag.

The radio warmed up and "Help!" blared from the speakers. The Beatles hit, combined with the night's events, was surreal. Freddy gave the foot feed a little gas and the tires slowly rolled over the soft soil.

In seconds he was at the bottom of the deep pit and killed the engine. Broken roots jutted from the sides like severed nerve endings in a raw, torn wound. The rich odor of damp dirt washed over him. There wasn't enough room to open the door. He climbed out the window and onto the roof.

He still half expected to feel a bullet in his own brain, but when he glanced up, the bulldozer was nearly overhead with a bucket of freshly turned dirt.

Frantic to get out of the pit, Freddy jumped onto the trunk and leaped out of the way as the first load fell. He stumbled out of the crater and across the broken ground. John T. steadied his balance. Another load fell onto the hood, and they watched the car disappear.

"I need to puke."

Without taking his eyes off the bulldozer, John T. shrugged. "Who's stopping you?"

Freddy stepped into the darkness and vomited over and over, until there was nothing left but thin bile. When he returned weak and shaking, the Impala's resting place was indistinguishable from the surrounding landscape. John T. handed him the bottle and Freddy rinsed his mouth with the harsh whiskey.

Beyond a nearby dragline, the storm approached with a rumble of thunder.

When the car was completely buried, Marty pushed a smoking tangle of thick limbs over the freshly turned dirt, repeating the process with a pile of unburned wood. Fifty yards away, debris burned fitfully, coals glowing as the half-green timber smoldered. Marty scooped a load of coals that fanned alive with fresh oxygen. He dumped the fire onto the brush pile and flames licked upward.

Finished, he backed away, killed the engine, and climbed down to join them beside the truck. "How 'bout that?"

"Smooth as a baby's butt." John T. handed him the open pint of whiskey. "Hey, did you see those kids we passed out on the highway?"

"Yep."

"Wasn't that girl Ned Parker's granddaughter?"

"Yep." Freddy stopped, afraid of what John T. was thinking, especially after what they'd done. "It could have been thomebody else, though." He shivered when John T. turned his dead gaze on him.

Thick smoke boiled as the rising breeze fanned the coals. Freddy shook his head. "Thoth men are justh *gone*."

Marty joined them and beamed, mistaking the statement as praise. As was his nature, he rebounded quickly from any crisis. "You're right." He took another long drink of bourbon. "Now we can go on home and nobody'll ever know what happened. We're 'bout done with this lake, and by Christmas, it'll all be underwater."

"But it wath murder!"

"Yep, that's a fact, sure as shootin', and we're all in it together. So the best thing to do is forget about it. What's done is done."

"Forget about it?" Freddy was stunned. "How'n hell can I *forget* about it? They're dead and their familieth won't never know what happened."

Their argument was interrupted as the coals burst into flame. The wood over the buried car quickly became a small inferno as the increasing breeze fed the fire.

Freddy wouldn't leave it alone. "Now we're going to drive off and thath's it?"

"It's over." Marty's patience was wearing thin. "We buried the bodies. We buried this conversation at the same time."

"Suits me." John T. paused and brightened, his mood warmed by the bourbon. "Let's go to Frenchie's café and get some eggs."

They climbed into the truck, with Freddy once again in the middle. He thought about the bundles of hundred-dollar bills he'd found in Harry Clay's inside coat pocket. Now, stuffed in his waistband, it was enough to get him out of their one-horse town and away from the sudden strangers sitting beside him.

John T. tossed out the empty bottle. "That was some quick thinking back there, burying the car."

"What makes you think it was the first time?" Marty asked. He liked the way it sounded, tough.

John T. shook out his last Camel as the truck reached the high ground and pulled onto the dirt road. "Son of a bitch."

Down below, wind sparked more than a dozen fires back to life, giving the devastation the eerie appearance of a battlefield, or an atomic bomb's ground zero.

Chapter Nine

It was a cloudy, drizzly morning and Ned couldn't put it off any longer, now that Leland was pronounced. "Cody, you want to go with me to tell Melva that Leland's dead?"

They were dreading the task. Though Ned had done it many times, such visits always took the wind out of him for days. This one would be especially difficult, because Melva was an odd woman, taken to nervous giggles at the worst times. Then, after a while, she might laugh before melting into long crying jags. Ned had seen it several times since Melva moved to Center Springs.

They had one son, a mama's boy named Marty Smallwood, from her first marriage. Marty was a little feller when they bought a few acres not far from Isaac Reader's house. Though a friendly guy, Charley was a half-hearted farmer and spent an inordinate amount of time in the honky-tonks across the Red River, where he drank gallons of 3.2 beer and shot pool until they closed at two in the morning.

They had a daughter together, whose name Ned couldn't remember because Charley ran off with the toddler one night, leaving Marty behind. Some folks said he took up with a Choctaw woman in Oklahoma. Others reported seeing him in Dallas a few months later, without his daughter, checking in the Adolphus Hotel with a colored woman on his arm.

Ned didn't care one way or another, but he hated the divorce for the little girl and Marty's sake, though Charley didn't seem to pay much attention to the boy anyway. Leland arrived a few months later and married Melva before the end of the year. Now *he* was gone.

Cody shrugged. "I guess we don't have much choice."

"Good." Ned led the way to Cody's Ford Galaxy on the side of the road. Bubble lights rotated on each side of the roof-mounted speaker. The threat of a shower had instead become a soft, soaking mist. "You can drive now that you're in a decent car."

Cody followed. "What don't you like about my El Camino?"

"Because this is a car for law work, not that half-breed truck of yours," Ned dropped into the cloth seat, "and I don't have to put it on, one leg at a time."

They'd been watching a steady stream of cars and trucks arrive at the peeling farmhouse on the far side of the pasture. The drive was short and Leland's yard was full when they turned off the red dirt road into the drive, telling Ned the country grapevine was working just fine.

"Not a one of these people knows Melva that well." Ned shook his head, threading through the haphazardly parked vehicles. "Half of 'em are folks who care maybe a little bit, the other half's nosey."

The porch flexed under their feet and Cody stepped carefully. "Watch that rotten place."

"Hell, most of the planks on this porch wouldn't make good firewood." Ned ground a foot on a rotting board that crumbled to dust over the floor joist, leaving two nails exposed. "Somebody'll have to come over and fix that for her now."

"She has a boy."

Ned snorted. "I know him, too. Like I said, somebody'll need to do it for her."

Hats in hand, they entered the living room. Melva was sitting on the couch between two farm wives. Winnie Louise's orangy-red hair was tied up in a scarf, as if she intended to get up at any moment and start cleaning house, and she probably would when the mood struck her. The other was Fannie, an interesting name for the Baptist preacher's wife and Cale Westlake's mama.

The trio watched Ned the way a dog minds its master when

a scolding is on the way. Their eyes filled when Ned stopped, though they had little use for Leland, and less for Melva.

Never one to draw anything out, Ned shifted from one foot to the other. "It's him, out in the pasture, Melva. Leland's dead. I'm sorry."

She wiped her moist eyes. Running ragged nails through her dishwater blond hair, Melva gave the lawmen a crooked grin. She shook her head. A shrill, self-conscious giggle became a guffaw. "He sure did love stewed prunes."

Embarrassed by the odd statement, Winnie Louise rubbed Melva's back in sympathy. "He's in a good place."

Fannie patted Melva's hand. "Better than this old world."

Melva giggled again and shrugged her thick shoulders. "I guess it's up to me now to milk."

"Why, honey, you can sell that old cow."

Another giggle, and then tears rolled down her plump cheeks. "Marty'll milk for me. I imagine he'll hang around the house more now that Leland's gone."

Those two were like oil and water, and Marty never much took to Leland after they married. Leland expected him to listen to him as a son would, but the youngster was turned in such a way that they never saw eye to eye.

Melva wiped her tears. "What am I gonna do about Leland?"

Ned cleared his throat. "We'll take care of that right now. He's on his way to Travers and Williams. They'll fix him up and you can go up there this evenin' or in the mornin' and pick out his casket."

Melva giggled again and everyone in the house was embarrassed.

Ned had all he could take. "Let's go."

"Bye, Melva." Cody touched her shoulder and followed. "Call if you need anything." They clumped down the steps, passing another couple on their way in with a fresh-baked peach pie.

Marty rested on the fender of Cody's sheriff's car, one heel propped on the front bumper and his hands cupped around a Zippo. He flicked it closed and exhaled a lungful of smoke toward the two lawmen.

Ned wanted to simply walk past the glower, but it wasn't polite not to say anything at all on such a day. "Sorry for your loss, son."

"I ain't your son." Marty hawked and spat. "Sorry is the best description for that man I can think of. He wasn't enough for my mama. She deserved better."

Cody tried to stay out of it and let his gaze rest on Marty's Dodge parked in the yard. He idly checked the truck's fenders, in case Marty might have run into something, but they were undamaged and freshly waxed. He tried to think of something to say, but everything sounded trite and dusty in his mind.

Ned slipped his hands in his pockets. "We'll do our best to find out what happened."

"I don't care one way or another. He never was much, no how."

To control his temper, Ned changed the subject. "You might want to replace some of them boards up there on the porch."

"I'll get around to it."

"Your mama's liable to fall through and get hurt."

As if that hadn't occurred to him, Marty straightened to better see the boards. "I'll get to it soon as I can."

"All right, then." There wasn't any point in standing in the wet, talking to a post.

Another couple arrived, the woman carrying a covered dish. After a somber exchange of howdys, the lawmen got in the car.

As soon as Ned slammed his door and was sure no one could hear him, he took off his hat and rubbed his head. "That woman's as crazy as a shithouse rat, and so is that no'count boy of hers."

Cody started the car and grinned. The wipers caught the water beaded on the windshield and flicked it away. Only then did Marty push off the fender, but he didn't turn around. Ignoring him, Cody saw an abandoned truck rusting to dust in a thick mat of coastal Bermuda grass. Beyond the fence, a weathered barn sat a hundred yards from the house with Leland's pickup parked inside.

"Hang on a minute."

Marty leaned against a porch post and watched Cody go through the gate and head for the barn, soaking the legs of his pants in the tall grass.

"You're supposed to have a search warrant for that, Sheriff."

"Not searching. Lookin'." Cody stepped inside and emerged minutes later and returned to the car. He gave a little wave that Marty acknowledged by thumping a butt in their direction. Cody shifted into gear, backed into the road, and headed toward town.

"The truck?"

"Nary a dent."

Chapter Ten

I was sitting alone at the top of the bleachers in our WPA gym, eating my sandwich and reading, when Cale Westlake and his friends saw me. They were going past the double doors on the Home side to find a place to smoke, and I doubt they'd have noticed me at all, except I took that exact moment to turn the page.

Cale came in to initiate the tired old ceremony that millions of boys have seen in their lifetimes. "Hey. Looky here, boys, what we have. It's little Mouse, all alone and huddled up."

He was pretty much right about the little part. I was still the smallest kid in my grade. "Why don't you mosey on off and leave me alone?"

"I don't think I want to. This is my gym too." He shifted from one foot to the other beside the wall separating the bleachers and the hard maple basketball court laid in the 1930s.

The Toadies, Frankie, Harlan, and Rex climbed up the two steps from the floor, scattered at the half-landing, and sifted upward through the bleachers. They settled around me like birds on tree branches. I put my sandwich down on the wax paper because I knew lunch was over. I should have been afraid, but I'd already seen them all run from a monkey and screaming like girls. I realized I wasn't as scared as I was before.

Frankie reached for my library book about a wisecracking private eye.

"Whatcha' reading, professor? A monkey primer?" He snickered at his own weak wit.

I yanked it out of reach. "Nothing you'd be interested in. There ain't no pictures, and all the words have more than three letters." I felt pretty good about that one. The book's character could have said that.

Cale stayed where he was, glaring upward. "Think you're pretty tough now, Mouse?"

I remembered how they ran away at the Ordway house. "Tougher'n you. I know about you and Pepper that night I got caught."

Something came over Cale's face. "What do you know? What'd she tell you?"

"You don't *get* to know what we talk about." Snapping the cover closed, I stood to leave and the others rose around me.

On the gym floor several rows below, Cale stepped into the bleachers' entrance, blocking the opening. "He scared us."

"*I* wasn't scared." It was an outright lie. That monkey terrified me.

"*You* didn't see him."

The conversation was confusing. "What are you taking about?"

Cale set his jaw. "John T."

"He wasn't there."

"We saw him. Me and Pepper."

"No he wasn't. And what if he was?" I started downward. "I'm gonna go."

"I'm not finished with you yet, Mouse."

"All right, guys. I give, if that's what you want. I'm outnumbered, so you're the winners." I stepped over the narrow bleacher in front of me, and down. As my foot landed, I was nose to nose with Rex. My foot slipped and the downhill momentum caused me to bump into him. Rex tripped and went a-flying backwards to land in a heap at Cale's feet.

Seeing it as an act of war, Frankie swung a punch toward my stomach. I instinctively moved the book to waist level. His fist hit it with a solid thunk, knocking me off balance again. He hissed, shaking his hand like it was broke.

Harlan swung too, but I was off balance and he completely missed. Barely staying on my feet, I bounced down the bleachers to the bottom like a ping pong ball. Catching myself with my free hand, I straightened my legs and jumped over the low wall to land inches from Cale. He was so startled, he stepped back into Principal Stevens, nearly knocking *him* down.

Not realizing it was an adult behind him, Cale jerked his elbow back, catching the principal hard in the ribs. He swung around and delivered a roundhouse blow that Principal Stevens caught with one hand.

Cale's action was so shocking the rest of us froze like statues.

The principal held Cale's fist. "Lunch is over, boys, and no roughhousing in the gym. Y'all are supposed to be outside anyway." Still keeping a tight hold on Cale's fist, the principal checked the Montique on his wrist. He was awful proud of that watch, and spent a considerable part of the day shooting his cuff to check the time. "Better yet. Class is about to take up. Everyone out."

Making like a patty, I hit the road and heard Principal Stevens. "Mr. Westlake, it'll be me and you and my paddle after school today."

When I peeked over my shoulder, Cale was getting a good butt-whipping while his friends tucked their tails and ran once again.

A minute later, Pepper walked into class at the same time as me. "Why are you so out of breath?"

"Your boyfriend."

She shot me a glare. "I don't have one."

"Cale Westlake. He thinks you're his girl."

"Well, I ain't. You still haven't said why you're breathing hard."

"I forgot my atomizer." That's what we called my "rescue" inhaler for asthmatics. I didn't go anywhere without the constant reminder of my frail lungs. Instead of a book satchel, I carried an army surplus backpack to hide the puffer. "Can you find some other boyfriend?"

She absently fingered her part, a habit that started about the time she started wearing hippie clothes. "I don't know what you're talking about."

I saw an opening I couldn't identify, but gave it a push because I was mad about her hanging out with him and ignoring me. "What y'all saw."

She gaped. "How do you know about that?"

"Cale told me."

"He promised he wouldn't ever say anything."

"Well, he lied. You better give me your version to prove he's lying about that, too."

"I don't know what he told you, but we were walking down the road and a car passed us with John T. in the backseat. Marty Smallwood's truck was following them into the lake. They were up to something, but we don't know what. Cale wanted to run off, but I wanted to wait, so we hid behind some vines and an hour later Marty drove out with John T. They drove real slow, looking for something, and we think it was us. What did Cale tell you?"

"Nothing."

"What?"

"He said John T.'s name and thought I knew something." I grinned. "Now I do." I glanced at the door, both to make sure Cale wasn't coming in, and to be sure Miss Rosalie wasn't ready to start class. "You oughta tell Grandpa or Uncle Cody what you saw."

Pepper rolled her eyes.

The fight was catching up with me as the adrenaline wore off and I felt like crying. I couldn't lean on anyone but my cousin for support and it worried me that I was losing my best friend. She was more fun than any boy I knew, always up for anything, no matter how dangerous or dull, with a mouth on her that got her jaws slapped. Grandpa Ned called her a pistol.

"I don't know what happened, but I don't want it to catch up with *you*."

Her face softened. "I know. I'm sorry you got a whippin'."

The class was filling up, and I wanted to get off that subject. "Anyway, stay away from him."

"I will."

But I knew she wouldn't.

Chapter Eleven

A low pressure system stalled over San Angelo made it seem as if rain was their new way of life. Ned met Cody in the sheriff's office parking lot and they drove through a light drizzle to both of Chisum's body shops to see if anyone had come in with damage to a hood or fender. No one reported repairs consistent with the hit and run, but they promised to give Cody a call if they ran across anything.

When they were back in the car, Ned shook water off his hat onto the floorboard and plucked the microphone off the dash bracket. "John, you listening?"

Thunder rumbled as Cody steered the sheriff's car onto North Main. It was gloomy enough that the lights came on in the stores and reflected off the wet concrete and bricks. Most of the people without umbrellas stuck to the covered sidewalks for shelter and avoided the open town square and its Italian marble fountain. "You could use his call numbers, you know."

"Yep, and he'd answer the same." Ned didn't like call numbers. He preferred to use the radio the same way he talked.

"Go ahead, Mr. Ned." Deputy John Washington's voice was deep and rich even through the cheap radio speaker. John was a mythical figure in Chisum, a giant of a man whose shoulders brushed most doorframes when he passed. He was the first official black deputy in the county, and though it wasn't written anywhere, Big John's assignment was to represent the law to the colored folks.

Ned considered John a family member. They worked closely together through the years, and had a reputation that covered northeast Texas. Both men were fair, but didn't take any nonsense from anyone, black, white, red, or green.

"Me'n Cody are heading over to Malcom Jackson's shop. You want to meet us there?"

"Sure 'nough. Trouble?"

"Naw. Checking body shops. You heard about the hit and run in Center Springs?"

"I did. A'ite. See you there."

Cody turned south. "Where's the shop?"

"You ain't been there?"

"Not that I remember."

They passed Nathan Jewelers. "Hit West Washington and keep going."

Cody glanced at Ned, and then did a double take that would have been funny any other time. "You okay?"

Ned wondered what Cody knew. He hadn't been feeling great for the past couple of weeks, and his stomach tingled deep inside where he'd been shot months ago. "I'm fine. Why?"

"Your face is beet red. Your blood pressure must be up."

"I feel a little flushed is all."

"You're more than flushed. You better run by Doc Heinz's office."

"You're bound and determined to get me into the doctor's office these days, ain't you?"

"It's not that, but you were supposed to go by a long time ago for him to check out that wound. I don't know why you don't do it."

Ned absently rubbed his belly where the bullet had caused considerable damage. "Because I've got better things to do than have him poke at me for a minute and then want ten dollars for looking at my tongue."

Pools of water spotted the broken streets. The houses changed from the Craftsman, Tudor, and Victorian styles to more modest bungalows and saltboxes. Fewer houses were painted, and those that were, boasted bright colors. They cruised down streets without curbs. In places, grass only grew in the ditches full of running water. Contrasting with other parts of town, the yards were mostly bare mud. Scattered among those who seemed to barely survive, other houses bloomed bright with late season flower and vegetable gardens.

Despite the weather, the neighborhood corner mom and pop grocery was busy. Ned pointed. "Across the street there."

What was once an unpainted livery stable had been converted to a garage. Wide oak trees shaded two bare dirt lots packed hard and black from years of spilled grease, oil, and traffic. Over the double doors, a hand-painted sign reading "Mechanic" hung on gray boards warped and rotting. Despite its age, the substantial structure was a testament to craftsmen from the past.

While a group of loafers watched through the open double doors, Cody pulled as far off the street as possible. It was Cody's first time in the "colored" part of town as the sheriff, and the looks thrown his way told him he needed to drop by more often, to get to know those folks.

"Howdy!" Cody waved toward the cluster of men sitting inside out of the rain. "Y'all doin' all right today?"

Ned stuck close to the side of the car, holding the fender for stability. "Howdy, men."

A couple of hands rose in return. Most simply watched. There was a tension in the air. The loafers appeared loose and comfortable under light from bare bulbs dangling from the grimy, open rafters overhead. But nearly everyone shifted in some way, far from their earlier relaxed positions.

A radio blared with colored music. Ned remembered that Cody called it Motown once when they were talking about modern music.

"I'm Sheriff Cody Parker."

"I know who you are." A barrel-chested man stepped around a jacked-up International pickup and through the open doors of the shop, wiping his hands on a greasy rag. "We do somethin' for y'all?"

As Ned turned toward the voice, a figure standing in the drizzle at the outside corner of the building seemed to evaporate behind a car on blocks.

Cody nodded toward Ned, letting him take the lead, since the hit and run happened in his precinct. Ned leaned against the garage doorframe, stopping under the eaves to stay out of the water dripping from the roof. The strong odor of old grease, gasoline, and mildew boiled out the door. "You're Malcom?"

The man stuck the rag in one pocket of his overalls. "Yessir."

"I knowed your daddy. Henry."

"He was."

"Henry was a good man."

"He was."

"We had a hit and run out toward Center Springs a day or so ago. A man was killed."

Malcom's experience with the law leaned more toward jailed kinfolk and friends than visits from the sheriff's office. "Was he colored?"

"No, white, and we don't know who did it."

One of the loafers raised his voice. "So y'all come out here to see if it was one of us done it?"

The man in his twenties, wearing black slacks and a white t-shirt wore the biggest, bushiest head of hair Cody'd ever seen outside of television or the newspaper. "No, not the way you put it."

"How come it's always a nigger done it?"

Ned felt his face fill with pressure. "You didn't hear that from us."

"I see the two of y'all standing *here*." He rose with two others of similar age. One bumped a cane-bottom chair as he stood and it fell with a clatter against a stack of car parts. The man's voice grew louder. "Y'all don't have no business accusin' any of us for runnin' anyone down."

Cody slipped both hands into his pockets of his khakis, hoping the move would show he wasn't aggressive. "We haven't accused anyone of anything." He dismissed them to address

Malcom. "Has anyone come in with a dented fender, or hood? Maybe said they run over a cow or a deer or something?"

The angry young man tugged at his t-shirt, as if to give his chest more room to puff out. "How about y'all takin' this somewheres else to *in-ves-ti-gate*?"

Ned's eyes grew cold, and his head felt as if it would pop from the pressure. He was suddenly aware of water splashing off the tin roof into a nearby catch barrel. Malcom remained still, waiting to see what might happen.

Ned raised an eyebrow at the younger man. "You got a name?"

"Yeah, what's it to you?"

"I always like to know who I'm talking to."

"You're talkin' to *me*."

Thunder rolled over the shop, vibrating deep in their chests. Malcom's eyes flicked to the man. "Dee-wight. We ain't doin' nothin' but talkin'."

"Yeah, and so'm I."

Cody met Dwight's gaze and held it steady. "We're checking all the shops, to see if anybody came in for repairs. That's all."

"I believe you're here trying to pin a killin' on somebody that don't look like you. That's it, ain't it? It's easier to convict one of us than it is one a y'all."

"You're wrong, Dee-wight." The deep rumbling voice sounding like it originated from deep inside a 55-gallon barrel came through the open back door of the garage. It for sure didn't belong to the slender black man who stumbled through the door, propelled from behind. Deputy John Washington pointed toward an overturned bucket beside an engine hoist. "Spec, you sit down right there. What'chu runnin' for?"

The gangly man who'd earlier ducked around the corner hung his head. "Nothin'."

"Not for that warrant for assault, or the one for suspicion of armed robbery outta Dallas? Your brother's name came up on that one too. Hubert Geroid, weren't it?"

"No suh. You got the wrong man for that, and I ain't seen Hubert in months." Spec rested his elbows on his knees.

John gave him the eye. "Uh, huh. You and me'll be talkin' later." He raised an eyebrow at the young man who'd been arguing with Ned and Cody. "Dee-wight White, why you squarin' off with them lawmen?"

"They here accusin' us…"

"Naw, you're talkin' to hear your head rattle on that one. I don't believe they here to *accuse* anybody about nothin'. They askin' questions is all."

Ned shifted his position to regain Malcom's attention. "Malcom, we've already been to two other shops in town. Now, all we need to know is if you've had anybody come by with body damage, like they might have hit something."

"Nossir. No body work. Most of our folks don't have money for such things, dents and all. We try to keep the motors runnin', that's all."

Cody stepped close to Malcom and extended his hand. "Since I'm sheriff, I'll be around every now and then to check and make sure everything's all right. Y'all need anything, you don't have to just call Deputy Washington anymore. The sheriff's department works for the whole town."

Malcom relaxed and returned the firm grip. "That'd be fine."

Cody smiled. "Ned, you ready to go?"

"I 'magine we better."

John cleared his throat. "Mr. Ned, if you don't need me to go with y'all, would you mind if I hung around here for a little while?"

Both he and Cody were grateful for the opportunity to back out gracefully before things escalated even further. "You go ahead on. I'll talk to you back at the courthouse."

"I'll see y'all in Mr. O.C.'s office if I get done here in time."

It galled Ned to leave, but staying and arguing wouldn't do any good with men already angry and itching for a fight. Rubbing his belly, he followed Cody to the sheriff's car.

Cody slammed his door and narrowed his eyes. "We're going straight to the doctor's office."

"No we ain't." Ned put his wet hat on the seat between them and slammed the door.

Cody tilted the rearview mirror toward Ned. "See how red your face is? That ain't a mad you got on there. It's something else."

Ned adjusted the mirror and sighed. "All right."

Chapter Twelve

James and Pepper were on the way home from her Grandpa Ned's house when he remembered Ida Belle's order to pick up a loaf of Ideal bread. He pulled into Oak Peterson's gravel drive and left the engine running while he went in.

Arms crossed in her usual aggravated posture, Pepper stiffened when she caught sight of John T. and Freddy killing time with the Spit and Whittle Club that had migrated from Neal's place. She didn't expect to see them, even though Freddy was local. John T. periodically attended the Center Springs school when he was a kid, but they'd moved away during his junior year and he seldom hung around either of the stores unless Marty was with him.

Pepper's heart jumped when Freddy glanced in her direction. She slumped down in her daddy's car like a rabbit in a briar patch, hoping John T. didn't recognize her.

Cale saw the car from the domino hall and came up on it from the off side. He spoke softly so the men nearly thirty feet away couldn't hear. "Hey, girl. I have the money to go."

Pepper kept her head down and didn't pay any attention to Cale. Her thoughts were on the two young men sitting in the middle of the farmers staying dry under the overhang. She knew almost everyone in Center Springs and wished she was more like Top. He wouldn't have recognized John T. that night, and he for sure wouldn't have known who Top was. Top wouldn't have been in the middle of all this.

Cale tapped her shoulder with his finger. "Hey, Earth to Pepper."

She had to bring herself back. "Huh?"

"I have the money. We can go."

"Where'd you get it?"

"Stole it."

She pushed him. "No you didn't."

"I did." He grinned and puffed up his chest. "I take care of my woman."

"So when are we going?"

"Uh, later, I guess."

Frustrated with the answer, she frowned and stared forward, refusing to further the conversation.

Half-listening to the story Frederick Winters was telling there in front of Oak's store, Freddy hadn't been able to take his eyes off James' car from the moment it pulled up, sure it was Pepper's white face he saw on Friday night as they flashed by on their way to the bottoms. He was wishing Marty was there, so he could ask him what to do, but since that night, Marty kept making up excuses to stay home and take care of his mama.

He figured Marty was scared, but that was all right with Freddy. It gave him more time to hang out with John T., who made Freddy feel tough, as long as he didn't have to talk much so's people would notice his lisp.

But he felt the bottom of his stomach fall out because Pepper didn't want to make eye contact, an insult in such a small community. Freddy glanced at John T. who was staring a hole through the car, not paying a bit attention to the lies swapping back and forth between the farmers.

Pepper's voice was soft. "In the morning."

"That's too soon."

"We have to get out of here." She pointed at John T. and Freddy, keeping her finger below the window.

Freddy nearly panicked, convinced that she was telling the boy beside her what she'd seen that night. His face prickled with heat.

Arms folded over his chest and ankles crossed, Colton Marsh tilted his head. "John T., me and the Wilson boys was trying to remember when y'all moved to Center Springs."

John T. pulled his attention from the car and focused on Carlton, wondering why the farmer had any interest in him. "I's in the third grade. The folks starved out of Tahlequah and had some kinfolk here at the time."

"That's what I was telling them. They remembered your mama and daddy as hard-working people."

"They were. Worked themselves to death picking cotton for other men. *Their* folks died in the Depression of the same thing. I don't intend to follow 'em. I'll probably go out behind the wheel of a car."

Freddy could tell Pepper was talking about him and let the front legs of his chair down with a thump.

John T. frowned. "What?"

The other members of the Spit and Whittle club noticed. "Why, that boy's white as a sheet."

"You all right, son?"

Freddy shook his head. "We got to go."

James Parker came out of the store with a paper sack in his arm containing more than bread. He stopped for a moment to speak with the farmers under the overhang. He also knew Freddy pretty well, and had a good idea of who John T. was, though he didn't care for the young man who most folks figured would at some point spend the rest of his life in Huntsville Prison.

John T. gripped Freddy's shoulder. "I believe I'll take him home." He flashed a grin at those around him, quickly making up an excuse. "I don't believe snuff agrees with him."

The farmers laughed. To a man they all knew the results of dipping.

John T. led Freddy away from the gathering. "Suck it up, stupid. What's wrong with you?"

He nodded toward Pepper. "They're talking about uth."

Pepper was pouting when Cale noticed Pepper's daddy coming toward them with John T. and Freddy following close behind. "Listen, I'll call you tonight." He spun on his heel. "See you."

James stopped beside the car and handed the sack through the window to Pepper. "Let's go, girl."

Freddy and John T. passed James on the way to John T.'s car and nodded hello.

"Howdy." James slammed the door and left without a backward glance. Pepper watched the two young men out the back window until they disappeared from sight.

She turned back around and shivered.

John T. and Freddy watched the car disappear. The heavy drizzle caught in their hair like dew on a spider's web. John T. unrolled a pack of cigarettes from his sleeve. "We might have to do something about her."

The pit of Freddy's stomach fell out. Now he was truly terrified.

Freddy wished he'd never gone to the movies that night. Hanging out with Marty and John T. suddenly wasn't worth it, even if they did pay attention to him.

Chapter Thirteen

After Ned and Cody left the garage, Deputy Washington leaned against a rough support post and crossed his arms. "What got into you, Dee-wight?"

"I'm tired of the white laws coming in here and accusing us of what we ain't done wrong."

"Then you ain't got no reason to get mad, because you're innocent."

"That's right. All of us are."

"Now you cain't speak for everybody here." He grinned at those sitting around. "Not meanin' any of y'all's done something wrong."

They laughed, the tension broken.

Dee-wight didn't laugh, though. "I'm not gonna take any more of this."

John cut him a look. "What you gonna do?"

"Why I'm…"

"You ain't gonna do nothing, because there's nothing to do. Mr. Ned's a good man, and he treats ever'body the same, no matter what color they are. Sheriff Cody's the same. He don't see no difference. You might try that yourself."

"John, it ain't *right* how they're always snoopin' around here, trying to lay blame on us for everything that happens, from stole chickens to bank robberies."

"Layin' blame and investigatin's different. What you talkin' 'bout? The sheriff ain't never been by here, far's I know, and Mr.

Ned don't have much business in this part of town. But it don't matter none. They're the Law, and when they ask question, you need to answer and don't give them no lip. It's the same thing as when I come around."

"You don't accuse us!"

"Did either of them say y'all was under suspicion?"

Dwight shrugged. Malcom and the rest watched, waiting. "No."

"Then you're talkin' to hear your head rattle, like I said." John nodded to end the conversation. "Now, y'all hear anything about that hit and run out by Center Springs, you let me know. Some of you have family out there that might know something."

Malcom picked up a wrench and stared outside at the rain as if it might offer a clue as to whether he should get back to work. "I hear you got a connection yourself out there."

John grinned, thinking about his girlfriend Rachel Lee. "We gettin' connected up all right."

"She's somethin' else." Linwood Carter chuckled. "My wife's second cousin was kin before her old man run off back to Jefferson."

"She's divorced now." It was the first time John had said the words, though he'd paid the court costs to finish the paperwork. It felt good to tell them she was free from any entanglements with her ex-husband. He headed toward the back door. "And you're right, she's a keeper."

He stepped outside, and then stuck his head back in the door. "Oh, and Spec, I reckon you oughta get that sorry-assed brother of yours and run over to the sheriff's office and turn yourself in to get all them troubles of yours straightened out. It'll go better for you if you do. If I have to run y'all down tomorrow I won't try to help a'tall."

Spec plucked at his shirt and then shrugged. "A'ite."

John grinned and disappeared. They heard his voice through the open door, over the suddenly heavier rain. "That's what I like to hear."

Chapter Fourteen

The day was about done when Ned and Cody dropped by the courthouse to see Judge O.C. Rains. He'd been at his desk all that day, trying to catch up on the mountain of paperwork that continually threatened to overwhelm his office.

The windows in his office were wide open, since the rain came from the west. There were no screens on the public building and flies buzzed in and out during the summertime without impediment. Fortunately, the rain beat them from the air, filling the room with the damp smell of paper, mildew, and old books.

Knowing his old friend hated for folks to come busting through the door, Ned walked in without knocking. He slapped his wet Stetson on the hat tree beside the door.

O.C. glowered upward from under bushy white eyebrows. "What's the matter with you?"

Aggravated that it showed, Ned grunted and picked up a pile of papers from a wooden chair. He put them on the worn oak floor and dropped heavily into the uncomfortable seat. "My bullet hole's hurtin' me today."

Cody closed the door. "Doc Heinz said it could be the weather making his wound act up, or it could be that he has some kind of infection, but this cranky old fart wouldn't let him do a complete exam."

"You ought to listen to him." O.C. screwed the cap back on his fountain pen. The wind shifted and O.C. twisted around and pulled the window to within an inch of the sill. Water streamed down the wavy glass. "You can't do much outside today anyways. Go back over there and let him check you good."

"Ain't got time." Ned shot Cody a couple of daggers. "What about these missing businessmen?" He pointed at the newspaper on O.C.'s desk. The headline in *The Chisum News* was large enough to read from across the room: *Two Disappear, Foul Play Suspected.*

O.C. tapped the paper with a thick fingernail. "Ask the sheriff there. All I know is what he told me, what's in this rag, and what I might have heard from other unnamed sources." It felt good to goad Ned with as little information as possible.

"Well, he's already told me a little bit, but I know *you*." Ned shifted his position, hoping to get easy. "This ain't a regular disappearance, so what'd you find out?"

"I talked to Willis Allen. We had lunch today at Frenchie's, and he told me they came up here to buy some land." Willis Allen ran the Chevrolet dealership and sat on the city council. "Said they intend to buy up enough farms to start up a big ranch, and they had cash with 'em to get people interested. Then they disappeared."

Ned rubbed his belly and hoped Cody hadn't noticed. "They ought not have been flashing money around."

"Well, they did." Cody said, absently.

Both of the elderly men were surprised. "What?"

"Gave Norm Hopkins five hundred cash of what they called 'earnest money.' He said they told him he could keep it, whether they did a deal or not."

"I never heard of such a thing." O.C. studied the sheets of rain through the window. "Not giving cash, anyway. Checks makes more sense."

"They're trying to close the deals fast, before other folks hear they're buying and up the prices on their land." Cody bit his lip, thinking. "Probably would have worked, too, if they hadn't disappeared. Even if they turn up, the cat's out of the bag and prices'll go sky high."

He stood. "I'll know more after I've had time to make some calls."

"You been kinda busy learning this business, and hiring that new female deputy," O.C. kidded. "I'm surprised you found out anything at all so fast."

Ned shot Cody a glance over his shoulder. "Yeah, and you're gonna get in trouble at home by hirin' some gal outta Houston."

"I hired a deputy named Anna Sloan, and not a gal."

O.C. chuckled. "Who'da thought about hiring a girl deputy? You might have done better if you hired one who leans toward the fleshy side."

Cody felt backed into a corner by the two old lawmen. "You two are barkin' up the wrong tree. She's a good deputy with five years of solid experience. Hell, I worked with women in 'Nam that made two of most men."

"And a lot more curves than we're used to." Ned gave O.C. a wink. "We don't need to borrow no trouble. We have enough of our own problems right here in town."

Cody flicked the switch on the metal table fan sitting on top of the wooden file cabinet. It hummed to life. "You hear something I need to know, O.C.?"

Thankful for the slight breeze as the fan oscillated, the judge tugged the window completely shut and studied the gray town outside. "Nary a thing right now. Y'all find anything new on that dead feller in Center Springs?"

Ned rubbed his scar. "There ain't much to find. Somebody run over Leland and he's dead. I don't know much else to do."

Cody opened the door. "I know, and it won't get done standing here talking to you two old farts."

"You gone to check on that new deputy?"

The sheriff grinned at the judge and flicked his hat toward Ned, sprinkling him with water. "Yep, and to try and solve a disappearance."

When he was gone, Ned rubbed his head. "That would have made me mad a few years ago. I used to have a temper."

"You still do."

"Not so's you'd notice anymore."

O.C. laughed and waved toward the door. "Get out of here, and go get that belly checked out."

Chapter Fifteen

Pepper and I were arguing about music again. The weather had us hemmed up inside and listening to music on Miss Becky's little plastic GE radio when "Jimmy Mack" came on. I always like the beat of that song, but Pepper started in. "That's nothing but bubble gum music. You should listen to songs that mean something to our generation."

"Like what?"

"Like 'For What It's Worth,' or anything by The Rolling Stones or Jefferson Airplane."

"Uncle Cody calls it long hair music."

"Hair doesn't have anything to do with it. It turns me off when they're always talking about hair."

A car went by on the highway and slowed. I could tell Pepper was afraid it was John T. coming to get her, but it was only the mailman.

Before we could go any further, Miss Becky came in from the kitchen. "Turn it off is right. Y'all turn off that radio and come with me."

I was glad for the excuse to do something. "Jimmy Mack" was over, so I clicked the knob and killed The Young Rascals singing "Groovin'." "What do you want us to do?"

"I need y'all to carry these buckets up to the garden for me."

"But it's raining!" Pepper stopped beside the chrome and Formica table. "We'll get soaked."

"No, we won't." Miss Becky tied a bonnet on her head, then handed one to Pepper. "Put this on. It's a mist right now, and we need to gather what we can that's ready."

Pepper held the homemade head-cover by the long ties like it was a dead rat. "I'm not wearing this ugly thing unless Top wears one too."

I grabbed one of Grandpa's stained old work hats from the rack beside the door and plopped it on my head. It was too big, but I knew it would keep the rain off. "I got this."

Exasperated at arguing with Pepper all the time, Miss Becky took the bonnet back from her and hung it where she kept her aprons, on a little cast-iron rack beside a wall holder full of wooden kitchen matches. "Fine, get your hair wet."

She handed us the empty galvanized buckets and led the way through the light drizzle. She unwired the gate into the pasture. Grandpa always used two or three strands of bailing wire to hold it shut.

A little bluebird fluttered out of the hay barn and landed on the top strand of bob-wire not ten feet away. Miss Becky stopped. "Why, ain't they the prettiest little things you ever saw?"

Pepper was still sulled up, so she didn't say anything. I liked the bird's bright color. "That'uns a different kind of blue."

"It'd be prettier if we had the sun."

We filed through the gate. I gave one wire a quick twist to keep it closed. The little bird watched with interest. I trotted past the chicken house to catch up, following a lane Grandpa cut through the grass from the gate to the garden, a little over a hundred yards away. I was glad for the lane, because our pants would have been soaked to the knees in the tall grass.

About the time we reached the old caved-in storm cellar that had been there since the 1920s, the bluebird fluttered past and sat on one of the wet boards sticking up out of the ground. We stopped again, because it was so close.

Pepper felt for the part on top of her head, making sure it was straight, then she adjusted her hair held in place by a braided cloth headband. "That bird's crazy."

"It's not a bit afraid." Miss Becky smiled and led off again. We stopped at the gate leading into the garden, waiting again while she untwisted two more strands of bailing wire. It was more than Pepper could take.

"Why don't Grandpa put a good latch on these and be done with it?"

"Wouldn't do no good." Miss Becky worked at the next wire. "He'd wire it up again the next time he took a notion the cows might get out."

"Some day I'm gonna make enough money to buy this place and I think I'll burn it down." She'd been mean-mouthing Center Springs for the past year or so, wanting to live somewhere else.

"Why, Pepper, that's a horrible thing to say."

Pepper frowned at the ground while Miss Becky twisted the wire. I knelt down to tie my sneaker, and was shocked when the little bird lit on my knee. I didn't move a muscle. "Miss Becky, looky here."

She put a hand on her face. "My lands. I never saw such a thing."

Pepper snorted. "A wild animal acting like that, it's probably sick with hydrophobia."

"Birds don't get rabies."

The bluebird fluttered to a bush growing up in the garden fence, and before I could stand back up, it came back to my knee. "It's not afraid."

"That sure is something." Miss Becky fiddled with the bonnet tie under her chin. "Wonder what's got into that little thing?"

I noticed something was tangled around his leg and wrapped around his toes. "It has something on its foot."

"Catch it. See if you can get it off."

I thought she was crazy, but the bird held still while I lowered Grandpa's hat over it and reached underneath to get a soft grip. With the bluebird in hand, I found a tangled mass of long animal hair around the leg that had been there so long it was cutting into the flesh.

"I think this is horse hair, or from a cow's tail." I carried it to Miss Becky.

"Poor little thing." She reached into her apron pocket for a tiny pair of pointed scissors. "Hold her still."

"What makes you think that bird's a she?"

"I don't, Pepper, but I reckon I call most birds a she if I don't know what they are." While I held the bluebird upside down, she carefully snipped at the hairs wrapped around its leg and toes. Even Pepper was interested, and drew close as the last bits fell away, revealing the raw skin underneath.

"All right. Turn her loose."

I released the bird and we watched it fly to a nearby bush. Satisfied that life was back to normal, it disappeared into the hay barn.

"That was the dandgest thing I've ever seen."

Miss Becky gave Pepper the eye, knowing that if she hadn't been there, my cousin's language would have been much stronger.

To save her, I stepped in. "I've never seen those little scissors before."

She returned them to her apron pocket. "I dreamed I needed them to cut one of you kids free, so I knew the good Lord was telling me something. That's why I put them in my pocket this morning."

"But you don't have our Poisoned Gift." I kinda wished Pepper wasn't with us, because I'd had another one the night before. I wanted to talk to Miss Becky about it, and knew that in the mood Pepper was in, she'd make fun of me and I'd get mad.

She handed the buckets back to us as the drizzle became a light shower. "Dreams aren't always bad."

That one was. Mama and Dad had died in a car wreck and I came to live with Miss Becky and Grandpa. I seldom dreamed about them, but in this one, I walked into Dad's bedroom to find him alive again and asleep on his side. Mom was yelling for me to be careful. I stepped close to the bed and Dad swung his fist so close I felt the wind in my dream. "Don't stop her, son, she has to go!"

I screamed and woke up.

Miss Becky went through the gate and stopped at the first row as the rain sprinkled our clothes and puddled between the rows of late-season peas.

"Damned bird," Pepper whispered. "If we hadn't wasted time with that thing, we'd be halfway through."

I felt good about helping the bluebird. "I love it here."

"I don't." Pepper put down her bucket and picked a handful of peas. She spoke softly. "It won't be long 'till I call this place Splitsville.

Chapter Sixteen

Cody went downstairs to find Deputy Anna Sloan sitting at his desk. She was on the phone and wiggled her fingers in a wave. "Yes ma'am, I understand. You said they had cash with them? How much?"

She listened, using one finger to absently move her pillbox uniform hat in a tiny circle on the nearly empty desk. Cody hung his wet Stetson on the hat tree and shifted uncertainly. He wanted to work through the growing stack of papers on the corner of the desk, but couldn't ask her to get up while she was on the phone. Hands in his pockets, he walked to the window and stared at the wet parking lot.

As she talked, he heard genuine concern in her voice. It was refreshing to have someone on staff who could relate to women in the course of an investigation. She filled a hole that was evident the day he took office. He needed to break up the men's club.

Judge O.C. Rains convinced the city council to appoint Cody Parker as interim sheriff after Sheriff Griffin's betrayal and death, knowing full well that come election time in May, Cody would be a shoe-in for the job. Cody in turn put the ex-sheriff's driver, Deputy White, back on the street before wading through dozens of applications to find someone with good investigative skills.

Anna's was the only one that stood out in a pile of applications filled out by men. He knew that hiring a woman was breaking dangerous ground, but he needed someone with experience in detail work to dig through facts and information to solve cases.

Anna came highly recommended from the Harris County Sheriff's Department in Houston where she'd broken half a dozen cases that stalled for one reason or another. When Cody asked her over the phone why she wanted to leave a promising career in the big city, she chuckled. "I'm tired of the humidity. It makes my hair swell."

Cody laughed. "All right. I'll get back to you tomorrow." He hung up and went straight home that night to talk it over with his redheaded wife, Norma Faye.

It was full dark when he arrived. She was setting the table after he washed up and joined her in the kitchen. "What would you think if I hired a woman deputy?"

"Is she pretty?"

"She's not hard to look at in the mugshot she sent with her application."

"Why a woman?"

"Because y'all pay more attention to the little details that men miss. I have enough hairy-legged boys to do most of the work, but I need somebody who'll stay at it until they catch what the rest don't see or think about."

"Why are you asking *me*?"

"Because folks will talk for one thing, especially after the way we got together. Even though we're married and she ain't my type, some will wonder what I'm up to since she's the first female deputy we'll ever have in the department."

Norma Faye stopped setting the table. "When you first started talking about needing people, I thought you were hiring a secretary, or someone else for dispatch. I never thought of a woman deputy."

"See? We may be riding alone sometimes. We might work nights. I may talk about her a lot, and I don't want you to get the wrong idea or to feel uncomfortable. I don't care about anybody but you."

"Idiot." She gave him a quick kiss. "I'll never be jealous, but you watch yourself with everyone else."

Relieved, Cody sat down to eat. "I'm crazy about you."

"I know."

Anna's tone dropped on the phone as she sympathized with the person on the other end of the line. "We'll do our best, but right now the investigation hasn't turned up anything that'll tell us where they are. I'll call you again in a day or two. All right, bye." She hung up and realized where she was. "Oh! Sorry." She hopped up and came around the desk.

"Don't worry about it." They traded places and Cody settled into the chair. He slid her little hat toward the edge. "Who was that? You find anything out?"

"Not a thing." She unconsciously smoothed her skirt. "That was the Dallas police. All they have is background information. Those missing businessmen drove out a few days ago. They were at the motel here in town one minute and vanished the next. The night manager said he remembers seeing their car pass by about dark and turn toward town, but that's all we know right now."

"They have family?"

"I'm sure they do, but they weren't married. Dallas is handling that end."

"So what's your plan?"

"I'm going over to the Ramada Inn and start there. Maybe I'll get an idea of where they might have gone or who might have seen them if I drive around."

"All right, let me know if you find anything out."

She secured the hat with a bobby pin. "Sure thing. Tootles."

The radio crackled. "Sheriff Parker, come in."

He lifted the handset. "Right here, John."

"Sheriff, we have a situation on the square."

"What's that?"

"There's some kids out there having a demonstration."

"In the rain?"

"Yep. I was driving past and saw 'em sittin' out there under umbrellas, holding signs about Viet Nam and peace this and peace that. I prob'ly don't need to handle thissun alone. They all look like you, not me."

It was John's way of saying they were white kids. Cody grinned at the rain as it fell harder. He checked the clock and saw it was six o'clock. "How many are there?"

"A dozen or so high school kids, but there are a couple of older ones, too. Probably the ones that thunk it all up. We gonna do something about it?"

"Nope. Go on home, John, and tell Rachel howdy. If they want to have a sit-in out in the rain, then let 'em. They'll give up before long."

Chapter Seventeen

"John T. West is for sure after us."

A shiver ran down Pepper's spine. "I was afraid of that."

Rain dripped off the eaves of the Baptist church not twenty yards from Cale's house. "He was asking around about you."

In his living room, Cale checked over his shoulder to make sure no one was listening in on their phone conversation. He spoke softly, because his own daddy sometimes had ears like a bird dog. He was pretty sure the reverend was in the church with a couple of ladies planning the upcoming Thanksgiving celebration, but he wasn't taking any chances.

"Sammy Dollins was there and heard John T. ask how many grandkids your granddaddy had."

Sitting at the telephone table in Miss Becky's living room, Pepper cupped the mouthpiece and barely whispered, even though her grandmother was outside, sweeping off the porch. "Maybe it's our imaginations. We didn't see anything but them going past."

"We know that, but they don't."

"What do you think they were doing?"

"I think it has something to with Leland Hale getting run over."

"Grandpa would have said something about that if he thought it was John T. or Marty. Him and Uncle Cody went over to Marty's house that day and I know good and well they would have checked Marty's truck. They've been watching every car and truck that's gone through Center Springs."

"You don't know for sure, though. Maybe that Impala hit Mr. Leland." Cale thought for a moment, wondering if the timing was right. He finally decided it was. "Let's go to California. I don't want John T. after me for any reason, and if we're gone, we won't have anything to worry about. You wanted to go. Now's the time to do it."

In a teenage moment of absurd rationality, she decided that running away was the best option. Butterflies filled her stomach when *It* was said, the thing she'd been talking about and leading up to for months. She couldn't run away alone, but Cale made it possible.

"Yep. That's how you do it. You don't announce it to anyone, you just split." She shivered. "San Francisco, here we come."

Chapter Eighteen

Anna started the engine, put the patrol car in gear, and pulled out of the courthouse parking lot. One of the other deputies pulled in at the same time and waved a finger when he saw the car. Then he shook his head and laughed, and Anna wondered if he was laughing at *her*.

It didn't bother her that much. She'd been in law enforcement for ten years, and dealt with her share of sexist comments and arrogant men. In Houston, it had taken three years before most of them gave up and treated her like one of their own.

There were a couple, though, who had to learn the hard way. One wouldn't keep his hands to himself one night after work in the parking lot, when he cupped her breast and squeezed like he was checking a cantaloupe for ripeness. After the cast came off his little finger, he absently rubbed it every time they passed each other in the station.

The other one was her partner, an old-school deputy who believed women belonged in the bedroom and kitchen. They rode together for two years and she endured a daily ration of ill treatment until the day she solved the murder of a ten-year-old child whose abused body was dumped beside a Houston bayou. When they arrested a local preacher for the crime, and he confessed to the murder, her partner never said another word again.

The ten-year-old had been his granddaughter.

Anna took the back way to the Ramada Inn because she wanted to start fresh in her thinking. Her idea of retracing the businessmen's routes came from those first couple of weeks in town when she knew no one and needed something to do in the evenings.

The rain increased still again as she parked near the motel's swimming pool in the middle of a large L. She watched rain dimple the surface of the heavily chlorinated water that was usually full of kids and parents. Then she pulled away.

The Motorola squawked with cop talk, most of it about car accidents and rising water. She drove down Highway 271, and under the loop's overpass. She passed the bowling alley, not knowing that one of Ned's cousins had come close to dying in the parking lot a year earlier, when his wife's boyfriend knocked him in the head with a crowbar. It was one of the hundreds of stories folks in Chisum and Center Springs knew about, but didn't discuss.

On an impulse, she stopped at the bowling alley for the second time since moving to Chisum. That first week, she bowled one game, but then realizing it was more fun with others, picked up a greasy cheeseburger in the coffee shop and left to eat it in her rented house. Anna occupied the next few nights by unpacking her few possessions, finding the right position for the rabbit ears antenna on her portable television, shopping at the Woolworth, Duke & Ayres, and Bealls, and going to the movies at the Plaza and Grand Theaters, both downtown, within two hundred yards of each other.

Inside, the noisy Bowl-a-Rama assaulted her senses with the familiar smells of popcorn, sweaty socks, the rumble of rolling balls on hard maple lanes, the solid crack of scattering pins, and the clunk of the new machinery resetting them for the next roll.

Harold Hollis was spraying disinfectant into shoes when Anna stepped up to the counter. "Is it Halloween?"

She frowned. "Excuse me?"

He gave her a long inspection, from the uniform cap bobby-pinned to her hair, to her blouse, and the skirt ending above her knees. "You're dressed up for something and I wondered if it was Halloween."

Her ears flushed with rising heat. "It's time for you to drop that crap and talk to me, that's what time it is." She pointed at the badge over her left breast, wishing she could wear it somewhere else. "I'm Deputy Anna Sloan, and I'm here to investigate a murder."

Harold put the shoes down and patted the air between them. "Keep your voice down. There ain't been no murders in here, and my customers don't want to hear anything like that."

Anna had to force the smile off her face. It didn't take much to back some fools down. She spoke softly, forcing Harold to mirror her actions over the counter. She was far enough back that it was uncomfortable for him, and that made her feel even better. "I didn't say it happened here. I'm working on a case involving two businessmen from Dallas."

The manager waited. "Okay?"

She held out a black and white photo that had been delivered from Dallas, a two-and-a-half-hour drive away. "Were these men in here?"

He studied the likeness. "Nope."

"You're sure?"

"I might not know shit from Shinola, but I'd recognize the noses on those two if they came in." His eyes slipped from Anna's face to her chest. "Ain't seen 'em."

"Hey, up here." When Harold's eyes rose, she continued. "Maybe you weren't working if they did and there's somebody else I could talk to."

"I open and I close. There ain't nobody works this counter but me. Bowling alleys run on a tight margin. Hell, I had to shell out a butt-load of money for them new pin setters so I didn't have to hire and feed a bunch of kids that wouldn't show up for work. Now it's me, Mary on the snack counter, and Slim back there on the grill, but I ain't never seen these two."

Deflated, Anna gave up. "All right, but if you hear anything, you call the sheriff's department."

"All right, missy."

She paused. "Answer me this, if a male deputy came in here, would you call him buddy, or feller, or bub?"

Harold raised an eyebrow in surprise, wondering at the question. "Nope."

"All right. That's good to know. Now, the next time I'm in here and you call me missy, I'm going to stick one of those size thirteen bowling shoes up your ass, got that, bub?"

Shocked that a woman would speak to him in such a way, Harold gaped like a fish out of water as she spun on her heel and stomped back into the rain. Anna had to sit in the car for a few minutes to cool off before pulling back into the light flow of traffic.

Chapter Nineteen

Ned pulled into the bottle-cap lot in front of Neal Box's store in Center Springs. The Spit and Whittle Club was on the porch and out of the incessant rain. A few trucks were parked in front of Oak Peterson's store, less than fifty yards away. Ned figured some were there to pick up staples such as bread or salt, and the others were folks getting their mail from the post office in the back. Oak was smart enough to know that most people preferred Neal's store, but he stayed in business because of the post office. He'd located it at the rear, though, so they would have to pass all his wares on their way in and out.

Between the two small businesses, the door to the domino hall was open and a soft light made the one-room building inviting.

Ned joined the loafers on the porch. Ty Cobb and Jimmy Foxx leaned against the wall in straight-back chairs on two legs, their muddy feet stretched out. "I swear, it's a risin' like nobody's business."

Rain dripped off the roof well away from the two-by-six porch railings they used as seats. Ned settled on one with his back to the highway. "What is?"

"The lake." Jimmy Foxx motioned toward the south. "We was down on the south end, huntin' coons on the creek when Ty Cobb damn near drowned."

"Aw, I didn't come close to drowning, but we was running

a branch down there that we've hunted for years. When I went lopin' over a little rise in the dark, I wound up swimming."

The men laughed. Isaac Reader, Neal Box, Wayne Simpson, Dub Hinkley, and Mike Parsons all loved a good hunting story, and none of them ever let the facts get in the way of telling it.

"Shoot, I know that trail like I know the back of my hand, and I'm a tellin' you, the water is comin' up so fast in them sloughs that you can watch it eat up the ground. I had to dog paddle back to the rise and Jimmy Foxx hauled me in like a big old gar. It won't be long before the creek gets out of the banks."

Mike Parsons leaned forward to speak. He always leaned into a conversation. "It's fillin' up faster than they want. There's a steady stream of heavy equipment coming up out of the bottoms. They ain't even finished with burning up all the trees, but if they don't get their rigs out pretty soon, they'll be underwater the way it's comin' down."

"I came over a while ago," Ned said. With the completion of the dam, there were now two ways to get to Center Springs off the highway running between Chisum and Hugo, in Oklahoma. The original two-lane road came from Arthur City, and now the cutoff across the dam originated in Powderly, about two miles south of the Texas/Oklahoma border. "All the fires are out and there ain't but a couple of draglines left. They're having to pull one out with a bulldozer."

"Yep, they've beat the ground up so much that's it's boggy from all this rain." Dub rubbed his three-day old whiskers. "The creek's up seven or eight feet, which ain't much down there in that big hole, but it'll be a sight deeper if it don't clear off soon."

"Listen. Listen. They say it's gonna rain for another week, at least." Isaac Reader cleaned under his fingernails with a pocket knife. It always made Ned nervous to watch him do that, because Ike's knives were sharp enough to shave with, and the jerky little farmer seemed to work way too deep under his nails.

Mike Parsons crossed his arms. "Hell, Ike, they don't know for sure. I can guess as good as the weatherman can."

"So what do *you* think, then?"

Mike scratched his head. "I think it's gonna rain for another week."

More laughter. A dented Pontiac Catalina came down the road from the dam and slowed at the stop sign, then accelerated across the highway and into Oak Peterson's drive. Ned hadn't yet become accustomed to so many strange cars coming through Center Springs. "Y'all know who that is?"

Jimmy Fox squinted past Ike. "That's John T. West." He resumed his position. "Most folks don't have any use for him."

"I don't neither." Ned said. "He runs with a couple of other no'counts."

Ty Cobb bit his bottom lip, thinking. "Yeah, I've always thought it was him and Marty Smallwood who was settin' fire to hay barns a few years back."

Marty's name caught Ned's attention. "That's right." He stood. "You know, I need to go. See y'all later."

He dropped heavily into the front seat of his car, slamming the door against the rain and rubbing his tingling scar for a minute. He slowly drove through the puddles in front of the domino hall and across the oil road between it and Oak's store.

He parked alongside John T.'s car and studied the undented front end for a moment before going inside. Unlike Neal Box's store, Oak's business seemed like a dungeon even on sunny days. Where Neal had three large double-hung windows on both sides of the frame building, Oak only had two thin, horizontal windows on the east side, up near the ceiling hanging thick with farm implements. The worn wooden floor sagged in places, and many of the dry goods on the shelves had been there so long they were dusty.

John T. was in the rear, talking to Oak through the iron bars of the post office counter. "Have you seen James Parker's little gal, Pepper?"

Oak shook his head. "Naw, not today. Why'n't you ask James, or Ned?"

"I will when I see 'em. I wanted to warn her away from that Westlake kid."

"Somebody needs to." Ned joined him at the post office window. "I ain't seen her today. Why?"

John T.'s face reddened. He moved to face Ned. "Well, uh, I don't think much of that Westlake kid and I think she needs to be careful."

"I'm all right with that, but I don't know much about you. Where do you live?"

"Down toward Cooper right now."

Ned's blue eyes took stock of the man in front of him and he didn't like what he saw. "I'd sooner you didn't have anything to do with my grandkids."

"That's fine, then."

"Where's your other runnin' buddy you were up here with earlier? What's his name…"

"Freddy." His eyes narrowed in frustration when he realized he'd done exactly what Ned wanted.

"Yeah, ol' Freddy. Where's he?"

John T. scowled. "Home, I guess. He tried snuff the other day, but it didn't set well with him."

"Ain't that the truth?"

Oak watched the exchange with one wandering eye through his coke-bottle-thick glasses. His sight was so bad he had to hold objects almost against his nose to read them. Tiring of the subject, he peered at an envelope through the thick lens. "Ned, you want your mail?"

"Probably just duns."

"Most likely. You need anything else, John T.?"

He started to say something else, but changed his mind. "Nope. I'm gone." John T. spun on one boot heel.

When he opened the door, James Parker rushed in, shouldering him aside. "Ned!"

The old constable's head snapped around at his son's frightened voice. "What?"

"Pepper's done run off from home."

"What are you talking about?"

"She left in the night."

Holding his belly, Ned rushed out the door, followed by James. Ned had no idea what to do first, other than get ahold of Top. He'd know what was going on.

John T. watched them go. With luck, Pepper and Cale would disappear forever, like a lot of kids who ran away from home.

At least he wouldn't have to deal with them.

Unless they returned.

Chapter Twenty

Once again on Main Street, Anna shook off her mad and passed a small, empty building that still harbored a mystery. A decade earlier, the owner of what then was a small fix-it shop was tied up, beaten, and left alone. By the time Ned and John Washington broke down the door, the owner was dead. They never knew if it was from the beating, asphyxiation, or the rats. The case was still unsolved.

She thought about turning into SkateWorld, but didn't figure grown men in suits would have any interest in roller skating. Her next stop was the Dairy Kreem drive-in. She parked under metal cover and ordered a burger, fries, and a Dr Pepper. The carhop hung the tray on Anna's partially opened window.

Anna held up the photo. "You ever serve these guys?"

The little brunette stood hip-cocked beside the car. "Yep. They've been in here a few times."

"Do you remember the last time you saw them?"

"It's been several days."

The hand-cut fries were still too hot to eat, so Anna separated the largest and balanced them on the side of the plastic basket, like cigarettes in an ashtray. "Did you talk to them?"

"No ma'am. Not more than taking their order."

Anna bit into the burger and chewed for a moment. "Do you always work this shift?"

"No ma'am. I work around my kids, and when Earl says he needs me, and that's pretty regular the way some of these gals are, not coming in and all."

"Did those guys ever stop here at night?"

The carhop thought for a minute. Another car pulled in out of the rain on the other side of Anna's patrol car. "Only once, last Friday. They came through about an hour or so before dark. Gotta go. Bye."

While she held the sweating Dr Pepper bottle and took a pull on the paper straw, Anna filed that little bit of information away. She made a note to come back and talk to the others later.

She finished her burger and the carhop picked up the tray. Anna backed into the rain and continued down the street to the Owl Drugstore. Neither the pharmacist or his employees recalled the brothers. That one was definitely a dead end.

Chapter Twenty-one

I was in the living room, scared and out of place. Pepper was gone and Miss Becky was cryin' to beat the band. Norma Faye, Uncle Cody's redheaded firecracker of a wife, at least that's what Grandpa called her when none of the family was around, was sitting beside Miss Becky on the couch and rubbing her back.

Pepper didn't need to be with me all the time, but by being close by, she made me feel better if I was down in the dumps, like now. Right then I was feeling so out of sorts I didn't know what to do. I was wishing Uncle Cody was there.

Miss Becky dabbed at one eye with a cup towel. "Pepper's gone, Top, and we need to go to church."

Of all the places Pepper might run off and hide, I knew it wouldn't be the Assembly of God church across the pasture. "She ain't there, Miss Becky."

It was like I said I'd hated her all my life. Her eyes widened and welled even more. She buried her face and bawled long and loud.

"What'd I say?"

Norma Faye blinked tears from her own eyes, shook her head, and laid her cheek on Miss Becky's shoulder.

Miss Becky's voice was muffled from inside the now damp towel. "I've failed with both of them. The Devil's done run off with one and the other'n don't know that our salvation and hope is in the church. Pepper ain't there, Top. Jesus is!"

I still hadn't learned when to talk, and when not to. "But you always said Jesus was right here with us, in our hearts, and all around us. What do we need to go to the church house for?"

"Hush, hon." Norma Faye rose and gently tugged me by the shoulder toward the kitchen.

I hadn't been there but for a minute before Grandpa and Uncle James pulled up in the drive. The wet gravel sounded completely different under the car tires than it does when it's dry outside. The back door opened and Aunt Ida Belle climbed out of the car. Her face was screwed up and she was crying too. They all came through the kitchen door, letting the screen bang shut.

Slap, clop, clop.

That's when I knew when things were really bad, adults lettin' screen doors slam.

They weren't no more'n through the kitchen and in the living room than the women commenced to wailin' like somebody had died. It made me feel even worse, listening to them like that.

Two marked cars came up the drive. Uncle Cody and Mr. John Washington finished filling up the living room with serious-faced adults.

Uncle Cody pitched his wet hat on top of the TV. "Does anyone know where she might have gone?"

Everyone shook their heads.

Aunt Ida Belle got hold of herself. "Don't nobody know where my baby girl is?" Her voice hitched like a kid's. She always gets her hair permed at Geneva's little shop by her house in Arthur City, but it was all wet and blowed up as if she'd been pulling at it.

"Top!" It was Grandpa and he sounded aggravated.

I knew that was coming. Here I was, all by myself and not knowing anything, but Pepper was still getting me in trouble. "Sir?"

"Tell me where Pepper went, son."

I tried on about three different expressions, trying to let 'em know I had no idea. "I didn't know she was gone until y'all did. She didn't tell me nothin'."

"If I find out you're a-lyin, I'll take my belt to you."

"I know, Grandpa. But I don't."

Uncle James rubbed his palms on his thighs. "Maybe she said something and you didn't much think about it. Is she staying with somebody from school?"

"Nossir."

Uncle Cody rubbed the back of his neck. "Maybe she's with kinfolk in Chisum."

I didn't know, so I didn't say anything.

Mr. John snapped his fingers. "I know. Mark Lightfoot. I bet she's gone across the river and is with him right now."

Aunt Ida Belle appeared hopeful. "I bet that's it. Do we have a phone number for anybody over there who knows him?"

"I'll find out." Mr. John put his hat back on and went outside.

"Top?" Miss Becky wiped her eyes.

"Honest! I don't know. We haven't talked to Mark since the powwow in Grant. I don't know no phone number for him. He said the house they were living in barely had electricity, let alone a telephone."

Conversation stalled while they studied the floor and each other.

Aunt Ida Belle took a deep, shuddering breath. "We need to do something. James, don't sit there like a bump on a log."

"What do you want me to do?" His voice told how miserable he felt.

She was lost. "I don't know."

The phone on the telephone table jangled loud enough to make us jump. I thought Grandpa would shoot it, even though it was our ring on the party line, and not two or three. It rang again, and again.

Uncle Cody sat down on the hard seat and answered. "Hello. No, this is Cody." He was mad at first, but then his jaw set and he listened. "Well, that explains a lot. No, Pepper's gone too. Do you have any idea where they went?"

We all watched him like an actor on a stage, hanging on to every word and trying to figure out what the person on the other end of the line was saying. Like Grandpa who rubbed his bald head when he was frustrated, Uncle Cody rubbed the back of *his* neck, where the hair used to curl over his collar. Now it was cut short, like the rest of the men in our community.

"Well, we don't, neither. That clears up a few things here, though. All right, we're working on it right now. Yep, I'll call you when we find something out."

Mr. John came back into the house as Uncle Cody hung up. Water dripped from his hat and his shirt was soaked. "Mister Ned, I got somebody from the sheriff's office in Hugo heading over to where Mark lives. He knows 'em, cause he has to go over there pretty regular to break up family squabbles and sometimes to haul off a drunk or two."

That made Miss Becky screw her face up even more. Mark lived with us for a while after his mama was killed, but we had to give Mark up when his family came to get him. Since they had the law on their side, Grandpa said we had to let him go instead of raising him as part of our own family.

Uncle Cody took a deep breath. "You can tell 'em to come on back. That was Cale's daddy. He said Cale's run off too."

Grandpa's face got red as a beet. "That little bastard! He took her with him."

Uncle James stood. "Let's go."

"Hold up, James." Uncle Cody held up his hand. "I said he's gone. Preacher Westlake don't know anything else and said he ain't got no idea where Cale might be. He's as worried as we are."

I've never seen so many adults in one place that didn't know what to do. Mr. John crossed his big arms and stared at the ground, studying on it.

The phone rang again, making us all jump. Uncle Cody eyeballed me and then answered. I raised both hands and shrugged, showing that I was telling the truth and still didn't know where Pepper was off to.

"Hello. This is Cody." He listened and then his eyes changed. "Thanks ma'am. I appreciate the call. No ma'am, I don't think it's wrong, and I'm glad you did, this time."

He hung up. "That was Miss Whitney."

"Aw, psssshhhhh!" It was Miss Becky's sound of disgust.

The old widow woman didn't have much family and couldn't get around much, so to fill the time, she liked to listen in on our party line. We all knew she picked up sometimes when we were on our call.

Grandpa took off his hat and rubbed his bald head. "Well?"

"She was listening to me talk to Preacher Westlake, and this time it's a good thing. She was listening a couple of days ago when Pepper and Cale Westlake were planning to run off, and she heard it all. They're on the way to San Francisco."

Both Miss Becky and Aunt Ida Belle wailed, and Miss Becky started praying loud and long.

Uncle Cody stood up. "Let's go."

It was the first time I ever saw Grandpa unsure of what to do. It took several long seconds before his face cleared. "Nope." He put his hat back on and set it right. "You're the sheriff now. You can't go off after runaways. Your job's right 'chere." He stopped Mr. John as he drew a breath to speak. "You too, John. Y'all have a hit and run to solve, along with two missing men. Me and James will take care of this.

"John, what you *can* do is put out an APB on the kids. Norma Faye, you come call the bus station and see if the kids showed up there. Mama, we've seen worse, just 'cause it's our baby girl don't mean…" He paused with a catch in his throat. Grandpa didn't say anything to Aunt Ida Belle, because all she could do was sit there and beller like a calf.

Norma Fay shooed Uncle Cody away from the telephone table. "I'll call the Dallas bus station, too. You're right Ned. Someone will remember seeing two kids buying tickets to California."

They all started talking at once and Miss Becky stood. "Come go with me, Top. We're walking over to the church to pray as hard as we can."

"Shit," I said under my breath, and Norma Faye whacked me a good one on the butt while she waited for someone at the bus station to answer the phone. It didn't hurt, though.

Chapter Twenty-two

Back on Main, Anna drove south. The rain slacked off to a light, misty drizzle when she glanced up at the 271 Drive-In marquee. *In the Heat of the Night* was the main headline. The story about murder in a racist southern town made her snicker, considering where she worked now. She didn't think there would be too many people that night. Even the second feature with Robert Mitchum, *Home From the Hill,* wouldn't be much of a draw, even though it was shot in Clarksville, only twenty miles away.

She was already past the drive-in when she realized it was the perfect venue for two men in a strange town and made a U-turn into the long gravel drive. It was still early and the ticket kiosk beside the giant screen was empty, so she crunched over the wet gravel and through the forest of short speaker poles. She parked near another car beside the concession stand and went through the front door.

Cecil Hutler was scrubbing the grill with a steel brush. He saw her and smiled. "Well, if you ain't a sight for sore eyes. I believe you're the prettiest deputy I've ever seen."

Anna took the compliment and smiled at the heavyset owner. "Thank you. I'm Deputy Anna Sloan."

"I've not seen you before."

"That's true. I only started a week or so ago. I'm here investigating the disappearance of two out-of-town businessmen." She held the photo out of reach, in case he was tempted to take it in his greasy fingers.

"I know. I saw the paper." Cecil showed his greasy hands. "Wish I had an exciting job as a lawman. What I have, though, is the glamorous life of a movie mogul. I keep the projector going up there," he raised his eyes toward to ceiling and the room above that housed the equipment, "order movies, keep the speakers going, replace the speakers when these idiots forget and drive off with them still hanging on their window glass, clean the grill, order food…"

She was afraid the list would go on forever and wiggled the photo. "Have you seen those guys that disappeared?"

Cecil lowered his hands. "Yep."

Anna chewed her bottom lip. "When?"

"They was here one night a couple of weeks ago. Maybelle was sick and I had to take tickets for a while until my wife could get up here to relieve me so I could get the first reel ready for the show…let me see, that was *Bonnie and Clyde*. I liked that one, 'course it's a real rip-snorter…"

"What made you remember them?"

"Why, they was dressed to the nines. You don't hardly see suits out here at the drive-in. They might have been to a weddin', instead."

Anna waited.

"One of 'em came to the concession counter. I remember, I went down for a cigarette and run a bunch of kids out of the bathroom. Them boys like to hang around in there and smoke."

Anna wiggled the image again. "Did you see them leave?"

"Lord, no. When the lights come on, it's a regular car race to the exit, and I'm usually packing up the reels by that time…now wait a sec. I came down for a minute, waiting for the projector to cool, and saw 'em in line to leave. I believe I saw someone get in their car before they reached the exit, but I can't be sure."

She felt a prickle along her neck and the unbelievably good luck. "Do you know who it was?"

"Lord, no. Somebody got out of a truck and in with them."

"Did you recognize the truck?"

Cecil scratched his shaggy head. “Naw. I see so many trucks and cars come through here every night, I couldn’t tell you who was driving it. I wouldn’t-a noticed, but some teenagers had one of them Chinese fire drills, where the doors on two or three cars all come open at once and everybody gets out, even the drivers, and they run around like chickens with their heads cut off for a minute and then pile back in. Drives me nuts, ’cause that kind of nonsense slows the line and the older folks complain about it, but they really ain’t doing nothin’ wrong, kids havin’ a little fun’s all. I only noticed ’cause it was an adult got in the car.”

She felt her hopes fall. “All right. If you think of it, give me a call at the sheriff’s department.”

“Sure will. Hey, do you want some free passes to the show? I’ll tell the wife to let you in any time you want. You can come tonight and see this new picture. I doubt we’ll have much of a crowd in the rain, but the kids who like to smooch will be here for sure. They don’t watch the picture anyways.”

“How about I wait till the weather clears?”

Cecil studied the big screen made gray by the falling rain. “That might be a while.”

Chapter Twenty-three

Ned pulled his Plymouth Fury to the curb in front of the Greyhound bus station in Chisum, the windshield wipers barely keeping up with the rain. Norma Fay hadn't gotten anywhere with them on the phone, so Ned gathered up James to do police work the only way he knew how, with shoe leather.

James never wore a hat, so he hurried out to stand under the neon-trimmed chrome overhead that extended to the curb. Ned circled around, stepped over the gutter running with water, and they pushed through the doors and into the station.

Two rows of uncomfortable blue chairs sitting back to back took up the center of the waiting room. Half a dozen people talked or read, passing the time until the next bus arrived. One man in wrinkled khakis and a worn blue work shirt sat facing the ticket window, reading a paper. He lowered it, saw the badge on Ned's shirt, and raised the paper higher. A couple in the other row waited for their bus, shoulders touching.

Ned's breath caught at the sight of an old man with an unusual black Stetson pulled low, hiding his face. It stood out against the small-crowned silverbellies worn by most of the men in Chisum. Ned stepped forward and touched the dozing man on the shoulder. "Tom."

Instead of Tom Bell, a stranger glanced up with a quizzical expression. "You talking to me?"

"Sorry." Ned felt his spirits sink. "Sorry. Thought you was somebody else."

The stranger grinned. "I reckon I am."

The oily haired ticket agent smiled at James through the window. "Howdy. Where to?"

"Not buying a ticket. We're looking for my daughter who took off on her own. She might have come here with a boy her age, about fourteen or fifteen, and bought tickets to somewhere in California."

The agent shook his head. "I'm sorry your little gal's gone, but I wouldn't sell tickets to a kid. Runaways come through ever now and then to catch the bus, but I send 'em on their way."

"Maybe somebody bought 'em for the kids."

He shrugged. "Might have happened. Lots of parents buy the tickets and put 'em on board to ride by themselves. Happens all the time, but they gen'lly tell me what they're doing. If they came through here during the night, I wouldn't know it no how. I get off at six. Hold on. He picked up a microphone. "All aboard for Dallas. All aboard for Dallas."

Ned stood to the side, hands in his pockets. Still keeping an eye on him, the man with the paper stood and headed toward the door leading outside. Ned scanned the others. They rose along with two scruffy young men who picked up small grips and filed through the doors and around the corner from where Ned parked the car.

He followed them outside under a second chrome overhang. After they boarded, Ned rested one foot on the bottom step. "Do you drive this route every day?"

The white-haired driver stuffed the tickets he'd collected into a pouch hanging from the dash. "Yessir."

"Did you have a couple of kids get on yesterday, boy and girl about the same age, fourteen or fifteen?"

"Nossir. Not yesterday."

"Did you drive last night?"

"Nossir. That'd be somebody else."

"Well, did you hear anybody say a couple of kids like that went to Dallas?"

"I wouldn't know."

"All right then." Ned's gaze rested on the man sitting on the front row, hiding his face again with the newspaper. "When'd you get out?"

Lowering *The Chisum News,* he squirmed. "Yestiddy. How'd you know?"

"McAlester?" The big penitentiary in McAlester, Oklahoma, a hundred miles north was as well known to Texans as Huntsville, farther south in Texas.

"Yes, boss." There was no pause between the words, as if they were one. The man's gaze slipped off to the badge on Ned's shirt. "I'm movin' on."

"Did your time?"

"Yes, boss."

"You see two kids, boy and a girl, fourteen to sixteen, come through here and get on a bus?"

"No, boss."

Ned studied on him for a minute, watching the ex-con grow more and more uncomfortable. "All right. Don't backslide."

"Yes, boss. Uh, boss? How'd you know?"

"I been at this business a long time, son. I don't know what you done since you got out, but you look awful nervous. I wouldn't do it again, at least not in this county."

The man's eyes slipped toward the floor. He had less than five dollars in his pocket, along with a Baby Ruth bar he'd snitched from the drugstore on the square, in case he got hungry on the way to Dallas. "Yes, boss."

Ned pushed away and the bus pulled into the rain with a roar. He met James back inside. "Dad, they don't know nothin' here."

"All right. Let's go check the train station, and if that don't work, we'll go to Dallas."

"Where in Dallas?"

"The bus station there, I reckon. They might have hitchhiked, and if they did, there's no way to know if anybody picked them up. The bus is our best chance."

"We might be going about this the wrong way."

"Why'd you say that?"

James rubbed the back of his neck. "I don't think these kids have enough money for bus tickets to Dallas, let alone California. Pepper couldn't save a dime. Every time she got any money, it'd burn a hole in her pocket until she spent it."

"Maybe that little shit Cale had money."

"He might, but do you think he'd have enough for *two* tickets?"

Ned drew a deep breath and thought. "It's the only thing we can do right now. If they hitchhiked, they could be anywhere. I'm hoping for the bus right now, and we'll see while I study on it."

"What if we split up? One of us tries the bus station, and the other'n follows the highway. Let me do that while you hit the stations. They might have started out thumbing, and then decided to catch a bus, or the other way around."

James watched Ned's face. Then the old constable nodded. "A-ite. I need to move. I'll follow the highway and you check the station in Dallas. We can keep in touch calling Miss Becky and leaving messages about where we are. We can meet somewhere along the way. Find our girl, Ned, before something happens."

Chapter Twenty-four

Anna's name came through the Motorola in her car. She picked up the microphone. "Go ahead, Cody."

"Ned's gone for a while and we got a theft report out of Center Springs. Run out there and talk to Oak Peterson. He owns the store with the gas pumps out front. Let me know what you find out."

It aggravated Anna to no end to get off the trail she was on, but it wouldn't hurt to be gone for a couple of hours. Chisum receded quickly as she followed the wet highway north through the country. A sign appeared through the rain, pointing the way to Center Springs over the new dam. Rain dripped from the needles of young pines recently planted along the two-lane road.

She emerged onto the dam, but it was hard to see the entire lake basin through the gray curtain of rain. All construction had stopped, and the dragline still rested far down below. Sanders Creek, stripped bare of vegetation, was already out of its ancient banks, and spreading. She wondered if the owners had good insurance, because it wouldn't be long before the heavy machinery was drowned in the rising waters.

She passed the hill where Ned's grandfather once lived. The house overlooking the creek bottom was long gone. Less than a mile further, the cotton gin belched smoke into the gray sky as it burned stems, leaves, and lint. The new road she followed dead-ended at the highway, directly in front of Oak's store.

A handful of farmers in overalls and khaki pants sat out of

the rain on benches under the porte cochere covering one side of the two gas pumps. Instead of driving under the shelter, Anna parked several feet from the covered area and walked through the falling weather.

"Hello, gentlemen."

To a man, they all waved or said howdy. One of the farmers leaning back in a cane-bottom chair dropped it to all fours and touched the brim of his hat. She could feel their eyes on her as she passed, but it was part of being an attractive woman in uniform, and as common as men staring at her chest instead of making eye contact.

She stepped through the wooden screen busy with flies. Even if he'd been standing in the middle of a dozen men, Anna would have known Oak by his description. He was behind the register, a notepad held barely an inch from his good eye.

He scratched through gray hair that hadn't been introduced to a comb or brush in months, and angled his head. "What can I do you for, ma'am?"

She glanced around the dark store. "Sheriff Parker sent me over while Mr. Ned's out of town. Said you were robbed."

He felt the countertop, and laid the pad down. Anna wondered how he could read the chicken scratches on the Big Chief pad. He dropped a yellow pencil beside it. "I was."

"At gunpoint?"

"Oh, no ma'am, 'round here, somebody'd get shot for that, if they was anybody around. Most of those boys out there either got a pistol in their pocket, or a gun of some kind in their truck. Nobody in their right mind would come in here waving one around.

"It happened when I was back 'ere in the post office. Y'know I cain't see good, but Cale Westlake was loafing around for a good while, and I believe he slipped around here and took money out of my cash box."

"When was this?"

"Day or so ago."

Anna saw the huge cast-iron cash register. "Didn't it ring when he opened it?"

"Why, no. That's small change in the register. I keep the bigger bills under the counter there in a cigar box. Cale's been in here since he was little, so he knows where I keep the larger bills. I didn't notice 'til I had to make change a little bit ago."

Anna took a slender notepad from her pocket and pulled the cap off a Bic pen. "Can you describe Cale Westlake?"

Oak appeared surprised. "You don't know him, do you?"

She tried not to stare at his wandering left eye. "No, I don't."

"Why, he's the Baptist preacher's son. Teenager with shaggy hair like them hippie kids grow today."

"A *kid* stole money from you?"

"Yes, ma'am. When I come out from behind the post office window, he was gone. I didn't know the money went with him 'til a little while ago, when I went to make change for Richard Sanderson out there. I swear, I wish he wouldn't come in here with them fifty-dollar bills. I gen'ly don't count the money ever night, 'cause it's so hard to see and my head hurts bad enough from it at the end of the day as it is, without counting money."

"Where does he live?"

Oak pointed back down the road. "Beside the Baptist church, but he ain't there. You passed it if you came over the new dam road."

"Where is he if he's not home?"

"They say he run off with Pepper Parker, Ned's granddaughter."

Anna slipped the pen back in her shirt pocket. "You don't know how much he took?"

"About a hunnerd and sixty dollars, I reckon." He angled the pad around so she could see it and thumped it with a yellowed nail. "I always write down my sales on this, so's I'll have a record."

Anna put two and two together and returned to her car to call in and tell both Cody and Ned that the kids were traveling with a pocket full of money. Then she went back to work on finding out what happened to the businessmen.

She didn't pay any attention to Marty, John T., and Freddy sitting on the domino hall's porch, talking with the other loafers about the runaways.

Chapter Twenty-five

The rain stayed on top of Ned all the way from Chisum to Dallas. Water stood in the middle of every plowed field, and the grassy bar ditches along both sides of the highway ran full. Swollen creeks threatened to escape their banks, evidence of even heavier rain only an hour west of Chisum.

As darkness approached, he stayed below the speed limit, uncomfortable with the increased traffic near the city. Highway 80 led him past the Sands Motel in the easternmost outskirts of Dallas. Only twenty years before, even that area was under cultivation by the children living at the Buckner Orphan's Home. Now, it was bright with the new motel, a drive-in theater, and a huge department store called Sage.

When he passed the cutoff for Fair Park, the site for Dallas' annual State Fair of Texas, gloomy low-hanging clouds hid the skyline and the red Mobil flying horse that was usually visible for miles.

He talked to himself as lightning fractured the clouds and thunder rolled through the city's concrete canyons. People hurried along the sidewalks, some sheltered under umbrellas and others with wet newspapers held overhead.

"I'god, if them fellers would wear hats like they're supposed to, they wouldn't be a-runnin' with wet papers on their heads."

Another light caught him in front of the Adolphus. The formerly grand hotel built in 1912 was so famous that Babe Ruth and Queen Elizabeth II once stayed there. Times hadn't been good to the building or downtown Dallas.

Before the light could change, a cocky black youngster in a blue, wide-brimmed hat rapped the silver-covered head of an ebony cane against Ned's window. "Hey, pops, you got a light?"

Ned rolled his window down and saw an unlit cigarette in the boy's hand. "No, and you're too young to smoke. How old are you, anyway?"

"Old enough to do what I want." Tucking the cigarette back into his shirt pocket, the boy leaned in. "You look like you right off the farm. You need some action tonight?"

"Action?" Ned judged him to be no more than fourteen, the same age as Top and Pepper.

"Yeah, action. A date...a woman."

"Lordy mercy." Ned was no stranger to Dallas pimps, but in all the times he'd brought prisoners to the Dallas jail, he'd never seen one so young yet hard and experienced from life on the streets. Ned's spirit fell when he realized his grandkids weren't prepared for the big city where people like this were waiting for kids fresh from small towns. "You get outta here before I take that cane away from you and blister your little ass with it."

Unused to such a direct challenge, the kid's eyes drifted to the gold badge on Ned's shirt. "You ain't doin' shit, old man." He tapped the brim of his hat with the cane and sauntered back onto the sidewalk and into the hotel.

Knowing where his temper would lead him if he followed the little smart-mouth inside, Ned decided it was best to go on. The light changed and he accelerated in the sluggish traffic. After a left on South Lamar, he found a parking spot at the curb outside of the brightly lit Greyhound station. Digging change from his pocket, Ned fed the wet parking meter and stepped through the revolving doors.

Unlike Chisum's, the once-classy Dallas Greyhound station built after WWII was buzzing with activity as travelers passed through, loaded with suitcases and paper sacks. Now the word *seedy* came to mind. The cracked and dirty floor was pocked with missing tiles. Dingy light fixtures, cut and torn seats, grimy walls badly in need of a fresh coat of paint, and an unidentifiable, musty odor all served to drain the spark out the proud old building.

It was loud and full of scruffy, long-haired kids staying out of the weather. The number of traveling families was noticeably lower because the kids' mere presence ran off the higher class customers, who in turn took to the skies and Braniff Airlines with their sparkling, sharply dressed stewardesses. To keep pace, the bus line introduced its own version of stewardesses who served sandwiches and light meals on longer trips, but it was too little and too late.

Ned's spirits fell at the sight of so many travelers, and he realized Pepper could have gone through the station without being noticed. His gaze wandered through the station to linger on what he took for an Indian in a lone chair against a dingy cinder block wall. The taut, muscular young man in his early twenties had hair down past his shoulders. Appearing to doze with his head against the wall, his folded arms rose and fell as he breathed.

The white kids dressed like their idea of Indians, and the only Indian in the station looked for all the world like a down-on-his-luck cowboy.

An elderly black man with a dust pan and broom fought a losing battle to keep up with the trash and cigarette butts on the floor. Ned touched his shoulder. "Excuse me, old timer?"

The janitor raised up from his broom to see the little constable's star on Ned's shirt, then the pistol in the holster on his hip. He ducked his head, reminding Ned of Old Jules, the elevator man back in the Chisum courthouse. "Yes, boss."

He held out Pepper's photo. "Have you seen this little gal come through here in the last couple of days?"

The janitor paused. "She looks like most of these kids passin' through."

"I 'magine."

"Nawsir, I ain't seen her, but that don't mean nothin'. I keeps my head down. She might have come through. Sometimes one'll stay outside while another'n buys the tickets, and then they go 'round the outside and board that-a-way."

Ned held out Cale's photo. "How 'bout him?"

"Nawssir. Him neither."

"All right then. Thank you." Ned slipped a folded dollar into the old man's hand.

"Thank you, sir."

When he was sure they weren't around, Ned threaded his way through people, legs, and luggage to join a line waiting to buy tickets.

A young man with long hair and the brightest clothes Ned had ever seen saw the Stetson and revolver. He raised a pair of granny glasses with blue lenses. "Hey man, you can't be the fuzz, you look like my Papaw."

Ned took in the long hair, the beard, beads, and sandals. He wondered if there was anyone in Dallas under the age of twenty-one who was respectful of their elders. "Fuzz?"

"Yeah, man. Like, pigs."

"Pigs?"

"Dude, are you some hayseed or something?"

That was a word Ned understood, and he bristled. "What do you want, boy?"

"Nothin, man. Don't go all ape on me. I'm diggin' the gun and hat's, all. You're not from around here, are you?"

"Nope. Chisum."

"So you traveling?"

"No. I'm looking for a runaway girl." Ned figured it wouldn't hurt to show him the photos. He held them out. "Have you seen either of these two?"

The hippie examined the pictures over the top of his glasses with exaggerated facial expressions. Ned recognized a smell coming from his clothes and realized he'd been smoking marijuana. "Haven't seen either one of them, but I wouldn't rat her out anyway."

"She might be in trouble, and I want to take her home."

"She could be anywhere in this town, Gramps. She might have crashed at somebody's pad when she got here, or bummed a ride or, don't freak out, but maybe she's somewhere on the make to pocket some bread. Who knows?"

"Don't you speak English?"

The hippie spoke quietly. "All right, what I mean is she could be anywhere, staying with friends, or if she's that kind of girl, she could be whoring to make enough cash to get by."

Ned flashed.

He balled the hippie's vest in his fist and pushed him out of the line. The guy's sandals slipped on the tile floor as he struggled not to fall.

"She ain't no whore! She's just a baby!"

"Chill *out*, *man*. I didn't mean nothing. What's it to you?"

The fear in his eyes was enough to back Ned off. He glanced around to see passengers watching in fascination, but none made any move to get involved. It was Dallas. The expressionless Indian against the wall barely opened his eyes, and then closed them again.

Ned let go, breathing hard. The exertion caused his stomach wound to ache, and he suddenly felt weak. "She's my *grand-daughter*."

"Aw man, I'm sorry. I'm sayin' man, that there are some dudes in here that wait on young girls to come through. See that cat over there?"

Ned cut his eyes toward a young black man. Unlike the hippie, he was dressed in bell-bottom jeans and a tee-shirt. His eyes were hidden by shades.

"He's a pimp. You know what that is, right, being the fuzz and all? He picks up one or two girls a week, on their way through to somewhere else. He gives 'em money or feeds 'em and gives 'em someplace to crash. He turns 'em on to heroin and pretty quick they work for him. You're in the city, man. It's that *way*."

"How do you know all this?"

"Man, I been here for over a week, trying to bum enough bread for a ticket to San Francisco." He grinned. "I guess I'll have to thumb it, though, 'cause all the money I score goes for weed and the munchies."

Ned didn't bother to ask him for an explanation. He started for the pimp who saw Ned heading in his direction. He jumped to his feet and quick-stepped outside.

Ned followed. "Hey, wait a minute, feller!"

Outside, the young man broke into a jog and disappeared into the dark alley behind the bus station. Ned followed much slower. In the dim lights, he saw another alley intersecting the first, half a block away. Polished shoes splashing in the stream of water flowing toward the gutters, he rounded the corner to find three men waiting with knives.

Ned stopped, holding the butt of his pistol. "Don't."

"What do you want old man?"

"I'm trying to find a missing child, that's all."

They snickered. Backlit by a yellow security light above a door, the pimp stepped forward. "So are we." The heavy mist caught in their hair and reflected the light in tiny sparkles.

"Careful, boys. This six-shooter ain't afraid of them knives."

The pimp's smile slipped. "I ain't your boy!"

The barrel of a pistol jammed into the back of his head told Ned he'd made still another terrible mistake. He was about to die in a Dallas alley, and Pepper would be lost forever.

"*This* pistol's in charge, old man." The voice was dark and rich. "Don't you pull that piece, or I'll blow your brains all over this alley."

Ned's mouth went dry, but instead of feeling afraid, heat prickled his face. "Don't want no trouble."

The pimp slid forward in a loose shuffle. "Let me see that picture you's wavin' around in there."

The man holding the gun to his head gave it a shove. "Turn loose of that pistol and give him the picture."

Slowly so as not to aggravate the gunman, Ned took Pepper's likeness from his shirt pocket and held it out. As he did, he felt the snap break on his holster and his pistol slip out.

The pimp flipped the photograph from Ned's fingers. He turned it toward the yellow light from a bulb above the nearest door. "Nice piece."

Ned's forehead throbbed. "No call to talk about her like that. She's a kid."

"That's how we like 'em." The pimp and his crew chuckled. "Ain't seen her, though. Wish we had. She'd be worth some money." He flipped the photo into the water streaming down the middle of the alley. "Speaking of that, why don't you give me your billfold and that badge? I'd like to have me a badge."

The pistol against the back of his head disappeared. Ned took the worn leather billfold from his left back pocket and held it out. "I got some cash here." He reached into his other, getting a grip on the leather sap.

Risking a glance over his shoulder to measure the distance between him and the most serious threat, Ned's eyes widened as a dark shadow rose and swung a short length of pipe. It connected with a wet slap against the gunman's head. He fell, arms stiff at his sides, unconscious before smacking his face onto the concrete with the sound of a dropped steak.

There was no time to think. In a practiced move, Ned pulled the heavy sap weighted with several ounces of lead and whacked the startled pimp on the temple. The street hustler's eyes rolled white and he went down as if he was poleaxed. Like a malevolent spirit, the shadow rushed past Ned and he caught glimpses in the darkness as the pipe rose and fell.

Only seconds passed, but in that time, grunts and shrieks filled the air, punctuated by one short, desperate plea. "Hey, wait…"

More blows fell, and then there was silence.

Heart beating wildly, Ned knelt and picked up his pistol and the one dropped by the now unconscious man. He tucked that one into his belt. Too old for street fights, he backed away from the alleyway's opening and against the wall with the sap and the .38 at the ready.

The Indian he'd seen in the waiting room emerged from the darkness, the length of pipe washing clean in the rain. "You all right?"

Ned cocked his head and lowered the pistol. "Who're you?"

"Crow."

"I don't know no Crow."

The taunt, muscular Indian pitched the pipe onto the concrete beside the unconscious pimp. "We can't talk here. We got to git."

Ned blinked and waved toward the bus station. "We need to call the laws on these punks and I still need to check in there to see if my granddaughter…."

"She ain't in there, sir."

"How…?"

Crow gently touched his shoulder and Ned felt an electric power in the man. "Because I doubt she ever came by bus. Now, let's go." He led the way and Ned followed on shaky knees.

Chapter Twenty-six

Cale couldn't *believe* the language coming from his girlfriend. Pepper was *pissed*. There was nothing to do but let her run out of steam, but he soon realized that might be a while.

She finally calmed down enough to talk in a slightly more civilized tone of voice. "I want my damn money back!"

"Listen kid. I don't give refunds."

They were at the counter of the Santa Anita Indian Trading Post on Route 66. Outside of the white building, signs abounded.

Watch Real Indians.

Trade!

Moccasins!

See Our Baby Rattlers!

Jackalopes For Sale.

She'd been excited long before they arrived at the quirky trading post late that afternoon. To that point, their road trip had been good, if not perfect. Earlier in the day they hitched a ride with a young family who left them off on the side of Highway 80, west of Dallas. At his wife's urging, the man pressed a ten-dollar bill into Pepper's palm and told them to be careful.

They hadn't been gone ten minutes when Pepper waved the bill at a passing eighteen-wheeler. The gray-haired driver shut the rig down and pulled over. The kids piled into the cab and Pepper stuck the ten into the driver's shirt pocket. "Nice ponytail."

"Thanks kid." With a hiss of air brakes, he pulled back onto the highway. "How far are you going?"

"The ocean."

"Hop in." Back on the highway with the kids sharing the passenger seat, Jimmie Ray Ozborne handed the ten back. "You don't need to pay me. I was on the road myself once. You can call me Oz. I'm heading for Albuquerque."

Cale and Pepper shared the passenger seat. She wriggled around to get herself comfortable. "Will you take us all the way?"

"Sure enough!"

Oz had the radio tuned to an outlaw rock 'n' roll station out of Mexico. With the cab filled with the Rolling Stones, James Brown, and The Doors, they rushed across the arid desert. True to his word, Oz dropped them off in Albuquerque an hour before dark, leaving Pepper with her ten bucks and some advice.

"Don't y'all get in no trouble."

They picked up another ride and would have gone farther with the man in the station wagon, but since Amarillo, Pepper kept seeing signs for Indian trading posts, and couldn't go another mile until she'd seen the inside of one.

And that's where the trouble started.

"No refunds, kid!"

She glared across the counter full of cheap knives, even cheaper bowls, fake Indian jewelry, Kachina dolls, rubber tom-toms and post cards. "You cheated me."

"You got your money's worth."

"The sign out front says 'Stop in and See the Baby Rattlers.'"

The man grinned. "So?"

"So them ain't nothing in the case behind that curtain but a handful of painted baby rattles."

"Right. Baby rattlers."

"I want my money!"

"Hell kid, it was only a quarter."

"That's not the point. You *cheated* me."

"Nope. Those are baby rattlers, like the sign said."

Worried because they were drawing a crowd, Cale pulled at the thin strap of her sack purse. "C'mon. You're spinnin' your wheels. He won't give you your money back."

"Well, I ain't buying a damned thing in here, and I was fixin' to try on some of those moccasins over there."

The manager's face hardened. "I'm done with you. Get out."

"We're gonna get gone, but this is a sorry excuse for a trading post."

Cale pulled Pepper outside, noticing that most of the adults were grinning at them. "You're gonna get us arrested."

Still mad, she pouted in the hot gravel parking lot. Fluffy clouds drifted overhead, scattering wide patches of shade across the desert. Not far away, a dust devil spun to life, reaching a hundred feet in the air.

"Look at that little tornado!" Pepper pointed.

"My people call them *chiindii.*" The black-haired boy in a headdress, bustle, feathers, and breastplate gave her a smile and did a little step to make his jingles rattle. "Hello. I'm Jonathan."

For a moment Pepper thought it was Mark Lightfoot in an Indian dance outfit, and felt a moment of sadness when she realized it wasn't him. "Oh, hi."

Cale stepped between them. "Yeah, and I'm her boyfriend, Cale."

Ignoring him, Pepper returned the smile. "I'm part Indian. What does chindy mean?"

He corrected her. "*Chiindii*, a ghost. They are bad. My people believe they are ghosts left behind after a person dies."

"My cousin sees ghosts."

"Many of our people do."

Pepper couldn't take her eyes off the young man. "Wonder who it was?"

"Doesn't matter. Don't let it touch you. Contact with a *chiindii* can cause illness. Even death, because they are everything bad about a person."

Cale couldn't take it any longer. "What are you all dressed up for?"

"I'm a dancer."

"Fancy dancer is more like it." Cale's tone was obvious. "Why don't you dance right out of here?"

Jonathan's eyes flashed. "I wasn't talking to you, but I'll cut you a deal. You pluck this white feather off my head and I'll leave. You can give it to her. If you can't in say, sixty seconds, you pay me twice what she paid to see the baby rattlers."

Seeing it as a way to get Pepper's money back, Cale nodded and grabbed for the feather.

Already anticipating the move, Jonathan danced away and bobbed his head. The parking lot was immediately filled with the musical jingle from the bell sets on his ankles, wrists, and waist. He held a fan in one hand and a bone whistle in the other.

Cale snatched at the bobbing feather again, but this time in addition to ducking his head, Jonathan blocked the grab with his forearm, sweeping the fan across Cale's eyes.

"Hey!"

Jonathan bent, danced, and bobbed. He sang softly to himself, keeping a constant beat with his feet. The jingling bells filled the hot sunshine. A crowd gathered, watching Cale dart in to snatch at the feather, only to be denied each time.

Pepper's breath came fast and she found herself rooting for Jonathan.

Thirty seconds later, Cale was pouring sweat and tiring. Head bouncing and bobbing, Jonathan spun left, then right. No matter how quick Cale's hands were, the Indian boy was faster. The vivid assortment of brightly colored ribbons, feathers and beads were a rich blur surrounded by the crowd of tourists who thought the confrontation between the two youngsters was part of a pre-designed show. Jonathan suddenly danced faster, his spins so pronounced that the feathers generated their own breeze.

Almost as if he had a stopwatch, Jonathan ceased to dance and stood upright. Cale grabbed the feather, plucking it from the roach on Jonathan's head. "Got it."

The Indian boy straightened. "No. The dance was over. You lost. Give it back."

Cale backed away. "You lose." He stuck the quill upside down under his own headband. "Let's go, Pepper."

He stopped. A dozen Indian boys in similar dress blocked his way. "Give it back."

Cale had never been on the receiving end of such a situation. Knowing he'd already lost, the bully quickly backed down. He jerked the feather out of his headband and threw it on the ground. "Indian giver!" He laughed at his own wit.

Jonathan's arm shot out and Cale recoiled as a painted stick lightly tapped him on the chest. "Hey! What was that?"

The Indian boy slipped the stick back into his waistband. "I counted coup on you."

"What's that?"

"Look it up."

Uncomfortable, Cale stepped back. "C'mon, Pepper."

She allowed him to grab her hand, and as he pushed his way through the line of dancers, she felt someone slip something into her free hand.

It was Jonathan's feather, and a Kennedy half dollar.

Chapter Twenty-seven

Ned's headlights lit the empty pavement. They hadn't passed but one car in a good long while. Behind the wheel, Ned Parker momentarily took his eyes off the wet road as they neared the small town of Denton on Highway 77. "Why are we going this way?"

Crow slumped against the door and crossed his arms. "I believe the girl you're after is heading for Amarillo."

"Her name's Pepper, and she's my granddaughter. How do you know where she is?"

"I don't, but I know where she ain't, and she hasn't come through that bus station while I was there." Crow handed him the picture he'd retrieved from the alley.

Ned shook his head, feeling a lump rise in his throat. This news on top of all the stress was taking its toll. His stomach ached worse than ever, making him feel bad all over. "How do you know that?"

"Because I come down from Oklahoma City a couple of days ago and I've been hanging out in the station to stay out of the weather."

"Why'd you set out with me?"

"Because I recognized you as a lawman from Chisum. You took my cousin to jail a couple of years ago and I come down when he appeared in court. You was there and he pointed you out. He said he was in the wrong and you was a fair man." Crow grinned. "That little stint in your jail did him a lot of good. He straightened right up after he got out. But Mr. Ned, you were as out of place in that city as a cat in a doghouse."

A dozen questions flashed through Ned's mind. He didn't know where to begin. "You an outlaw?"

"I'm not wanted for anything, if that's what you're thinking. I'm not running *from* anything, other than boredom."

Ned mashed the dimmer switch on the floorboard when a car appeared on the horizon. The click was audible. The oncoming car didn't reciprocate and it nearly blinded Ned as it passed. He switched back to high beams as the car disappeared in his rearview mirror. "Tell me what's going on here."

"I saw you in there and heard what you were doing." Crow shifted in the seat to get comfortable. He reached over his shoulder to push the door lock button. "I've seen that pimp and his friends working the station. They picked up a few girls who thought they could make it on the street. That's how I know your girl didn't come through, because they'd-a been on her like a chicken on a June bug."

Ned shivered, thinking what could have happened. "She's only fourteen."

"They don't care."

"She's with a boy a little older."

"He couldn't have stood up to those guys. They fight for a living."

"You were better."

"I've had to make a living."

Ned studied on the implications of that statement. "Start with you and your name."

"My name ain't important. Crow is enough, but I ain't Crow, I'm Comanche."

"I've known some folks up in Tahlequah by the name of Two-Crow."

"Nope. Just Crow."

The rain slacked once again and Ned turned the wipers to low. "You know so much, where we going?"

"Amarillo, first. The kids moving through Dallas are trying to get to California for the most part. I've watched them, and listened to what they had to say. If they aren't taking the bus, some of 'em are thumbing it. You're thinking old school. You need to think like they do."

"I cain't. I'm too old."

Crow nodded. "I understand. We need to get ahead of them if we can. Since Amarillo's the next biggest town, they'll most likely stop there for a little while before hitting sixty-six and taking it to California."

Route 66 was already a legend before it became even more appealing by the television program a few years earlier. The highway stretched from Chicago to Los Angeles. Other routes existed, of course, but Crow figured the runaways would follow the rest of the counter-culture kids funneling toward the Promised Land.

"My son, James, is checking different places."

"That's good. You know what highway he's following?"

"Not for sure. I'd expect this one, but he could be anywhere. We're supposed to call in to the house ever so often to check in."

"Well, when you do, tell him I think they're going to San Francisco."

"What makes you think that? Why not Los Angeles?"

"All these kids want to go where the action is."

"I'd bet Los Angeles."

"You'd bet wrong."

They drove in silence for several minutes. Few cars were on the road, so Ned kicked his speed above seventy. The farther west they drove, the less it rained. "Why'd you step in back there, and what are you getting out of this?"

"I was bored, for one thing, like I said, and I don't like to be bored. I don't like to see a man outnumbered, neither." Crow closed his eyes. "Besides, I've been thinking about going to California myself."

Chapter Twenty-eight

A steady stream of people came through our house, bringing food like somebody'd died. The women cried with Miss Becky about Pepper and held her hand. I tried to stay out of the way and spent a lot of time sitting alone in the hay barn, missing my cousin and wishing she'd at least call.

For the first time in a couple of days, the house was empty. I was on the couch and feeling pretty blue when Miss Becky came out of the kitchen. "Top, it's quit raining for a while. I need you to ride up to the store and get me some flour and baking powder."

She didn't drive, so I was her only hope. I heard she'd driven the tractor once or twice before I came along, and steered the truck in the pasture while Grandpa fed the cows, but she didn't have a license and had no intention of getting one as far as I could tell.

The phone rang, so when she sat down to talk, I jumped on my bike and coasted down the drive. The wet highway hissed under my tires as I pedaled past the ditches full of water. The weather kept a lot of people from running the roads, so not even one car passed me the whole way.

A handful of loafers sat under Oak Peterson's overhang, in the same postures I'd seen time and time again. Some sat on the benches, hands or elbows on their knees. One or two rocked back and forth on the back legs of cane-bottom chairs. I waved as I passed, and most waved back, but they didn't stop talking.

I didn't go into Mr. Oak's store because he scared me. I pedaled on past and leaned my bike against Uncle Neal's porch.

Thunder rumbled up on the river as I climbed the steps and went inside. For once there wasn't anyone on the porch. I hadn't seen that but a time or two. Uncle Neal was there at his counter with his wavy white hair sticking straight up, slicing rat cheese with his electric slicer.

Marty Smallwood leaned on the chest-type Coke machine, smoking a cigarette. I picked up a bag of Gold Medal flour and can of Clabber Girl and put it on the counter. I wanted an RC, but he didn't show any intention of moving out of the way. Not knowing how to go about asking, I stood there for a long minute.

"What do you want, kid?"

"I'd like an RC."

He uncrossed his ankle and flicked an ash on the floor. With the toe of his boot, he kicked a wooden case of warm RCs. "There you go."

Uncle Neal spoke over his shoulder. "Marty, come here and see if this is enough."

With a smirk, he pushed away from the cooler and sauntered to the counter. Running fingers through greasy hair, he dropped the butt on the floor and ground it out with his boot. "Yeah, that'll be enough. You ain't been across the river in a while."

Uncle Neal cut his eyes toward me and gave his head a little shake. "I got a pound of cheese here."

Marty sure didn't take the hint, or as I figured, he didn't care. "Some of the boys were shootin' dice the other night and said they missed your money."

I knew a lot of folks went across the river to drink, dance, and gamble, but it never occurred to me that Uncle Neal liked to play dice. Grandpa always had two sayings, "Some people just need killin'," and "Small towns are like stock ponds and you never know what's going on under the surface."

I had to think about Uncle Neal gambling, and I knew it was a sin, but I couldn't figure out if it was as bad as drinking. I put my dime in the machine and found an RC cap. Using two fingers, I slid the bottle through the puzzle of metal tracks to where I could yank it out of the machine. I pulled the cap on the opener mounted on the front and it clattered into the box. I decided I'd stay right where I was, drinking my RC as long as Marty was in the store.

"Marty, how's your mama?" Uncle Neal changed the conversation again and wrapped the cheese in white paper. There were two other packages already finished, waiting to be rung up.

His face softened. "She's fine."

"We don't see her much."

He glanced over at me. "How often do you see *this* kid's grandma in here?"

The sharp question caused Uncle Neal to raise his eyebrows. "Good point. That'll be two dollars and thirty cents."

"Put it on Mama's bill."

"All righty." Uncle Neal flipped through his book and wrote in pencil.

Marty picked up the packets and left. I saw Freddy Vines on the porch. Past him was John T. West, leaning against Marty's Dodge truck. They must have been in the cab and I hadn't noticed when I rode up. I'd been concentrating on missing the muddy red puddles in the lot. Freddy was a droopy little guy with a lisp, and he was complaining about something.

Marty pitched the packets through the open window. Freddy got in and slid across the bench seat to the middle, and John T. slammed the door. Something about that guy scared me, and I stared like an idiot. They sat in the truck for a minute, and I got the idea they were watching me back. It was so cloudy I couldn't see them, but standing in the lighted store, I must have been clear as could be.

"That all, Top?"

I shivered. "Yessir. Miss Becky said put it on our bill."

"Sure will." He put them in a paper sack and rolled the top down so I could carry it easy. Thunder rumbled again. "You better pedal hard."

I took the bag.

"Hey, any news on Pepper?"

"Nossir."

He shook his white head. "All right. Get gone before it starts raining again."

Moving at a pretty good clip, I hurried off down the steps. Marty's truck was still there, and the three inside were arguing. I swung a leg over my bike and pushed off. At the same time, I glanced into the cab to see that Marty was pretty mad and Freddy looked like he was about to cry.

With his arm hanging out of the passenger window, John T. gave me a dead stare.

"Hey kid. They find Pepper yet?"

"No."

"No, sir."

I gulped. "Nossir."

"Whyn't you go with her?"

"She didn't tell me she was leaving."

"She tell you why she was going?"

"No…nossir."

"Is that the truth?"

"Yessir."

He gave me those dead fish eyes again, and when I was sure he wasn't going to say anything else, I pedaled hard, trying to beat the rain.

Chapter Twenty-nine

The glitter was already worn off their road trip by the time Pepper and Cale arrived in Gallup, New Mexico. Her unwashed hair hung limp and she smelled of sweat. Her bell-bottom jeans were dirty from mid-calf down, heavy with road grime and dust. Cale fared no better, except he had to listen to Pepper.

"I'm hot, tired, and hungry. I need a bath."

He stopped in front of a Texaco station with a sign out front that said, "Try Our Lousy Coffee." Other signs also advertised diesel, a restaurant, and tires. "What do you want me to do about it?"

"I don't know." She paused, exasperated. Their whole adventure wasn't what they expected. Everything she'd seen on television featured happy teenagers dressed in beads, singing, dancing, and laughing. Everyone was so *clean* in the pictures and on television. She hadn't cracked a smile in miles, she was grimy, and with her transistor radio in pieces on the highway back in Center Springs, there was no music. "I expected this to be fun."

Cale wiped sweat from his forehead. "It ain't that bad."

"Is that the best you can do?"

"What?"

"Conversation. You don't never say anything."

He shrugged, watching a couple of hippie kids walk around behind the gas station. "I bought you those Indian beads back there in the curio shop." He'd paid a ridiculous amount for the fake beads, significantly shrinking the wad of cash in his pocket.

With her back to the station, Pepper didn't see a girl rise from the shade of the tall sign out front and follow the boys around back. "How about you get us a room somewhere…with two beds."

"You know no one's gonna rent to a couple of underage kids. Look, those guys over there live on the road and seem to be doing all right."

She followed his point to see a youngster with long blond hair lean on the back corner of the station, appearing to keep watch. "What is he doing?"

"Let's see."

Around back, the pair found the three boys and a girl washing up in the one smelly bathroom. The key attached to a large chunk of wood dangled from the lock. Pepper and Cale joined the line, glad for the opportunity to use clean water because most of the other gas station attendants refused to give kids the bathroom keys.

Pepper was the last to use the sink, washing her thick hair with cheap gas station soap. The light was out, so she couldn't completely close the door for privacy. Unlike the girl before her who took her shirt off and washed nude from the waist up, Pepper kept her shirt in place and did the best should could with handfuls of soapy water. Finished, she pulled on the dispenser to reveal a fresh section of the cloth towel loop for her hair.

Her shirt was still dirty, but at least her pits were clean. Finished, she felt bad about so many using the restroom. She wiped the lavatory down with a handful of soap and dried it with half a roll of cheap toilet paper.

Cale and the kids were in the front when she took the key back around to the attendant. He hung it on a nail behind the counter. "You ain't the one I gave it to."

"Right, but I'm the one brought it back."

"You didn't buy anything."

Still feeling guilty, she used her Kennedy half to buy snacks. She and Cale finished them before joining the group of kids standing near a line of highway smudge pots that would be lit at dusk to warn drivers of road construction.

"Hi. I'm Pepper."

"Cool." The girl brushed her long blond hair. "I'm Amanda."

"This is Cale. Where you guys headed?"

"San Francisco."

"We are too."

"You want to travel with us?"

Pepper thought about how easy it was for Amanda to take her shirt off in front of the other boys. "We like to travel alone."

"At least go with us tonight." One of the boys gave Pepper a good, long appraisal. "We're gonna crash at this pad we heard about a mile from here. Hoof it with us for a while."

Cale took an immediate dislike to the young man in the crushed and lopsided straw cowboy hat. Greasy brown hair hung to his shoulders and the sparse beard did nothing but make his face look dirty.

"We'll thumb a ride and get down the road." The boy took Pepper's arm. "I'm Barry. These guys are Mike and Owen. Come with us for the night and you can take off in the morning. I hear they have some good weed where we're going."

Even though he didn't like the guy, Cale thought about free marijuana. It was the one thing he hadn't yet tried, and the lure was irresistible. "All right."

"Shit," Pepper said under her breath and allowed Barry to lead her off down the highway.

The snacks hadn't lasted long, and she was hungry by the time they arrived at a stucco house that was old during World War I. The bare yard did nothing to improve the appearance of the structure. A leafless cottonwood looked as listless as the neighborhood.

Hoping they had food inside, she quickly changed her mind about staying the minute they stepped through the front door. The house reeked with the thick smell of incense. Music like the country kids had never heard blared from a console record player in the dimly lit living room. Young people slept on cast-off couches and broken-down chairs. A black light caused people and clothes to glow with an eerie incandescence.

She stopped, mesmerized by the guitar rifts. "Who is that?"

A shirtless boy sitting on the floor glanced up. He was surrounded by other kids, curled up like kittens on the hardwood. Cale instantly disliked him, more for his filthy feet than anything else.

"Dude's name is Jimi Hendrix."

A girl giggled, stoned out of her head. "He's so far out."

"I've never heard..."

"That's right, little girl," Shirtless said. "You've never heard him before because that's an album I got from my cousin who lives in England. Jimi's hammering them Beatles into the ground over there."

Stomach growling, Pepper slid down the grimy wall and Barry sat beside her. Cale wedged himself between her and Shirtless, receiving a glare for his effort.

The cherry on a joint flared red, and then floated through the smoke as it passed from one person to the next. Another made its way to the new arrivals.

Pepper wished there was an adult somewhere close. "Who's house is this?"

Barry shrugged. "Who knows?"

The joint was suddenly in Cale's hand. He took a shallow hit and coughed most of the smoke back out. He passed it to Pepper. She cupped the joint and instead of inhaling, gave it a puff, keeping all the smoke in her mouth. She blew it into Barry's face and handed it over. He grinned at the flirtation, drew deep, and passed it on.

The joints made another revolution and Pepper was convinced she could feel the effects. Her head buzzed. She felt something and glanced down to see Barry's hand on her leg. At the same time, someone untied her shoe.

She squinted through the smoke to see Shirtless on his stomach. He gave her a grin, his teeth glowing in the black light. "Hey baby, I bet your feet are tired. Let's get these off and I'll give you a massage."

Stunned for a moment, Pepper didn't know what to do. Then she threw her head back, laughed, and kicked his hands away. "Get your damned grubby paws off me."

Interested in one of the other girls in their circle and already buzzing from the grass, Cale missed the exchange. He was startled when Pepper shot to her feet. She stepped over Shirtless. "I'm gonna get something to eat."

"Get me something, too."

Her response to Cale was a snort. Jimi Hendrix ended and with a screech of the needle across the record, Grace Slick blared from the speakers, asking if "you want somebody to love." Pepper was relieved to find gray light coming through the dingy kitchen window. Dirty dishes filled the tiny counter, and cold pans crusted with unidentifiable solids occupied all four burners of the filthy gas stove.

The twenty-year-old Frigidaire was empty, except for a jar holding one pickle. She fished it out with two fingers and found a half-empty bag of Fritos on the table. The pickle disappeared in seconds. Munching the stale chips and sipping at the pickle juice, Pepper wandered into the hall. The bathroom door was closed when she passed, the shower running. She almost moaned at the thought of a hot shower. Instead of returning to the living room, she waited against the wall for a turn.

Barry joined her in the narrow hallway. He gave her a crooked smile and stroked her arm. "Hey baby. How about you and me go in one of these rooms and get it on?"

She backed away. "No. I'm not into that."

"Sure you are." He closed the space and slipped his arm around her waist. He nosed her ear.

Frightened, Pepper pushed against his chest. She realized it was only her against the larger boy. "Look…"

"C'mon baby. You know you want to."

Pepper trembled. Her breath caught. "No." She pushed again.

He rubbed his cheek against hers, his hat brim bumping her head. "I am so into you right now."

She smelled old sweat, oily hair, cigarette smoke, and marijuana.

"You really turn me on. Do what you feel, Pepper."

It was the absolutely wrong thing to say at the wrong time. Barry's free hand slipped up her arm, under the strap of her bag, and across her shoulder. He stopped directly over the scar burned there by the Skinner and pulled her close.

That rainy night in the creek bottoms, the Skinner scarred Pepper's shoulder, but he also damaged her deep inside where dark corners held secrets and recollections best not recalled.

Pepper whimpered as the memory welled of Top handcuffed and nearly dead, and the helplessness she felt, half-naked and tied face-down on a fallen log. She thought she'd pushed that night away, but Barry brought it back when he ground his pelvis against her. She pushed again, barely stifling a scream. Then he kissed her.

It was too much and Barry's face became the mask of the Skinner.

"No!" She threw a right uppercut that would have made her Uncle Cody proud.

Barry's head snapped back and he bit his tongue. He dropped to his knees and fell against the wall, holding his bloody mouth. "Are you *crazy!*"

"*Yes!*" Furious, Pepper kicked at him and he rolled away. "I *am* crazy! I'm *insane!*" She stomped down the hall and through the smoky living room, kicking people out of the way. "Move!"

While Scott McKenzie sang about going to San Francisco with flowers in your hair, stoned youngsters recoiled from Pepper's assault by curling into balls or drawing their limbs as close as possible. They rippled away like rings on the surface of a pond.

"Hey girl, uncool!"

"Chill!

"She doing acid?"

"Yeah, bad trip, man."

Furious, Pepper stopped beside Cale and kicked the sole of his shoe. "I'm leaving. Are you going?"

He squinted in the weak light, trying to focus. "Whatever you want. I'm feeling pretty good right now, though."

With a growl that scared everyone within hearing distance, she grabbed his shirt and yanked Cale to his feet.

Moments later, they were breathing fresh air and back on the road.

Chapter Thirty

I hadn't hardly been back at the house for twenty minutes before Norma Faye pulled up in the drive. I waited for her and Aunt Ida Belle to get out, but Miss Becky came out of the kitchen and clicked the TV off. "Come go with me."

In the silence, I heard rain running off the roof and drumming on the water cooler hanging in the window. It had been thundering long and loud and the next line of storms wasn't too far away. "Where we going?"

She untied her apron and hung it on a hook, trading it for a bonnet. "We're going to see Melva Hale."

I saw the flour and baking soda still sitting on the table and knew she'd sent me off to get me out of the house. "Aw, let me stay here."

She thought about it for a minute, then changed her mind. "No, not with everybody gone. I don't want to go, neither, 'cause I don't feel like it, but they done buried Leland in the rain and I know she's hurtin' like we are. Now, come on."

There wasn't much talk while we drove. I could tell none of them wanted to go, but they went anyway, because that's the way they lived life.

I've never felt as uncomfortable as I did when we walked into that old house. Melva didn't act like she wanted us there, but she opened the screen door. Folks usually smiled and said something like "come on in this house" or "howdy, y'all, good to see you." She didn't do anything except back up to let us in.

Marty was laying on the couch, not reading or nothing. The house was silent, with not even the tick tock of a clock to fill the emptiness. When Marty saw me, he swung his feet around and without saying boo to anyone, walked into a bedroom.

Melva giggled. "That boy's something, ain't he?"

Aunt Ida Belle and Norma Fay exchanged looks while Miss Becky put a foil-covered dish on the empty table. "How you doin', hon?"

"I'm fine. How're you?"

"Holdin' up. Pepper's gone, you know."

"Who?"

Aunt Ida Belle sat on the couch. "My girl, Pepper. She's run off with some boy."

"Well, I 'spect she'll come back with a baby then."

All three women gasped. "It isn't like that," Norma Faye said.

Melva's smile reminded me of that painting the *Mona Lisa*. I couldn't believe she'd say something so mean. I tried to find some way to change the conversation and saw a faded photograph. "Is this Marty when he was a baby?"

Melva shook her head. "No, that was my other boy. It died not long after its daddy took that picture.

"I'm sorry." Miss Becky patted her hand.

"Oh, that's all right. It was a long time ago and I reckon it was for the best. It didn't have a chance to grow up to sin, and run off."

Aunt Belle's mouth was a thin line. "There's no reason to talk like that. We came 'cause of Leland."

"They're both dead and buried, and ain't no one on this Earth can do nothing about it, so we need to go on. In a hunnerd years, it won't make no difference anyways."

I kept staring at the baby in the photo, and didn't like that she'd called that little thing an *It*. "Didn't you name him?"

"Hush, Top." Miss Becky's expression flashed me a warning.

Marty came through in boots that sounded a size too big. They were squared off at the toes with a chain going across the top. "Jerry. His name was Jerry." He didn't stop, letting the screen door slam behind him.

"It cried all the time." Melva shook her head as a tiny giggle rose in her throat. "Never saw a baby cry so much."

I couldn't sit there anymore with that crazy woman. "I'm going outside."

Miss Becky nodded. "There was a lot of folks at Leland's funeral, Melva. It was good to see so many."

I knew better than to let the door slam when I went out. Marty was on the porch, smoking and watching the rain drip off the edge of the roof. "Why were you staring at us so much up at the store?"

I couldn't meet his eye. "I wasn't staring."

"I guess you heard what we were talking about?"

"It was probably about money or girls—Grandpa says that's what trouble's usually about."

Marty took a long drag and let the smoke out through his nose. "Your grandpa talk about me?"

"What for?"

"Does he?"

"No. Why would he?"

"Where is he?"

"Gone." I didn't want to tell him anything. I didn't trust the guy any farther than I could throw him, and I didn't like him one little bit. Even for a kid, I knew he was trying to lead the conversation somewhere, and I didn't know why. I wished Uncle Cody would drive up and take him to jail, for anything. For some reason though, the way he kept staring at me, I felt like I needed to explain what I'd seen up at the store. "You guys were sitting out there, and I couldn't help but wonder what you were doing."

He smirked. "Yeah, I know about doing things you can't help." He took a deep drag and let the smoke out through his nose in a long cloud. "Want a drag?"

"Nossir."

He snorted again. "I was smoking half a pack a day by the time I was your age."

"I have asthma."

He finished the cigarette and flicked the butt into the wet dirt beside Norma Faye's car. "I'm going for a ride. You want to go?"

I sure didn't, but I was afraid I'd look like a baby. "I'll have to ask."

"Go ahead on."

I went back inside and stood beside Norma Faye's chair for a long second. They glanced up at me, but no one said anything. Acting bored, I went back outside.

"In or out," Miss Becky said.

I stepped around a rotting board and faked a sigh. "They won't let me."

He nodded and patted his hair greasy with HA hair lotion. "Didn't think so. Your cousin's still gone, huh?"

"Yep."

"She left in a hurry, I hear."

"She left. That's all."

He studied me for another second before getting into his truck and backing onto the dirt road. Shifting into gear, he pulled out in a spray of muddy water.

I stayed on the porch, wishing we would go, too. After I'd cranked the washing machine ringer a couple of times and poked through a wooden box of wrenches, I laid on my back to see what the yard looked like upside down. It seemed like an hour before they made their goodbyes, and we hurried through a heavy shower.

Me and Miss Becky climbed into the backseat. She folded her hands in her lap. "Norma Faye, drive us to town. I want to talk to O.C."

Both her and Aunt Ida Belle flicked their eyes to the rearview mirror at us back there. Aunt Ida Belle twisted halfway around. "What good will that do?"

"None at all, but at least we'll be doing something."

While Norma Faye drove, I closed my eyes and listened to them gossip about how odd Miss Melva was, until the conversation drifted back to Pepper. I dozed on the way to town and dreamed she was back with me and we were laughing like we used to.

Chapter Thirty-one

Miss Becky opened the door to Judge O.C. Rains' office without knocking. He glanced up and pitched his pen onto a stack of papers. "Have any of you Parkers ever learned how to knock?" His eyes told me he wasn't really aggravated.

She stopped, wondering if it was a serious question. "Why, it had your name on the door and I figured you'd be in here."

He sighed and waved at the only empty chair in the office that smelled like old books and damp paper. Miss Becky sat down. Norma Faye and Ida Belle stayed by the door. I perched myself on a stack of law books beside his desk, drinking a Mountain Dew. It didn't taste near as good as it would have if Pepper'd been with me. She always liked those bottles because they said "It'll Tickle Yore Innards!" and had a picture of a cork going through Willy the Hillbilly's old slouch hat.

I suddenly realized I missed her so bad it hurt. My stomach knotted up, and for a second I thought I'd cry, but I wouldn't do it in front of all those adults.

"Did you bring me a Coke?" The judge's white eyebrows met in the middle, but I knew he wasn't mad.

"I'll go get you one. What kind do you want?"

Folks who aren't from around out part of the world sometimes have trouble with how we talk. If I went up to the store and asked for Coke, Uncle Neal would ask me what kind. Coke's a general word for soda pop. I'd seen the judge drink Dr Peppers, oranges, grapes, and root beers, but there were others in the machine downstairs like RC Colas, Double Colas, Big Reds, and cream sodas.

"Aw, I reckon I don't need one right now, but I might take a sup of yours after while."

Ida Belle was dabbing at her eyes with a lace handkerchief. "O.C., can't you put out one of those all calls to tell everyone to look for my baby?"

"Hon, we've done done it." I could tell it about broke his heart to see them in his office, desperate for information. I wasn't sure why we were in there in the first place. Uncle Cody was sheriff, and I knew for a fact that he was doing everything he could to find Pepper. I guess they were reaching out for whatever they could find. "There's men watching for them all across Texas. I've seen half a dozen reports about little gals they've picked up that fit Pepper's description. None of 'em was her. Have you heard from Ned or James?"

Miss Becky nodded. "They split up for a while, but they haven't found her. Have you heard from Cale's mama'n daddy?"

"Yep." Mr. O.C. rocked back in his chair. "Talked to them several times, and he's asked the same questions as y'all. We're doing what we can." He pooched his lips out to think. That's when the phone rang.

"This is Judge Rains."

Judge O.C. didn't hold a receiver tight against his head like some folks. He kinda rested it on his shoulder and angled the whole thing away from his face while he rocked back and forth in his creaky old desk chair. I was sitting close enough I could hear snatches of the man's odd way of talking. It was as if he were reading and stumbling over a written speech.

"Hear what I am telling you—"

"Who is this?"

"—don't matter. Them two men you're looking for are buried by the dam and equipment at the new lake."

O.C. frowned. "How do you know that? You don't sound right."

"Near to the heavy equipment."

"That's a pretty big lake bottom. Can you give me a little more to go on?"

Aunt Ida Belle had heard enough to scare her. "Oh my God! They've found my baby in the bottoms!"

They all three set up to start wailin', but Judge O.C. covered the mouthpiece. "Y'all hush and settle down. This is about something else." He went back to the caller. "All right. Them two men are buried by the heavy equipment close to the dam. Who is this?"

"You need to hurry…ah…due to the water coming up."

"Wait." Mr. O.C. stopped rocking. "Why'd you call *me*?"

"Ned Parker ain't here and them men need to be burried right."

Something about that voice was familiar.

"How do you know about them?"

Silence.

"Did you call the sheriff's office?"

"No, I'm talking to you, ain't I?"

"Who killed 'em? Was it you?"

There was a long silence before the line went dead.

Judge Rains pushed the disconnect button with his finger. The caller hadn't given him much information, but I was sure of one thing, he was from Center Springs. No one else would know Grandpa was out of town and I didn't think it came from town, because it wasn't raining hard right that minute.

Judge O.C. dialed four numbers real quick. Someone answered on the other end. "Who's this?"

"Cody." His voice was as clear as the man's had been.

"Good. I got a call, said them businessmen you've been trailin' are buried in Center Springs."

"Where?"

"Said somewhere in sight of the dam. You better get to rolling. With all this rain, the creek'll be out of its banks by now and I'd imagine it's gettin' close to where he said they're buried. Get John Washington to go out there with you."

"Wonder why they called you and not me?"

"Can't say. I asked him, but he didn't give me no answer."

"All right. I'll get Anna, too. We need to move fast."

Mr. O.C. hung up without saying goodbye and scowled. "Becky, I hate to run y'all off, but that was an important call I gotta get on right now."

She gathered her purse and stood. "Dead men buried in the lake. Daddy said that lake would claim folks pretty quick, but I doubt he figured it'd be this soon."

"It wasn't the lake that took 'em."

Norma Faye shoved a strand of red hair behind her ear. "Was Cody in his office?"

"Yep."

"We were going by to say howdy, but I guess we'll need to go on home."

"That'd be best. He's gonna be pretty busy for the next little while."

Instead of going to see Uncle Cody, we went downstairs, our footsteps echoing on the black and white tile floor. All that time, I kept playing Mr. O.C.'s conversation over in my head.

I'd heard that voice before, but I couldn't place it.

Chapter Thirty-two

Cody hurried out of the courthouse, taking the back steps two at a time. He jogged across the parking lot to his sheriff's car and picked up the microphone. "John."

He was on the wet road by the time Deputy Washington came back. "Go ahead, Cody."

"I'm on the way to Center Springs. We got a call saying those missing businessmen are buried in the lake bottom."

"Anything else? It'll be hard to find them out there."

"Not much. The caller said they were somewhere in sight of the dam, where the heavy equipment's been working to finish up. I've called some other folks, but you probably need to meet me."

"I'll be there directly."

Cody keyed the microphone again, thinking hard. "Anna."

She came on immediately. "Go ahead. I heard what you told John."

"Good. I need to talk to you about what you've found out."

"Quite a bit. See you there."

It was raining hard by the time he was north of town. The bar ditches ran with water, a clear indicator that the new lake would soon cover the Sanders Creek bottoms. He drove over the dam twenty minutes later. From that high vantage point, the empty bowl of the future lake emphasized the clouds hanging low overhead.

The lake bed was easier to access on the far side of the dam, opposite the overlook. There was another way into the bottoms, but it was farther west and wound through some rough country before opening to where they were going. Cody drove past the old house place where his grandfather once lived, then down the sandy incline rutted with deep tracks from heavy vehicles.

He stopped the car beside a cluster of pickups, afraid of getting stuck if he went any further. The wipers slapped a beat to the radio tuned low and buzzing with static. Two bulldozers chained to a dragline poured black smoke into the rain and towed the dragline free of the mud toward higher ground.

John and Anna arrived and more trucks parked behind them. Cody opened the trunk and pulled on a long yellow rain slicker. His shirt was already wet, but it would at least turn water for the rest of the time they were out there.

In her own raincoat and Stetson, Anna gave him a grin when she noticed him eyeing the hat. "I needed a little more brim for all this water."

"I can see that. It probably makes more sense for you to wear that anyway."

Isaac Reader, Dub Hinkley, and Mike Parsons closed in to hear. Buck Johnson parked close and joined them. With nothing else to do in town on such a rainy day, he dropped by to offer his services if they were needed.

Cody waved a hand. "Y'all, all I know is that someone called and said the bodies of those businessmen are buried somewhere out there."

John whistled, appearing twice as large in his own loose slicker. "That's a lot of blowed up country."

"Listen, listen, this is a big lake." Ike Reader stated the obvious, as if the rest of the people around him hadn't noticed. "Do we spread out and start kicking the ground?"

"I don't believe that'd work, Ike."

"Well, they might not be buried deep and we might see some clothes, or an arm or something."

"We might, but I doubt that, too."

Anna shoved both hands in her pockets. "Then why are we here?"

"Well, I guess we had to come out. I wanted to see how high the water's getting, and *second*, I had an idea." He pointed at a battered farm truck rattling down the hill toward them with Ty Cobb Wilson behind the wheel. "They may have our answer."

The Wilson boys stopped and detrucked. Not minding the rain, Jimmy Foxx tromped through the mud and lowered the tailgate while Ty Cobb walked down to meet them. Both wore thigh-high waders, folded down at the knee and flapping like bell-bottom jeans around their calves. "You must have something special going on to be out here in this weather."

Cody watched Jimmy Foxx open the door to one of the dog boxes. "Yep." He explained about the call and why he'd contacted them. "So I heard you had this dog that can smell dead people."

Jimmy Foxx led a soaked Brittany spaniel on a leash. "Sure do. Cracker here, we call him that 'cause it's short for Cracker Jack, well, we can't hunt quail anywhere near a cemetery because he'll run to a fresh grave and start digging."

John's eyes widened in horror at the thought of digging in a grave, fresh or otherwise. "Lordy mercy, what's *wrong* with that dog?"

"Nothing that we can figure out." Ty Cobb rubbed Cracker's ears. "He's got the best nose I ever saw for a retriever. He ain't much at pointing birds, but by God, once we get one on the ground, he'll find it. We've used him to track all kinds of wounded game, but if he gets a whiff of something dead, you cain't hardly drag him away." He looked sheepish. "Brother Hill at the Methodist church said we couldn't hunt anywhere near the cemetery anymore, though that's where two or three big coveys hang out. Said it wasn't right to see a dog nose-deep in a fresh grave. He's done it twice."

Ike stepped back from the dog, as if it might sniff at him. His fears ran deep, and often involved clowns. He'd never thought to worry on a dog that pointed dead people, though. "Listen, you don't think he can point at folks who might be sick or dying?"

Cody bit his lip to hide a grin. "You feeling all right, Ike?"

"I'm fine now, but I'd die right here and now if that dog was to lock up on *me*. Listen, listen, you know, Mr. Messer out in Ragtown can smell cancer and he can tell when folks are ready to die. They bring him out to some people's houses ever now and then who're in bad shape to see if they'll make it."

Anna raised an eyebrow at the thought. "You're kidding, right?"

"If I'm lyin', I'm dyin'…" Ike trailed off when he realized how the words sounded. "Listen, I heard tell they took him to the cancer ward in Dallas and he 'bout had a seizure pickin' up on all them old folks that didn't have much longer in this old world…" he stopped again, thinking about what he'd said.

The guys would have left him dangling, but Anna felt sorry for the sun-baked little farmer, so she tried to get Ike off the hook. "So you called them to find the bodies, Cody?"

"That was my thought."

John shook his head. "I don't rightly know if he'll be able to smell in all this rain. It's been coming down for so long."

Cracker sat in the mud and scratched an ear with one hind foot.

"I understand, but we're talking about *two* bodies, and I doubt they were buried that deep, if they're here at all."

Ty Cobb waved an arm in the rain. "I hope you have a starting point. There's a lot of country out there."

"Not much of one." Cody jerked a thumb. "Get down toward the creek, because the water's rising and I think it'd be best if we covered the ground there first, then y'all can work out this way."

Jimmy Foxx released the dog and whistled. He waved an arm and called to Cracker in a singsong voice. "Look *fooor* it." The Brit put his nose to the ground and sniffed his way toward the creek that had already slipped its banks. The dam was finished and the Corps of Engineers had closed the gates. For the first time, all the water that should have eventually emptied into the Red River two miles away was creeping toward what would soon be the permanent shores of Lake Lamar.

The Wilson boys followed, slogging their way between half-burned brush piles, following the dog working toward the distant ribbon of muddy water. The spaniel loped ahead for several yards with his nose to the ground.

Ike remained rooted to the muddy ground, glad the dog had gone the other way, but fully prepared to run for his truck if it started back toward him.

John shrugged his shoulders, threatening to split the slicker at the yoke. "That poor old dog's gonna wear his sniffer out, prob'ly for naught."

"Could be." Cody turned to Anna. "All right. What have you found out?"

"Those guys have been here for a long while. Judge O.C. recalled seeing one of them down on the square one day, taking pictures while he was talking to Mr. Ned, and you, John."

"I remember that. Mr. Ned kept watching that guy making pictures with his camera. He worried on that for a long while."

"I don't know why he was taking pictures. They came to buy land and from what I hear, brought a briefcase full of money."

"That'll get you killed pretty quick, if you're flashing it around." Cody watched Cracker lope to another brush pile.

"I don't know if they were flashing it, but they had it. They stopped for a burger the night they disappeared, and then went to the drive-in to see a movie. The owner said he remembers them and saw someone get out of a truck and jump in the car with 'em." She held up a hand. "No, he couldn't recall the truck, or who was in it."

"That don't surprise me. Half the people who go to the drive-in take their trucks."

Anna absently chewed a painted fingernail, then quit when she realized she was damaging the finish. "Did you know the kid Pepper's with stole money from Mr. Peterson's store?"

"I knew someone did, but not a name." Cody shook his head. "I'll have to let Ned know that it was Cale."

"Any news about the kids, John?"

"Not yet. I should have gone with them."

"Nope. I know you wanted to, and I did too, but we have to stay here."

"Mr. Ned ain't feeling too good. He might need me."

"His bullet wound is still acting up." Cody had his eye on the dog and stopped talking when the spaniel became interested in a half-buried log. The others followed his gaze and tensed, waiting for a reaction from one of the Wilson boys. Then the dog raised his leg to pee and took off again.

Cody chuckled. "This might take a while."

John watched the spaniel. "Can't be too much longer if he keeps histin' his leg on every stick he smells. That little dog'll be plumb wrung out before he's done."

Chapter Thirty-three

High, thin clouds scudded over Amarillo, a welcome departure from the depressing clouds sitting over most of east Texas for more than two weeks.

James Parker waited against the fender of his Bel Air in front of Peggy's Coffee House and watched Ned pull his smoking Plymouth off the two-lane Route 66. He expected James to be there because he'd stopped at a drugstore phone booth in Quanah, Texas, to call back to Center Springs. Ned learned from Miss Becky about the search for the missing businessmen, Cale's theft of the money, and that James planned to meet him at the Amarillo coffee shop.

It had been a long two-day trip from Dallas to Peggy's parking lot. While Crow spent most of his time dozing against the passenger door, rousing only when they slowed down in every small town that seemed to be spaced exactly thirty miles apart, Ned steered past fields of endlessly rocking jack pumps and isolated farmhouses protected by tall fences of cedars that broke the constant wind. As they neared the Texas panhandle, the landscape shifted from groves of shin oaks and ever-present mesquite trees to grain silos, round fields watered by irrigation, and cotton gins.

The Fury started knocking outside of Estelline and by the time they reached the outskirts of Amarillo, black smoke poured from the tailpipe. Adding to his worries about the car, Ned was dismayed with the number of diners and motor court motels that lined up on both sides of the highway.

He showed Pepper's photo over and over to the mom and pop motels and coffee shops beckoning weary travelers with neon cowboys, teepees, or wagons flickering in the darkness. In the daytime, the same colorful signs vied for attention by announcing refrigerated air, swimming pools, and the newest attraction, color television.

No one recalled seeing the runaways.

He killed the engine and it rattled to death. Ned stepped out, bent from the pain in his stomach. The constant ache was taking its toll, draining him of energy. James was torn between concern for his dad and the need to know about the big Indian getting out on the other side. He chose Ned and pushed off from the fender.

"What's wrong?"

"Stomach's aching. It's been acting up." He rubbed it for a moment, then forced himself to straighten up. "What have you found out?"

"Nothing." James' hands didn't seem to know what to do. "Nobody knows nothing. How about you?"

"Didn't find anything out in Dallas, and we stopped in near'bout every town between here and there. I don't know where those kids might be."

James jerked his head. "Who's that?"

"Crow." Ned waved him over. "Hey Crow, this is my son James, Pepper's daddy."

James watched him come around the car, thinking to himself that Crow was made of spring steel and actually *flowed* instead of walked. They shook, each taking the measure of the other man. Complete opposites, both liked what they saw.

"You're helping us find my daughter?"

"That's why I'm here."

"You think you have something we don't?"

"I can talk to these kids, something y'all can't do. You guys are looking in the wrong places. They won't be in motels, or diners, or on busses."

"How do you know that?"

"Have either of y'all ever lived on the road?" He continued when they shook their heads. "I do. I spend a lot of time moving from one place to another. You learn a lot of tricks right quick, like where to sleep and eat, or get out of the weather."

"You running from the law?"

"People keep asking me that." Crow tilted his head toward Ned, his black hair momentarily hanging over one eye. He pulled it back with a finger. "Now it looks like I'm running *with* the law."

Ned removed his Stetson to rub his bald head, feeling dampness that could only be associated with the way he felt. "So what do you think?"

Crow waved a circle in the air. "They won't be inside, if they're here. They'll be around back."

James frowned.

"They'll either be hoping for a handout from the kitchen, or going through the garbage cans."

James' eye narrowed. "Digging through the trash? She wasn't raised like that." He felt sick at his stomach to think his baby was eating from trash cans.

"I'm sure she wasn't, but it's free, so they save their money for when times get hard. Folks throw away a lot of good food, or the cook in the back'll give them a handout, if there haven't been too many through already."

"They don't sleep back there."

"No, James. They'll sleep with other kids they find. They might be in someone's house, or in the backseat of a car, or a van. They might spend a night or two under a bridge or maybe hitch a ride with a trucker and sleep while he drives. Those guys are pretty good about picking them up."

Ned deflated. "Why didn't you tell me all this in the car, instead of letting me stop so many times on the way here?"

"You needed to see for yourself how hopeless your way is, and I wanted to talk to both of you at the same time."

"It *is* hopeless." Tears welled in James' eyes.

The tendons on Crow's crossed arms bulged like thick ropes. "No, my way ain't and it works by talkin' to the right people." He jerked a thumb toward a pair of attractive teenage girls walking down the street. Dressed in bell-bottom jeans patched with bright material, flowered shirts, strings of colorful beads, and long, straight hair held back with bright headbands, they carried sack purses with long straps over their shoulders. Both were barefoot. "These guys are travelers, too. Gimme a minute."

They watched as Crow's demeanor completely changed. He walked toward the kids in a loose shuffle, bouncing on his toes. He bobbed his head as if listening to music. When the distance closed, he raised two fingers.

"Peace, ladies."

The dark-haired girl in granny glasses flashed the peace sign back. She peered over the top of the round lenses. "Hey, man." It was obvious they were both interested in the young man with the long, black hair.

"You guys on the road?"

They nodded. The blond girl tilted her head to study Crow. "We're hitching to San Francisco."

"Cool. Hey, my name's Crow."

The brunette stood hipshot. "Far out. I'm Dona, and this is Kandi."

"Ladies, don't take this the wrong way, because I'm looking at a couple of very hot mamas, but I'm trying to find my girlfriend. We had a bad scene and she split on me a couple of days ago. I'm sure she's chilled by now, but we need to get back together. Do you guys know of a place around here where she might have crashed?"

Ned and James exchanged a puzzled glance. It was as if they were talking in a completely new language.

Kandi flicked her hair and indicated Ned and James. "Bummer. Who are they?"

"Couple of dudes I hitched with to get here."

Dona pulled her granny glasses even lower with one finger. "That one's wearing a badge."

Crow knew better than to tell them the truth. If they knew the older men were searching for Pepper, the conversation would be over. "He's cool. Says he's on the way to California himself, I think for some kind of convention or something. They said I could bum all the way, and baby, that beats riding my thumb from here to there."

"Dig it." The girls turned their attention back to Crow. "We heard of a pad not far away. The guy who owns it's pretty cool. We're going there ourselves."

"Far out. How about you cop a ride with us and I can check it out."

"They'll take us?" Kandi wasn't convinced. "What's their angle?" She'd been on the road long enough to know that older men sometimes expected certain forms of payment for a ride.

Crow grinned. "They don't have one. They're a couple of cool dudes is all. You in?"

Dona chewed a thumbnail, thinking. "I'm hip."

"Cool. Come on." Crow led them back to the cars. "Mr. Ned. This is Dona and Kandi. They're gonna show us a place where Pepper might have hung out." His back to the girls, he frowned and gave the tiniest of head shakes to warn them not to say much.

Dona used her middle finger to gently poke at Ned's gold badge. "I've never been this close to the fuzz without being in trouble."

He suddenly became conscious of the badge and gun on his hip. "I don't have any jurisdiction here."

When she reached toward the pistol to give it a poke, Ned put himself between them. "Y'all get in the Chev-a-lay."

Crow opened the back door. "I'll ride in the back with these two. James, you get shotgun."

Dona shrugged and slid smoothly into the seat. Crow followed, pulling Kandi in after him. Confused, James started to argue about who was going to drive his car and then changed his mind. Without a word, he went around to the passenger side and dropped heavily into the seat, muttering to himself.

The neglected frame house was only a mile to the southwest, tucked into a neighborhood built immediately after World War II. All the windows gaped open and cheap curtains moved in the slight breeze. Rock 'n' roll music filled the air. Only Crow and the girls recognized the Strawberry Alarm Clock singing "Incense and Peppermints."

Crow spoke over the seat. "Thanks, Mr. Ned, for the ride. Why don't y'all grab a bite to eat and come back in an hour or so?"

Not knowing what else to do, Ned scratched the stubble on his cheek, then absently rubbed his aching stomach. "A'ite. You girls be careful with these people."

Kandi gave his shoulder a pat as they slid out of the seat. "Thanks, Pops!"

They watched the trio disappear into the house and went back to the diner to decide what to do with Ned's Plymouth.

Chapter Thirty-four

Realizing it wasn't smart to stand in the rain while the dog worked, Anna and John joined Buck and Cody in his car to watch through the windshield. Rain thundered on the roof and the wipers barely kept up with the big drops slapping the glass.

Anna fidgeted in the passenger seat. "This is like watching grass grow."

"This rain is something, though." John shifted in the back to stretch his legs.

"We had falling weather like this in Viet Nam." Cody shivered at the thought. "You'd be walking along under a cloudy sky and it'd come a frog strangler for a few minutes, then it might get sunny for a while. The humidity was so thick you couldn't breathe. We could actually see the water hanging in the air. Other times, it'd rain for weeks. We couldn't keep our feet dry, and guys fell out with all kinds of foot problems. We called it jungle rot. Buck, didn't y'all call it something else over there in Japan?"

The former marine nodded. "Trench foot. Bad stuff. I've seen the flesh fall off feet from it. I remember one ol' boy took off his socks and his feet should have been attached to a dead man. The doc used a brush and scrubbed off chunks of…"

Anna held up a hand. "Boys, I know this is probably some kind of rite of passage, but there's a lady in here. Can we change the subject, like back to where we started?"

They laughed and Cody slowed the wipers as the rain slacked off. "I saw on the weather that this is all coming from a hurricane that came out of the left coast of Mexico and then across the desert."

"I didn't think it rained in the desert."

Cody glanced into the rearview mirror to see John, instead of turning around. "This one dumped a lot of water there, and now they say it might fall here for another week."

John crossed his arms, staring out the side window. "Where we're sitting'll be underwater in a week."

"Maybe sooner than that." Anna wiped the foggy glass to better see the Wilson boys and their dog through the gray curtain.

Cody's radio came alive. "Sheriff?"

It was Martha Wells in dispatch. A longtime veteran in that position, she was cool and calm in a crisis, but everyone knew she'd break down and cry like her heart was broke when it was all said and done. "Go ahead."

"Is Anna with you? I tried both her radio and John's, but they're not answering."

Cody mentally kicked himself for not letting her know the other two deputies were out of their cars and with him. "They are."

"Anna, we got a call here a little while ago from Cecil Hutler at the drive-in picture show. He says he needs to talk to you as quick as you can."

She took the microphone from Cody's hand. "All right. I'll head on over there right now. Did he say what he wanted?"

"Nope. Wanted to talk to you."

"Fine. Thanks."

"Cody?"

Anna passed him the microphone. He mashed the button. "Go ahead."

"We've got half a dozen wrecks and there's high water down south toward nig…on the other side of the tracks. You want me to send someone down there?"

John was already opening the back door. "I'm gone."

Anna climbed out. "I'll get someone to work the wrecks." She closed the door and trudged back to her car through the mud.

"Y'all drive careful." Cody rehooked the radio and cracked the driver's window for ventilation. "Buck, you wanna get up here?"

With John gone, Buck stretched both legs across the seat and pulled his hat down low. The justice of the peace sounded a lot like Judge O.C. "Naw, I'm comfortable right 'chere."

Outside, light rain pattered on the car's roof and Cracker sniffed the wet ground for dead people.

Chapter Thirty-five

The glittery Silver Spur Cafe and Coffee Shop in Santa Rosa bustled with activity when three other buses disgorged dozens of passengers. They scattered with their Brownies, lined up at the cafe door for a table, or drifted into the curio shop to browse the same Japanese-made "authentic" Indian souvenirs they'd seen at other stops.

Pepper had an idea and grabbed Cale's hand. They joined a group of tourists going through the front door and entered the New Mexico cafe fragrant with bacon, fried onions, hamburgers, and cigarette smoke. Red and orange vinyl booths filled the right side by the windows, and a counter lit by large round chrome and glass globes took up the left. The clatter of dishes coming from behind the counter proved how busy the tourist stop was at that time of day.

When it came their time to be seated, the harried waitress in a white uniform saw two teenagers standing alone. Her scratched nametag identified her as Molly. "We don't serve hippies…"

Pepper's eyes flashed and she jerked a thumb back over her shoulder. "We're not eating with our parents! They're losers, making us go on this stupid trip. We want to sit at the counter!" Standing on her tiptoes, she pointed a finger down the line of tourists. "Put *them* on the other side of the cafe!"

Pepper's shrill voice cut across the crowd. Some stopped to stare, others examined their feet, and a few laughed. "Right, dear old mom and dad?"

Molly followed Pepper's aim and caught the eye of a middle-aged couple embarrassed by the scene in front of them. The man in a crew cut raised an empathetic eyebrow toward the waitress that said, "What are you gonna do with kids these days?"

Molly sighed and waved toward the crowded counter. "Come on, kids. Sit at the end down there, and keep your voice down, hon."

Pepper led the way past the line of people perched on red stools. She whispered. "If we play this right, we can eat for free. I'll tell her to take the bill to our parents over there."

Cale laughed. "That's pretty smart."

They plucked menus from the holder and when Molly came around back, ordered the daily special.

She watched Molly swing back toward the booths to deliver plates. "You know, I think we're gonna walk this check instead. No need to stick those folks with the meal. They didn't do nothin' to us."

The cafe buzzed with conversation. A kid in a nearby booth stuck a dime in the tableside jukebox. Bobby Bare filled the air with "Detroit City." Pepper wished there was a little jukebox on her end of the counter so she could play some rock. She figured that was exactly what this bunch of squares needed to hear.

Another bus arrived bringing a fresh rush of hungry travelers. The kids were halfway through their gray meat loaf when Molly came around to refill the glasses and coffee cups lined up along the counter. She was pouring hot tea over what was left of the ice in Cale's glass when her eyes hardened. She gave her head a stiff shake.

Pepper noticed and spun on her stool to find a black family in line had finally reached the cafe's glass vestibule. The dad's face fell. He spoke softly into his wife's ear. Her shoulders slumped and the couple gently guided their three children out the exit door. Suddenly furious, Pepper spun back on her stool. "What'd you do that for?"

Molly met her gaze. "For *them*, honey. It would have been embarrassing if they'd gotten all the way inside. My manager don't allow no coloreds or Indians."

Pepper felt her face drain of blood. For the first time in her life, she realized what Miss Becky, a full-blood Choctaw, and Grandpa Ned had known all along about the world. "You better run me off, too, then. I'm a quarter Indian."

"But you can't tell. Hon, your back was to me when I pointed for them to come to the back. They can get something there, but coloreds can't eat in the cafe."

"Damn the back door. I won't eat here, neither."

"You already have."

She threw down her fork. "C'mon Cale. Let's get gone."

"But I'm not done with my dinner."

"I am."

"You're gonna leave hungry because of some niggers you don't even know?"

The air around Pepper sucked away, leaving her in a silent vacuum. Not trusting herself to speak, she stalked away.

"Fine," Molly said, picking up Pepper's half-eaten plate.

She was outside when Cale caught up to her. "Where are you going?"

"I want to see."

"What?"

They rounded the corner. She stopped, drained of all energy. "That."

People ate in haphazardly parked cars and trucks. An Indian couple squatted in the skinny shade of the wall, while a line of little barefoot kids sat on a tailgate, swinging their legs and devouring sandwiches from a bag. A Mexican family walked past a hippie couple sharing a hamburger and knocked on the back door.

The colored family wasn't there, but a well-dressed middle aged black man smiled, nodded, and kept eating behind the wheel of his Oldsmobile.

Pepper started for the open back door, but Cale grabbed her before she blew past the Indians and into the kitchen. "You can't go in there and stir up a stink. I know you're madder'n an old wet hen, but they'll call the laws on us. Let's go."

Pepper spun to give him what for when she stopped, hearing Molly crying inside the door. "Those kids walked the check." She sniffled. "Dammit. I should have known better, but they tricked me and I can't afford to pay for another meal out of my own pocket. That's three this week, and Don'll take a quarter of my check."

Her voice moved away to disappear in the clatter of dishes. Unsure which way to turn, Pepper stayed in one spot for several seconds. Then she held out her hand. "Money."

"What?"

"Give me that money you got squirreled away."

"Why?"

She snapped her fingers.

Cale reached into his pocket and dug out several bills. Pepper glanced at them, then went inside. When she came out, her eyes were full of tears. "Come on."

"What'd you do?"

"Paid for our dinner."

"After what she said about them colored people?"

"Don't matter. She's trying to get by, same as the rest of these folks." They walked back to the highway and Pepper stuck her thumb out. "This ain't no better'n where we come from."

Chapter Thirty-six

I was bored stiff with all the rain and Pepper being gone. Even school wasn't the same without her. At least one thing had changed, though. With Cale gone, his toadies pretty much left me alone.

The day passed with the smell of chalk, lunches, and mildew. Everything around us was souring from the dampness. Kids' shirts and pants smelled musty, because most people in Center Springs depended on the sun to dry their clothes. With the weather like it was, folks had to dedicate one room in the house to racks of still-damp clothes, but unless they had good circulation, things like towels soured in a short time.

Miss Becky had a wooden rack she set in front of the open oven to dry ours. Other folks might smell mildewey, but not *her* family, because she also went through a lot of Mrs. Stewart's Bluing.

After school, I went into my back bedroom to read. I hadn't felt much like doing anything since Pepper left, but I had a pretty good book called *The Year of the Jeep*. In it, a kid named Cloud needed to make money to buy parts for an old jeep he was fixing up. Because of him, I'd considered getting a job for my own spending cash.

I flopped down on the bed with my head toward the foot while rain drummed the roof. I punched a feather pillow into shape and tilted the book toward the window for more light.

When I opened it, a sheet of paper from a Harold Hodges notepad fell onto my chest.

I didn't use it for a bookmark, so I laid the book down and opened the folded paper to find a note from Pepper.

> *Hey butthole. I've had enough of this hick town, so I'm leaving with Cale. He's not really my boyfriend or anything, but we're going just the same. I bet he tries to kiss me, but he better not. I know everybody will be worried and it'll get on you, so I'm sorry. Cale has a cousin we're going to meet, then on to San Francisco. This will be a great adventure. Love you.*

It was signed with a heart and a lot of Xs and Os that I didn't understand.

My eyes burned. I wiped them with the back of my hand. Swinging my legs over the side of the bed, I sat there to think for a minute. It was a private letter, but I had something that Grandpa and Miss Becky would want to know, not to mention Aunt Ida Belle and Uncle James.

I knew where they could find Pepper.

Chapter Thirty-seven

Crow was waiting in front of the house when Ned steered the butter-colored Bel Air around the corner over an hour later. They were down to one car after a mechanic finishing his lunch in the diner agreed to give the engine a once-over. He started the car and listened for only a moment before slamming the hood and calling a tow truck.

James rode with his elbow hanging out the window. This time, instead of only Dona and Kandi, Crow was standing in a small crowd mostly made up of young women. Ned pulled to the curb beside them. Everyone in the yard took notice until they realized the men weren't getting out, then returned to their animated conversation.

Their clothes were a riot of color selected by a blind man. There was no definition to wardrobes of patched jeans, sandals, and a wide array of oversized shirts. The only thing the girls had in common was their complete abandonment of brassieres, which shocked the older men.

A girl with curly hair barely restrained by a yellow headband pointed. "Is that them?"

Crow didn't acknowledge the car and ignored the obvious question. "You see her, or this Cale kid, you call the sheriff's department for me."

Kandi grimaced. "We don't talk to the fuzz."

"I know, darlin', but do this one for *me*."

"What about your girlfriend?"

Crow ran his hand up and down her side. "I'm getting close to forgetting her."

She melted into him. "Will you be coming back this way?"

"You can count on it."

"All right. Maybe we'll find you in San Francisco, though."

To Ned and James' shocked surprise, Kandi slipped her arms around Crow's neck and gave him a kiss that should have been delivered behind closed doors. She didn't turn him loose for a long moment, and when she did, both grownups in the car realized they'd been holding their breath.

Crow spoke softly into her ear, gave her a pat on the backside as if he didn't care who saw the intimate gesture, and waved to the rest. Most flashed peace signs, and one of the boys gave Crow a handshake. He climbed into the backseat. "Found what I was looking for! Winslow."

Ned glanced over the backseat. "Arizona? There's a lot of other places between here and there."

"There's a lot of big empty and nothing else. Pepper's been here, with that boy…"

James' voice choked. "Cale." She'd been right there, only yards away, and now she was gone again.

"Yeah, Cale. They crashed here but nobody remembers when and that's all anyone knows. One of the girls said she left in a car with some kids heading for Winslow first, then on to San Francisco."

"They're following sixty-six?" Ned studied Crow's eyes.

"That's the way."

"Sixty-six don't go to San Francisco," James said. "It goes to Los Angeles."

Crow nodded, watching the girls walk back into the house. "That's right. And we'd better get going. Our best chance to catch them is Winslow. If we miss her there, we'll be playing catch up, and if they get to Barstow ahead of us, they might take any way to San Francisco. They may head up to Bakersfield and north, or cut across to Highway 5, so there's no telling what they'll do."

"We might find 'em in San Francisco, if they get that far."

"Two kids in that city will be like finding a needle in a haystack," Crow said. "There are tens of thousands there already, and more are coming. Once they get off sixty-six, they can go whichever way the wind blows."

Without a word, Ned aimed the car toward the Texas/New Mexico line. He pegged the speedometer at eighty on the straight highway leading to the distant horizon.

The two-lane held straight and true, occasionally cresting a ridge, then revealing a shallow drop through the desert with a view so wide open it took their breath. Used to small, curving roads through landscapes of trees, pastures, and farms, the vast spaces drew their eyes to distant blue ridges shimmering in the sun.

Crow slid to the middle of the seat to see down the highway. "There's a slight chance we'll find them in Santa Fe, but the kids told me the best place they can crash is Winslow."

"Crash?" James cracked the window for some air.

"It's a place they can sleep."

"Is that where they take that dope?"

The slight frown on Crow's forehead was the only indication of how he felt for James. "There's drugs there."

"I hope they don't make her take none."

"James, these kids live for grass…marijuana. *Most* of 'em smoke it, and they'll take pills too, and LSD, and about everything else you can think of, but they don't *make* anyone do it."

"She wasn't raised like that."

Nothing Crow could say would sound right, so he kept his mouth closed.

They shot across the state line into New Mexico, and passed a highway patrol car heading in the opposite direction. Driving with his arm out of the open window, the trooper waved downward in an exaggerated patting movement, telling Ned to slow down. He took his foot off the accelerator, flicked a wave back to the trooper as they passed, and once he was over the hill, he slammed the hammer back down.

Chapter Thirty-eight

Rumbling thunder drummed beyond the distant treetops. Occasional bolts of brilliance punctuated the day as Cody fidgeted in the front seat, occasionally turning on the wipers to clear the rain sluicing down the windshield. One of those times when the glass cleared, he saw Cracker locked up as if pointing a covey of birds.

"Buck."

Cody opened the door before the justice of the peace could rise and tilt the hat back on his head. Outside, he lit a cigarette and watched the Wilson boys slog their way to the dog. Cracker broke his point and dug in the soft ground.

Buck cleared his throat, spat, and lit a Camel. "Whadda ya think?"

"I think they're awful close to that dragline. I'd a thought they'd have found something farther out toward the middle of the bottoms."

The Wilson boys conferred, then pulled Cracker away by his collar. They tried to coax the dog to toward another pile of cold, wet charcoal, but he ran back to the original site to dig. Jimmy Foxx knelt beside the wet dog and ruffed his sides.

Ty Cobb waved at the sheriff's car.

Another door slammed, and Ike Reader joined them carrying a bildukey. Those who'd been waiting in their trucks sloshed through the mud to Cody's side. Ike took the lead, waving the skinny shovel like a sword.

"What now?"

Cody took a drag on the cigarette and squinted through the smoke hanging in the moist air. "The rest of y'all get your shovels and let's see what we can find." He pondered Ike's shovel and the long, thin blade sometimes called a sharpshooter. "Uh, Ike, I doubt they'll be buried in post holes."

He examined the shovel as if it had materialized in his hands. "Uh, okay. I'll get another'n. Hey, Cody, listen, you think they'll put that dog in his box?"

"Don't see any reason why not. He's done his do."

"Well, if it's all the same to you, I'll wait until they get him in it first."

Cody took a shovel from Buck. "That'll be fine, Ike."

"Listen, I'm not tryin' to get out of workin', ner nothing."

"I know that, Ike. I'm glad you're here. Let's go, boys."

The digging was easy in the soft ground. The problem was that water quickly filled the growing excavation. Ike soon joined them, and half an hour later, they had a mud hole.

Chapter Thirty-nine

James saw a sign outside a small Sinclair Station near the New Mexico/Arizona border. Last Chance for New Mexico Gas. "We might ought to fill up."

Ned's patience was short, and when the attendant didn't arrive in what he considered a reasonable amount of time, he got out of the car. James followed suit and stretched to work out the kinks.

A man in filthy overalls popped out of the garage, wiping his hands on a rag as oily as his clothes. "Help you?"

Ned was already around the back of the Chevrolet, reaching for the gas nozzle hanging on the side of the pump. "Gas."

"I'll do it. We're full service here."

"All right. We're in a hurry."

The attendant with the name Duke sewn onto his coveralls dug in his ear, leaving a smudge of oil on the lobe. "Regular, or ethyl?"

"Regular."

"Figured."

Duke removed the cap, jammed the nozzle into the tank, and gave a lever on the pump a flip. Internal machinery meshed and the numbers reset. "Travelin' far?"

"A fer piece."

Duke scrubbed at a particularly stubborn bug smear on the windshield. "There's drinks inside."

James gave the fender a slap. "That sounds good."

Crow emerged on Ned's side. He stretched as well and noticed that for the first time Ned wasn't wearing his badge or pistol. Ned saw him glance at the empty space on his shirt, and started to comment but he stopped when an old DeSoto fifty yards away coughed, slowed, and coasted toward the drive. There wasn't enough momentum to carry it any farther, and the car died in the middle of the lane.

Crow shaded his eyes, making Ned think of an old painting he'd once seen of a Mohawk brave squinting into the distance. "That's an old lady driving."

James trotted over to help. The two-lane highway was momentarily empty, but he knew a car would be along any minute. The woman's mouth was a tight line and her fingers fluttered over a strip of lace at the top of her blue dress. "I'm out of gas."

"I see that. You steer and we'll give you a push. Put 'er in neutral."

Crow joined them and she forced a smile at the hippie. James and Crow planted their feet and found a place on the sloped rear end. The black metal was hot against their hands. The heavy car moved slowly at first, then picked up momentum as they dug in to gain as much speed as possible to overcome the drive's upward slope. Moving like molasses in the wintertime, Duke joined them.

The car was rolling at a pretty good clip when Ned gave a wave. "Turn!"

Using both hands inside the wheel, the elderly woman put every bit of her ninety pounds into the turn. Puffing and pushing, the trio managed to subdue gravity. The car rolled to a stop at the pump opposite Ned's sedan.

With the same lack of interest, Duke moseyed over to her window, breathing hard. "Regular or ethyl?"

"Regular."

"Fill'er up?"

"You give green stamps?"

"Nope."

"How far is the nearest gas station that gives S&H Green Stamps?"

Duke scratched at the stubble on his chin. "About half a mile back the way you came."

"Then give me a two bit's worth."

He blinked in surprise. "Two bits?"

"Young man. You should give stamps." She handed him two quarters. "There. Payment in advance. And you should wash up every once in a while."

Ned chuckled, then rubbed his stomach, now a steady ache punctuated with knifing pains. Duke pumped two-bits' worth of gas and hung up the nozzle. Without a word, the woman started the car and drove off.

"I never seen anything like it." Duke absently rubbed his hands on the oily rag and raised Ned's hood. He pulled out the dipstick. "You're about half a quart low."

"Put some in, then."

It was silent under the hood for a moment. Duke stuck his head around the hood. "It's a good thing y'all pulled in here when you did. This belt's broke." He held it by both ends.

Ned tilted his head. "That so?"

"Sure enough. I have one in there that'll fit, though. It'll be two and a half, plus another two and a half to put it on. Won't take but a minute."

A sudden sharp pain slashed through Ned's side, making him gasp. He leaned on the car for support. "Go ahead."

Duke met James and Crow coming back outside. "Belt's broke. I'll get another one."

James started to answer, but saw Ned leaning on the car with a stricken expression on his face. He rushed to him, setting two Coke bottles on the roof. "What's wrong?"

"I don't know. It felt like somebody's twisting a blade in my guts."

"We might need to find a doctor."

Ned straightened with a wince and shook his head. The pain had eased. "Nope. It's better now. Probably something I ate. Besides, we don't have the time right now."

Torn, James paused. "All right, but if it keeps on like that, we're doing something about it."

"All right, then. We can't go anywhere right now anyway."

Carrying the new belt and a handful of tools, Duke came outside, stepping faster than before, followed by Crow. "Be done in a jiffy, fellows." He dove under the hood. Crow stood in the shade of the overhead, watching Duke work on the fan belt while he chewed a Baby Ruth. He drained his RC cola, dropped the bottle into the wooden case sitting beside the station's door, and settled into the backseat to wait.

Ned and James were in the front twenty minutes later when Duke slammed the hood. He stepped smartly around to Ned's window and paused, oddly bent. "There you go."

"What do I owe you for the gas and belt?"

"Not a thing, gentlemen."

"What?"

"Well." Duke paused and glanced at Crow waiting with the back door open and one foot on the ground. "Y'all did for that old lady and you didn't need to."

"That don't make no sense." Ned tilted his head upward, confused. "We owe you for your time, at least."

"Nossir. We provide service with a smile. Uh, y'all can help someone else down the road and that'll be payment enough for me."

Thinking the man was crazy, Ned glanced at the pump, shook his head, and opened his billfold. He handed him six one-dollar bills. "This is for the gas. You keep the change. I'm at least gonna pay *that*."

Another glance into the backseat. "You sure?"

"Of course I'm sure. Thanks." Ned pulled away and when he glanced at his side mirror, Duke was standing right where he'd been, rubbing his stomach and watching them leave.

"That was the damndest thing I've ever seen," Ned said. "Why wouldn't he take any money for this new belt and the work he did?"

Crow met his eyes in the rearview mirror, thinking about the cleanly cut fan belt he'd seen Duke throw into the trash. It didn't take but a second to convince him that he'd made a serious mistake. "I guess he liked your looks."

Chapter Forty

The rain slacked off, following the pattern that seemed endless. Cody leaned on a shovel beside what that might or might not be a quickly filling grave. "All right. This ain't working like it should."

Buck lit a cigarette off the butt in his hand. He flicked it onto the ground and took a deep drag from the fresh one. "We're spinning our wheels here."

Cody glanced over his shoulder at the dragline crawling behind the two growling bulldozers. "Ike, would you go wave down one of those drivers and tell him I'd…the sheriff…would like for one of them to come over here and dig us a hole?"

"Sure 'nough." Ike took off across the muddy distance, glad to be away for a few minutes.

"That don't hardly seem the right way to dig folks up, son."

Cody met Buck's eyes. "We don't have time to be finicky." He motioned toward the creek that was noticeably closer than when they'd arrived. "If those men are down there, we need to roll them out pretty quick. They can be gentle at the funeral home, when the medical examiner in Dallas releases 'em."

"That dozer might tear them up."

"At least we'll have what we find. If not, they'll be underwater in a couple of days and we'll always wonder."

Buck studied the rivulets leading toward the creek. The dozer slowed and in the distance, they watched the driver speak with Ike. The engine's timbre changed again to an idle as he climbed down. The other drivers conversed before removing the huge chains tethering them to the dragline.

In minutes both bulldozers cut across the barren terrain. Ike followed and came around when they stopped. He beamed. "Listen, listen, how about two of 'em?"

"Good job, Ike." Cody stepped between the monstrous machines and shouted. "Can y'all cut us a big hole here?" They nodded. "Be careful. There may be some bodies down there."

The older of the two nodded and gave Cody a thumbs-up. In tandem, they lowered their blades and pushed forward, immediately enlarging the shallow mud hole. Buck winced, thinking about what might happen as the blades tore through the ground. They continued for twenty yards and slowly dumped the contents of the shovels. Buck watched the mud and water spill out, then shook his head when he saw nothing else.

They reversed their engines, backed up and repeated the process. Again, the results were the same.

Buck studied the hole. "They may not be down there."

"They may be deep. The ground sure seems soft in places, like it's been dug before."

The bulldozers backed up again.

"Probably because it's been tore up so bad already when they pushed all the trees down."

Muddy water seeped into the wide scar.

Cody waved them forward again. The drivers conversed, separated slightly, and the shovels dug in again. This time the metal tread of the bulldozer on the right, the one driven by the older driver, sunk deeper than the other. The driver throttled higher and they rolled out to dump the mud.

Again, Buck shook his head.

Instead of backing up, they separated, split around Buck, and circled back to the deep gash. Cody waved at the older driver and gave him a signal.

One more time.

The driver made his own signal toward the other dozer, indicating that he wanted to go deeper. He nodded and working at slight angles to each other, they dug in again, this time in a slight V from their starting point. Black smoke poured out of both stacks as the shovels took deeper bites.

At that same moment, Cracker streaked around the machinery, aimed directly at Ike. Seeing the dog appear out of nowhere, Ike recoiled and gave a little bleat, throwing up his hands to ward off the attack.

Ty Cobb leaped forward, grabbed, and missed the dog. Cracker raced toward the little farmer who froze in place. The dog shot between Ike's feet as the man's eyes rolled back his head. Ike fell backward in a dead faint. Lucky for him, the tortured ground was soft as a feather bed, and he landed with a muffled thump.

Cracker didn't slow. He dashed into the middle of the huge hole and started digging. Frantic, the dog threw wet dirt between his hind legs like he was trying to outdo both bulldozers.

"Hold it!" Cody waved the dozers still.

Jimmy Foxx jumped into the hole and grabbed at the dog. Whining, Cracker dodged, spun in a circle and stopped to dig again.

"Come here you little idiot!" Ty Cobb joined his brother.

It was a greased pig contest in the muddy hole, with Cracker dodging and digging while the boys threw themselves at the wet Brit. Cody laughed as they whooped encouragement at the brothers to catch the little dog. Jimmy Foxx lunged again and caught Cracker by the collar. Whining deep in his throat, the dog wriggled to get free, but Ty Cobb got a good hold and they had him outnumbered.

Cody nudged Ike with the toe of his muddy boot and wiped a tear from his eyes. "That was the damndest thing I've ever seen."

Buck took a knee beside Ike. "He's already coming around. I never."

Regaining control, Cody waved everyone back, and seeing that the dog was well in hand, waved for the dozers. The engines roared, belched smoke, and dug in.

Grinning, the younger driver rolled up dirt and fresh roots.

The older man's smile quickly faded when his machine slowed and stalled. When he throttled higher, it shuddered. The ground beneath the shovel moved in an unnatural way. The broken surface rippled several feet away. The ground swelled, making Mike Parsons shiver with unease.

"Must be a big damned log," Buck said.

"Why would it be buried that deep?"

"Well, they probably…"

Buck quit talking when the mud-covered tail fin of an Impala erupted from the soil. Rain washed some of the mud away, revealing more of the trunk. Glass exploded from the stress and the gagging odor of death swept over those standing around.

Cody waved at the driver to stop. He shifted into reverse and backed out. Cody dropped into the hole, and struggled toward the door with the busted glass. On one knee in the mud, he braced himself against the car and held his breath. He winced and backed away.

"This is what we came for, Buck. You want to make this official?"

The justice of the peace joined him as the bulldozers coughed and died. Rain pattered in the sudden silence. "Well, I don't need to officially pronounce them dead, that's for sure." He backed out of the way and nodded.

Cody called up to the older driver. "When I tell you, see if you can get that blade under the front end of the car there and raise it up." He addressed the younger driver. "When he does, back up to it and we'll throw a chain around the axle, then you can pull it out. Don't stop till you get to the highway."

The engines roared to life again. Fifteen minutes later, the car with its gruesome cargo wallowed behind the dozer like a ship in a gale.

Cody and the men followed the car in silence. Moving on weak knees, Ike walked between Mike Parsons and Dub Hinkley. When they reached the parked vehicles, the bulldozer operators climbed down and unhitched the car. Cody made it a point to shake the hands of both men and thank them. Visibly relieved that it was over, they returned to the dragline and a job preferable to digging up bodies.

The Wilson boys promised Cracker both a good meal and the threat of spending a week without hunting.

The first, for finding the bodies.

The second for scaring Ike half to death.

Chapter Forty-one

While Crow took a shower and James watched Walter Cronkite give the nightly Viet Cong body count on the black and white television, Ned made a long-distance collect call to Miss Becky. As he waited for the operator to make the connection, he had an uneasy feeling all this had happened before.

This time, though, he wasn't planning to invade Mexico.

After a series of clicks, she answered. The operator asked if she'd accept the call. "Sure 'nough, hon."

"Howdy Mama."

"Where are you, Daddy? Have you found her yet?"

"Not yet, but we know somebody who's seen her and she's all right."

"Praise the *Lord!* Who'd you talk to?"

"I didn't. Crow did."

"Who?"

Ned realized he hadn't caught her up on their companion. He explained, but could tell that she was waiting for him to take a breath so she could say something. He stopped when she made that little sound in her throat that always meant she wanted to break in. "What is it?"

"Top knows where you can catch her."

Ned glanced at James. "Come over here and listen to this."

James swung off the bed and joined Ned. They put their heads together with the receiver between them. "Go ahead, Mama. James is listening."

"Pepper left Top a note that he found this afternoon. She said Cale has a cousin out west somewhere. I talked to his daddy and asked him. He said they have a cousin in Flagstaff who has a boy about Cale's age." She gave them the address and the phone number. "He's been trying to call, but no one's answering."

Relief flooded through Ned, and James dropped into a chair. "We're liable to get ahead of them."

Ned listened to Miss Becky as the bathroom door opened and Crow walked out in a cloud of steam. He was back in his same jeans, but carrying the wet shirt that he'd obviously washed by hand. His long hair hung on his shoulders, water dripping on the towel slung around his neck.

He threw them a curious glance as he passed and stepped out the door. He hung the fancy shirt on a nail partially driven into a rough-cut cedar post holding up the long overhang sheltering the Western Skies doors. He stayed there, watching kids swinging on the equipment in the horseshoe-shaped center of the courtyard.

James returned to the bed. "Ask her if Ida Belle's there."

Ned nodded and listened some more about Top, the rain, and how the folks at church were praying for them.

"All right, Mama. We're gonna stay here tonight in Winslow. I plumb wore out today and we can't go no farther. Flagstaff ain't far, so we'll get up early and be there pretty quick. Is Ida Belle with you?"

He shook his head at the answer. Relieved, James turned his attention to the television and President Lyndon Johnson's struggle with the war.

"Oh," said Miss Becky remembering something else. "Cody found them missing men. They was buried in the lake-bottom."

Ned shook his head, both relieved that they'd been found, yet even more uneasy that the killers were so close to the house. "Does he know anything else?"

"Not that he told me. Well, they was buried in their car."

"What the hell?"

"Watch your language. The Lord's a-listenin'."

"How do you bury a *car?*"

"Cody says they figure someone did it with a bulldozer or dragline, and that's what they used to dig 'em out with, a bulldozer."

"All right. I'll call him when we hang up." He glanced at the alarm clock beside the bed. "It's late enough that he should be home by now. Y'all lock the doors tonight."

"We will. Be careful on that old highway, and find my girl and bring her home."

"All right."

Ned hung up by pushing the disconnect button. When he released it and the dial tone sounded in his ear, he dialed O for the operator and made a second collect call to Cody's house.

"All right. Mr. Parker, your party is on the line."

There was a click as she transferred the call. "Heard you found them two that was missing."

Cody smiled, thinking that Judge O.C. would give Ned a dressing down if he launched into a conversation like that with him. "Yep. Had to use a dog to sniff 'em out, and a bulldozer to dig 'em up, but we found 'em. Buried in the lake bottom, in their car."

"You said you used a dog?"

"Yep. The Wilson boys have a little Brittany spaniel that can smell dead people, even under the ground."

"I never heard of such a thing."

"Me neither, but it worked."

"Well, tell them to stay away from the Methodist cemetery, and the Presbyterian graveyard, too. I don't want to get any calls about a dog diggin' up coffins."

"Ned, they call them caskets now."

"Uh huh."

"I sent the bodies to the medical examiner in Dallas. They'll get back to us, but the only thing they'll be able to tell is how they were killed, and it don't matter to them none. I doubt it'll matter to us, neither."

"You're right about that. I guess you know about Pepper headed for Flagstaff."

"Yep."

"All right, I'll let you know when we get Pepper. Becky told me about the note Top found. We're in Winslow." He paused to hang up, and then thought better. "Listen, I still think those businessmen are tied in to the way Leland Hale was run over."

"I don't see how."

"I don't, neither, but something's been digging at me like a rock in my shoe and I can't figure it out. Did y'all check on the buried car's fender?"

"Of course." Cody paused, waiting on Ned to ask a dozen questions about the investigation, but he was unusually quiet on the other end. He wondered if it was just the cost of a long distance call, or something else. "You keep studying on it, and I will too. Y'all be careful out there."

"Ain't nobody gonna mess with the three of us."

"Three?"

"Yeah, oh, I ain't told you about Crow." Ned took a quick moment to explain.

"Crow, how much?"

"He didn't give me anything but Crow."

"Maybe Two-Crow."

"I'd-a said that if he'd told me Two-Crow."

"Where's he from?"

Ned sighed in exasperation. He hated being questioned on the phone. He glanced out the open door to see Crow sitting with his eyes closed in an orange shell-back lawn chair in the middle of the courtyard, listening to the kids squeal in the playground. "Up around Tahlequah. He's Comanche."

"I'm gonna contact the sheriff up there to see if he can tell me anything about him."

"He's all right." Ned grunted at another sudden pain. This time his forehead broke out in a sweat. His eyes flicked toward James, who was absorbed in the local news.

"What was that?"

"Clearing my throat's all."

"I'm gonna talk to the Tahlequah sheriff anyway, to make myself feel better."

"I'd feel better if you figured out who ran over Leland."

"Workin' on it."

Ned hung up without saying goodbye.

The sun went down, but Crow stayed in his lawn chair long after the neon Western Skies Motel sign flickered to life. James went to sleep sitting up in one of the full-size beds. Ned laid down beside him, still in his clothes, too, and closed his eyes, leaving the other bed for Crow.

Morning light showed the bed hadn't been slept in at all.

Chapter Forty-two

Anna killed her engine beside the 271 Drive-In concession stand. Water stood ankle deep between the elevated rows of posts and speakers. The rain had slacked to a heavy mist, but the radio said it was only a matter of time before the next wave came through.

Cecil Hutler, the drive-in's owner, was in a lawn chair underneath the overhang facing the huge blank screen. There were three rows of shell-back metal chairs for those who preferred to sit outside instead of in their cars. "Howdy, gal."

Long used to being referred to as "gal," Anna sat in the chair beside him. It rocked and that pleased her. She pushed lightly with her foot to enjoy the experience. "You called me?"

"Sure did. Did you see the movie we're running?"

She'd barely paid attention to it, but several people in town were excited to have *Home from the Hill* showing again. It was based on a book by William Humphrey, a local boy, and had been filmed a few years earlier in nearby Clarksville, with parts shot in Chisum. "Sure did."

He nodded and fished in his pants pocket for his pipe. His teeth clicked on the stem and he dug a tobacco wallet from the other side. "Yep, and for the first time in a long time I got to watch some of it."

"Okay."

He opened the wallet and packed the pipe, then returned everything to its proper place. While she waited with dwindling patience, he scratched a kitchen match alight and puffed until fragrant blue smoke surrounded them both.

Despite herself, Anna took a deep breath of the cherry mix and relaxed. It really wasn't so bad sitting in the silent drive-in, in what was quickly turning into a fog.

"I'm usually in the back, cooking, or taking money, so even though I show these films every day, week after week, I usually don't get a chance to watch them. Last night was different. It was so slow, the wife left the ticket booth and came out here with me. We had us a big time

"Now I'll tell you, that movie came pretty dern close to what it's really like around here. Hell, some of the folks in town even got to be in it. Extras, they call 'em in the movies. They mostly stand around as background, but it was fun while they was here.

"Anyway, I'm sitting here eating my own popcorn, when this truck comes on the screen. Mama recognized it right off. It was the same kind of truck, a fifty-one Dodge them people was in who was talking to the businessmen that disappeared. Right down to the light ivory color."

Anna sat straighter and faced Cecil. "And?"

"Why, little missy, Mama remembered who was in it. Marty something-or-other, and a mean son of a bitch named John T. I know him, cause he's gotten in some trouble here in town before. I run Marty off one night a year or so ago."

Gears began to mesh. "Do you have a last name for either one of them?"

"Nope. There was another'n sitting in the middle, but Mama said she didn't see him. Said they was all squeezed in that cab pretty tight."

Anna rested her elbow on a knee. "Would she be able to pick him out of a picture?"

"Which one?"

"Either."

"Sure."

Anna was confident that the name John T. would be familiar to someone in the sheriff's office, if he was mean as Cecil said.

There couldn't be anyone else in tiny Center Springs named Marty, either, that drove an ivory '51 Dodge. "All right! Thanks."

Cecil winked. "You could stay for the picture and see the truck for yourself."

"I wish I could, but I need to get this information to the sheriff."

He puffed his pipe, staring at the white screen. "Suit yourself."

Chapter Forty-three

Their ride dropped Pepper and Cale off in front of the Hopi House, still another tourist trap sitting by itself ten miles west of Winslow. The Arizona sun beat down, heavy on their shoulders. On the opposite side of the dusty highway, two Indian women in a wooden stand knocked together from scrap lumber sold turquoise jewelry and painted bowls displayed on bright blankets.

Pepper absently read the familiar signs advertising gas, food, curios, Indians, and moccasins. "I thought we were gonna get away from two-lane country highways, but that's all I've seen since we left."

Cale pulled a renegade strand of hair out of his eyes. "What do you expect? It's a road and it leads to California. That's what you wanted."

A '53 Dodge and a Fairlane passed, blowing up enough dust to make them squint. "I wanted to be in San Francisco. I didn't know it'd take this long to get there."

Pepper stopped, glaring at Cale. "Here's one thing I know for sure. We're going to find somewhere to sleep tonight. I'm tired, hungry, and want a bath."

"So where is this magic place?"

She sighed. "We'll find some kids and bunk in with them, I guess."

She had no intention of sleeping in a culvert under a bridge. Full of despair, they hoped the next town was bigger. A Mustang roared on the highway, its mufflers clattering, followed in quick succession by a Dodge Dart and a Ford Sunliner pulling a teardrop trailer. No one paid any attention to Pepper's thumb.

Frustrated, she glanced back, hoping to see a friendly driver and instead, caught sight of a desert thunderstorm in the near distance, dropping a blue-gray veil of rain on the desert.

It was headed directly toward them.

"Well, shit."

Chapter Forty-four

Miss Becky was wound pretty tight, and for the first time in my life, I heard her say a bad word.

I was on the porch, missing Pepper and swatting flies to keep boredom at bay and to cut down on the number getting into the house every time someone opened the screen door. It had been a few minutes since I'd slapped one, because I was watching a fox work its way down the fence line across the highway. We didn't see too many foxes, and that one surprised me. I wondered if it was sick, walking around in the daylight like that, but before I thought to call through the screen and ask Miss Becky to get the .22 rifle, I heard a jar crash to the floor.

"Shit-fire!"

It was like a bolt of lightning struck the house. In my worst nightmares, I'd never thought to hear Miss Becky say anything such as that. Lest lightning really strike and hit me instead, I held my breath. It was a long moment of silence, and then a groan.

"Sweet Jesus, forgive me for backsliding." Her voice was low, because we all knew Jesus could even hear us think. She started sobbing.

Her crying brought tears to my own eyes, and they burned both for her and the emptiness I felt with Pepper gone. I doubt she even knew the words came through the screen. I slipped off the end of the porch and went through the wet grass to the smokehouse where I stayed for a good fifteen minutes. When I came back, I glanced inside and saw her dump a dustpan full of glass into the trash.

"Top." Her voice sounded hoarse. She sniffed a couple of times like she had a bad old cold. "Hon, run up to the store and get me a box of yellow cake mix."

"Yes ma'am."

"Don't tarry. It's liable to start raining again at any time."

"I'll be right back."

My bike was leaning against the outside kitchen wall. I climbed on and pushed off as she came to the door. "Hurry back. We're walking over to the church house when you get back."

I knew why, and I also knew better than to argue.

It didn't take more than five minutes to pedal down the wet highway to Uncle Neal's store. A couple of men were sitting under the overhang at Oak Peterson's. Uncle Neal's door was open and the lights were on inside, but for the first in a long time, there wasn't a soul on the porch. I leaned my bike against the steps and took them two at a time.

"Uncle Top!" Uncle Neal's booming voice seemed especially loud in the empty silence. For some reason he liked to hang an "uncle" on me, and I never knew why.

"Howdy Uncle Neal. Miss Becky wants a box of yellow cake mix."

"I ain't sure what I have right now, but it'll be on that shelf on the backside of the beans there. Down low, on the bottom."

I went around to the other side and found the flour, baking soda, and sugar.

"Raise your hand."

I did, and realized Uncle Neal could see it over the shelves.

"Move down a ways."

I did, and found the mixes. I wiggled my fingers to show him I'd seen it, then squatted to read the labels. The light wasn't particularly good back there in the corner, so it took a few seconds to find what he had in stock.

There were more mixes than I expected, chocolate, lemon,

and spice. It was aggravating to want a stupid *color*. To me, cake was cake.

"Howdy!" Uncle Neal always greeted his customers like they were long lost friends.

"Howdy back. I came to get thome thliced ham and a loaf of bread."

I froze at the sound of that voice. It was the one who called Mr. O.C. about the bodies buried in the lake bed.

Trembling, I knew I couldn't stay there, hiding on the floor. Uncle Neal would sure 'nough wonder where I was and would call attention to me. I figured it'd be best if I got my mix and went up to the counter like everything was hunky dory. I tried to speak, but my mouth was so dry it came out a croak. I cleared my throat like there was something in it, and tried again.

"Found it."

"Good. You all right? Some of that dust get in your craw?" Uncle Neal laughed and I heard him turn on the slicer. "I reckon I need to dust under there. No tellin' what might be living in the back of them shelves."

I rose and came around the end of the row. A young man stood there with his back to me, waiting on his order. I recognized him as the one sitting between John T. and Marty. I stopped beside the Coke cooler and waited, absently rubbing my foot back and forth on the raw floorboards.

Uncle Neal talked while he sliced. "I hain't seen you in a coon's age, Freddy."

"Nothir. I've been laying low for a while."

"I heard you was asking for a job here while back."

"Thill am, only I don't need one ath bad as I did. I decided to thart college next themester, in Commerce, and there aren't too many folkth want to hire thomeone who talks like me and ith gonna quit in a couple of month."

"Ain't that the truth?" Uncle Neal weighed several slices on a piece of white paper in his hand. He stopped. "I meant about working such a short time. This enough?"

"Aw, give me a half a dothen more thlices. Money ain't burry good if you can't thpend it."

Uncle Neal laughed again and turned off the slicer. "You must have put some back to pay for college."

Freddy was silent for a second. "I made a little hauling hay, bought a car'n got me a thcholarthip to boot."

"A scholarship! I'll be damned. Not many folks around here get one of them. You must have been something special."

Freddy rubbed the back of his neck, and I could tell he was uncomfortable with the conversation. "I juth lithened in class. I thouldn't have thaid anything about it, Neal. Don't thay nothing."

He frowned. "Oh, well son, don't worry about that. The truth is that scholarships aren't handouts."

"I know. I don't like to talk about my bidness."

"Well fine, then." Neal glanced toward the door, as if expecting someone to walk in. "You might want to go it alone for a while. Some folks tend to hold you back, if you know what I mean."

Freddy watched at the door. "You may be right."

Finished with his slicing, Uncle Neal wrapped the ham in another sheet of butcher paper and used a piece of masking tape to hold the flap closed. He wrote on it and rang up the sale on his old metal register. The heavy clunk of internal machinery sounded normal to me, and I suddenly realized everything *was* normal. It was me that was acting and feeling different.

Freddy passed him some change and left without paying any attention to me. He went down the steps and got under the wheel of an older model Chevy sedan.

Uncle Neal saw the car too. He rubbed his chin. "Well I'll be. He must have a hauled a butt-load of hay to make enough for a car *and* college money."

"Miss Becky said to put this on Grandpa's account."

He forgot the car and licked the end of a pencil stub. "Will do. Any news about Pepper?"

"Nossir."

"She making a coconut cake?"

"She didn't say."

"Well, if she is, see if she'll cut me a slice. I dearly love Becky's coconut cake."

"I will." I stepped out on the porch and saw the Chevy turn onto the highway, heading west toward Forest Chapel, but he could have also been going to Belk, Direct, Monkstown, Tigertown, Ragtown, or even Ivanhoe for all I knew, not to mention the little dots I couldn't remember.

Chapter Forty-five

"Painted desert, my ass." Pepper grumbled as they walked down the Flagstaff sidewalk. "It wasn't nothin' but sand and rocks."

Cale tried to keep things upbeat, but she seemed to be a thousand miles away. "Hey, where's my girl?"

Tired and dispirited, Pepper didn't stop walking. "I never was your girl."

"Sure you are. You came with me, didn't you?"

"We came together on this trip, that's all."

"C'mon. We're over halfway to San Francisco. You'll feel better when we get there."

"No I won't."

"Sure you will…"

"It's all bullshit."

"What?"

She stopped and waved her arms, hands flapping like they wanted to take off on their own. "This. Everything. This trip, this hippie shit, living on the road, whatever you call it. I'm done."

"You're tired."

"You're damn right, I am. Nothing's different out here except we're in the *goddamned* desert and I'm hot and dirty and tired and I want to lay down and go to sleep for a while."

Cale patted his pocket. "We have a little money left."

"What are you gonna do with it? We gonna get a motel room?" She pointed at the Western Skies. "Are *they* gonna rent us a room?"

"Well, no."

"That's right. How about down there at the El Rancho, or that way, at the Pony Soldier, huh? I wanted to stay in one of them giant teepee rooms we saw in Holbrook back there, but that ain't gonna happen, neither."

"You're missing the point of this trip, to get away from the establishment and help change the world. Look, we'll find out where the kids hang out and crash with some of them."

"Not me, bub. I've thought about it and I'm done with being groped and expected to put out to sleep on a dirty mattress on the floor and wake up to get groped again."

"It's called free love."

"It's called something I don't want to do...not after that night in the bottoms. If that's sex, I've had enough of it already."

Exasperated, Cale threw his hands in the air. "Well, what, then? What do you want to do? There's a bus station down there. How about...?"

"*No!* I'm not washing up in another dirty bathroom or sitting in a damned bus station to get out of the sun."

"I'll buy us tickets, then. How about that? We'll get on a bus to San Francisco."

Her temperature cooled. "You have enough?"

"I think so. We're halfway there, so we can go on, or back home."

Mollified, she struck out for the station. When they arrived it was busy with travelers waiting on the next bus. They stepped into the small, stifling lobby. The rooftop water cooler did little more than move the air.

Cale chewed his lip. "I bet that ticket agent's mean. He won't sell tickets to a couple of kids."

"Try." Pepper's glare cut a hole through him.

The unshaven agent was writing on a pad when Cale reached the window. "Can I get two tickets to San Francisco?"

The man adjusted a pair of glasses that immediately slipped back down to the end of his nose. "No, and you'd better get on out of here before I call the police. You're as underage as I've seen 'em, and I don't intend to get in trouble. Go on back home till you grow up."

He didn't have to tell Cale twice. Tail between his legs, he returned to Pepper. "Outside." When the door closed behind them, he kicked the wall. "That old fart in there wouldn't even think about selling us tickets."

"That's it, then." Pepper stalked away, back in the direction they came from. "I've had it."

Cale followed. "Hey, it'll get better. Let's go scrounge some food and..."

Despair welled. Putting both hands to her cheeks, Pepper screamed as Cale backed away in terror. Their situation, the scar on her shoulder, John T., and the realization that no matter where she was in the world, she'd never shed her roots, all added gasoline to the fire that suddenly erupted through the wall so carefully built since that terrible night in the bottoms.

She bent her knees and screamed again toward the hot sky, trying to rid herself of the demons she'd carried for the past three years.

Her third scream came from deep inside and lasted as long as her breath, then it died away, to be replaced by the hiss of cars passing on the highway.

Spinning on her heel, she wiped away what welled in her eyes and stalked off down the sidewalk. Block after block, Cale followed like a whipped puppy, head down and both hands in his pockets.

They eventually reached the outskirts of town, where she stopped beside a colorful Volkswagen van parked on the street between The End of the Trail motel and a Texaco station. Pepper's spirits had recovered when she uttered the first calm words in an hour. "*Psychedelic*."

"Ain't she a beaut?"

She flashed the long-haired boy a brilliant smile. "You're a tall drink of water."

"I wish I had a nickel for every time I heard that."

"This yours?"

"All mine."

"Where you headed?" Pepper spoke over the roar of motorcycles pulling up to the curb. A line of bearded, leather-clad bikers rumbled around the van and parked in front of a nondescript bar.

"California." He stuck out a hand. "I'm Kevin."

"Hi, Kevin. I'm Pepper. Where in California?"

A bearded giant swung a leg over his bike. "Hey, pretty little girl. You can ride on back with me."

Pepper's disgust at his dirty jeans and matching shirt was obvious. She noted his leather vest and dismissed him, turning her attention back to Kevin. "San Francisco?"

She felt Cale pluck at her sleeve. "Hey, I thought you were done."

"Shut up, Cale." Pepper ignored him and yanked her arm free. "Do you have room for any more?"

Irritated at her disinterest, the biker stepped close to Pepper. "Yeah, shut up, Cale."

One of his friends snickered. "Careful there, Griz. She might be mean."

For the first time in his life, Cale did the right thing, only at the wrong time. "Hey, back off, Fatso." He stepped between Griz and Pepper. "We're not talking to you."

Griz popped Cale in the chest with the flat of his hand, knocking the lippy youngster backward. He landed hard on his butt. Through the years Cale had won his share of fights against country boys bigger and tougher than himself. Jumping to his feet, he threw a hard right that thumped solidly against Griz's big gut. The biker grunted and swung his own right, catching Cale on the forehead. This time the kid dropped like a sack of feed.

Griz bent over to grab Cale's shirt, but the boy was game. He hit Griz on the jaw with everything he had, but there wasn't much power behind it. The only thing the punch did was finally make Griz angry.

"You gonna let that little piss-ant beat you, Griz?" A muscled biker leaned back and laughed.

Saving face, Griz squatted and gripped Cale's shirt with two big fists. In that second, a sneaker whistled out of nowhere. Pepper's kick held all the anger and frustration she built up on the road. Griz's nose exploded like a rotten tomato. Off balance, he staggered sideways and dropped to his knee. Cale kicked out at a blue-jeaned leg, connecting with an unidentified shin. A sharp yelp filled the air and then a flurry of boots hammered him from every direction as the gang members jumped in to protect their friend.

"Let's get!" A set of twin boys with blond hair to their shoulders pulled Pepper inside the van as Kevin jumped in and started the engine.

"No!" Struggling to stay with Cale, she cracked her head on something hard and lights flashed behind her eyes. She collapsed on the floor and more hands held her as the van's door slid shut.

Outside, Cale curled into a ball as the bikers kicked him unconscious.

The van sped away from the street fight and for Cale, everything went black.

Chapter Forty-six

Ned's stomach hurt so bad he could barely get out of bed. James paced the floor. "Let us take you to the doctor."

"Hell. no. We need to get to find Pepper, *then* you can take me to the doctor, but not before."

"Why not?"

"'Cause we need to move, for one thing, and for the other, they might want to put me in the hospital or something for this belly-ache. You know how doctors are, if they think they can get you in a hospital bed, they'll dern shore do it. Then that'll leave you and Crow without me."

Crow was waiting in his favorite lawn chair when Ned and James emerged. He rose and watched Ned take the backseat for the first time. Only then did Crow begin to worry about the old man. "You don't want to ride up front?"

"Nope. I'm gonna lay back here and see if I can get easy. I took a dose of Pepto-Bismol Bismol. It should start working before long."

Crow raised his eyebrows and James sighed. "I don't know how many times we've told him there ain't no second Bismol, but he says it anyway, like he's hard-headed or something."

James started the car as Crow climbed into the passenger seat. They drove through Meteor City before the town came awake. A fading sign for the town of Two Guns and a large building advertising mountain lions grew smaller in their mirrors. Giant red and yellow arrows nearly twenty feet in length outside of the

Twin Arrows Trading Post faded into the distance. They were most likely the only people from out of town that day that didn't stop at the stark white café and gas station.

Flagstaff eventually rose in the distance. Not long afterward, James steered into the parking lot in front of the courthouse. "I'm going in to talk with somebody about this address for Westlake's relatives. I want a police officer to go with us."

Crow was silent, but in the backseat, Ned spoke up. "Find us a city map. We can go it alone."

"I think we need the law with us."

"Son, I *am* the law."

"Dad, you're Texas law, and sick to *boot*."

"That don't make no difference. I'll rally when we get there."

James drummed the steering wheel in frustration. "Crow, what do you think?"

He flicked his eyes toward the front door beneath the tall clock tower, wondering if the police department was housed inside the red brick building. If nothing else, there would be sheriff's deputies inside. "I'm with Ned. This is family business, and you don't need the local fuzz to go with you."

"Family? Ned, you didn't say anything about family. You said he was Comanche."

"I believe he means it in a way other than blood."

"I do."

James studied Crow for a long minute. "You're on the run from the law." It wasn't a question, but a flat statement.

"I'm on the run from life."

"Ned, we truly don't know this feller. It could be he's a fugitive."

"Right now, he's a man helping us, son."

"But," James stopped, watching a kid walking down the street. "...I'll be damned."

Ned raised up on one elbow in the backseat to see where James was pointing. A teenager hurried toward them at a pretty good clip. The boy didn't see them in the car, and James realized he was on his way into the courthouse.

Crow followed James' point. "What?"

"That's Cale Westlake."

For the first time since they'd met him, Crow showed surprise.

Before they could react, Cale opened the door under the clock tower and went inside.

Chapter Forty-seven

Instead of going straight back home, I cut off the road at the catch pen a hundred yards from our drive and pedaled down to Uncle Cody's house. I knew he wouldn't be there, but figured Norma Faye would be. She was sitting on the porch, shelling peas.

"What are you doing out cattin' around in this weather?"

I dropped my bike in the yard and joined her. "Miss Becky sent me to the store for some cake mix."

Surprised, she glanced up at the gray sky. "She must want to bake awful bad. She always makes her cakes from scratch."

"I think she made it up because she wanted to get me away for a little while. She dropped a jar and I heard her cuss."

Norma Faye's hands went limp in her lap. "She never."

"She did. She said 'shit-fire,' and then went to crying."

Norma Faye bit her lip. She was wearing lipstick, even at home alone, and her top teeth scraped some off her bottom lip. Her eyes filled. I couldn't go anywhere without women spilling tears. "She's worried sick about Pepper."

"She's all right, now that she's cried, I 'magine."

"No, she isn't." Norma Faye stood. "I'm going over there. You can ride with me and leave your bike here."

"She said she's going to church when I get back."

"She can, but we probably need to talk first."

"I didn't come here to tell you that."

She raised her eyebrows and waited.

"I need to talk to Uncle Cody, but I don't want to do it when Miss Becky's around."

Norma Faye didn't bat an eye or even take a second to think. "You want to go inside and call him?"

"Can I?"

"Sure." She sat back down without questioning me like anyone else would. "I'll finish shelling these peas and then we'll go to the house together."

Their phone was in the kitchen, at the back of the house. I walked through, remembering what it was like when Mr. Tom Bell, the old Texas Ranger, was rebuilding the place that had fallen into ruin. His trunk still sat against the wall in the living room with a crocheted drape over it, like it was a little casket, and maybe that's how they felt about it. I only remembered it was full of guns when me and Pepper snuck in one day while Mr. Tom was gone. When we lifted the lid, we found his pistol, holster, badge, and a big, mean-looking rifle.

I knew the number by heart, and spun the dial five times.

"Sheriff's Department."

The voice didn't sound like anyone I'd ever talked to. "Is this Martha?"

"No, hon. This is Deputy Anna Sloan. Who do you need?"

"Uncle Cody, uh, I mean Sheriff Cody Parker."

"You must be Top."

"Yes ma'am."

"Your Uncle Cody's not here right now. What can I do for you?"

"I really need to talk to him about something really, really important."

"Really?"

I knew right off she was making fun of me, and it made me mad. "What'll it take for you to have him call back, or come home?"

"Well, he's in Dallas right now, with some bodi…on official business."

"Can you radio him?"

"Is it that important?"

"Yes ma'am."

"I'll holler at him. Are you all right, hon?"

"Yes ma'am. I have some news that he might be able to use."

"Can you give it to me?"

I caught myself biting my lip like Norma Faye. "Will you tell him?"

"Sure will. He's my boss."

"I think I know who called Judge Rains and told him where to find the bodies of those missing men."

There was a long moment of silence. "How do you know that?"

I explained what I'd overheard on Mr. O.C.'s phone, and again in Neal's store.

"How sure are you?"

"Sure enough to call you."

"I've heard stories about you and Pepper, how y'all get in trouble sometimes."

"We aren't wrong, though." I thought about telling her about my dreams, but I didn't know her well enough and was afraid she'd laugh at me.

"All right. I'll see what I can do."

Relieved, I hung up. I'd done everything I was supposed to do, and she was right, without Pepper there, I was out of it.

Norma Faye was waiting when I came out on the porch. She'd been listening. "Why didn't you want to make that call at home?"

"I believe Miss Becky has enough on her plate as it is, so I don't want her worrying about me getting involved in something like this again."

She raised an eyebrow and studied me for a while before standing up. "You're quite a little man, you know that?"

It made me feel good for her to say that, and I felt better as she drove me home without asking me a single question.

The three of us went to church an hour later to pray. Mine was short, and I probably could have made it in the living room instead of the church house.

Miss Becky took a long, long time at it, though, and I reckon she needed the altar as a pipeline to be heard, after saying such a bad word.

Chapter Forty-eight

Ned and James followed Cale Westlake into the Flagstaff police station. Crow stayed outside, in the car.

Slower because of the pain in his stomach, Ned came in last. They stopped at the sight of Cale standing in the lobby, apparently trying to decide where to go. The youngster saw them when he heard the glass doors close.

They were shocked at his appearance. Two black eyes and a split lip highlighted the huge lump on his forehead. His shirt was splattered with blood.

Before Ned could grasp the sight, James lost control and launched forward. "You little bastard!"

Cale recoiled as if a snake struck at him. Before he could get away, James grabbed a handful of hair and shook the boy like a rag doll. "Where's my daughter?" His voice echoed throughout the tile lobby.

"Wait!" Cale's eyes went wide and filled with water. He tried to twist out of James' hands, but James shook harder.

Ned stepped between them, bunching up his son's shirt and trying to separate them. "James! Back off!" Cale's tennis shoes squeaked on the floor as he fought for balance. "Son!"

Two sheriff's deputies shot out of a nearby courtroom and seeing the apparently violent situation, plowed into the three of them, knocking Ned on his backside. Ned grunted as he hit the hard floor and a lance of pain shot through his tailbone. His Stetson went rolling across the floor.

James went down hard, taking Cale with him. Growling like a mad bear, he refused to let go of the boy's shirt and struggled to pull him closer. "Where's my girl?!"

The lobby was suddenly filled with shouts and orders as more people poured out of nearby offices. Half a dozen uniformed men joined in to separate the two.

A young police officer planted one foot between Ned's outstretched legs, pushing him back with the point of a billy club. "Don't move old man!"

James continued to struggle and a deputy on the ground got him in a choke hold from behind. The deputy bent backward, pulling the stricken father into a painful arch. James ducked his chin and twisted, fury overriding good sense. Another deputy twisted James' arm until it came close to breaking. He released his hold on Cale's shirt and disappeared under a pile of even more lawmen who rolled into the fray like an offensive line.

Ned struggled to push upright. "Hold it! I'm the law! That's my son you've got!"

The officer with the baton increased the pressure on Ned's chest. "Fine sir. When we separate your son from that man, you can get up and we'll figure all this out."

"No, the *grownup* is my son, James. The boy is a runaway."

"Stay right there."

"I said he's a runaway!"

"I said don't move!"

Ned's face flushed with heat. "*I* told you I'm a lawman. My badge is in my pocket."

Ned tried to reach for it and his arm went numb when the officer swung the wooden club against his shoulder. It impacted with a thick, meaty sound. "Don't reach into that pocket old man!"

"You son of a bitch! You hit me again and…"

"Dad!" Still struggling to get free, James saw the officer use two hands on the baton to strike Ned a second time and managed a croak. "Dad!"

The old constable's blue eyes flashed, as if taking a photo of the officer standing above him with the baton raised for another strike, then he relaxed and laid back, groaning.

None of them saw Cale Westlake run out the door.

Chapter Forty-nine

Two hours after he got a radio call from Anna, Uncle Cody's tires crunched up the drive. It was nearly dark, and I was waiting on the porch. Hootie roused up, but he recognized the car and rested his head back on his paws. He didn't move again until Uncle Cody trailed around the car and up on the porch.

"Deputy Sloan told me what you think you found out." Cody dropped into the cane-bottom chair beside me. Hootie stood, turned around three times, and laid back down to watch the road. "Well, at least this time you didn't go off trying to solve everything all by yourself. I guess Pepper not being here made a difference."

"I'm not sure what difference that'd be. It seems like I'm right back in the middle of stuff I don't want to be in by being up at the store and hearing Freddy. You know how he talks, well, I recognized him right off."

"You sure about what you're saying?"

"Sure enough."

"On your word I'm taking him into custody. That's a big responsibility for a kid."

"I know his lisp. He says 'very' funny, like 'burry,' and 'bidness,' too. Let Judge Rains talk to him and he'll recognize his voice like I did."

"You know that's what I'll do, but the judge didn't say anything about a lisp."

"It's 'cause of the way he talked, like he was careful. The judge'll remember that."

The rain had stopped, but the world was heavy with water. It dripped off the house, from the trees, and from the thicket of sand plums beside the hay barn. The long grass in the pasture lay droopy and green. A thin stream ran from the hill where the barn sat, down the ruts made by Grandpa's truck, under the pipe gate, and then down the gravel drive to join a thicker stream flowing in the ditch. The water streamed over the drive toward the slough below the house that eventually ran off into Sanders Creek, a mile away.

A cow lowed in the distance, and a hoot owl tuned up. I guess he was impatient because it'd been cloudy for so long and he was all mixed up. Behind the house, a whippoorwill called. It all sounded so normal, but at the same time wrong, because the storms weren't past, Pepper was gone, and Grandpa and Uncle James weren't there.

I couldn't meet Uncle Cody's eyes. "What are you going to do with Freddy?"

"Anna's on the way to pick him up, and then we'll take him in for questioning."

"Will you tell him how you know?"

"I don't know." He paused. "We'll see how it goes."

"Do you think he did it?"

"Can't say. He might have. He might know who did it, or he may be telling stories."

That was our nice way of saying he might be lying.

"Am I gonna get in trouble?"

"For what?"

I shrugged. "I don't know."

He gave my neck a squeeze. I realized how skinny I was when his hand slipped down to cover most of my shoulder. "You don't ever get in trouble trying to do the right thing."

"I didn't know for sure where Pepper was going."

"Oh, *that's* what we're talking about." It was quiet for a moment. "Did she tell you she was leaving?"

Chapter Fifty

After Anna promised to pass Top's information to Cody, she made a call to a friend in Houston. The crusty old deputy's gruff demeanor changed when he recognized her voice on the phone.

"How you doing, gal?"

"Fine, Burt." They exchanged pleasantries for a moment before she went to the reason for her call. "Listen, I'm working on a couple of cases up here in Lamar County, but this department is more than a little behind the times. I need anything you can find out about a guy named Leland Hale, and his wife, Melva." She spelled it to make sure he didn't write down Melba.

"What else?"

"There's something about him and that woman that bothers me. He's dead now. Hit and run. She's the strangest woman I've ever met, and acts even stranger when she talks about Leland. I'm wondering if he had any kind of criminal record that she's hiding for him."

"I'll do what I can. When do you need it?"

"Yesterday."

Burt laughed. "You haven't changed a bit. I figured country living would slow you down some, but it sounds like you're still the same old Sparky."

"I'm Anna here. Don't you be giving these guys that nickname. Thanks, Burt."

Half an hour later, she followed the winding country road through the river bottom on her way to John T.'s house. She

"No. She's been talking about California for a good long while, especially after...after we were took." A painful lump rose in my throat and my eyes burned. I didn't know where it came from. One minute it wasn't there, and the next minute I wanted to bawl like a baby. I kept those feelings packed down most of the time, but every now and then they'd well up like spring water. "She don't talk about it."

"Do *you* want to talk about it?"

I had to swallow twice before answering. I was afraid someone was listening through the screen door, but the kitchen was dark. "Everybody worries about what happened to Pepper all the time. It's always poor Pepper this, and poor Pepper that. She don't want it, but she never says anything."

"So what do *you* want?"

"I wanted someone to ask me how *I* felt after the Skinner took us...how *I* feel. No one ever does, though."

It was quiet on the porch while Uncle Cody digested our words.

"Do you need to talk about that night?"

"I want to talk about a lot of things."

"Like what?"

"That, and Hootie getting chewed up." The Brit perked up his ears at his name, then sighed and went back to watching the road. "Like us almost letting that killer Kendal get away, or Grandpa nearly dying down in Mexico." I tried to swallow the lump, but my chest was full of pain and my voice broke. "Or about Mr. Tom Bell. I loved him and now he's gone, and here I am, sitting here all alone. Everything I love and need keeps getting hurt in some way, or killed."

"I know, but you're not alone. Let's talk."

That stubborn Parker streak rose up then and I shook my head and wiped the tears off my cheeks. "No. Pepper's gone, too. It's about her right now...again." A good mad replaced my tears, because it was always about her. That was something about me I never understood. When I got mad, I'd get to crying. I wiped my cheeks dry. "I should have told someone what she was thinking."

"It's not your fault. She does what she does."

"She has a hurt deep down inside. It ain't all about that scar on her shoulder. You know, the Skinner did things to her, too."

"Do you think she needs to talk to a doctor?"

"They said the scar wouldn't be a problem."

"I'm talking about a head doctor."

"She ain't *crazy*!"

"Never said she was. People can get hurt inside their heads and talking it out helps."

"Do they have those for kids?"

"Yep."

"Boys *and* girls?"

I could feel him studying me. "Both, if they need it." He gave my neck another squeeze and it told me he understood the weight of everything that was resting on my shoulders, from my parents dying, something I never talked about, to that terrible night in the bottoms when the Skinner did those things to me and Pepper.

We set there quiet for a while before the tightness in my chest eased. I finally broke the silence. "There's something else."

"A'ite."

"That dream I keep having. A horse is talking to me, leaning his head against my chest and whispering."

"You have a horse talking to you now?"

I smiled, feeling the dried tears pull at the skin of my cheeks. "Stupid, ain't it? I've gone from dreaming about drowning in the Rock Hole to Mr. Ed."

We both laughed about the talking horse on television.

"Your horse is like Mr. Ed?"

"No. I'm not dreaming about that stupid show. Horses don't talk, but the one in my dreams does, and he knows Grandpa."

"I've been having dreams, too."

"What about?"

He was silent for a moment. "Dead babies."

I shuddered.

"Only you'd understand. Dead babies that keep poin
west, past Neal's store."

"What does it all mean?"

He sighed. "It means the Gift is trying to tell us somethin

crossed the swollen Sulphur River and came to the little wooden post office.

A stout woman wearing a tight bun on top of her head smiled wide when Anna stepped up to the scarred counter.

"Howdy, Deputy. What can I do for you?"

Anna returned the smile. She unfolded a sheet from a notepad and slid it across so the woman could read it. "I'm looking for this address."

"Well, hon, that's off the main road a piece, but it ain't far."

"Can you tell me how to find it?"

"Sure 'nough." The postmistress closed her eyes to visualize the route. She pointed into the air with an arthritic hand. "You go right down the highway to the next road and turn right. Then you follow it for a piece and turn left at Carson Taylor's barn. Go on past two gravel roads to the third one and turn left. There's a big pecan tree there and you won't miss it. Cross a plank bridge and turn right again, I believe, and you'll pass Nellie Renshaw's house. I swear, that woman makes the best sweet tea I've ever drank. Past there you see a big pool, but you don't turn anywheres near it, but it's deep, it's an old gravel pit they used to build this here highway—so you'll know you're on the right road. Go on a piece past a growed-up pasture, then a little field that ain't no bigger'n a minute, and I swear, I don't know why Daniel Spears wastes the gas to plow it ever year, and this year I believe it was peas that didn't make good—but anyway, go on a little fu-ther to the Crawford cemetery, you'll know it's the right one 'cause of the fresh grave right there beside the road. That was Miss Millie Bills, she was a sweet old soul and we're all gonna miss her, bless her heart, but then you'll see a little house off to the left with some big oak trees on the south side for shade. That's where you're going."

She opened her eyes, pleased with the directions.

Anna blinked. "I got most of that, could you write it down for me?"

"Why sure 'nough, hon. Better yet, let me draw you a little map." She cheerfully drew several intersecting lines, making small notes to identify the landmarks. She slid it across the counter. "There you go."

Anna folded the map and put it into her shirt pocket. "Thank you so much. Do you know John T. West?"

The little woman's face changed in an instant. She held one gnarled hand in front of her mouth, as if the actual name shouldn't be spoken. "John T. I know him. That's where you're going, ain't it, to pick him up?"

"What makes you think that?"

"'Cause you wouldn't be going there for nothing else. He's been in the pen. What's he done this time?"

"I can't talk about that. I need to find him."

The postmistress patted Anna's hand that was resting on the counter. "Hon, you be careful out there with him. That boy is mean as a snake. I ain't never heard of him working a lick and, you know, he drinks."

Anna captured the hand between her own and gave it a soft rub. "I'll be all right. Thanks."

"If I'd-a thought about that house being John T.'s, I might not have told you how to get there all by yourself. I don't want to have that on my conscience if you was to get hurt."

"There's nothing to worry about."

"Yes there is, when it comes to John T."

Chapter Fifty-one

Ned held an ice bag against his bruised shoulder and listened to both the Flagstaff sheriff and police chief apologize. “It don’t matter none.”

The chief, a young man with close-cropped hair shook his head. “It does to my department, Constable Parker. It was a bad mistake all around, on our part, and yours.”

Completely wrung out, James slumped in a chair beside a worn wooden desk that had seen better days during the Garfield administration. “Cale Westlake got away. That boy was beaten, and I’m scared to death for my daughter.”

The sheriff laced his fingers on the desk. “We have men on the way to the address you gave us. They’ll pick her up if she’s there. We’ll find Cale, too.”

“I doubt she’s there.” Ned winced and rolled his shoulder. “Something’s happened. That’s why he was here, and now he’s gone again.”

“You should have asked him what was wrong.”

Ned’s blue eyes iced the distance between him and the youngest police officer who’d spoken, the one who’d used the billy club. He wished he could return the favor. The sheriff had called Chisum at Ned’s urging, and talked to Judge O.C. Rains. He was still smarting from the dressing down he’d gotten from the old judge.

The officer finally dropped his eyes. Ned grunted. “Have you ever gone after a runaway child that was blood?”

"No."

"That'd be no *sir* to you, and the truth is that you don't know what the *hell* you'd do in any such situation, so if I's you, I'd sit right there with my damned mouth closed and let my betters do the talking."

"Easy, Constable Parker." The chief agreed. "Lester, why don't you go outside?"

Ned remembered the police car parked next to theirs. "No. We're leaving." His harsh outburst stunned them all. "Are you finished with us?"

The sheriff shrugged.

The chief tapped a yellow pencil against the desk. "We are too." The phone rang. He answered and listened. "All right." He hung up. "Mr. Parker, they went to the address you gave, but the house is empty. It appears they've moved."

James deflated even more. "All right. Let's go."

Ned wrote on a piece of paper.

The sheriff shifted, his leather holster creaking. "What's that?"

"My number in Center Springs, Texas. Give my wife a call if you find anything out. She'll tell me the next time I call home."

"Where are you going?"

Ned rested his blue eyes on the sheriff. "After my granddaughter."

When they were out of the office, the chief thumped a forefinger on the desk. "We need to find Cale Westlake before they do."

The sheriff shrugged. "They have as much chance as us, though."

◇◇◇

Their car was gone when they stepped outside. Ned tilted the Stetson back on his head. "Well, son of a bitch."

"Crow stole my car." James' head felt like it would explode as anger flashed once again. "I told you he was a crook. Now what are we going to do?"

"I don't know." Ned needed somewhere to sit, but the city fathers apparently didn't want anyone loafing in front of their courthouse.

"I'm going back in and file a report on my stolen car."

"Wait."

"Wait, *hell*. Dad, he stole our car and now we don't have any way to find Pepper."

Another sharp pain shot through Ned's stomach, and he bent over to brace himself on both knees. "Let me think." He took a deep breath once the pain settled back to a more tolerable level. "All right." He pointed to a diner down the road. "Here's what we're gonna do. I want to go in there and sit down and order a Bromo-Seltzer. Then we'll figure out our next step."

"Crow could be a hundred miles away if we wait for you to drink a powder."

"I don't believe he stole it and run away. Let's think a minute while we walk."

James finally gave in. "All right." He rubbed his throat, sore from being choked down. "I could use something to drink anyway. You think they have sweet tea out here?"

"Of course they do."

They were halfway to the diner when Crow steered the Bel Air around the corner. He shot over to the curb, reached across the seat, and gave the door lever a yank. It opened with a squall. "Get in. Quick."

Ned jerked the back door open. "See, I told you he wouldn't run off."

Without a word, James dropped heavily into the passenger seat. Ned stopped at the sight of Cale Westlake in the floorboard. He had a second lump on his forehead, and his hands were cuffed.

Ned got in, slammed the door, and Crow quickly pulled away from the curb. He smoothly accelerated away from the courthouse. Ned nudged Cale with the toe of his shoe.

"You stay right there and get to talking."

Chapter Fifty-two

It was full dark when Anna rolled into Ned's drive. Cody was still sitting on the porch with Top. They weren't alone, of course. Miss Becky, Ida Belle, and Norma Faye had taken turns coming out to check on them. It was obvious they wanted to know what Cody and Top were talking about, and Cody gave them enough information to satisfy the curious women, but not what Top said in confidence.

Anna killed the lights and Cody trailed around the front of the car to talk through her open car window. He saw someone in the backseat, lit by the dash lights.

"Howdy, Freddy."

The dejected man barely raised his head. "Cody."

"You know why I had Deputy Sloan pick you up?"

"I don't have any idea."

"Sure you do." Cody waited.

"Why'd you thend a girl to get me? Thath embarrathing."

"I didn't. I sent a deputy."

"I'd as thoon be taken in by that nigger John Wathington."

Anna caught his eye in her rearview mirror. "Don't make me have to drag you out of that backseat."

"What'd I do?"

"Don't use that word around me."

"What?"

"That word you used referring to Deputy Washington."

Chapter Fifty

After Anna promised to pass Top's information to Cody, she made a call to a friend in Houston. The crusty old deputy's gruff demeanor changed when he recognized her voice on the phone.

"How you doing, gal?"

"Fine, Burt." They exchanged pleasantries for a moment before she went to the reason for her call. "Listen, I'm working on a couple of cases up here in Lamar County, but this department is more than a little behind the times. I need anything you can find out about a guy named Leland Hale, and his wife, Melva." She spelled it to make sure he didn't write down Melba.

"What else?"

"There's something about him and that woman that bothers me. He's dead now. Hit and run. She's the strangest woman I've ever met, and acts even stranger when she talks about Leland. I'm wondering if he had any kind of criminal record that she's hiding for him."

"I'll do what I can. When do you need it?"

"Yesterday."

Burt laughed. "You haven't changed a bit. I figured country living would slow you down some, but it sounds like you're still the same old Sparky."

"I'm Anna here. Don't you be giving these guys that nickname. Thanks, Burt."

Half an hour later, she followed the winding country road through the river bottom on her way to John T.'s house. She

"Only you'd understand. Dead babies that keep pointing west, past Neal's store."

"What does it all mean?"

He sighed. "It means the Gift is trying to tell us something."

crossed the swollen Sulphur River and came to the little wooden post office.

A stout woman wearing a tight bun on top of her head smiled wide when Anna stepped up to the scarred counter.

"Howdy, Deputy. What can I do for you?"

Anna returned the smile. She unfolded a sheet from a notepad and slid it across so the woman could read it. "I'm looking for this address."

"Well, hon, that's off the main road a piece, but it ain't far."

"Can you tell me how to find it?"

"Sure 'nough." The postmistress closed her eyes to visualize the route. She pointed into the air with an arthritic hand. "You go right down the highway to the next road and turn right. Then you follow it for a piece and turn left at Carson Taylor's barn. Go on past two gravel roads to the third one and turn left. There's a big pecan tree there and you won't miss it. Cross a plank bridge and turn right again, I believe, and you'll pass Nellie Renshaw's house. I swear, that woman makes the best sweet tea I've ever drank. Past there you see a big pool, but you don't turn anywheres near it, but it's deep, it's an old gravel pit they used to build this here highway—so you'll know you're on the right road. Go on a piece past a growed-up pasture, then a little field that ain't no bigger'n a minute, and I swear, I don't know why Daniel Spears wastes the gas to plow it ever year, and this year I believe it was peas that didn't make good—but anyway, go on a little fu-ther to the Crawford cemetery, you'll know it's the right one 'cause of the fresh grave right there beside the road. That was Miss Millie Bills, she was a sweet old soul and we're all gonna miss her, bless her heart, but then you'll see a little house off to the left with some big oak trees on the south side for shade. That's where you're going."

She opened her eyes, pleased with the directions.

Anna blinked. "I got most of that, could you write it down for me?"

"Why sure 'nough, hon. Better yet, let me draw you a little map." She cheerfully drew several intersecting lines, making small notes to identify the landmarks. She slid it across the counter. "There you go."

Anna folded the map and put it into her shirt pocket. "Thank you so much. Do you know John T. West?"

The little woman's face changed in an instant. She held one gnarled hand in front of her mouth, as if the actual name shouldn't be spoken. "John T. I know him. That's where you're going, ain't it, to pick him up?"

"What makes you think that?"

"'Cause you wouldn't be going there for nothing else. He's been in the pen. What's he done this time?"

"I can't talk about that. I need to find him."

The postmistress patted Anna's hand that was resting on the counter. "Hon, you be careful out there with him. That boy is mean as a snake. I ain't never heard of him working a lick and, you know, he drinks."

Anna captured the hand between her own and gave it a soft rub. "I'll be all right. Thanks."

"If I'd-a thought about that house being John T.'s, I might not have told you how to get there all by yourself. I don't want to have that on my conscience if you was to get hurt."

"There's nothing to worry about."

"Yes there is, when it comes to John T."

Chapter Fifty-one

Ned held an ice bag against his bruised shoulder and listened to both the Flagstaff sheriff and police chief apologize. "It don't matter none."

The chief, a young man with close-cropped hair shook his head. "It does to my department, Constable Parker. It was a bad mistake all around, on our part, and yours."

Completely wrung out, James slumped in a chair beside a worn wooden desk that had seen better days during the Garfield administration. "Cale Westlake got away. That boy was beaten, and I'm scared to death for my daughter."

The sheriff laced his fingers on the desk. "We have men on the way to the address you gave us. They'll pick her up if she's there. We'll find Cale, too."

"I doubt she's there." Ned winced and rolled his shoulder. "Something's happened. That's why he was here, and now he's gone again."

"You should have asked him what was wrong."

Ned's blue eyes iced the distance between him and the youngest police officer who'd spoken, the one who'd used the billy club. He wished he could return the favor. The sheriff had called Chisum at Ned's urging, and talked to Judge O.C. Rains. He was still smarting from the dressing down he'd gotten from the old judge.

The officer finally dropped his eyes. Ned grunted. "Have you ever gone after a runaway child that was blood?"

"No."

"That'd be no *sir* to you, and the truth is that you don't know what the *hell* you'd do in any such situation, so if I's you, I'd sit right there with my damned mouth closed and let my betters do the talking."

"Easy, Constable Parker." The chief agreed. "Lester, why don't you go outside?"

Ned remembered the police car parked next to theirs. "No. We're leaving." His harsh outburst stunned them all. "Are you finished with us?"

The sheriff shrugged.

The chief tapped a yellow pencil against the desk. "We are too." The phone rang. He answered and listened. "All right." He hung up. "Mr. Parker, they went to the address you gave, but the house is empty. It appears they've moved."

James deflated even more. "All right. Let's go."

Ned wrote on a piece of paper.

The sheriff shifted, his leather holster creaking. "What's that?"

"My number in Center Springs, Texas. Give my wife a call if you find anything out. She'll tell me the next time I call home."

"Where are you going?"

Ned rested his blue eyes on the sheriff. "After my granddaughter."

When they were out of the office, the chief thumped a forefinger on the desk. "We need to find Cale Westlake before they do."

The sheriff shrugged. "They have as much chance as us, though."

Their car was gone when they stepped outside. Ned tilted the Stetson back on his head. "Well, son of a bitch."

"Crow stole my car." James' head felt like it would explode as anger flashed once again. "I told you he was a crook. Now what are we going to do?"

"I don't know." Ned needed somewhere to sit, but the city fathers apparently didn't want anyone loafing in front of their courthouse.

"I'm going back in and file a report on my stolen car."

"Wait."

"Wait, *hell*. Dad, he stole our car and now we don't have any way to find Pepper."

Another sharp pain shot through Ned's stomach, and he bent over to brace himself on both knees. "Let me think." He took a deep breath once the pain settled back to a more tolerable level. "All right." He pointed to a diner down the road. "Here's what we're gonna do. I want to go in there and sit down and order a Bromo-Seltzer. Then we'll figure out our next step."

"Crow could be a hundred miles away if we wait for you to drink a powder."

"I don't believe he stole it and run away. Let's think a minute while we walk."

James finally gave in. "All right." He rubbed his throat, sore from being choked down. "I could use something to drink anyway. You think they have sweet tea out here?"

"Of course they do."

They were halfway to the diner when Crow steered the Bel Air around the corner. He shot over to the curb, reached across the seat, and gave the door lever a yank. It opened with a squall. "Get in. Quick."

Ned jerked the back door open. "See, I told you he wouldn't run off."

Without a word, James dropped heavily into the passenger seat. Ned stopped at the sight of Cale Westlake in the floorboard. He had a second lump on his forehead, and his hands were cuffed.

Ned got in, slammed the door, and Crow quickly pulled away from the curb. He smoothly accelerated away from the courthouse. Ned nudged Cale with the toe of his shoe.

"You stay right there and get to talking."

Chapter Fifty-two

It was full dark when Anna rolled into Ned's drive. Cody was still sitting on the porch with Top. They weren't alone, of course. Miss Becky, Ida Belle, and Norma Faye had taken turns coming out to check on them. It was obvious they wanted to know what Cody and Top were talking about, and Cody gave them enough information to satisfy the curious women, but not what Top said in confidence.

Anna killed the lights and Cody trailed around the front of the car to talk through her open car window. He saw someone in the backseat, lit by the dash lights.

"Howdy, Freddy."

The dejected man barely raised his head. "Cody."

"You know why I had Deputy Sloan pick you up?"

"I don't have any idea."

"Sure you do." Cody waited.

"Why'd you thend a girl to get me? Thath embarrathing."

"I didn't. I sent a deputy."

"I'd as thoon be taken in by that nigger John Wathington."

Anna caught his eye in her rearview mirror. "Don't make me have to drag you out of that backseat."

"What'd I do?"

"Don't use that word around me."

"What?"

"That word you used referring to Deputy Washington."

"No. She's been talking about California for a good long while, especially after…after we were took." A painful lump rose in my throat and my eyes burned. I didn't know where it came from. One minute it wasn't there, and the next minute I wanted to bawl like a baby. I kept those feelings packed down most of the time, but every now and then they'd well up like spring water. "She don't talk about it."

"Do *you* want to talk about it?"

I had to swallow twice before answering. I was afraid someone was listening through the screen door, but the kitchen was dark. "Everybody worries about what happened to Pepper all the time. It's always poor Pepper this, and poor Pepper that. She don't want it, but she never says anything."

"So what do *you* want?"

"I wanted someone to ask me how *I* felt after the Skinner took us…how *I* feel. No one ever does, though."

It was quiet on the porch while Uncle Cody digested our words.

"Do you need to talk about that night?"

"I want to talk about a lot of things."

"Like what?"

"That, and Hootie getting chewed up." The Brit perked up his ears at his name, then sighed and went back to watching the road. "Like us almost letting that killer Kendal get away, or Grandpa nearly dying down in Mexico." I tried to swallow the lump, but my chest was full of pain and my voice broke. "Or about Mr. Tom Bell. I loved him and now he's gone, and here I am, sitting here all alone. Everything I love and need keeps getting hurt in some way, or killed."

"I know, but you're not alone. Let's talk."

That stubborn Parker streak rose up then and I shook my head and wiped the tears off my cheeks. "No. Pepper's gone, too. It's about her right now…again." A good mad replaced my tears, because it was always about her. That was something about me I never understood. When I got mad, I'd get to crying. I wiped my cheeks dry. "I should have told someone what she was thinking."

"It's not your fault. She does what she does."

"She has a hurt deep down inside. It ain't all about that scar on her shoulder. You know, the Skinner did things to her, too."

"Do you think she needs to talk to a doctor?"

"They said the scar wouldn't be a problem."

"I'm talking about a head doctor."

"She ain't *crazy*!"

"Never said she was. People can get hurt inside their heads and talking it out helps."

"Do they have those for kids?"

"Yep."

"Boys *and* girls?"

I could feel him studying me. "Both, if they need it." He gave my neck another squeeze and it told me he understood the weight of everything that was resting on my shoulders, from my parents dying, something I never talked about, to that terrible night in the bottoms when the Skinner did those things to me and Pepper.

We set there quiet for a while before the tightness in my chest eased. I finally broke the silence. "There's something else."

"A'ite."

"That dream I keep having. A horse is talking to me, leaning his head against my chest and whispering."

"You have a horse talking to you now?"

I smiled, feeling the dried tears pull at the skin of my cheeks. "Stupid, ain't it? I've gone from dreaming about drowning in the Rock Hole to Mr. Ed."

We both laughed about the talking horse on television.

"Your horse is like Mr. Ed?"

"No. I'm not dreaming about that stupid show. Horses don't talk, but the one in my dreams does, and he knows Grandpa."

"I've been having dreams, too."

"What about?"

He was silent for a moment. "Dead babies."

I shuddered.

Freddy grunted at Cody. "What'th thith all about? Ith thith woman crathy?"

"Nope. She's a long way from crazy. I sent her to come get you. What do you know about some bodies we found today?"

The expression on Freddy's face was a full confession, but expressions can't be used in a court of law. Cody's prompt caused Freddy to shrug.

Cody opened the back door. "Get out."

The porch light snapped on as Freddy slid out of thc seat.

"Shut that off and stay in the house!" The light immediately went out and Cody was about to order Top inside, too, but he wasn't on the porch.

The boy's voice made him jump. "I know it was you, Freddy."

"Top, go in the house." Cody spoke automatically.

Anna opened her door and joined them. "Top, hon, you shouldn't be out here."

"I recognized his voice."

Top was determined to make them listen. He planted his feet, squared his shoulders, and lifted his chin. He was just as much a part of this as anyone else in the yard, and he figured that if he could get Cody to listen to him, as he'd done earlier that evening, they might see that he was standing up like a man.

Anyone else would have glared daggers at the youngster, but thoroughly humiliated by his arrest at the hands of a female deputy, and identified by a kid, Freddy simply stared at his feet. It was one more in a long line of embarrassments. "I didn't do nothing."

"Then why do you think you're here?"

"I'm here becauthe thith woman picked me up, in front of my frienth."

"Any idea who his friends were?"

Anna dug a notepad out of her back pocket. "He was in front of the skating rink in town, talking to some girls about half his age. I didn't get their names, but three young men that *were* about his age were there too." She tilted the pad to read by the dome light. "Kenneth Lee Williams, Eliott George Hestor, and Peter Dale Heslink. They volunteered to follow John to the courthouse for questioning. We didn't put them under arrest."

"They didn't do nothing, neither."

"Good. That takes a load off my mind." Cody gave Freddy a smile. "Now, tell me what you know about the bodies we dug up in the lake bottom."

"We don't know nothing about them, nor any *other* bodieth you find."

"What other bodies?"

Freddy was confused. "Theriff, any *other* bodieth, I reckon."

"I didn't say anything about anyone else."

"I know, what I'm trying to thay ith that *I* didn't thoot nobody."

"*I* didn't say you did."

"Then let me go."

"I will when I'm sure I can. Did you make any calls to Judge Rains about knowing where some people were buried?"

"No."

"You know something you aren't telling."

"I honesthly don't know what you're talking about."

Anna stepped in. "Who *would* know, then?"

Freddy hung his head. "I'm completely innothent. I didn't thoot nobody."

"What do you do for a living?"

"Huh?"

"I'm asking what you do for a living."

"Whatever. I got out of thchool and hauled hay all the thummer long. Plow thome. I'm pretty good with my handth, tho I work on carth."

"You ever work on the lake? You know, run some of that big machinery to push over trees, like draglines or bulldozers?"

Freddy narrowed his eyes. "No."

"Anybody you know who does?"

He shrugged.

"Could you?"

"Prob'ly, but I didn't."

"Didn't what?"

"I didn't bur-ry nobody with no bulldozer."

"Know who could have?"

Freddy shrugged. "Bunch of people been working down there. You bedder ask thombody else."

"Uncle Cody. He told Mr. O.C." The boy was determined to tell Cody what he knew. No more hanging back.

"Top, if you have something to say, stand right here and speak up." Cody noted the change in the boy, and decided to listen.

"He said burry."

"Huh?"

"He said *burry*, instead of bury, and he says *bedder* for better. I heard him say it on the phone. I know good and well it's him, even though he was trying to disguise his lisp."

Uncle Cody raised an eyebrow at Freddy. "Well?"

"I ain't been talking to that boy."

"Didn't say you was."

"Well, he'th thaying like I did."

"Did what?"

"Talk to him on the phone about burrying them men down there."

"Where?"

He jerked his head toward the lake. "You know, where you found 'em."

"How much money did y'all get out of this?"

"Money? What-choo talking about, money?"

Cody caught Anna's eye. "Bet they split it three ways."

"There wathn't no money."

The yard was suddenly silent as thunder rumbled in the distance.

Cody smiled. "You devil, you. They didn't know about the money, did they? You kept it all."

"They…." He stopped like he was trying to organize his thoughts.

Anna and Cody didn't say a word. Top glared at Freddy, sure that Cody had him in a box. A drop of rain landed with a splat on the roof of her car. Another splatted on the gravel between them. One hit the tin roof of the chicken house, then the hay barn. More fell, scattered, but landing with force.

"They'll kill you when they find out."

Freddy stared at his shoes.

"I think I'm gonna let you go. Then I'll tell the papers about the money that's missing." Cody crossed his arms. "They haven't released that information, yet. I'm gonna tell them down to the dollar how much those men had in their briefcase. After I tell the *Chisum News*, I'll call Channel 12. Before you know it, everybody in Lamar County'll know there'd been a buttload of money in the empty briefcase that we found in the car. Your buddies don't have it, and they'll sure start thinking."

Freddy started to shake.

"We're gonna release the bodies to their families here in a couple of days, and they'll come get them to bury those men back home, thanks to you. You wanted them to get a decent burial, and they will. But now you need to fess up. If I don't decide to let you go so your friends can find you, I'm going to charge you with murder, and if you keep quiet to save your friends, you'll go to the chair."

Cody knew full well that the state didn't electrocute prisoners any longer, not since 1964, but most folks still remembered Ol' Sparky, and he figured that Freddy wasn't one hundred percent sure that the electric chair wasn't still in use.

"Freddy, you're between a rock and a hard place. I have enough on you right now to serve as a full confession. You've slipped up half a dozen times. You aren't that quick, son. Tell me who was with you, or I might let you go and wait until it all comes out in the news. They'll do the dirty work for me."

Freddy licked his lips, studying Anna, then Cody, and settled on Top there at the edge of the darkness, ten feet away. "Would I be thafe in jail?"

"Safer'n you'll be once word gets out."

He licked his lips again, like the sun was blazing overhead. His shoulders drooped and the lisp became even more pronounced, if that was possible. "It wathn't me. I didn't thoot them, but I wath there. I couldn't thop them."

Anna put her hand on Freddy's arm, and that light contact was all he needed. "Who are they, hon?"

"Marty Thmallwood and John. T. Wetht."

There it was. The confirmation she needed.

Now all they had to do was find them.

Chapter Fifty-three

It was nearly dark as they drove between the one-story buildings lining the busy Flagstaff street. Neon lights flickered in a blizzard of color, shapes, and sizes.

"This is kidnapping."

James heard Ned tell Cale to get to talking, but he thought the statement was directed toward Crow. At the sound of Cale's voice, James twisted over the backseat. "How the hell???"

Crow checked the rearview mirror. "Where have y'all been?"

"We had a little trouble in the courthouse."

"For two *hours?*"

"We're lucky that was all."

James re-learned how to get his jaws moving again. "How'd this happen?"

Crow checked the speedometer, slowing until he was satisfied with their speed. "Y'all went in, and about a minute later this little shit came boiling out the door, running like the devil himself was on his tail."

Ned studied the boy at his feet. "What'd you do, run him down with the car?"

"Naw. I opened the door and hollered at him to get in. I guess he thought I was one of them hippie friends of his, so he came charging over, but then when he jumped in and saw your handcuffs in the backseat, he must have put two and two together. He tried to jump out, but I convinced him to stay."

"With what?"

Crow held up his fist, flexing his fingers. "He has a hard head."

Ned nudged Cale again. "It ain't kidnapping, you little fool, because I'm putting you under arrest. Start talking. Where's Pepper?"

"He hit me. That's against the law."

"I didn't see it, and I'd have probably done the same thing when you resisted arrest, and I'm sure I would have thought you were trying to get away."

The air went out of Cale. Still curled up in the floorboard, he rested his head on the seat. "I don't know."

He yelped when James reached over the seat and grabbed a handful of hair, yanking Cale's head up. "Don't dick with us, boy! Where's my daughter?"

Tears filled his eyes, either with pain or recollection. "I really don't *know*." He yelped again when James gave his head a shake. "Mr. Parker, we hitched with some kids and they let us out about a mile away from here. We were going to walk, but then some guys on bikes stopped while we were talking to some other kids in a Love Machine…"

"What's that?"

Cale realized he was treading on dangerous ground. "It's a Volkswagen van, all painted up with 'love' and 'peace' written on it."

"Go on, then."

"We got into a mess with the bikers and they beat me up. When I came to, Pepper was gone and there was a crowd of people around me."

Ned tried to understand what Cale was saying. "Kids on bicycles beat you up?"

"No, motorcycles. It was a motorcycle gang. I tried to fight, but they all joined in. They're grown men and I didn't have a chance. While they had me down, she kicked one guy in the nose. Then someone hit me in the head and lights flashed. My money was gone when I woke up and I went to the courthouse to make a report and that's when y'all came in."

The cords in James' arm stood out over the seatback as he gripped Cale's hair even tighter. "You let them take my *daughter?"*

Cale's mouth opened at the pain and he pushed up with his legs. Hands cuffed behind his back, he could do nothing to relieve the pressure. "Mr. Parker, I really tried to stop them. Really. Those guys are *tough*." He started crying. Broken, with all the false bravado and arrogance beaten out of him, Cale realized most of the world was a lot tougher than he ever imagined. "I did what I could."

Crow made a left, driving aimlessly. "What colors were they flying?"

"I didn't see no flags."

"No, stupid." Crow sighed. "What did they have on the backs of their jackets?"

"I didn't get a good look. Seems like the one I saw had a rattlesnake on it."

"Did the snake have horns?"

Cale sniffled. "Yeah."

"Who're *they*?" James released his oily hair in disgust.

Crow frowned. "Demon Rattlers. They're out of California."

"How do you know that?"

He paused for a beat, thinking. "I saw 'em clear out a little dive in Scottsdale one night, the first time I came out this way."

Numb, James scanned the buildings around them, as if the answers were posted on the brick walls. "She was right here. Right *here*!"

"Son." Ned understood his fear and frustration. "Why don't you go on to the station and get them to put an APB on Pepper. Tell 'em she was kidnapped by some motorcycle gangsters and that Demon name."

"You'll have to go without me." Crow slowed for a light, thinking. "It'll be you guys and them, then."

"Nope. Me and tough boy here are going with you. Splittin' up will double our chances of finding her."

"Give me a minute." Crow pulled to the curb in front of a nondescript entrance with a blue neon sign with the simple word "Bar" over the door. Half a dozen Harleys were parked on the sidewalk. "Wait right here and talk it over while I go inside and you better thank your lucky spirits their jackets didn't say Hell's Angels."

Ned and James waited at the curb, like they did outside the house in Amarillo. James stared through the windshield. "What's hell's angels?"

Ned shrugged and rubbed his belly. He needed to lay down.

Half an hour later, Crow returned to the car to talk through the window.

Frustrated because he'd been gone so long, James snapped a question. "What'd you find out?"

"The Demon Rattlers hang out in Barstow. That'll be where they're headed."

Ned laid his head back on the seat and held his stomach. "Shit."

Chapter Fifty-four

It was twilight when the Love Machine pulled into the gravel parking lot of a Mexican restaurant with a pulsating red and yellow neon sombrero. The door slid back and Pepper boiled out, fighting and cussing.

She landed on her feet and aimed a forefinger back toward the shocked hippie kids. "If any of you sons a bitches want to get out and try again, then have at it!"

She didn't know where she was, or how long she'd been in the van. While she regained her senses, they'd driven around for an eternity in a fog of paranoia, thinking the bikers were after them. Kevin drove down so many side streets that he was lost for nearly half an hour before finding his way back to Route 66. All the while, Pepper raged at the others, demanding that they go back and find Cale.

None of the flower children in the van had any interest in getting near the bikers again and unanimously decided to head straight for San Francisco.

Here was her ride, but she couldn't leave Cale.

Over Pepper's demands and tears, they argued all the way to the next town before pulling into the restaurant's parking lot. They were as glad to get shed of her as she was of *them*.

One of the girls slid the door closed. "Sister, you are uncool!" She flashed a peace sign. "Go home and peace out."

"I didn't ask for any of you to save me!" She kicked at the rocks. "Cowards!"

The van pulled away in a wash of dust, leaving Pepper in the parking lot. She didn't need their saving. Their "make love, not war" interference caused her to lose the only friend she had on the road. Regaining control, she studied the restaurant's sign against the purple sky, wondering how to find Cale. She figured the police had already picked him up.

A quick check of her pockets revealed nothing but lint. Her purse contained only a few items, her eagle feather, and a handkerchief. She didn't have a dime to make a call. Hupping deep in her chest in an effort not to cry, she crossed the highway, stood on the eastbound side leading back to Flagstaff, and stuck out her thumb.

Chapter Fifty-five

The motel room smelled like stale cigarettes, Pine-Sol, and old hamburgers. The same smell of every room on Route 66 from Chicago to Los Angeles. Outside, the sun rose on the dusty desert town of Barstow, California.

James had driven all night, arriving at the Stardust Inn while the stars twinkled overhead. It was almost a carbon copy of the Western Skies in Winslow. The annoyed manager hadn't yet taken his first cup of coffee, and after some negotiations regarding the time they were checking in, took an extra three dollars for the following night.

Despite their location, the Mojave Desert had cooled from the summertime temperatures of over a hundred, to a pleasant fifty-five dry degrees when the sand and rocks glowed orange with sunrise. The dry wash of the Mojave River defined the town's north and eastern borders. Low scrub bushes and creosote seemed to be the only plants that flourished in the harsh environment.

Ned lay on a threadbare bedspread covering one of the two full-size beds. The now-constant pain in his stomach rendered him virtually helpless. Cale lay on the other with a washrag full of ice over his black eyes.

Crow and James were arguing about who would go to the bar where the Demon Rattlers hung out. Standing beside the window, James fumed. "It's my *daughter* in that saloon!"

Expressionless, Crow nodded. "I completely understand. But

for one thing, we don't know for *sure* she's in there, and I kinda doubt it. What do you do for a living?"

"What? I run a hardware store."

"Ever been in a fight, other than the one in the courthouse?"

James squared his shoulders. "Yeah. More than one, too."

"Um hum. I meant after you got out of school."

"No."

"Any experience in law work, like your daddy there?"

"No."

Crow tapped the dresser with a fingertip. "Come here."

"What?"

Softly. "Come *here*."

James stood and joined him. Crow pointed at the mirror opposite the beds. "Tell me what you see."

"Us."

"Right. Tell me what you really see. Truthfully. Describe… us. Start with you."

"This is ridiculous."

"It'll explain what I'm trying to tell you, James. What do you see? Describe your head."

James Parker considered the mirror. "A head."

Crow nudged him with his shoulder.

"All right. Short, graying black hair of a man in his late thirties. Cowlick. Two eyebrows, also black. Brown eyes. A nose. Two ears that need trimming, I guess. Lips, and a chin with a dimple."

"That's about right. Now, describe me."

"A guy with long hair."

"More detail. Lots of detail, more than you used on yourself, but don't stop at my chin."

James growled in frustration, low in his throat. He drew a deep breath. "Long black hair, like an Indian."

"I *am* Indian, but you're right. Keep going."

"Hippie hair, then. A scar across your forehead from the middle to your temple. Black eyebrows. Dark eyes. Indian cheekbones. No mustache or beard, though, like those hippies, but that's because you're Indian again. A nose that's been broke before…"

"Twice."

"Huh. Square chin with a horizontal scar in the cleft under your bottom lip and one on your ear. Wide shoulders. Some kind of necklace under your western shirt that needs washing better than the last time, but it was expensive when it was new. Shirt's hanging outside your jeans." He glanced down. "Levis and work boots."

Crow flexed his hands. "These?"

"Big hands. Big knucks. Lots of scars."

Crow flipped them over.

"Rough. Calluses."

"So between me and you, who do you think has more luck walking into a rough bar full of bikers?"

"That don't make no never mind." James spread his hands, talking to the two images in the mirror, as if Crow wasn't standing right beside him. "I'm Pepper's *daddy*."

"And I'm not. That makes me the best man for the job. I'm not mad. I'm not scared. I'm not worried. The minute you walk in the door and into a nest of Rattlers, they'll know for sure that you don't belong. If they *just* kick your ass, you'll be lucky. They can do much, much worse."

"Ned has guns in the turtle hull."

"I'm sure he does. But a trunk full of guns won't get it all done. One man can't walk in a bar and start threatening people, or shooting. Hell, if they don't kill you, the law will when they show up. And there's no bet Pepper's *in* there. Those guys hang out in bars, but they don't *live* in them. What I need to do is find out where she is and I don't need *you* in there with me to worry with."

"I don't get it. Why are you doing all this for us?"

Crow's eyes went flat. "Trying to right a wrong. Ned, am I right, about him staying?"

The old constable opened one eye. "He's right, James. We don't know this world, or them people. Let Crow go and come back and tell us what he's found. Right now, *I* cain't do nothin', that's for sure."

Crow spread his hands to punctuate the statement.

"All right." James plodded back to the table like an old man, worn out and aching. "Go. Tell us what you find."

"Oh, you're going with me. I need you to drop me off and wait. We might have to move fast."

Chapter Fifty-six

"We're turning off here." The man Pepper knew as Jeff pulled his Oldsmobile station wagon into the parking lot of the Jackrabbit Curio Shop. A canvas water bag hung over the car's front grill, a common sight on Route 66. Advertised by dozens of stores and trading posts along the route as emergency gear, the bags full of water stayed cool by condensation as they drove.

His wife, Brenda, twisted around in the front seat. "We're going to make some miles while the kids are asleep." Behind Pepper, two pre-teens slept on a thick pallet of quilts covering their suitcases. "You be careful who you take rides from, honey."

Pepper threw the strap of her sack purse over her shoulder and slid out. "I will. Thanks for the ride."

The car pulled away and vanished. Pepper's mouth was dry as cotton and she hoped they'd have a water fountain. Across the road, still another rough roadside stand sold hand-painted pots. The Indian family under the brush arbor watched with impassive expressions as she waited for a long moment, indecisive. It reminded her of the mom and pop vegetable stands back home, where the owners supplemented their income.

The trading post museum was busy with travelers. The Navajo woman behind the counter barely glanced at one more kid fed up with The Establishment and passing through on her way to… somewhere. She went back to ringing up a cheap rock sample collection, three postcards, and an empty water bag similar to the one on the Oldsmobile.

Pepper realized that it was mistake to come inside. The aroma of fresh popcorn and signs for ice cream bars and candy made her stomach grumble. She turned away from the corn popper and drifted aimlessly down the aisles without seeing any of the items. There was no water fountain. She was on her way out when a voice stopped her.

"What can I do for you?" A chunky guy with a beer belly blocked the aisle, and the path to the door.

"Nothing, thank you." She tried to step around him.

He didn't move. "I think we need to talk."

Still not understanding, she shrugged. "Not really. I'm leaving."

"What do you have in the purse?"

"Nothing."

"It's heavier than nothing."

"I mean, there's stuff in there, girl stuff."

"Anything else?"

"What do you mean?"

He'd somehow moved closer. "I mean is there anything else in there besides brushes and lipsticks?"

"I don't have any lipstick. I don't wear makeup."

"Then show me."

"No." Pepper's famous anger rose. "Get out of my way."

Beer Belly didn't move. "I think you took something that you didn't intend to pay for. I want to see it."

"Why don't you wish in one hand and spit in the other and see which one fills up the fastest? Who are you, anyway?"

"The owner." Beer Belly grabbed her arm. "I've seen you in here before, and I'm tired of you hippie shoplifters."

Pepper jerked her arm away. "I've never been here, and I haven't stolen anything, either."

Moving faster than she could have imagined, Beer Belly snatched the thin strap off her shoulder and stripped it from her arm.

"Hey!"

As the shop full of customers watched, he blocked her reach and shook the contents onto a display of rubber tomahawks and plastic snakes. Pepper tried to shove around him to grab her purse, but he held her arm in a rough grip.

He picked up the eagle feather Jonathan had given her. "There, you stole this feather off one of those displays." He pointed to a line of cheap feathered headdresses and brightly colored felt pennants hanging on the wall. "Ethyl, call the police! I'm tired of these damned hippies stealing us blind."

"That's no painted chicken feather. It's real." She pulled and he increased his grip. Pepper knew it was useless to argue that the feather was a gift.

Her Uncle Cody once showed her how to break a hold and it came to her in a flash. She dropped and at the same time twisted her arm, pushed her elbows outward. Breaking free, she snatched the feather from his hand, hit the floor and shot under the display table to come up on the other side. Beer Belly grabbed for her over the table as she broke for the door.

A tourist playing good Samaritan held his hands wide, thinking she'd stop. Pepper leaped like a deer, dodging the man's grasp and landed on top of a display of Kachina dolls barely out of Beer Belly's reach. The decorated dolls crunched underfoot as she took two running steps toward the door and jumped. At that moment a customer came in and Pepper darted under the jangling bell.

She hit the sidewalk in a sprint. A shout followed as she cut around a corner and disappeared.

Chapter Fifty-seven

The Black Cat Saloon sat outside of the Barstow city limits on an unincorporated, sun-blasted spit of sand beside the highway that shimmered even in the late October temperature. Crow smiled at the sight of two dozen Harley-Davidson motorcycles already in the desolate dirt lot. "Go on past and drop me off down there."

James took his foot off the accelerator and coasted onto the shoulder.

Crow opened the door. "I didn't want anyone in the bar to see me get out. Turn around after I get inside and pull up on the side of the road, like you're having car trouble, but not so close they can see you from the inside. Be ready. I might come out a-runnin'."

He hiked back to the Black Cat. The front door gaped open and the dark interior was worn, and old, and dirty, smelling of mildew and spilled beer. A loud rooftop water cooler rattled and blew damp air into the bar. Crow stopped inside the door to let his eyes adjust to the darkness crammed with loud music.

He threaded his way across the gritty floor and ordered a Miller High Life. The bartender popped the cap and set it on the bar in front of him. "You might want to drink that outside."

"That'd be against the law."

"It'd be safer."

"Thanks for the advice."

Several customers watched him take the bottle to an empty table. He sat with his back against the wall. Jefferson Airplane blared from a scratched jukebox on the other side of the room, filling the smoky air with "Somebody to Love." Crow figured that song played about every half hour.

Wearing filthy jeans and an equally dirty shirt underneath a sleeveless leather jacket, a skinny little bearded guy made of twisted steel rose from a table and pushed his way across the bar. Beard stopped in front of Crow, belched, and rolled his shoulders beneath the Devil Rattler jacket. "Do I know you?"

Crow shook his head and tilted the bottle. "Nope. Never been here before."

"So what are you doing in our bar?"

"Looking for someone." He shrugged. "That's about it."

"That's our beer."

"I paid for it."

The man noticed the leather thong disappearing under Crow's shirt, thinking it might hold a surfer's cross. Even though Crow wasn't wearing love beads, the biker identified him as one of the thousands of kids involved in the counter culture. "We don't want you *flower children* in here." He spoke the words with disgust. "This is a *man's* bar. A bar for real men who ride bikes."

"I'd ride one if I had it. It'd sure beat riding my thumb."

The biker chuckled. "Maybe one of us will ride *you* and pull that pretty hair while we do it."

Crow watched to see what the rest of them were doing.

They were watching him back.

Jefferson Airplane gave way to Buffalo Springfield's "For What It's Worth." In an odd corner of his mind, Crow thought the song was incredibly appropriate.

"I think you need to leave, now, while you can walk."

Crow gave the bottle a slight wave and sat it on the table. "Hey, I don't want any trouble from you guys. I like bikes, *and* bikers. I'm hoping to find a friend of mine."

"Who?"

Crow shrugged and raised his voice over the music. "I don't

see her. I was thinking I might ask one of the ladies in here if she's been through."

Beard laughed. "He wants to talk to the girls. Hey, Griz. C'mere." Beard jerked his thumb at another biker who was big as a bear, then turned back to Crow. "I got a deal for ya. This big bastard is Griz. Convince him that you're okay, and you can ask the girls all the questions you want." He laughed. "Hell, you can do anything you want with any one of them if Griz says you're all right."

His clothes an exact copy of Beard's, Griz bounced on his toes and moved around the table to sit beside Crow. He grinned wide underneath a swollen nose broken only a couple of days earlier. A hayseed teenager and his girlfriend had been at the wrong place in the wrong time when the Rattlers were in the mood to hassle someone.

He picked up Crow's mostly full bottle and took a drink. Letting the beer backwash into the bottle, he stuck his tongue down the neck, licked the top, and thumped it back down, allowing some of the beer to trickle out of his mouth and down his thick beard. He grinned wide at Crow and waited for a reaction.

It came like a lightning strike.

The brown bottle slammed across the bridge of Griz's nose, breaking it again, and exploding in foam and glass shards. Griz's head snapped against the cinderblock wall. While still seated, Crow threw an uppercut that popped his head against the wall a second time. Before the crowd could react, Crow hit him a third time with everything he had, driving the man out of the chair and onto the floor. He landed with a thud and lay on his back, groaning and cradling his bloody face.

Crow shifted his gaze back to the bar full of standing bikers. "Well, that went sour pretty damned fast."

The room exploded.

Crow became a black hole that sucked in all matter. Every male in the bar converged in a rage. Crow kicked the table toward their charge, splitting the flow. He threw a chair and the crush on his right piled up when the lead biker tangled in the legs.

Crow slammed his fist into Beard's face. The little guy had never been hit so hard in his life. He dropped like a rock. Moving like liquid mercury, Crow planted one foot on a chair and jumped on top of the bar. After only two running steps, a hand reached out and grabbed his boot, tripping him up. Instead of fighting the fall, Crow went with it like an acrobat, pitching forward and rolling into a complete flip. Bottles crashed. He felt glass cut deep through his shirt.

Regaining his feet, Crow took three more steps down the bar, inches away from the reaching crowd. He leaped off the end, dodging as the bartender swung a sawed-off bat at his legs. The jump carried him into a short hallway leading toward the bathroom. A back door offered escape.

Praying it was unlocked, he made a split second decision and hit it with his shoulder. It slammed open and Crow shot out into the sunshine. Ducking around the corner, the roar of a bike told him that running was out of the question. He stopped, ready for the next chapter when a raked Hardtail slid around the corner.

A biker with hair dramatically shorter than the Rattlers' motioned with his thumb. "Get on!"

He had no time to think. Crow grabbed at the man's shoulders like a cowboy leaping on a horse. The big engine roared as the back tire threw a rooster tail of red dust into the still air. Hands grappled at him, and someone snatched a hank of hair. Crow's head jerked back when the hunk was ripped out by the roots.

Eyes watering, Crow hung on as the Harley shot across the dirt parking lot, and onto the hot highway. "Shower down on it. They're after us."

Instead of accelerating, the biker backed off the throttle while two highway patrol cars passed, heading in the opposite direction. The biker spoke over his shoulder. "No they won't."

Crow twisted to watch the patrol cars sweep into the Black Cat's parking lot in a boil of dust. It hit him that James wasn't parked where he told him. In fact, the car wasn't anywhere in sight.

Crow gave his rescuer a pat. "Rocky, my man. Good to see you again, brother."

Rocky raised his voice to be heard over the engine. "You almost got your ass kicked in there."

"You were inside?"

"Yep, in the corner by the door."

"So you left when the war started?"

"Before. I've known you long enough to expect you'd either come out the front slow and easy, or out the back a-runnin'. Seems like I guessed right."

Crow noted the different colors on the back of the man's jacket. "Outlaws?"

"Yep. They're from Detroit."

"How'd you get the jacket?"

Rocky checked the highway and spoke loudly. "Joined up a while back. Some of the guys wanted to come with me when I got your call, but I told 'em I had to take a road trip to clear my head."

"They give you any trouble back there?"

"Naw, those guys are pretty territorial, but they tolerated me. It's been a long two days, waitin' for you to show up. I found out pretty quick they aren't my kind of people, though."

"Mine either. You can drop me off in town. I need to call back to the motel and find out where James went."

"James?"

"Yeah, one of the guys I hitched up with." Crow saw a telephone booth and pointed past Rocky so he could see. "Pull over there."

"Nope. I'm taking you where you want to go."

"Where's that?"

The Outlaw jerked a thumb. "Their house." He accelerated toward Barstow. "You be ready to get in and out, though. We won't have much time."

"I'm bleedin' through the back of my shirt and somebody's gonna notice. You have a spare on you?"

Rocky pointed down and back. "Saddlebags."

They passed James' sedan parked in front of a single-pump Gulf station. Crow recognized it, waved as they passed, and James pulled out to follow at a distance.

Chapter Fifty-eight

Cody met Anna at the new Lake Lamar overlook. Slamming her car door, she ran through the rain and joined him in the front seat. He pulled back on the highway and drove over the dam.

Any other time, Cody would have told her to meet him at Leland Hale's house to pick up Marty Smallwood, but he wanted the time to talk with her first.

She flipped through papers in a file resting on her lap. "It didn't take long to find out that Marty's been working on the lake for the past couple of years, driving a dozer."

"That piece of the puzzle fits pretty good. Marty or John T. used the dozer to bury the car after they killed those men."

"That's what I think. Freddy says they did the shooting, but he had a part in burying the Impala. I went by the Corps of Engineer's office, but they didn't have any idea where Marty is. Most of the trailers are gone now that they finished the job. The guy I talked to said they haven't seen him, not since they started pulling the rigs out of the lake bottom when the water started to rise."

"Did John T. work there?"

"Nope. I can't find anywhere he's worked." She took out a sheet of paper and read from it. "Marty's another story. They hired him fresh out of high school and he worked his way up to driver. The foreman didn't think much of him, but he always showed up on time. Picked up his check regular as clockwork, but he hasn't been by to get the last one."

They passed the stores, following the winding road west. Water filled the ditches on both sides. "John T. lives south of the Sulphur River in the bottoms."

Cody steered onto the dirt road leading to Leland's house. He pulled into the drive two hundred yards later. The only vehicle in sight was the old truck in a nest of grass.

"I don't believe Marty's here." Cody shifted into park.

"What do you want to do?"

"Let's go in and ask Melva where he is." Talking to the strange old giggling woman was far down Cody's list of things to do, but he thought she might know when he was coming back.

When they stepped up on the porch. Cody pointed down at the rotting boards. "Watch your step there. All this rain will make those old planks soft."

Cody rapped on the frame and waited. It didn't take but a second to tell there was no one in the house. People give off a certain vibe, even if they're trying to be quiet. Not even a ticking clock broke the stillness. Doors in Center Springs were seldom locked, so Cody hooked a finger in the handle and opened the rusty screen. The tired spring screeched in protest.

"Are you going in?"

"Yep. Serving a warrant here." The door was unlocked, so he swung it wide to step into the gloomy interior. He paused. "Anybody home? This is Sheriff Parker, Miss Melva. I'm coming in. I have a warrant for Marty Smallwood."

The floorboards squeaked under Cody's boots. Anna stayed where she was, breathing the musty air that smelled of dust, soiled sheets, and material long folded and forgotten. All the lights were out. The only illumination came through the dirty windows covered with equally grubby flour sack curtains.

Knowing the layout of the house, Cody went through the living and dining rooms, and into the kitchen. Scummy dishes filled the sink and countertops. He jumped when the Frigidaire's compressor kicked in and rattled to life. Anna followed.

They exchanged glances and chuckled. Cody pointed at the

back door. "Check out the back, and I'll finish in here. They aren't here, though."

The hinges squalled when she went out. The land sloped sharply away, and the porch was six feet off the ground. The boards weren't any newer back there, so she took care to reach the ground. The slope behind the house was covered in rotting food. Some of it still in plates and casserole dishes once covered in foil. Anna realized it was food brought by well-meaning neighbors.

Inside, the beds hadn't been made in days. None of Marty's clothes were in the pasteboard wardrobe, or in the rickety chest of drawers.

Cody came back through the living room, wondering at the number of romance magazines scattered on the furniture and crammed into a wooden rack beside the couch. Anna met him in the front yard.

"The chickens in the brooder house need water."

Cody studied the pasture beside them. Leland's cows grazed on the lush grass, their coats soaked from the constant rains. The saturated pasture on the far side of the truck was empty, except for an old swayback mare scratching her neck against a bois d'arc tree. It was the highest point in the pasture, and the driest.

He pointed at the ground. "Tracks there that don't belong to my car. They ain't been gone long." Cody chewed the inside of his lip. "All right. We'll find him, but being here convinced me that we've waited long enough to find out who killed Leland. There's a connection here. Him getting run over and Marty helping kill those businessmen makes too much of a coincidence."

Cody's Motorola came to life, blaring through the one-inch gap at the top of the drivers' side window. "Sheriff Parker." He crossed the yard, opened the door, and reached inside for the microphone.

"Go ahead, John"

"We need assistance one mile east of town on Highway 82. Two tow-truck drivers are fighting over a car stalled in high water. It's raining to beat the band and everyone else is working wrecks."

Ambulances in Chisum were owned by the two funeral homes in town. Wrecker drivers constantly monitored the police and sheriff departments' radio broadcasts, so when calls came in for accidents, they raced to the scene to take the tow. It was first come, first served. Disagreements often dissolved into fisticuffs.

"We have to do something," Cody told Anna. He keyed the mike. "I'm in Center Springs with Anna. It'll be over by the time one of us gets there."

"All right. Y'all need to know that we're having more and more roads to flood, 'specially my side of town. It won't be long 'til this whole county is underwater, if this rain keeps up."

Cody pitched the mike onto the bench seat. "Climb in." Anna slammed her door. "I've been thinking. We have enough people out there working car wrecks. I want you to go pick up John T. at his house. After I drop you off, I'm going back up to the store to see if anyone's seen Marty. He's mine, yours is West. Let's pick these guys up today."

"That's Hopkins County, you know."

"Yep. I'll give the sheriff a holler and let him know you're coming. You need someone to go with you?"

She rolled her eyes and gave him a grin. "I'm not a guy, but I can serve an arrest warrant."

"Fine, but you be careful. It'll be you and him down there in the bottom, and I've heard you don't want to fool around with this guy."

"Don't worry."

"I always worry."

It was still raining when they reached the new Lake Lamar dam. Anna glanced out the window to see the dragline was safely out of the lake, and the water already covered the hole that held the Impala.

"You know what?"

"Hum?" He kept his eyes on the wet road. The long dam with the curve in the middle always made him nervous.

"I had a thought. What if there's others buried down here at the lake?"

"What makes you think that?"

"Nothing really, but Freddy was talking like he knew something else. It made me wonder if we'd have ever found them once it was all underwater. Do you think that was the only time somebody was buried down there?"

"Who knows?"

"Burying the car looks a little slick to me, like maybe it wasn't the first time Marty or John T. could have done that, don't you think?"

Cody shrugged, slowing to make the bend. He shivered. "Lord, I hope not."

Chapter Fifty-nine

Careful to watch the speed limits, Rocky steered through Barstow. Crow rode easily in the back, hands resting on his thighs. They ended up at the parking lot in front of the Skateland roller rink.

Only a few cars were scattered around and no one paid them any attention as Crow swung off the Hardtail and waited for James to pull up in his car. He was out in a split second. "What the hell went on in there? Did you find her? Who's this guy? Why did you leave so quick? The cops barely had time to show up."

Crow held out a hand. "Slow down. Was it you that called the cops?"

"Sure was." James didn't take his eyes off Rocky and the silver earring in his left ear. He'd never seen a man with an earring before. "I didn't like that place one little bit, so I went back to that gas station we passed and made a call. I told them my fourteen-year-old daughter was in that bar. They came pretty quick."

Rocky frowned at Crow, who wanted to be mad because the arrival of the police might have caused problems. Instead, James' unexpected move saved his bacon.

"What do *you* have to do with this?" James radiated anger, but it had no effect on the biker. "What do you know about my daughter?"

As if James wasn't grilling him, Rocky absently dug a red bandana from his back pocket and twirled a finger. Crow made sure his back was away from the road while Rocky lifted his shirttail and pressed the bandana against the cut. That done, he answered James. "Cool down, man. I'm on your side."

"Take it easy, hoss." Crow pulled the bandana tight with his shirt. "He was there when things got out of hand. If it hadn't been for him, I'd be dead and on my way out into the desert to dry up and blow away."

James aimed a finger at Rocky. "He's one of them motorcycle gangsters."

"He knows where Pepper might be."

Like he'd been slapped silent, James gaped a moment, then swelled up again. "Did you have anything to do with her being there?"

"Dude, you are *angry*." Rocky rolled his eyes. "I've never laid eyes on the girl."

"James." Crow's voice was sharp for the first time since they met. "Rocky'll tell you what he knows if you'll let him."

He took a deep breath. "I'm listening."

The biker jerked his head to the north. "I heard them say they have a house here in town. One of the girls invited me to party with them."

"Where is it?"

Rocky shrugged. "I'm not sure."

"Oh, great! You think we'll go door to door and ask people if a motorcycle gang lived there?"

"Man, would you back off? I need to get my bike out of sight. I'm going to pull it around back there. Then we're going to wait in your car and watch the highway. Those guys'll come by on their way to the house, and we'll follow them. But I need to get this thing out of sight right now, and Crow needs to get in the car before somebody asks him why he's bleeding."

"Good idea."

Crow opened the passenger door as Rocky kicked his bike to life and disappeared around back of the huge Skateland building. When James dropped into the seat, his demeanor completely changed. "Great idea. Now we're getting somewhere."

"Following them to the house will be the easy part," Crow said.

"Why?"

He winced when the bandana pulled the cut. "Because if she's there, and not by choice, getting her out's gonna be a bitch."

Chapter Sixty

Pepper finally arrived back in Flagstaff with the aid of an elderly couple driving from California to Missouri. She felt like screaming again when they saw the sign for the Tomahawk Trading Post and pulled off the highway. She wanted to go home, and here they were stopping for souvenirs.

"I need gas, Little Missy." Earl's blue eyes in the rearview mirror reminded Pepper of her Grandpa. "I haven't seen a Conoco station for a while, and Mama wanted to pick up a couple of things for the grandkids."

He pulled up to the ethyl pump behind a pair of ten-foot-high plaster Indians. A sign beside them read, "San Francisco Peaks, 32.9 miles." In that moment Pepper realized she was as close to anything named San Francisco that she would reach.

Her energy drained away. Ready to cry, she sat with her knees together in the tuck-and-roll-covered backseat.

"Honey, why don't you go in with me and get something to eat?"

Pepper knew the woman had other plans, most likely to call the police and hold her there as a runaway. Neither of the adults believed the story she spun about being separated from her truck-driving brother one stop back.

"No, thank you. This is where I'm supposed to meet Bobby Clifford. We always said that if we got separated, we'd meet up at the next town."

"That's a hard, dangerous life for a little girl."

"I'm seventeen. That's an adult in…Arkansas."

"You're awful little for seventeen. Why, you haven't even filled out yet."

"I come from a family of late bloomers. I'm all right, really. Thanks."

While Earl filled the gas tank, "Mama" gave her shoulder a pat. "Well, if you're still here by the time we leave, I might need to call someone."

"You won't." Pepper pointed at a dusty eighteen-wheeler pulling up to the diesel pump on the far side. "There he is! Bobby Clifford!" Catching sight of the gesturing girl with an eagle feather woven into her hair, the truck driver gave her a friendly wave back.

"See? Bye, and thanks!"

She trotted past the giant plaster figures and an out-of-place totem pole. She ducked behind a covered wagon with two kids sitting on the seat. Their mother snapped a picture with a Polaroid. Catching the familiar and surprisingly comforting aroma of fresh manure and hay, Pepper was drawn to a weathered pen made of rough boards.

"Welcome to the OK Corral."

"Authentic Buffalo! Do Not Pet!"

She glanced back to see Mama gone and Earl alone at the pump. She rounded the corral and sank down out of sight, overwhelmed with homesickness. A ragged old buffalo lay in the pen devoid of shade. The water trough was empty, with no sign of hay or grain.

Eyes closed, the bull's head drooped.

Pepper's eyes welled. "You poor old thing."

Her mood shifted as anger took over. She found a cheap plastic water hose attached to a faucet. She stomped around the pen and twisted the handle. When the water gushed out, she dragged it across the open space and shoved the end through the slats and into the dry trough.

Smelling the water, the buffalo huffed and struggled to its feet. It crossed the pen and nosed the gurgling water, then drank deep.

Seeing red, Pepper stomped around the building and found a feed barrel. She flipped the top off and filled the bucket beside it.

Half a dozen trips later, the feed trough was full. Tourists snapped pictures of her as she broke a bale of dusty alfalfa and threw the whole thing into the pen, scattering the squares.

A tourist wearing a cheap tourist cowboy hat from the gift shop pointed at the buffalo. "Can I pet it?"

Her eyes flicked to the "Do Not Pet" sign. The old Pepper that she thought was almost gone resurfaced. "Sure."

He turned to a plain woman standing beside him. "See? I knew those signs were for show. They put them up so the buffalo seem dangerous. It's all for the tourists who don't know different, right?"

Signs.

Little bluebirds dusted in a corner of the corral.

Pepper paused, thinking about the different kind of signs which had been in front of her nose for the past few days. She absently touched the eagle feather in her hair and came to a decision.

"Mister, Old Buff there is as gentle as a kitten. See those little bluebirds dusting there at his feet. He's so easy going, he don't care about anything." She flashed the tourist a brilliant grin. "Climb on over there so she can take your picture. Get on his back if you want to. He won't care."

He gave her a frown. "You sure it's all right?"

"Of course it is. It'll make a great picture. But one thing, though."

"What?"

"I'd turn that hat around. You have it on backwards."

His wife snickered as he took it off and replaced it. "I was doing it for a picture."

Pepper winked. "I knew that."

As the man reached for the latch to open the gate, Pepper left, heading down the street toward the twin rows of motels and cafes.

There was a spring in her step, because she was going home.

Chapter Sixty-one

Cale made a complete turnaround and found his true calling, taking care of Ned. Frightened at the shape the old man was in, he stuck close, bringing him water to wash down the aspirin that seemed to do no good. Whenever Ned needed assistance, Cale was right there.

A string of motorcycles rumbled past Skateland not far away. Down Route 66, past motels sitting shoulder to shoulder with names like The Cactus, The Torch, and of course, the Route 66 Motel, James and Crow slumped down in the front seat of the car and watched the line of roaring Harleys.

Rocky positioned himself in the middle of the backseat so he could see. "There they go."

Without having to be told, James waited until the last bike passed and pulled in behind them. He wasn't worried that they'd see him. The traffic had increased on the busy highway and he blended right in.

The last bike was driven by Griz. He had a rag tied over his nose like a bandana that had slipped down from his forehead. It was stained dark with blood.

James slowed to let them get ahead. They didn't need to worry about losing the gang. With the windows down on the sedan, the roar was like following a jet.

Griz's brake light flashed and he entered a neighborhood of small houses. James followed them for another block and then saw the taillight flash again as Griz stopped in a yard full of bikes.

"Y'all get down. I have to drive past. If I turn around, they might notice."

Rocky lay flat across the backseat and Crow ducked. It was dark enough that when they passed, only James' silhouette was visible in the car. Trying to take in as much as possible without turning his head, he passed and stopped in front of a vacant house a block away.

"Now what do we do?"

Crow sat up. "Sneak a few peeks in the windows when it gets dark."

James shook his head. "You'll get caught."

"We don't have much choice."

James took a deep breath. "I can't believe I'm saying this, but we need to wait until tomorrow."

Crow studied him with newfound respect. "I'd think you'd want to go blasting in there."

"I do. But somebody'll get hurt or killed, and I can't afford to lose either one of you."

Rocky rested his arms on the seat back. "Hey man, I told you I'd help find the house. That's all."

"He's right." Crow nodded. "He's done his part. It's you and me again. The best thing to do is wait until they leave tomorrow. With the numbers down, we stand a better chance of getting her out, if she's in there."

James put both hands on the wheel. He needed something to hold himself steady. "She is. I can feel it."

Chapter Sixty-two

Cody went back to Leland Hale's house. This time Melva was home and had the lights on inside. He killed the engine and got out. A cat shot off the porch and disappeared under the derelict truck.

Once again being careful of the rotten steps, Cody stepped up on the porch and knocked on the door. "Miss Hale? Melva? It's Sheriff Parker."

He saw someone moving past the window and waited, standing to the side. The wooden door opened and Melva peeked out. Dim light spilled out. "What is it sheriff? What's wrong?"

"Howdy, Melva. Is Marty home?"

"You don't see his truck out there, do you?"

"No ma'am."

"Then he ain't here."

"I didn't figure. Can I come in for a minute?"

She thought about it for a second, then stepped back. Cody hooked a finger in the screen's handle. It opened with a rusty squall that he didn't remember being so loud. He pushed the wooden door open against the wall and gave the crack a quick glance to be sure nobody was hiding back there.

The radio was on, playing music through a filter of static. Melva returned to the couch and picked up her crocheting. Romance magazines were still scattered around the coffee table and couch. Cody stayed by the door, shifting from one foot to the other.

"Have you seen Marty lately?"

"He comes and he goes. Now that he ain't workin' no more, he's gone most of the time."

"Did he lose his job?"

"The lake started to fill up, so they're done." She giggled. "I don't know what he's gonna do for money now. Might have to move. I don't intend to, less I have to, but I'm 'bout tired of feedin' 'im."

"You've lived here a while."

"Yep, since before Charlie run off."

"Marty was little."

"Yep, Charlie brought me here from New Boston, probably to get closer to the river and them beer joints. That place was a misery."

"The beer joints aren't good places, that's for sure."

"I was talking about New Boston." Her annoying giggle burst from her chest and was gone. "Lost two daughters there. Food poisonin', but them joints are trouble, too."

The small community was seventy miles east of Chisum. Cody glanced out the front window, watching for headlights in the dim light. "I didn't know that. I'm sorry."

She kept crocheting. "After the girls was buried, my husband took the baby and run off, but he didn't want Marty. I'm tired of raising him, but he won't leave."

Cody frowned. "That was Charlie?"

She giggled. "No, Harry Clay."

"I'm confused."

"I's married 'fore Charlie, to Harry Clay. He never could keep a job, then he run off and took my baby. Don't know where he went. Charlie come along and we married."

Cody wondered if she'd officially divorced Harry Clay before she and Charlie wed.

"Did you work there in New Boston, before Marty came along?"

"Had to. Took a job in the tomato house packing 'maters. That's where I met Charlie."

Cody shook a cigarette from the pack and lipped it out. “So Marty’s the only one of your kids you have left.”

Melva pulled a long string of yard from the skein beside her. “No. I have an older girl, but she don’t have nothin’ to do with me. I never was married to her daddy.” A giggle. “Ain’t that a scandal?”

Cody wondered how many husbands and kids Melva’d had through the years. “Do you know where she is?”

“Waco. She went to Waco after I helped deliver her baby that was born dead. It was a blessing, ’cause when it was born she wasn’t married and there was no way she could have raised a baby. The Lord works in mysterious ways.” She giggled. Her strange behavior grated on Cody, and he could see why it was a chore for Miss Becky to gin up enough enthusiasm to visit. “Like Leland gettin’ killed the way he did. I reckon his time was long past when that truck hit him.”

“I guess you figured everything should have worked out for y’all when you came here from New Boston. Starting fresh and all. I’m sorry it turned out this way. I hope you can keep up with the farm.”

“Probably need to sell it. I doubt we’ll get what we paid for it.”

Cody frowned. “I’d think you’d make enough money off the sale to pay it off with a little bit left over.”

She giggled, but this time it was one he recognized. It was punctuation of fact. “We *oughta* make enough. It’s paid for. But it wasn’t Leland’s nohow. Me and Charlie bought it with some insurance money. He run off after we got settled in, and *then* I married Leland. I won’t be able to keep up with the taxes when they come due, though. We’ve been behind on them for six-seven years or so, and the gov’m’t won’t wait much longer. Letter in there on the table makes it so. I hope I can get the money out of Leland’s life insurance policy, then we won’t have to move.”

“You paid cash for this place?”

“Yes I did.”

“Y’all must have done pretty good in New Boston.”

“We wasn’t doing good, but Harry Clay had policies on both the girls.”

Cody felt like his head was spinning from all the information and he paused for a moment as cogs clicked into place. He started to ask another question, but headlights turning off the highway made him pause. Instead of Marty's truck, a sedan passed, driving slowly down the muddy road.

Melva giggled again, then took off her glasses and rubbed her eyes. "I wish I could do without these spectacles, but they seemed to help my headaches."

"You farsighted?"

She giggled. "Nor nearsighted neither. It's hurting something fierce right now."

"You probably need more light. You should get a stronger bulb."

"It ain't the light. I keep a headache all the time, but some days it gets so bad I have to go to bed. I hit my head when a horse throwed me into a fence post when I was fifteen and it's hurt ever since." She giggled and replaced the glasses. "Well sir, after I got up, I marched myself right in the house and got Daddy's pistol and shot that damned horse right between the eyes." She stretched out more yarn. "That's the gun that went off and killed Daddy later almost a year to the day."

Cody needed an ashtray. Finding none, he flicked the long ash into the palm of his hand.

"Use the floor. Ashes from a cigarette ain't no wors'n ashes from the stove."

He figured she was right about that. The wood stove's door was partially open and ashes littered the floor underneath. It was an odd dichotomy. The house was clean and tidy in a number of ways, but in others, it was downright dirty. The sink and counter was full of unwashed dishes, but the table was dusted. The living room was fairly tidy, but magazines littered all the furniture, and newspapers were stacked at the end of the couch. The rug under the coffee table didn't have a spec of dirt on it, but ashes and bits of charcoal made the floor in that corner gritty.

Instead of dropping the ash, Cody kept it in his palm and added another.

She produced another giggle. "It don't matter none."

"What doesn't?"

"I'll find me another husband sooner or later. I know what men want." This time Cody would have thought her giggle was self-conscious, but he decided it wasn't. "I'm gonna put me an ad in the personals in one of these magazines and 'fore you know it, I'll have me another man. That helps my headaches."

"Being married?"

"In a way." She lowered her voice in a little girl whisper that sounded creepy coming from a woman nearly sixty years old. "It's the relations that takes this headache away for a little while."

Giggle.

Feeling uneasy at the turn of the conversation, Cody used his thumb and forefinger to grind out the cherry on the cigarette butt. "How many times you been married, Melva, to know that much about men?"

"Five, no, six, if you count my first one when I wasn't but sixteen, but he run off on me not a month after we took our sacred vows. There's been some men in between, if you know what I mean."

Another set of headlights lit the dirt road. This time the vehicle stopped for a moment, then backed up and drove off.

"All right." Cody opened the door, forgetting the ashes in his hand. "Gotta go." He was off the porch in a flash and running through the rain. Starting his car, Cody backed out of the yard, his headlights sweeping across the house, the broken-down truck, and the propane tank near the fence.

He hit the highway, fishtailed slightly on the wet pavement, and shot away to catch the truck that turned out to be Ike Reader, who'd driven by to check Leland Hale's fence.

Chapter Sixty-three

Following the hand-drawn map, Anna found the rented house with very little trouble and parked in the empty front yard surrounded by trees on three sides. In the late afternoon light there were no other buildings in sight except for a ramshackle barn in the distance. She didn't know what kind of vehicle John T. drove, but he obviously wasn't there. She drummed her fingernails on the cloth seat, thinking.

"Dispatch, this is Deputy Sloan."

"Go ahead, Anna. Remember, you can call me Martha."

"I'm serving a warrant at…" she read the route number on the mailbox.

"Ten-four."

She stepped out, her foot squishing in a sea of red mud. Eroded car tracks crisscrossed the yard. A light shower dimpled the puddles. She paused, listening to the sound of high water in the roaring creek not half a mile away. A darker line of clouds moved from the southwest, followed by the grumble of distant thunder.

The house was a typical salt-box Texas farmhouse with a small inset porch in the left front corner. One peeling, shiplap-covered wall bowed outward and from the long perspective from the front, curved up and down like rolling hills. She'd already seen the other side when she pulled in. There were no ruts leading to the back.

Grit on the concrete porch steps scraped under her shoes. Once there, she checked the window to her immediate right.

The paper shade was drawn and still. Angling her body so as not to stand directly in front of the door, she banged on the screen with the heel of her hand.

After a long, silent moment, she banged again. "John T. West! Sheriff's department! Open up!"

She banged again, harder. "Sheriff's department, John T.! I have a warrant for your arrest! Come to the door!"

She bent outward to check the length of the house. Nothing moved. No one sprinted out the back toward the woods, at least no one she could see from where she stood.

She rapped her knuckles on the loose glass in what she expected to be the living room window. The paper blind blocked her view there as well. "Sheriff's department!" Anna tugged at the screen door. It opened easily. Propping it open with her foot, she twisted the knob on the wooden door.

"Search warrant!" For the first time she drew her pistol and pushed at the unlocked front door. Stiff, it only swung open for about ten inches. The part of the living area within her view was completely empty. She peeked inside and because she was small, slid sideways through the opening.

The wooden door swung wider and the world exploded as a booby trap triggered both barrels of a sawed-off twelve-gauge pointed at the door.

Chapter Sixty-four

"Cody."

"Go ahead, Martha."

"I can't raise Anna, and it's been half an hour."

"Where did she last report?"

She gave him the route number for the house. "She went there to serve that warrant on John T. West."

"I'm on the way. Did you call the constable in Cooper?" It was the nearest town to John T.'s house.

She heard his engine roar as Cody pushed the accelerator to the floor. "Sure did. Jim Ed Hathaway. No answer at his house, and I can't raise him on the radio, neither."

Cody flipped on his siren. "Did he go out there with Anna?"

"Can't say."

"All right. Let me know if you hear anything else. I oughta be there in twenty minutes or so."

He was about to hang up the microphone when his Motorola squawked again. "Cody."

"Go ahead, John."

"I'm hitched to your bumper."

Cody checked his mirror. "Hang on tight."

Five minutes later his radio squawked. "Cody, this is Jim Ed."

"Where are you?"

"Pulling a car out of a low place not far from Cooper. The water's rising so fast that it's cut folks off all around me. Why?"

"You know where John T. West lives?"

"Yessir, that mean son of a bitch lives on a back road south of the river, but it's getting' out of its banks now and spreadin' fast. It's raining like hell here."

All the creeks in that part of the county drained into the Sulphur River, a deep, winding cut with steep banks sometimes twenty feet from top to bottom.

"I'm gettin' it pretty good myself." Feeling the sedan's front end slip, Cody backed off the gas. "I'm driving as quick as I can, but this highway's slick as glass."

"I know it. I'm having to find a way around Springhill Slough. I'll be coming up on the post office in about five or ten minutes."

"That'll be about when I get there."

Cody dropped the microphone in his lap and concentrated on his driving. The water seemed higher on that side of Chisum and the fields were shallow lakes. It hadn't rained this much since the night the kids were taken, nearly four years earlier.

Minutes later, Cody rounded a curve to see flashing lights as Jim Ed pulled on the highway a quarter mile ahead. He flashed his headlights and Jim Ed's voice came over the radio. "I see you. We're gonna lose some time when we get off the highway up here. I sure hope these roads ain't washed out."

"You get me to my deputy. I believe she's at John T.'s."

"You figure she's hurt?"

"I hope not, but she still hasn't checked in." Cody prayed that her car was stuck somewhere between them and John T.'s house, but that wouldn't explain why she hadn't called.

Jim Ed knew where he was going, so the only thing slowing them was the road conditions. He stopped at a submerged plank bridge not far from John T.'s house and got out, slamming his door in frustration. Rain hammered his hat and bounced up from the stream of roiling, glassy water.

Cody braked and opened the door. "What's the matter?"

"There's a bridge under here somewhere."

"How deep is it?"

He studied the glass-slick surface. "Not quite deep enough to worry about, yet."

"Is there another way around?"

"Not that'll be any better than this. I'm gonna see if I can feel the edge with my feet. You get in my car and follow me. If we make it, you can wade back and get yours." Jim Ed opened his trunk and took out a shovel. Like a man walking on ice, Jim Ed eased forward in the strong current, feeling for the solid oak boards underneath the ankle-deep water.

He jabbed downward, feeling for the edge of the rough bridge. He felt the shovel miss, as the water caught the wide blade. "Here it is! Come on."

Leaning into the current, Jim Ed stood at the very edge of the bridge. The water pushed at his legs, and he knew it wouldn't be much longer before it gained enough power to take him down.

Barely touching the gas, Cody eased forward and passed so close to Jim Ed that he thought the side mirror would push the Delta County constable off into the current, but he missed by inches and continued several yards onto slightly higher ground.

Leaving his car, Big John waded onto the bridge. The current pulled like a live thing against his legs. He took Jim Ed's arm. "C'mon. I've watched this water climb your britches while you stood here. We'll leave the cars here and ride in your'n."

When they were inside with Cody, Jim Ed pointed. "Turn up there past the graveyard." The slough was out of its banks and headstones jutted from the water. "Hope it don't wash Miss Millie Bills out of the ground. She ain't been down there long enough to set."

By then, Cody saw Anna's sedan parked in front of the house. He pushed the car as hard as he dared, and a minute later they stopped in the flooded yard. Three doors opened simultaneously as the men jumped out of Jim Ed's sedan.

"Anna!" Cody rounded the car and splashed through the ankle deep water. "Anna!" He saw her on the porch, lying on her back, her fingers dangling only inches from the rising water. "John! She's shot."

The big deputy jumped the steps and landed on the boards. Drawing his pistol, he faced the destroyed door. "She alive?"

Cody pressed his fingers under her jaw, feeling for a pulse. His voice choked. "I think she's dead."

John growled and pushed through the ventilated door. A shotgun was tied to a step ladder. A limp line running from the trigger to the door showed how the contraption was rigged to fire. "No one did it by hand. They's a booby trap here."

Cody moved his fingers on her neck, pressing harder. "C'mon kid."

John disappeared into the house and Jim Ed followed, a shotgun ready in his hands.

Cody checked again. This time finding a pulse so weak that he barely felt it. "Thank God!" He grabbed her shirt and ripped it open, buttons rattling across the porch. Three small holes seeped blood. Another hole at the bottom of her bra bubbled through the material when she took a wet, shallow breath.

He ripped his own shirt off and used it as a compression bandage. He figured it was useless, but it was the only thing he could think to do.

John and Jim Ed came back outside after clearing the house. Jim Ed frowned when he saw Cody in his undershirt. "What are you doing?"

"Trying to stop the bleeding."

"I thought you said she was dead."

"Thought she *was*. We gotta get her out of here. She's about bled out, and I think there's a hole in her lung."

"Is it bubbling?"

"Yeah."

Jim Ed launched himself off the porch and opened the trunk. He rummaged around for a second and ran back through the rain with a roll of silver tape.

"What's that?"

"Duct tape. Where's the hole in her lung?"

"Through her brassiere."

"Take it off." Jim Ed ripped off a piece of tape.

Cody dug a pocketknife out of his pants pocket, selected the largest blade, and cut Anna's bra off to reveal the bullet wound.

Jim Ed wiped the hole with the palm of his hand, brushed her breast upward, and slapped the tape over the round wound. Anna immediately convulsed and twisted in Cody's hands. She gasped, breathed in, and then coughed blood.

Jim Ed nodded. "That'll seal it for a little while."

Big John shouldered past. "Let's go." He picked up the petite deputy and rushed toward the car. Jim Ed opened the back door as Cody hurried around to the drivers' side. John fell backward into the seat and Jim Ed piled into the front.

Cody slammed the shifter into reverse then paused. "We can't go back the way we came. The water'll be too high."

"Turn left and pray the slough hasn't trapped us here."

Chapter Sixty-five

Pepper was gone and I was getting punished for it in more ways than one.

I was missing my best friend so bad it hurt, and she was off somewhere without me.

Second, I'd spent my time in church while Miss Becky prayed, and I admit, I prayed some too, but not as hard as she did. Now, here I was again sitting in that crazy woman Melva Hale's house while Miss Becky and Norma Faye talked to her about how hard it was to live alone.

When Miss Becky called Norma Faye to come get her, she said it was because even though we had problems, other folks like Melva Hale did, too, and she thought the Lord wanted her to do for others and maybe he'd make sure Pepper was okay.

I'm sure Norma Faye was feeling a little put upon, too, having to haul Miss Becky everywhere she wanted to go while Grandpa was gone.

I couldn't take that old woman's giggles anymore, so I went outside to watch it rain. I was feeling pretty sorry for myself, because there weren't any chairs to sit on, not even one with a cane bottom, and I couldn't hang my legs off the edge of that raggedy-assed old porch for the water running off the roof.

I hadn't even brought a book with me, but I'd seen all those romance magazines scattered around in Melva's house and thought about going inside to get one of them. I struggled with the idea of reading love stories, and decided that at least it was *something* to read. I was ready to go through the trash and read the labels on soup cans.

When I came back inside, Norma Faye waved at the screen. "In or out."

"I need something to read."

She softened. "All right hon. Miss Melva, is it all right if he reads one of your magazines?"

She was sitting there, rubbing her forehead. Her eyes were closed. "He can have all he wants. I've done read 'em up."

A couple of magazines on the couch had covers I was interested in, but wouldn't pick them up with Norma Faye and Miss Becky watching. One called *Daring Love* reminded me of a comic book with a drawing of a smiling blond woman in a pile of hay, with a guy leaning over her like he was going for a kiss. Her shirt was unbuttoned down far enough to see her brassiere.

There were others; *Western Romance, The Love Book, True Romance*, and *True Confessions*. It seemed like they ran toward what might be the truth, so I steered away from them. A cheap magazine rack was stuffed full of even more titles, and I saw something like a newspaper with the title of *Police Gazette*.

It had women with big boobs on the cover, too, but I took it anyway to read about police stuff. Tucking it under my arm, I jumped off the porch and ran through the rain to stretch out in the backseat of Norma's car.

The headline read, "The Lure of LSD." In a little box toward the bottom I saw a story about hippies. When I opened the paper to that double page spread, there were a dozen pictures of hippies, and most of them were fighting with police officers.

The headlines screamed "Youth Goes to Pot" on one page, and "Cop Fighters" on the other. The first story was about something called "love-ins" and "sit-ins" and hippie girls who smoke cigars. The cop fighters' side was mostly pictures of colored people hitting police.

I'd never seen anything like that paper, and disappeared into a world I didn't know existed, the world that Pepper had left home for. It didn't take long for me to think she'd made a big mistake.

I jumped when Marty knocked on the glass with a knuckle. I rolled the window down enough to talk. His eyes were dull, almost dead. "*Now* what are y'all doing here?"

"Miss Becky's in there with Norma Faye. They came to visit with your mama."

"You damn Parkers are over here too much."

"You ain't a woofin'. I didn't want to come in the first place."

"Hey, you seen my lighter? I lost it the last time y'all were snoopin' around over here?"

I shrugged, but he took it the wrong way.

He studied me for a long moment with dead eyes. "Yep. Keep it, and I don't want y'all back over here."

I didn't try and explain. "Believe me, I'm with you on that one."

He straightened up and headed toward the barn. I saw a pistol sticking out of his waistband as he walked away. I made sure he was gone, then went back to my magazine. Rain drumming on the roof made me sleepy and I put the magazine down. It was pouring so hard that I couldn't see through the water sluicing down the windshield, so I closed my eyes.

I dozed and slipped outside and into the air. It wasn't raining and the talking horse was whispering in my ear. "*See it?*"

I tried to rouse up, but sleep pushed my lids back down. They were so heavy…

"Don't you see?"

Grandpa appeared and rubbed the horse's ears. "It's hard to see." The horse squeezed against Grandpa, pushing him into a barbed-wire fence so hard it started cutting through his clothes. "It's right there in front of us all."

He held up a Police Gazette. The headline was fuzzy.

The car door opened and jolted me awake. I sat up quickly, rubbing my eyes. Miss Becky slammed the passenger door.

"You ready to go home and get some supper, sleepyhead?" Without waiting for an answer, Norma Faye started the engine and backed up. When she did, I saw the old swaybacked horse standing beside the barbed-wire fence.

Chapter Sixty-six

"There's an old iron bridge up ahead. It'll take us across the river, and maybe we can get out that way."

"Maybe?"

Jim Ed keyed the microphone. "Dispatch. This is Jim Ed. I have an officer shot and we're in need of emergency care."

"Where are you, Jim Ed?"

"Not at the scene. We're about to cross the old iron bridge over the Sulphur. Everything's flooded out east of Cooper. If it's not underwater, we're gonna go hit 2675 and take it toward Roxton."

"Ten-four. Who's shot?"

Jim Ed raised his eyebrows. "Anna…Anna how much?"

"Sloan."

"Deputy Anna Sloan."

"I'll notify St. Joseph's emergency. They'll be waiting on you."

"She's 'bout dead."

"Better be quick, then."

Filled with anxiety, John shifted his weight in the backseat and bent his knee, forcing her legs higher. "Jim Ed. Get back here and hold her head up. She's as limp as a rag doll and she cain't breathe good with her head back like that."

John cradled Anna in his arms while Jim Ed crawled over the front seat, knocking his hat off in the process. What little cowlick he had left was standing straight up on his forehead, and the big empty patch on the back was white as a fish's belly.

"Lordy, we got to cover this gal's titties up. This ain't right."

His chest tight, Cody didn't take his eyes off the road. "Don't worry about that. They can cover her up when we get to the hospital." He braked hard when they came around a wide curve. "Well, *shit!* Jim Ed, you think this bridge'll hold us?"

The swollen river, full of branches, trash, and logs, washed from the damaged earth overcame everything it touched. Water boiled around the rusty structure that had been built over the deep riverbed not long after the Civil War. Logs and whole trees washed up against the railing and white waves lapped over the top, mixing with muddy water bubbling like a gurgling cauldron.

"It's been here over a hunnerd years."

"That's what I'm afraid of. Can we go back around?"

"This is the best and quickest chance we have."

From their position, the bridge seemed to bend in the middle. The railing vibrated like guitar strings as if the whole thing would go at any second, as soon as the water stacked a few more trees against the side.

Driving blind and hoping all the grid plates were still in place, Cody eased forward and paused, testing the weight and stability of the crossing with the front wheels, prepared to quickly back up if there was any question of continuing.

Anna grunted and gave a weak, wet cough. That was all he needed. "Y'all hang on."

Swallowing his terror, Cody drove onto the old bridge in a slow roll, focusing his eyes on the far side, allowing the car to maintain a constant speed while the water gushed only inches under the floorboard. The sedan plowed a wake ten yards, twenty, and they were halfway across when he heard John's voice. "Oh, my God."

Cody's head snapped to the right, stunned to see a huge oak tree rolling in the current, heading right for them. They all knew that when it hit, it would take the bridge down as if it were made of matchsticks.

Chapter Sixty-seven

The minute we got back home I told Miss Becky I needed to call Uncle Cody.

"He's working."

"I know, but this is about law work."

Norma Faye thought for a moment, fingers stuck in the front pockets of her jeans. "Can it wait?"

"No. I don't think so."

Miss Becky tilted her head toward the telephone table. "Go ahead on, then."

I dialed the sheriff's office, but it was so late no one answered. I tried dispatch. "This is Top Parker."

Martha Wells' voice softened. "Top, hon, I can't talk right now."

"I need to tell Uncle Cody something."

She hesitated. "Hon, he can't talk right now. He's on the way to the hospital with someone who's hurt."

"Who?"

"Somebody, but it's gonna be all right. I'll take a message and give it to him."

"No. Thanks."

I hung up and dialed again, a number I'd memorized a long time ago.

"What? It's late."

"Judge O.C.?"

His voice changed. "Top?"

"Yessir."

"You all right? Is Becky okay?"

"Yessir, we're fine, but I have to tell you something to tell Uncle Cody. It's the only way I know to get the message to him."

"He's busy right now, son."

"I know it, that's why I'm calling you."

"I'm listening."

I told him about my dreams, about the horse, and the grass. "Mr. O.C., it all means something, but I don't know what."

He knew all about our family's Poisoned Gift, and how it figured into the Rock Hole kidnapping a few years earlier. I could hear his chair creaking through the phone line while he rocked back and forth, thinking.

"All right. I'll let him know as soon as he gets to where we can talk."

Not having anything else to say, I simply hung up. The phone jangled with our ring. "Hello?"

"I have a collect call from Flagstaff, Arizona, from a Miss Beatrice Parker. Will you accept the charges?"

I laughed out loud. "Sure!"

Beatrice Parker.

It was Pepper.

Chapter Sixty-eight

Rain continued to fall.

Torn from its roots by the floodwaters a half a mile upstream, the great oak tree joined a mass of limbs, smaller trees, boards, and other debris rushing downstream over the deepest part of the old channel. Weighing well over forty tons, the old goliath headed directly toward the weakest portion of the bridge, a questionable point in the arch that long ago had rusted badly enough to lose over half of its original strength.

If the oak didn't take the bridge out upon impact, the sheer weight of the water against the tree's mass would quickly shove it completely off its already compromised foundations.

"Cody, go." Not taking his eyes off the oncoming tree, John's deep voice seemed abnormally calm, given the situation.

Terrified, Cody mashed the accelerator and the car's rear end immediately slid sideways. He gripped the wheel tightly and forced himself to let off the gas to increase his speed with agonizing deliberation as the tires dug in. Staring out of the passenger side window, John and Jim Ed couldn't take their eyes off the approaching tree.

Growling deep in his chest, Cody gave it more gas, feeling the tires slip for a frightening moment, and then regain tenuous traction. He tore his eyes off the far end of the span when an unseen log leaped out of the muddy water like a porpoise and rode over the rail. The angle was such that it rose high overhead, then the submerged portion slammed against the bridge's substructure. The entire bridge shuddered as the log stood straight up like a telephone pole.

They passed close enough to touch it.

Only a third of the way across, more water shipped through the tangle of debris against the passenger side rail. The powerful current pushed the car, and Cody instinctively steered into the flow as if he were sliding on ice, for all the good it did.

More gas.

They were halfway across and the tree seemed impossibly close.

"Gogogogogogo…." John spoke softly.

Jim Ed groaned. "Faster, hoss."

Their speed increased on an incline so slight that none of them felt it. In addition to pushing the bridge sideways, the heavy press of water against the old steel caused a sag in the middle of the supporting arch. Feeling the tires grip, Cody sped up. Taking a chance, he glanced over to see the tree was almost on top of them. The wide branches spanned over half the width of the bridge, reaching toward them in a great swath of leafless wood.

The tree slowed as the trunk slid underneath the bridge, two-thirds of the way across with a solid crunch. The oak clutched at the structure to keep from being dragged beneath the surface and shuddered to a stop as the bridge groaned and shifted.

"Gogogogogogo!" John's voice rose.

Someone in the car made a steady, *ahhhhhh* sound. Cody barely realized it was coming from him.

They were close, damned close to the other side, when the bridge surrendered to the pressure. Bending in the middle, it sagged out and down. The main supports pulled the concrete foundation completely out of the soft ground. They rose like long, cylindrical caskets dragged out of a grave, bringing tons of dirt with them.

"Hang on!"

The car's front wheels thumped across the widening gap as the bridge separated from the crumbling pavement. The entire structure pulled free and for a moment they were twenty degrees off square. Cody stomped the gas, snatching enough momentum to carry the car over the widening void and onto level ground.

As Cody mashed the pedal to the floorboard, Jim Ed looked down at Anna's head in his hands. "She's barely with us."

John faced forward. "Sweet Jesus!"

Chapter Sixty-nine

"What are you doing answering the phone? I figured it'd be Miss Becky."

I couldn't believe Pepper was on the other end of the line. I must have gaped like a fish for a second, because she didn't wait for me to say anything. "Hey, I need somebody to come get me or something. Who's there?"

"What?"

"Well, Jesus. You got wax in your ears? I need to talk to Grandpa or Daddy."

"Who is it?" Miss Becky asked.

Wait a second, I mouthed while Pepper kept talking.

"Give the phone to somebody else, will ya? At least *they'll* talk back. Where *is* Daddy anyway, or Mama? I called the house but it didn't do nothing but ring and ring. I want somebody to come get me. This idea wasn't all it was cracked up to be."

The back door opened behind Miss Becky and Norma Faye, and Aunt Ida Belle came through the kitchen. Setting her purse on the table, she paused. "What's going on?"

"Are you gonna say something, or what, dumbass? This is a collect call! I've never made one of them before."

I grinned wide. "Sure. Where are you?"

"I'm in Flagstaff, Arizona, and believe me, this ain't no place I want to live, that's for damn sure."

Aunt Ida Belle came into the living room. "Did something happen?"

All three women were staring at me and I grinned wider. "Wait a minute." I enjoyed the moment, because I knew that in about two seconds I was gonna make their day. I held the receiver out and put one finger in my ear. "Which one of y'all wants to talk to Pepper?"

Chapter Seventy

It took longer than Cody had hoped to find a way back to the highway and on to Chisum. From there it was a short drive along the nearly deserted highway. Several Catholic sisters were waiting outside St. Joseph Hospital's emergency room entrance along with a doctor when Cody came in fast and skidded to a stop in front of the emergency room.

Despite being highly trained and experienced nurses, Sister Angelica yanked the door open and hesitated, stunned at the sight of the bloody, half-nude woman in the arms of the black deputy. Anna's clothes were tangled around her shoulders and when they reached in to take her from John's arms, they rode up even higher. It took the sisters a full second to snap out of their shock and swing into action.

One of the nurses attempted to throw a blanket over her as they laid her on the gurney, but the doctor took immediate control. He pointed toward Anna's chest. "What's this tape for?"

"Lung wound." Jim Ed climbed out of the backseat. He was as bloody as John. "She took a shotgun blast."

The doctor studied Cody, then John. "Good work, men."

With practiced moves, they all disappeared into the elderly hospital, leaving the three lawmen standing alone in the empty entrance. Protected from the rain by a large overhang, Jim Ed shifted from one foot to the other. "Well, I guess we can go back to see if your cars are there, but I wouldn't bet a plug nickel on them be anywhere's close by."

"Not in this rain." Cody shook his head. Torrents of water splashed off the roof and onto the pavement, running in streams under their feet and out the other side. "Could you take us by the courthouse? I need to get a shirt and then we can come back up here to see how she's doing. She don't have any family or anything, so I'll need to hang around. Better get on the radio and tell dispatch where we are, and John, you can go on home if you want to. I bet Rachel's worried sick about you. The water could be coming up y'all's house, too."

He nodded. He'd been thinking the same thing. "I can stay if you want."

"We'll get you a car so you can go on."

"Ain't you worried about your house, and Mister Ned's?"

"Naw. Their house has never flooded up on that hill, and with the new dam in place, I doubt the Sanders bottoms on the other side of the new dam will flood anyway, unless the Red backs up."

Jim Ed radioed in, telling them that all three were safe and Anna was in the hands of the hospital staff. "I'm bringing Cody and John in with me. They don't have any cars."

Instead of getting a response from Martha, Judge O.C.'s voice came on instead. "Sorry about Anna. Cody, you there?"

He and Jim Ed exchanged places. "Go ahead."

"Good news! They found Pepper and she's fine."

"Thank God." Cody wiped his face with suddenly trembling fingers.

John's face broke into a wide grin.

"More news, too. If y'all are coming this way, I'll tell you when you get here."

Cody bit his lip, knowing something else was coming his way. "Be there in a minute."

Chapter Seventy-one

I thought there was going to be a fight to see who could get to the receiver first. Of course it was Aunt Ida Belle who wound up with it, 'cause she was her mama. She didn't hog the phone, though, but tilted it upwards so we could all hear. All three of 'em were cryin' and snifflin' to beat the band, so loud I could barely hear.

When Aunt Ida Belle started talking, it was hard to understand her through the tears. "Where are you baby? Are you all right?"

"I'm fine. I'm in Flagstaff in the Doo Bo Motel."

Aunt Ida Belle drew a sharp breath. "Are you and Cale in the same room?"

"I ain't with him at all, and what do you think, that I have money for a motel?" I could hear the old anger in Pepper's voice. It made me so happy that my chest felt like busting wide open. "What? Oh, the manager says I said it wrong." He spelled it for her, and she spelled "DuBeau" back to us. "I don't even have enough money to make this phone call. I'm standing here in the lobby. The manager's letting me call y'all."

We heard him in the background for a second time. "Yeah, and that phone's for paying guests, so you better get off pretty quick."

The next few words were muffled, so I figured Pepper moved the phone, giving the guy a piece of her mind, or a good cussin'. I hoped it was a small piece so he'd let her keep talking.

Norma Faye leaned in. "Hon, is Cale all right?"

"I don't have any idea. I'm worried sick about him. We got in a little trouble…"

"Trouble? Oh my God!" Aunt Ida Belle liked drama, and she was so scared of the least little things that she made you want to slap your head. She was afraid of kittens, because one jumped on her leg when she was little and it scared her so bad that she couldn't even have one in a picture on a calendar. "You sure you're all right?"

"Mama, I'm fine, and I don't want to talk about it right now…"

"Is Cale in jail?"

I could hear the frustration in Pepper's voice. "I don't *know*. I don't have any idea where he is. We got crossways with these guys on motorcycles and I busted one of 'em in the nose and some other kids in a van drug me away and took off like a bunch of stripe-ass baboons and they wouldn't let me go back to get Cale because they were as afraid as we were of them bikers and the next thing I knew…well, there's a lot that's happened, but it wasn't all bad. The thing is, I haven't seen him since."

"Don't you take no drugs at any of them dope houses, hon."

I'm sure my expression would have gotten my jaws slapped at any other time, but none of the three noticed it. "I 'magine she's had every chance in the world to take…"

They shushed me like I was a little ol' jabbering baby.

I heard Pepper draw a big sigh on the other end. "Did you miss the part about me being in this motel lobby? Can you have Daddy or Grandpa come get me, or send me some money to get home?"

Aunt Ida Belle shook her head like Pepper could see her. "They're out there somewhere right now, trying to find you."

"Here in *Flagstaff*?"

"They were, but the last we heard, they were in Barstow. Now, you stay right there, hon, until they come and get you."

"This guy's not going to let me stay here that long, and besides, I'm starving to death."

"Give me the phone." Norma Faye held out her hand. Her voice was strong and flat, like my teacher sounded when she intended to quiet the room down. She put the receiver to her ear. "Young lady, you get that manager on the other end of this line and stay right where you are."

There was a pause and she raised her eyebrows at us. For the first time ever, I saw a redhead's temper.

"Mister, I am Norma Faye Parker, wife to Sheriff Cody Parker here in Texas. That little girl there is his niece, so you give her a room and then you give her some money for food, and don't you let her go wandering off to get it neither. I'm good for every penny. Do you have a diner around there?"

She listened for a second, and I could tell she cut the guy off.

"I'm sure you have a wife, or a maid, or a housekeeper, or a grandmother around there somewhere. Send one of them out to get it and bring it back to her. Now, I'm going to the bank right now to wire you enough money for *two* nights and a dozen meals and…" She listened for a moment. "No, I don't care if she *is* fourteen, I don't want her waiting at no police station. You heard me say our people are coming for her and one of them is a lawman, Constable Ned Parker. Now, you'll have your money in an hour and after you take out for the room and food, you can keep whatever's left over. Give me the name of your motel again and the phone number and the address." She wrote it all down. "Now, give the phone back to Pepper."

She passed the receiver to Aunt Ida Belle and gathered up her purse. "I'm going to the bank."

She stomped out and was gone, and I had to listen to Aunt Ida Belle fuss over Pepper. "Is that motel a clean place? You know we're clean people. Now, don't you do nothing ugly with nobody, and don't be drinking beer, neither. Drinkin's a sin…"

I was thinking that when Pepper finally got home, everything wouldn't be sunshine and roses, not once they got hold of her. Then I heard something that about broke my heart. Pepper was sobbing into the phone, saying she was sorry, and I knew my cousin had turned a corner.

Chapter Seventy-two

No one slept in the motel room that night in Barstow, over three hundred and fifty miles west of Pepper's Flagstaff motel.

Ned was feverish, tossing and turning, tortured from within.

James worried all night on the other side of the bed, wondering if he'd made the right call not going in the house after Pepper, once he knew where it was.

Cale's head throbbed behind his black eyes, making breathing difficult. He was afraid to ask anyone to take him to the doctor, so he endured the pain, figuring it was part of his punishment. Lying in the darkness, he vowed never again to think he was tough or above the law. The fight with the motorcycle gang proved to him once and for all that there were a lot of people in the world who were tougher than he'd ever imagined.

Shirtless, Crow sat in the courtyard, this time in a yellow chair, watching cars pass on Route 66. He was sure the Rattlers didn't know where he was, but then again, he figured you never went wrong being extra careful. He threaded a needle from the motel room's sewing kit and went to work patching the clean cut on the back of his still damp shirt that would soon dry in the desert air. The long slash across his lower back stung.

In a green chair, Rocky drank from a paper bag. "You gonna tell them?"

"I've told them enough. I'm gonna handle this myself, in my own way."

"You didn't say nothing about me?"

"Didn't think they needed to know, and I wasn't for sure you'd make it anyway."

"Why wouldn't I?"

"We haven't talked much in the last couple of years, and I barely knew where you were. I wouldn't have, if Tammy hadn't gotten that letter from you before she left."

"Well, I'm here. Those guys are gonna be tough to handle."

Crow angled the patch job toward the light over the playground. He took another stitch that would have made his mama proud. "Once I know she's in there, we'll handle whatever comes up." He bit off the thread and held the needle out. "Here."

"Bad?"

"Enough."

"Stand up, then and turn so I can get the light." Rocky took the needle. "Shoulda done this earlier. Might be too late."

"No later'n the last time."

Rocky handed him the paper sack. "Draw on this."

Crow took a long swallow, the liquor burning all the way. He flinched at the first stitch in his back, but caught himself and remained still until Rocky finished. *His* stitches would have made their mama proud, too.

◇◇◇

Rocky was long gone at daylight, so Crow didn't know if he slept or not. They decided that Rocky should watch the house for a while, hoping to get a glimpse of the girl. Patience seemed to be the best option, and Crow had been patient for a long time.

When the sun rose, Crow stood and stretched, feeling tightness in his back.

The motel door opened and James stepped outside. "You ready?"

"Nope."

"Why not?"

"Because it's barely light, and those guys aren't going to be up over there until later in the day."

James rubbed at the back of his neck, an unconscious Parker mannerism that he never thought about. "So we have to sit around here some more?"

"At least until noon."

"Why then?"

"Because that's check-out time, and I don't think we'll want to spend another nineteen dollars on a room for no more'n an hour or two before we leave."

"I was thinking we'd leave Ned here in bed. Cale can take care of him until we get back."

"Nope. We'll need to move fast, and I don't know which direction. We can't take a chance on coming back through here to get them. We take 'em with us and they wait in the car."

"They might get hurt."

"We *all* might get hurt."

"I've been thinking. Let's call the cops and have them go over there to check and see if she's in there?"

"Good idea."

James waited, frowning. "Is it that simple?"

"I've been thinking about it. What do we have to lose?"

"Well, all right. I'll go in and call them right now."

"Fine."

"Somehow I think you're not serious."

"It's your daughter. Do what you think is right."

James hesitated. "I'll go in and call them right now."

"You said that. Go ahead on."

James was barely inside when Rocky rolled up. "She's there."

Crow felt a prickle down his spine. "You saw her?"

"Yep. It was her. She came outside with another girl and they rode off with a couple of old boys I hadn't seen in the bar. They met some hippies, sold 'em some grass, took the money, and got some groceries. I left 'em back at the house and came to get you."

"All right. Let's go."

When James came back outside after making the call, Crow was gone.

And so was James' car.

Chapter Seventy-three

It was still raining the next morning. The weatherman said it was about done, but we still had at least one more day and night before the storm passed. He warned that didn't mean the flood was anywheres near over with. Water would continue to rise for days.

Uncle Cody spent most of the night at the hospital, waiting to hear about Miss Anna. She was alive, but the doctors still weren't making any promises. It was daylight, or what there was of it on that rainy morning, when he got to the house. He and I were eating bacon and fried eggs at the table, talking about the dreams we still couldn't figure out. I didn't mind discussing it then, with him there with me.

While we talked, Norma Faye washed dishes and Miss Becky listened and cleared the table, happy that Pepper was found, but I could tell she was still concerned. She for sure knew something she wasn't telling, and every time there was a mention of a horse, her eyes snapped like fire.

Aunt Ida Belle rocked back and forth in Grandpa's chair, being mad. She'd already talked to Pepper and she was fine, but neither Uncle James nor Grandpa had called to check in. "If they don't call in an hour, I'm fixin' to fly out of Love Field and get my baby. She's sitting in a motel room in a strange town."

"Get two tickets," Norma Faye said. "I'll go with you."

Miss Becky took down a red syrup can, removed the lid, and plucked out her butter and egg money. She counted it. "I have enough here for the two of you."

They both started to argue, but Miss Becky shut them up with a frustrated wave. "I ain't-a flyin' with y'all, but I'm-a payin. Be careful. There's a lot of dark places in this old world."

I wanted to ask her if I could go, but I decided it'd be better if I stayed right there and kept my mouth closed.

Uncle Cody knew better than to say a word.

The phone rang and Aunt Ida Belle answered it. "Cody, it's for you. They was calling for Mr. Ned, but I told them you're here instead."

He took the receiver and listened for a couple of minutes. Then he drew a long breath. "All right. Thanks." He came back and sat down to finish his coffee. "That was O.C. Said he heard John T. and Marty robbed a store in McKinney."

Norma Faye raised an eyebrow to ask a question.

"They know we have Freddy. They'll be hard to catch now with getaway money in their pockets." Uncle Cody studied the yellow smears on his plate. "Marty's not as bright as folks think he is. He's such a mama's boy, I bet he comes back sometime, at least for a minute or two. He hasn't let go of her dress tail once in his whole life. He'll be back."

"Until then, what are you gonna do?"

Uncle Cody was surprised at the question. I'd never heard Norma Faye get into his business before. "Keep looking, I reckon, and keep trying to figure out this dream Top's having. I've had a little of the same thing myself, and the whole thing's sitting on the edge of my mind. It seems like a little bitty thing and…"

I piped in. "Like a little speck of dust out in space."

"That's right. A tiny speck of dust."

"And at night, if you think about that little green speck out in the stars long enough, it gets enormous, like the biggest balloon in the whole universe that somebody is blowing up and it gets bigger and bigger until it makes your chest ache."

Norma Faye put one fist on her hip. "What in the world are you two talking about?"

We said the same thing at the same time. "We aren't sure."

Chapter Seventy-four

Crow rolled past a police cruiser driving slowly through the biker's neighborhood. He parked at the end of the unpaved alley to think. There were no fences, and little vegetation behind the houses. From the tracks, it was obvious that bikes routinely used the alley as well as the street out front. It was only three doors down from the corner, so anyone popping out the back was less than eighty yards away. He was confident that most of the people who might run would instinctively turn toward the shortest escape route, only to find the Bel Air blocking the exit.

Their brief moment of indecision was all he needed.

Rocky pulled his bike into the other end, not blocking the alley, but enough to keep an eye out. Crow waited fifteen minutes before deciding that something was wrong. He backed up and drove slowly toward the street. When he stopped at the intersection, the officer standing beside the car was talking with two sleepy Demon Rattlers in jeans and bare feet.

The officer pointed to the sidewalk, obviously ordering the two to stand in one particular spot. He reached in and pulled the microphone through the window.

One of the bikers noticed the car idling at the residential intersection. He shaded his eyes, but Crow was confident that the man had no way of seeing inside.

Crow accelerated through the intersection and made a quick loop to watch the street from a different direction. Five minutes later, the police cruiser left and headed back to the highway.

Rocky rode past, giving Crow a little wave that said they'd have to come up with another plan.

Irritated, Crow followed the cruiser and tapped his horn at a stop sign. The policeman glanced up into his rearview mirror and waited. Crow put the car into park and walked up even with the officer's car door.

"Can I ask you a question?"

The policeman hung his elbow out the window. "Sure."

"Listen man, I know you got a call from someone to check out that house for a runaway girl."

"How do you know?"

"She's my friend's girl. He's the one who called you, right?"

"I don't know the specifics of the report. I was told to check out the house and see if there were any underage runaways."

"Well?"

The man didn't like being questioned by anyone, especially a long-haired hippie with a once-fancy shirt that might have been dragged out of a ditch. The officer shifted into park and opened the door, forcing Crow to step back. He adjusted the gun belt at his waist, a practiced habit that usually made people take note of his authority. "What's your name?"

Crow spread his hands, realizing the conversation wasn't going where he wanted. "Dude, I'm asking a question here for my friend. He's been trying to find his little girl, a fourteen-year-old named Pepper. See? That's odd enough for someone to actually be named Pepper. I'm for real here."

"I asked your name. Show me some ID."

"I don't have any."

The officer jerked a thumb toward the car. "Driver's license? Registration? *Draft* card?"

Crow spread his hands.

"Get over here against my fender."

"Aw, man." Instead of following orders, Crow moved toward the Bel Air. "Dude, look."

At the end of his patience, the officer slipped his baton free and let it swing beside his leg. "I'm not telling you again."

With a rumble, a cluster of Harleys came around the corner. The officer ignored them, but from the corner of his eyes, Crow saw more than one familiar face from the bar. There was Griz, who resembled a raccoon under the bandana bandage still tied over his nose. He built a smile as they passed.

"Against the car. Now!"

Crow held up both hands. "Please listen to me."

The officer advanced, the baton held ready. He'd been on the streets for years, and wasn't falling for one of the oldest tricks in the books.

The line of bikes filed past, a procession designed to show no fear. Women rode behind, some holding onto the men's belts, others riding casually, hands on their thighs. The bikers shouted and laughed.

"Good morning, officer!"

"Need any help, officer?"

"Watch him. He's a bad *man*."

Arms around a red-bearded Rattler, a woman's mouth opened in shock.

"Crow!"

His head snapped around as the officer swung. Instinctively trying to block the blow, Crow caught the baton on his forearm which immediately went numb. He groaned and slipped inside the swing, ducking and coming up under the officer's chin with his head. It wasn't a solid hit, and the man twisted back, raising a knee and trying for Crow's groin.

He twisted, blocked the knee with his thigh and dropped his shoulder. He punched the officer in the stomach. It felt like hitting a sack of cement. The man swung with his left fist, catching Crow in the side of the head. His eyes jolted in their sockets and he staggered, seeing stars. Crow kicked sideways, catching the officer's knee. It gave with a sickening crack and he went to the ground. Still in the fight, the policeman fumbled for the revolver in its holster. Crow kicked him in the stomach, knocking the air out of him. Gasping, the man tried to make his paralyzed lungs work while Crow unsnapped the strap over his pistol. He dropped the cylinder, ejected the bullets, and flung them into the street.

He raised up, breathing hard and expecting to see the bikers. Instead, he saw a number of cars that had slowed on the highway.

Crow waved the pistol at the gawkers and they quickly accelerated. He threw the revolver hard, landing it on the flat roof of a nearby house. He reached into the police car, ripped the mike cord free from the radio, then pulled the keys from the ignition.

"Stay down! Bury your face in that concrete!"

The man rolled slowly onto his stomach. Crow jumped behind the wheel of James' car and pulled around the officer's still form. He sped away, following the tiny speck that was the last bike in the gang.

He had to keep up with them, or he'd lose the girl he'd been trailing for weeks.

Chapter Seventy-five

Cody was sure of one thing. Marty would eventually come back to his mama's house. The best thing for him to do was to put more pressure on her.

The skies were heavy and gray, but the rain had stopped for the time being. He drove into the boggy yard and sat there with the engine idling, thinking.

What's been bothering me about all this?

Top dreams of talking horses.

He said something about grass.

He shuddered, thinking about the deep cuts on Leland's body from being thrown through the barbed wire fence. They were no closer to figuring out who'd run over him that night on the highway than they were at the outset.

Cody sent men as far away as Dallas, Bonham, and Clarksville to talk with body shop owners. Officers even went to wrecking yards and parts houses, asking if anyone had recently purchased replacement bumpers, headlights, or fenders, then they cross-checked with those customers when they could.

Nothing.

The possibility existed that the driver simply kept going, too drunk or scared to stop. Maybe it was a tourist, or simply someone passing through Center Springs that one and only time, never to return. No matter what, Leland sure didn't deserve to die that way.

He studied the dilapidated truck in Melva's yard, thinking he should offer her a couple of hundred dollars for the old wreck.

A used pickup like that would be perfect for a young boy like Top, growing up in the country. All it most likely needed was an engine overhaul and new brakes.

Since it wasn't raining at the moment, he climbed out of the car and walked over to the old mare cropping grass. She stuck her head over the top strand of wire and he absently rubbed her ears and soft muzzle.

"You the horse Top's dreaming about?"

She jerked back and nodded.

He laughed. "I don't believe it."

"Sheriff?"

Cody was startled to see Melva on the porch. He hadn't noticed that she'd come out. "Morning, Melva."

"Somebody ought to shoot that old mare. She don't do nothing but stand around and eat."

"She's old. I imagine she's worked pretty hard most of her life and now she's enjoying retirement."

"Useless things don't need to take up space."

"Well." Cody tracked around the truck, absently checking the condition of the tires that looked pretty good despite their age. "How about this useless thing? Would you think about selling it?"

"No."

"I'll pay you a fair…"

"I said no. You need something else?"

He stopped in the yard, not far from the porch. "Have you seen Marty since I was here last?"

"No."

She didn't giggle, which concerned him.

"Melva, tell me the truth. Has he been by here?"

She rubbed her hands. "I been here by myself all this time."

"Well, you know, I'd like to believe that." His gaze drifted to a big yellow cat on the porch. Slinking against the wall, it reached the open door and darted inside. Cody's eyes found a pasteboard suitcase sitting a piece back in the living room. "You going somewhere?"

She hesitated. "Why?"

The hair on the back of Cody's neck tickled. Melva wasn't usually prone to one or two word sentences, and she still hadn't giggled. He rested his right hand on the butt of the Colt 1911 on his hip. "I believe I see a suitcase sitting there."

"I'm going to…to Waco, to see my daughter."

"The one you haven't spoke to in a while? Y'all make up?"

"That's my business."

"It sure is. Not meanin' to pry, but I'd like to come in and poke around if I can."

Standing ramrod stiff, she tilted her head to the side with an odd, jerky twist. "Do you have a warrant?"

"Sure do." Cody started toward the car and thought better of turning his back on the house. He squared himself toward Melva.

There was a long pause. "Show it to me, then."

Cody decided right then and there he was going to stand where his feet were planted until the sun came back out, if he had to. "Come on down here. It's in the car and the way you're acting, I don't want you up there right now. You can wait in the backseat 'til I'm through."

"You don't have no call to arrest me."

"You're right about that. You're not under arrest. I want you here so I don't have to holler at you to talk. Now, quit being stubborn so we can get this over with and you can go on to Waco. How're you getting there, anyway?"

Her mouth gaped like a fish out of water and Cody knew in that second that Marty Smallwood was inside. His truck wasn't there, and there were no tracks in the mud, but he was sure of it all the same.

The yellow cat shot back outside and streaked off the porch. One part of his subconscious saw it flash across the wet grass and dart under the pickup, while another took a snapshot of the event.

A shape appeared at the door with astonishing speed.

Cody registered the pistol in Marty's right hand.

Snapshot.

A bright muzzle flash.

The shot seemed to surprise Marty, too.

Snapshot.

Melva, giggling, raised both hands to her face.

Marty took a step out the door and *intentionally* angled to get his mother between them.

Cody felt his knees bend. He was moving into a shooting stance as he drew the Colt automatic from its leather holster.

Snapshot.

A drop of rain struck his hat and another, his shoulder.

Marty fired again, his arm straight out as he moved, but the shot went wild. His mother moved to her right without visibly walking. Marty planted his foot and angled behind her.

One step.

Two.

The Colt rose and he found Marty in the sights.

Snapshot.

Marty was fuzzy, as he should have been, when Cody concentrated on the pistol's sights.

He fired, and at that same instant realized that Marty wasn't there. He simply disappeared. Cody shifted his focus and saw Marty's surprised expression as he dropped through the rotten porch, landing with a foot on either side of the joist. His momentum slapped him forward at the waist, slamming his chest and face against the boards. His nose instantly exploded.

Suddenly off balance, Melva stumbled down the steps. With the agility of a young girl, she caught her balance and took off. Cody grabbed her arm as she passed and slung her to the wet ground. Agility or not, the momentum was too much and she landed hard, rolling twice.

"Don't you move!"

Keeping his Colt aimed at Marty, Cody opened the car door and took cover, expecting John T. to start firing at any minute. Seconds ticked by as he kept the Colt trained on the house. Melva lay on the ground moaning.

Straddling the joist, Marty heaved and retched. His body slid sideways and disappeared from view under the porch.

"Dammit!" Cody knelt, his Colt aimed at the shadowy figure lying still under the porch.

"My baby. You shot my baby."

"Shut up, Melva."

Marty didn't seem to be making any attempt to move, so Cody took a chance and reached inside the open door for the microphone. "John."

The big deputy came back immediately. "Go ahead, Cody."

"Where are you?"

"Pulling on the highway from Rachel's…my house."

He was only five miles away.

"Get over here to Marty Smallwood's place. We've done shot it out and he's down, but I don't know how bad. John T. could be here, too."

"You hurt?"

"No."

John's siren wailed as he came back. "On the way. Hang on."

"You might better hurry."

Chapter Seventy-six

James trembled in rage. "I'm calling the cops."

"You already did." Ned was propped on the bed, feeling slightly better, but still feverish.

"To report our stolen car."

"I imagine Crow wanted to do it by hisself."

"I was going with him."

"That's why he went on."

"You taking his side in this?"

"There ain't no side. It's common sense. He'll be back with her in a little bit."

Cale cleared his throat. "Mr. Parker?"

Both men answered. "What?"

"Uh, I'm sorry for butting in and all, but I'm pretty hungry. None of us has et anything in a long while, and we're out of aspirin, and you need 'em."

James wanted to give the boy a dressing down, but he paused. Even though Cale had been part of the launching mechanism for the entire disaster, he was still a kid and doing a good job caring for Ned with what little they had.

He dug the wallet out of his back pocket. "All right. Run down to that diner east of here and get us whatever they'll let you take out."

"Make sure to get some coffee." Ned pushed himself higher in the bed. "I'd dearly love a cup of black coffee."

Cale blinked at them through his raccoon mask of bruises. "Uh, I, uh, I wanted to say I'm sorry."

Neither of the Parkers spoke.

Cale took a deep breath. "I'm sorry for running off with Pepper and for getting' y'all out here." His voice broke. "I'm sorry for everything I've done, and I'll do better, if y'all can give me a chance."

Unsure of what to do or say, James gave him an awkward pat on the shoulder.

On the bed, Ned closed his eyes. "If you was mine, I'd give you a whipping, and if I felt better, I would anyway." He opened them. "We'll talk later, but if you straighten up and fly right from now on, we'll be done with it. Now, go get me that coffee."

Cale darted out of the door, hurrying toward Highway 66 and the diner. Neither of the adults worried that he'd run off by that time. He'd already learned his lesson.

James watched him through the window. "So you want to wait some more." It was a statement, not a question.

"What can we do? Even if we call the police to come out here, we still don't have a car. Let's give it a little while and see what happens."

"All right, then. But I don't want to."

"Neither do I."

Chapter Seventy-seven

True to his word, Deputy John Washington arrived in minutes. He rolled out of the sedan and into the rain, dragging a shotgun with him. Melva still lay in the yard as if she were dead and Cody knelt behind the open passenger door, his Colt trained on the house.

John shouldered the pump shotgun and moved forward. "Where is he?"

"Under the porch."

"You ran him up under the *porch*?"

"Naw, the dumbass fell through it. He's laying there, hurt. I may have shot him. I don't know, but what I do know is that he busted through and straddled one of them two-by-sixes when he did. He keeps gagging and puking, but I didn't want to take no chances."

"Did you shoot *her*?"

"Threw her down. It might have knocked her out, but I don't know."

"What do you want me to do?"

"The light's so bad I can't hardly see him under there, and he may have a pistol pointed this way. I'll go around to the long side where he can't get a shot. Pour it on 'im with that scattergun if he starts shooting."

John settled one butt cheek on the seat to get as much car between him and Marty as possible and laid the shotgun across the door frame. He saw a slight movement and drew a bead on Marty's shapeless form. If he had to start unloading Number 4 buck under there, something was going to die.

After waiting so long for John, Cody was certain John T. wasn't in the house or he'd have already tried shooting it out or running. Cody jogged around to the left side, putting as much of the rotten floor as he could between him and Marty. He might hear Cody coming, but he couldn't see to shoot until he was right on top of him.

John didn't intend to let that happen. "Marty Smallwood! Don't you move a muscle, you hear me? Throw me out that pistol!"

Watching both the rotten boards and the hole that swallowed Marty, Cody tiptoed across the porch.

Marty didn't answer.

"Throw out that gun, now!"

All John could see was movement in the shadows. A trickle of rain funneled off his hat. Even if it had been a bright, sunny day, John doubted if he could have seen him under there anyway. The shape was odd, and he couldn't identify head nor tails.

Marty raised a shaking hand. "Don't shoot no more."

"I said throw the gun out."

"All right!" The sudden clap of a gunshot from under the porch made Cody jump. "Shit!"

John opened up with the twelve-gauge. Dust and splinters jumped as the pellets impacted the wood.

From the porch, Cody fired half a dozen times through the rotten boards.

Melva held her head. "Stop! Stop! You're a hurtin' my ears!"

Someone else was shouting too. "Stop shootin'! It was an accident!" Marty's pistol flew out the hole to land at Cody's feet. "I didn't mean to shoot! This damn thing's got a hair trigger on it!"

Stunned that Marty was still alive and talking, Cody crept forward to peek over the ragged hole while John thumbed fresh shells into his shotgun. "Let me see your hands!"

Shaking, Marty did what he was told.

"Climb out of there."

"Sheriff, I busted my nuts so hard when I fell that my stomach's cramping something fierce. I doubt I can walk."

"Keep 'em up there, then." Ready to shoot again, Cody peered over the hole to see Marty lying in a two-foot deep wallow in the dirt made either by dogs or hogs. The mounded dirt absorbed the pellets from John's shotgun. From his angle, Cody's bullets impacted the floor joists and nothing else.

Chapter Seventy-eight

Crow steered into the Western Skies motel, off the highway alive with a mix of new and old cars sporting fins, two-tone colors, long hoods, and deep trunks. He had unfinished business with the Parkers behind the chipped red door and felt bad about the way he'd left them.

James was watching out the window and yanked the door open before Crow could get out of the car. He checked the front seat, but Pepper wasn't there. "What happened? Where is she?"

Glancing over his shoulder, Crow pushed past him into the room. "Y'all need to get your stuff and get out of town. Right now. Listen to me, James, you do the driving and stay below the speed limit. If y'all get pulled over, you don't know me and whatever they ask you, say you ain't got no idea what they're talking about. You've been in this room all morning and now you're leaving, on your way back home 'cause Ned's sick."

Ned *was* sick, but he raised up on an elbow, jiggling the paper cup half full of cold coffee. Cale hadn't noticed the waitress added cream and sugar, and that, in Ned's opinion, ruined it. "What are you talking about?"

Crow pitched the keys to James. "The less you know, the better." He was already leaving when James grabbed his arm in a surprisingly firm grip.

"Where the hell is my *daughter*?"

"I don't *know* where she is."

"You went to get her."

"No, I didn't." Crow gently pulled James' fist from his sleeve. "I went to get my *sister*! Pepper's not there. She never was."

The strange turn of events made Ned's feverish head spin. Still, he swung his legs over the edge of the bed, groaning at the pain in his stomach. He couldn't straighten, and instead tilted his head to see. "Clear this up, Crow."

"We don't have time to talk. I gotta get gone before the police show up. They pulled me over and I fought with a cop. They're probably looking for James' car right now."

He turned to leave and froze at the distinctive sound of a cocking pistol. The muzzle of Ned's .38 was less than ten feet away. The old man suddenly appeared much healthier than he had only moments before.

"You ain't going nowhere till you tell us what happened this morning." He couldn't miss at that range. "If you try to leave, I'll shoot your kneecap off and you'll wind up under arrest anyway, and I have a good idy that you've been in trouble with the law before, so you better start talking, boy."

Cale's eyes were wide as saucers. "Uh, Crow, you better do what he says. That old man means every word. I know him." He paused and licked his lips. "He's the best pistol shot in the county."

Holding the doorknob, Crow sighed. He didn't want to stay, but for the next couple of minutes, he told them everything that had happened from the time he left.

"Fine, then." Ned lowered the pistol. "You fought the police. If they show up I'll tell them you're under arrest for warrants back in Texas and I'm taking you in. That might keep you out of jail here for now until we can sort all this out. But you still ain't told us all you know about Pepper."

"You don't get it, Ned. Pepper ain't *here*. She never *was* here as far as I know. I used y'all to find my sister. She disappeared after a guy come through Tahlequah on a motorcycle a few months back. We all thought she'd been kidnapped. You know Oklahoma law, Ned. They don't care about a Comanche girl disappearing these days. Said she probably run off with some hippies like so many kids do these days.

"But I didn't believe them. She'd never done anything like that before, so I called my brother Rocky and told him where I was going, then I started working my way west. I saw you with a car and a badge, and figured you had money." He shrugged. "That's all."

James rubbed his unshaven cheek. "How'd we come to be in Barstow? You said Pepper was here."

Unable to meet Ned's eyes, Crow settled on talking at Cale because it was easier. "I heard what Ned was doing in the bus station back in Texas. I needed the car and I was flat broke, so I threw in with him. When we got to Amarillo, those gals in that little house there told me where most of the kids were going. One said she'd seen what she took for an Indian girl on her way through, but hell, today all these hippies dress like Indians, so it could have been anyone."

He shifted toward the window to watch the courtyard. Two or three families were packing their cars to travel. He was glad to see a big Buick had pulled up beside James' sedan, partially blocking it from the street.

"Hey guys. I'm a son of a bitch for it, but I used y'all. Hell, I didn't think I'd give a damn about any of you, but you grew on me."

James balled his fist and stepped closer. "Pepper! My *daughter*."

"I don't *know*, man! It was a damned miracle that this boy showed up right at our fingertips. When he mentioned the bike gang, and told us about the Rattlers, it was like a gift from God. *Those* were the guys I was looking for."

Out of nowhere, James caught Crow a lick on the ear. "Don't you talk about God to *us*. You talk about Pepper."

Staggered by the blow, Crow balled his fists, and then relaxed and held up one hand. His suddenly numb ear rang. "*Dude!* You still don't get it, do you? She ain't here, not as far as I know. She's lost in a stream of kids on their way to California. Your best bet is to wait until she calls home for money like they all do."

Movement outside caught James' eye. Noticing, Crow followed his gaze. "I told you we shoulda split."

A police car cruised through the motor court and stopped behind their sedan.

Chapter Seventy-nine

Wearing Cody's cuffs, Marty sat with his feet through the hole in the porch. Soaked and muddy, Melva was in the back of John's cruiser. Standing with one foot on the floorboard, John was once again wearing his yellow slicker. "I'll follow you to town."

"You go ahead on." Cody eyed Marty. "I'm gonna have a talk with this dumb bastard before we leave."

John nodded and dropped into the seat. "You think this rain might hold you up a little?"

"That's exactly what I was thinking, big guy." The brief exchange spoke volumes.

As John backed out, Cody opened the trunk of Deputy White's car, sick at his stomach over what he was about to do. He came back with a roll of duct tape. "You're under arrest for a whole list of things, buddy. Number one is murder. Number two is attempted murder of a peace officer. Then you have assault, evading arrest, attempting to flee, and I probably have you for jaywalking somewhere."

Marty shrugged. "Don't mean nothing to me. Who says I killed anyone?"

"Someone who knows you. You've been accused of two murders."

"I didn't kill anybody. What you have ain't the truth. Anybody can point a finger. You don't have any proof."

"Proof enough that you shot at me. You don't do that for jaywalking."

"It's the damn hair trigger on that pistol. Sometimes it'll go off when it's cocked. I was running. I didn't intend to shoot at you."

"You shot at John."

"It was an accident, too. I don't remember cocking it."

"Well, you did. Now, fess up about the murders and where I can find John T."

Marty found a point on the ground at the bottom of the wallow and studied it. "I don't know about any murders, nor John T."

Cody twirled the roll of tape on his index finger. "You know, I saw how good this stuff sticks yesterday, so I got me a roll. I learned something in Nam that most folks around here don't know." He tore off a long piece and knelt in front of Marty. "You can spend a lot of time dicking around with something and still not get anywhere. Know what I mean?"

Eyes hooded, Marty gave a slight nod even though he had no idea what Cody was talking about.

"See, we're fighting over there in that little piss-ant country, but not really trying to win. I believe we'd be done already if the right folks would let our soldiers do their job. Now, personally, I want to be through with a fight as soon as possible, and I think I know how to end this one. Be still." Cody quickly slapped the tape across Marty's mouth and smoothed it against his cheeks. "There we go. Can you breathe all right?"

Fear in his eyes, Marty nodded.

"Good. Remember how that feels. I really don't think you have the sense God gave a goose, but now's when you can prove me wrong. I'm gonna ask you again. Where's John T.?"

Marty shrugged, breathing hard from fear.

"That's the wrong answer, hoss. You know good and well where he's hiding. Now think. Do you see how well you're breathing right this minute?"

Another nod.

"If it was me, I'd start having trouble. See, I've broke this nose a couple of times and it makes it hard to get enough air. Sometimes I have to open my mouth and take a deep breath.

That sure is a good feeling, drawing a deep breath when you can't get enough air through that nose."

Cody tore off another long piece.

"Now, you can shake your head till it falls, off, but you need to act like you got some sense and tell me where I can find him."

When Marty shook his head again, Cody slapped the tape across the bridge of his nose and pushed it down over the first strip. Realizing what was about to happen, Marty lunged upright, but Cody drove his fist into the punk's stomach, not hard, but with enough force to double him over.

Marty *oomphed* and convulsed, trying to draw air into his lungs.

"Marty, John T. nearly killed my deputy. She's a little ol' gal, but she's one of the best folks I've ever met. If she hadn't been there, it might have been me, or John Washington that soaked up some of them pellets. You might think John T.'s tough and all that, but he ain't dog shit on my boots. You thought *you* was tough, but you see how you are right now, trying to breathe? Well, I'm tired of foolin' with you."

With both hands he quickly reached out and folded the long flap of tape over Marty's nose and pushed hard. The terror in his prisoner's eyes told Cody that he'd found the exact thing to make him talk.

Leaping to his feet, Marty rolled back onto the rotten boards. Desperate for oxygen, he convulsed, rubbing his face on the porch to free the tape.

Cody twirled the roll of tape in his hands and watched as if Marty was a dying roach. Eyes glassy and chest heaving, Marty made horrific noises deep in his throat, he folded and went back down.

"Had enough?" Cody knelt with his knee on Marty's chest. He pinched one corner of the tape over his nose and peeled upward, allowing him to take in a deep breath. Crying, Marty pumped air in and out of his oxygen-starved lungs.

Cody tore off a fresh strip of tape and watched Marty's eyes lock onto it. "I'm gonna ask you one last time, then I'm gonna bust you in the nose and put this tape across it again. You can't breathe blood. You gonna answer?"

Frantic nodding.

"You know where I can find John T.?"

More frantic nodding. Marty wasn't paying attention to Cody, he was staring at the tape as if it were a live cottonmouth. Cody stripped it off his mouth like pulling off a Band-Aid.

Marty drew in great lungsful of air, whooping in and out.

Cody held the long strip of fresh tape in two hands between them. "Now, tell me where to find John T."

Chapter Eighty

Ned answered the knock on their motel door. The police officer looked surprised to see an old man in an undershirt. He cleared his throat, then glanced back over his shoulder at the parking lot. "Sir, is that your Chevy right there?"

Standing in his sock feet, Ned scratched at an armpit. "Yep, that belongs to my son."

"Sir, is he in there with you?"

Ned stepped back. "Sure is." The officer scanned the room. "That's my son right there on the bed."

Also in his sock feet, James gave a little wave. Ned plucked his shirt off the only chair in the room and shrugged it on. His badge caught the light and the officer took note. Ned stayed in the doorway. "We have a teenager in there in the shower." The water quit running a second later.

The second officer joined the first. "What's your name?"

"Ned Parker. Constable Ned Parker." He tapped the little badge on his shirt.

"Mr. Parker, did either of you loan your car out today?"

"Naw, I don't loan my car to nobody, but that's my son's. Why?"

The bathroom door opened in a rush of steam. One towel wrapped around his waist, Cale stepped out, drying his long blond hair with another and keeping his left side to the cops so they wouldn't see the bruises on the other.

The second officer addressed Ned. "We're after the driver of a pale yellow Bel Air who assaulted an officer."

"Well?"

Uncertain what to do next, the cops shifted from one foot to the other.

"Don't y'all have the license number of the car?"

"No. We didn't get it."

"Well, that's the first thing you do when you pull a car over. Didn't they teach that to y'all at the academy? Did you get a good description of the driver?"

"I didn't pull him over. He flagged another officer down, then attacked him. Big guy with long, black hair. Six-six, six-seven."

"Lordy, that's a hoss." Ned figured the cop in front of him was more Crow's size at less than six feet. "I haven't seen anybody that big since we left Texas. Have you, son?"

"Nope." James shook his head.

Ned buttoned his shirt. "Your man hurt bad?"

"Bruises. Shattered knee." The first officer paused, realizing he was talking too much. He figured it was probably Ned's badge that caused him to open up. "Well, thanks." He stepped back outside, leaving the door open. "Report says the car we're after's like that one."

"Well, that's a pretty popular model, and since it's a few years old, I 'magine there's a lot of them on the road." Standing in the door, Ned rubbed his bald head. "Well, I figger a guy who beats up a police officer'd take off for somewhere else and not check into a motel, do you think?"

"Maybe you're right. Sorry to bother you, Constable."

"That's fine." Ned patted his arm. "That's fine, son. Hope you catch him."

"We will." He stepped onto the walk and Ned waved goodbye. He opened the curtains and sat at the table. "Stay in there till I tell you to come out." He waved again at the officer outside and folded at a sharp stab of pain.

From the parking lot, Ned appeared to be writing, or reading, or praying.

Chapter Eighty-one

Lying on one of the double beds in the motel room, Pepper twirled her eagle feather by the quill and watched a rerun of "The Real McCoys," but her mind was a million miles away.

Six bottled cokes sat on the dresser, sweating through the cardboard carton. Ice shifted in the bucket beside them as it melted. Snacks were scattered across the remainder of the space, along with empty wrappers from Sugar Daddy's, Oh Henry!, Lik-M-Aid, Butterfingers, and Turkish Taffy.

The trash can was full of greasy hamburger bags and used paper cups.

Outside, kids squealed and splashed in the pool.

She was on the road, surrounded by the Route 66 culture of glitz and kitsch, and she was bored to death.

Tears ran down her cheeks and she wiped them away with the wrinkled sheet. Pepper simply wanted to go back to Center Springs, and home, because she hadn't gotten one damn thing out of the entire trip that she expected.

Though the motel advertised color television, "The Real McCoys" was in black and white. Pepper took a deep, shuddering breath and paused, listening to Luke tell Kate that she was the strongest of the two of them.

His words struck a chord and Pepper realized that she wasn't weak at all. Far from it, she'd been the leader of the trip out west. Though they hadn't reached San Francisco, she'd taken care of herself, fought a motorcycle gangster, defended herself from unwanted advances, and even, however briefly, stood up in the civil rights movement for those not allowed to eat in a "whites only" café.

With those thoughts, her chest swelled and a new strength filled her with power. She took a deep breath and changed channels. She was growing up.

She turned to Merv Griffin, something they weren't allowed to watch in Miss Becky's house, and watched him interview someone she'd never heard of, George Carlin.

Chapter Eighty-two

Cale took Ned's place at the table, keeping watch out through a crack in the drapes. The police car was gone, lights flashing when it pulled back on the highway.

When the parking lot was clear, Crow stepped out of the bathroom, his clothes limp with steam. It was his wet hair that stunned them all. Instead of the long, black strands that once rested on his shoulders, it was now short with a self-administered haircut. He built half a grin. "I didn't think you'd lie for me, Ned."

"Didn't lie." He was on the bed again, exhausted and feeling older than he did fifteen minutes earlier. "Said there was a kid in there taking a shower and James was here and we hadn't loaned the car out. The truth on all counts."

"Why do this for me? I used y'all for myself."

Ned spoke with his eyes closed. "I cain't say."

"I say we kick his ass to the street." James tried to burn a hole through Crow.

Crow caught his glare and paused, knowing James had no chance against him in a fight. "I'll go." He started for the door with his usual rangy ease.

"Wait." Ned spoke from the bed. "Let me think a minute."

James still wasn't over his mad. "I've thought all I'm going to."

The phone between the beds jangled, startling them all. James answered and held the receiver out toward Crow. "It's for you."

He listened. "You sure it was Tammy?" He listened some more. "That'll work." Hanging up, the smile on his face spoke volumes.

James felt empty. "You find your sister?"

"Yeah."

"And?"

"She's for sure with the Rattlers and they went to the desert."

"You sure Pepper ain't with 'em?"

They still didn't get it, or wouldn't admit that she'd never made it that far. "I'm sure."

"How does he know where they are?"

"He paid some hippie kids to let him ride in their Love Machine. They drove past the Black Cat and saw the Rattlers there, probably stopped for beer. The kids went to a gas station not far away and the Rattlers passed them heading into the Mojave. I figure they intend to camp out there until they find somewhere else to go, now that their house is hot."

Crow peeked through the drapes. "The cops aren't going to buy that story about your car for long. If I was him, I'd talk to the manager who'll remember seeing me. Y'all need to get out of here and I'm going to get my sister."

"How you gonna go?"

"Rocky'll be by to pick me up. I'll go out this back window in the bathroom and wait for him in the alley."

"How are you gonna find them?"

"Well, James, it's the desert. A lot of bikes pulled off the pavement onto a dirt road that leads back into some of the meanest country in this state. Their tracks'll be easy to find."

Ned rubbed his flushed face with a wet washcloth. "You gonna just walk up and ask them to let her go?"

"No." Crow took a deep breath. "We have the guns from your trunk."

"You stole Dad's guns?"

Crow shrugged. "Stole, borrowed. What's the difference at this point? We need them, and y'all don't." He pointed at the holster on Ned's belt. "You have that one."

"It don't make no difference, James." Ned held his side as if it were going to split like a ripe watermelon and felt wrung out. He laid there for a long moment, thinking. After a while, they thought he'd dozed off, but he surprised them. "Crow. Can you be certain that Pepper's not with them, since they have your sister?"

"Ned, my sister's there, but I can't say for sure that it's her idea, or theirs."

"No matter. Pepper might be there, right?"

"She *could* be, but I'd bet against it."

"Then we need to go with you either way, and James, I don't want to hear a word out of you about it. Whether Pepper's there or not, them rough people have his sister, and helpin' them's the right thing to do. We'd want someone to do the same for us. We're going to do for that little gal, at least, then we'll go on after Pepper."

James picked up the phone. "I need to call and tell Ida Belle what we're doing."

Ned shook his head, tired, but trying to gather enough strength to get started. "They'll take the fire out of us when they hear what we're gonna do, and you know they're gonna ask. I'd rather not call until we know something."

Unconvinced, James stared at the phone.

Cale spoke up. "Can I go?"

"You'll have to. I'll figure out what to do with you when the time comes."

Thirty minutes later the phone in their empty room rang and rang and rang.

Miss Becky finally hung up and waited with her news about Pepper.

Chapter Eighty-three

No matter what month, the Mojave Desert is a harsh environment full of sand, yucca, creosote bushes, catclaw cactus, rattlesnakes, scorpions, and Gila monsters. Most of what exists there can hurt you, kill you, or eat you.

It was the perfect place for the outlaw bikers to hide out for a few days. Their camp was above the basin floor where it was cooler, near an abandoned mine once named The Money Spring. More of a trickle really, the nearby spring provided cool, clear water, allowing the bikers to live there until their food ran out.

Under the bright light of a full moon threatened by the near sunrise, Rocky and Crow lay on a slight rise above the quiet camp. Chin resting on his crossed arms, Rocky didn't take his eyes off the glowing coals of a campfire. His whisper seemed to carry as far as a shout in the pre-dawn desert silence. "They've done this before."

"They can make as much noise out here as they want, and no one will complain."

"It's quiet now."

"That's the best time, when they're all asleep, or passed out."

"See anything?" James' voice startled them both. Crow gestured toward the ground. "Damn, boy. Can't you make any more noise?"

"I've being as quiet as I can. What do you see?"

"Not a damn thing right now, but we'll see them all up close if y'all don't keep your voices down." Rocky laid his head on an arm.

They were lucky to have such a bright night. The silvery light was going to be a boon to their plan, what there was of it. They couldn't be sure there were no guards, but Crow was convinced everyone was asleep. There was no need to post guards, and these guys weren't even close to military. Instead, they partied until after midnight while the three men waited and watched.

It was time to move, for sunrise wasn't far away. Rocky sighed. "You're sure about this?"

Crow nodded. "Yep. Sometimes being too sneaky and making a complicated plan is the wrong thing to do. I believe I'm going to walk in there and see if I can find her."

"How you gonna do that?"

"James, lower your damn *voice*. I'm gonna get a jacket from the first guy I find. If anyone rouses up and sees their colors on me in this light, they're not going to think a thing about it. They'll go back to sleep."

"And I'm gonna look for Pepper?"

"No. You're staying right here with Ned's shotgun and a pistol. If anything happens, you start shooting. There's enough light to do some damage. They'll grab the ground and we'll head back for the car."

Ned rested in the Chevy's backseat a mile away. Rocky's Harley and the car were already pointed toward the highway. Cale's job was to stay where they were with the motor running. When they came back, no matter the outcome in the camp, they'd need to hie out of there as fast as possible.

Crow and Rocky rose and crept forward on bent knees, trying to move as quickly as possible while staying low. Muffled by sand, their footsteps were soft. The biggest danger for the moment was walking into something sharp and dangerous.

James watched them disappear and wiped his sweaty palms on his khakis. Pepper was his daughter, and it didn't feel right to have two strangers doing his job. The one thing James *did* know for sure was that he wasn't as dangerous as the two men moving slowly toward the camp. He'd chosen a different lifestyle than Ned's law work, or Cody's military experience. He wished he was tougher, wished he'd had more schoolyard fights as a kid, and wished Ned and Cody were there with him. He waited and worried.

Crow and Rocky came to a deep arroyo south of the camp. They squatted in the shadow of a Joshua tree and listened. Crow whispered in Rocky's ear. "See where they parked the bikes?"

Rocky nodded. The Rattlers had circled the camp to line their bikes up facing away from the cut. Only yards from the edge, their positioning was perfect for what Rocky had to do.

"Once we come up out of there, you can do your thing pretty quick. If it all goes south, jump back into the wash and haul ass for the car. They can't make this drop, and even in this light I doubt they'll try to chase you."

"You're coming back through here, right?"

"Right. When I find her, we'll pick you up in there," Crow jabbed a finger toward the arroyo, "and we can slip away. Work fast and keep an eye out for us."

"Don't get anything started. You *know* I'm not a great pistol shot." He gripped the thin butt of the revolver stuck in his waistband.

They found an incline that was less steep than the wash's walls, providing a small, loose trail to the bottom. Rocks rattled down, despite their caution. With each small, clattering avalanche, they paused and listened.

At the bottom, another unanticipated source of noise came from loose gravel and dry vegetation left from the last flash flood. The two men carefully worked their way across the wash to the far wall.

The access to the lip was a soft spill fanning at the bottom and narrowing to a tiny exit between a boulder and yucca plant. Pebbles and stones trickled downhill. Breathing hard from exertion and fear, they reached the top and paused.

Crow pointed toward the bikes and slipped Ned's largest sap from his back pocket. A proven weapon in countless fights, it was the perfect device for the situation. Rocky peeled off and disappeared.

It was difficult to place his feet, watch for cactus, and keep an eye out of the leading edge of the camp and the sleeping Rattlers all at the same time. Crow had no idea where they were, but figured that most had passed out near the fire. The ancient part of the human brain sees fire as safety and security, and most people want to sleep as close as possible to the flames.

At least that's what Crow was counting on.

But then there's always that one guy that breaks all the rules. This one was either sleeping in a semicircle of catclaw for privacy, or had passed out there by accident. Crow missed seeing him, but the man's heavy breathing gave his position away.

Loose-limbed and rawboned, Crow flowed through the night like a panther, reaching the biker in half a dozen steps. He raised the sap and brought it down with all the force he could muster on the side of his head. The biker twitched, quivered, and lay still. The blow was loud enough to wake the dead, and Crow readied himself to face any attack that might rush from the shadows.

When nothing happened, he stripped the sleeveless jacket from the man's dead weight and found a .38 revolver under his belt. Crow stood and slipped his arms through the holes. Shells weighted the jacket on one side. He tucked the revolver in the small of his back. Carrying .38s and camouflaged, he entered the camp.

James was tortured by an internal tug of war. Obviously out of place in such a situation, he knew that covering Crow and Rocky was the best he could offer. At the same time, he was afraid Pepper was there, and his job as a dad was to find her and bring her to safety.

He couldn't pull his attention from a crumbling rock structure on the opposite side of the camp. The roof was long gone, as well as part of the nearest wall and half of the back. A buzz deep in his head kept telling him Pepper was in there, held against her will.

The more James thought, the more he convinced himself Pepper was inside, and here he was laying around and watching the camp. He rose, made sure the pistol was tucked in his waistband, and threw the shotgun across his shoulder.

James went to find his daughter.

Chapter Eighty-four

Dawn on that gray morning wasn't much more than a slight difference in the light. Cody, John Washington, and a dozen Oklahoma sheriff's deputies stopped on a dirt road out of sight from a cluster of fishing cabins of the Choctaw Fish Camp not far from the Kiamichi River. Some of the Oklahoma deputies were eyeing the big Texas deputy.

"I'god it's raining up here, too." John's voice was filled with disgust as they closed the car doors softly and gathered with the local deputies.

"Don't worry, that black won't wash off," someone said quietly and snickered.

Sheriff Quinn Davis dug a chew from a wrinkled BEECH-NUT packet. He tucked it into his cheek and spoke around the fresh wad. "Finny. Go wait in my car."

"Why?"

Davis spat and rested his gaze on the deputy who'd spoken. "'cause I told you too."

Jaw set, Finny stalked away.

"Cody, it's a good thing y'all got here when you did." Sheriff Davis chewed for a moment. "They'll have to close the camp pretty soon if it don't quit raining. The river's about out of its banks and it'll be here before you know it."

The local game warden, Ricky Garfield pointed. "Cody, I believe he's in the cabin at the far end. I called Edgar Sampson who owns the place and described West. He says that's where he put him. Quinn had sent men around back already, but John T. couldn't go far no-how. The river's not twenty feet from the back door now."

Cody wished for another cigarette, but the rain made it impossible to light up. "Do you have a plan?"

"I thought we'd drive Ricky's truck up to the cabin beside the one John T.'s renting." Sheriff Davis waved toward the thick stand of pines. "In this rain, they won't be able to tell us from anybody else wearing hats and rain gear. That'll at least get us close. The deputies can work their way through the woods, and when we're all near enough, we'll call him out."

"He'll come out shooting."

"We'll shoot back."

Cody bit his lip. "How about letting me try something first?"

John growled deep in his chest. "That ain't a good idea."

"You don't know what I intend to do."

"Yeah, but I know *you*. You tend to bull into things and think later."

"That's not true."

"The Cotton Exchange."

Cody paused. It had been his fault when he and John found themselves trapped in the Cotton Exchange with a lunatic murderer two years earlier. "Well, that one time."

"You boys gonna stand here and visit in this rain, or can we get going?"

Cody saw a deputy with a brown canvas, Western-style slicker. He stood out in a group of yellow rain gear. "Trade with me, would you? And guys, y'all are gonna remind me of a bunch of Easter eggs walking through the woods in all that yellow. You need to get rid of it. A little water won't hurt you. Yours, too, sheriff. He ain't stupid."

Cody shrugged into the smelly canvas and pointed toward one deputy in a billed cap. "Switch with me."

The man traded, happy for something to block the rain from running down his neck.

Stripping off the last of the bright rain gear, Ricky climbed into the driver's seat as Sheriff Davis took the middle and Cody quietly closed the passenger door. They drove in like registered guests and pulled up in front of the cabin nearest John T.'s. Cap pulled low to hide his face, Cody stepped out and went around to the tailgate. A wooden box of trash was closest, so he reached over the gate and lifted it out, as if it were something they needed inside.

Sheriff Davis unlocked the cabin and Ricky followed him inside. Cody sat the box on a rickety wooden table, and returned to the truck. He fumbled in the cab for a second in case someone was watching and headed toward what they thought was John T.'s hideout. Head low, he walked across the bed of pine needles to the tiny porch. Because the sandy ground drained well, it was like walking on wet carpet.

He rapped on the door with a knuckle and moved the long slicker to free his Colt, still keeping the handgun out of sight. The door opened and he paused at the sight of a barefoot young Indian woman standing there with a wet towel in her hand.

"Help you?"

"Yeah." Cody stumbled. "Uh, I was wondering if we could borrow some…coffee? We left the house to set up camp and didn't bring any. It sure would be good this rainy day." He quickly swept the tiny cabin with his eyes.

She smiled, showing brilliant white teeth. "We don't have any. John T. hates the taste of it. Besides, y'all got here too late. We're all gonna have to leave pretty soon. The river's up and the manager said he's closing down today."

Cody started to answer when the woman's expression went from pleasant to furious as she glared over his shoulder. He followed her gaze to see a flash of yellow in the woods. Trying to maintain the moment, he came back to her with a smile, "Anyway."

She tried to slam the door in his face. "John T.!!! Run!!!"

Shouldering her aside, Cody slammed the door open while drawing the Colt. Bowling her over, he stormed into the one-room cabin and realized it was empty.

There was no other door. Cody lunged back onto the porch to see John T. starting a beat-to-hell two-door Pontiac Catalina parked on the off side of the cabin. He'd been examining a Route 66 roadmap when Cody walked up. Concentrating on whether Pepper could be found after so much time, John T. really hadn't worried too much about the fisherman knocking on his door.

Cody pointed the .45. "John T.! Get out!"

Instead, John T. threw the map aside, started the car, and punched the accelerator. The tires spun on the wet needles.

"Hold it!" Cody jumped off the low porch and hit slick needles. His feet went out from under him and he landed flat on his back.

Realizing he was about to get stuck, John T. reversed, backed up, and shifted again. The car started forward. Sheriff Davis and Ricky Garfield darted around the corner, demanding that he surrender.

Still on the ground, Cody raised his pistol as John T. finally convinced the car to move. "I said hold it!"

The fugitive gained speed, steering directly at the two men who opened fire through the windshield, then split up in front of the oncoming car.

The big .45 bucked in Cody's fist. His first round shattered the driver's side glass, but John T. didn't slow. Cody fell and fired again at the same time the Indian woman in the cabin threw a shot at the lawmen in the trees. The deputies in the woods opened up on the cabin and the car.

It would have been suicide to rise into the barrage of bullets zipping by only a couple of feet overhead. Rolling onto his stomach, Cody added to the din as John T. stuck his left arm through the shot-out the window and blasted away toward the woods. The return shower of lead snapped holes in the sheet metal as John T. struck Garfield, throwing him over the hood. The game warden shrieked and convulsed in pain.

Sheriff Davis leaped against the cabin's wall.

Incoming rounds punched holes in both the car and the cabin behind Cody. The woman screamed, adding to the cacophony.

Partially blocked by the truck parked in his way, John T. aimed the Pontiac at Sheriff Davis, but instead of crushing him against cabin, John T. went limp and turned the wheel, sliding sideways and stopping only inches from the building. The engine knocked, rattled, and died.

John T. slumped against the door as he absorbed round after round of suddenly accurate fire.

"Knock it off, you dumb bastards!" The gunfire trickled off as Sheriff Davis' voice finally got through to the men. "I said knock it off! I'm under here!"

The last shot was late, and the lonely report echoed through the woods. Cody rose and rushed to the Catalina, the muzzle trained on the still form in the front seat, but it wasn't necessary. John T. West was shot to pieces, his cheek resting in the shattered glass of the window.

Cody dropped to his stomach to see Sheriff Davis lying partially beneath the car, pinned against the building. "Quinn, you hurt bad?"

"Only my pride."

"Hang on a minute 'til we get Garfield out of the way." Cody knelt beside the game warden. "How bad you hurt?"

Moaning in pain, Garfield rolled onto his back and gasped. "My whole leg's broke."

Big John trotted up. "We'll get you to the doctor right quick."

While two deputies rushed forward and pulled Garfield out of the way, another joined John to move the Pontiac. Cody reached over John T.'s corpse and steered the car as it rolled back far enough to free Sheriff Davis. With the Catalina out of the way, he sat up with a sick grin.

Cody knelt beside him. "What's so funny?"

Davis hung his head between bent knees. "I swallowed my chew, but hang on. It'll be back up in a second."

Chapter Eighty-five

Moonlight illuminated the sleeping bikers. Crow worked what he hoped was a consistent search pattern that brought him from the outer edges of the camp toward the fire.

Even though he was concentrating on finding an adult woman, he kept an eye out for a girl Pepper's age. A couple of underage girls were passed out with a bottle of Jack Daniels lying between them. One had dark hair and he turned her head to see her face.

She didn't match the photo.

The stained bandana across his broken nose, Griz snored softly. Crow studied him for a moment and moved on past two Harleys parked beneath a makeshift sunshade. Two more shapes slept nearby. Nearing the glowing coals of the campfire without finding who he was looking for, Crow knelt for a moment beside a piñon pine to think. Stomach clutched with nerves and fear, he started over, working a different pattern through the camp, finding others that he'd missed in the shadows.

The colorful eastern glow reflecting off high, thin clouds told him he'd run out of time. Coyotes yipped somewhere in the distance, following their prey through the scrub. Feeling empty, Crow took a wide circular route to check the outer edges of the camp one last time.

"Damn, man. You stepped on my hand." Groggy and angry, a redheaded biker sat up, holding his fingers. "Get your ass away from here."

A slim hand rose up and rubbed his beard. "What's the matter, sugar?" The woman's sleepy voice was clear in the still morning air, and Crow recognized it right off.

"Nothing. This dumb bastard stepped on me. Get away from here!"

Mumbling apologies, Crow backed away, but stopped after only a few feet. The couple became still and silent. He waited until he heard heavy breathing once again and crawled back to where they lay on filthy blankets spread beside a cluster of tall brittlebushes.

He reached out and took Tammy's hand. When she opened her eyes, he was smiling with one finger to his lips. She gasped and he put his fingers against her mouth. Maintaining the grip, he indicated that he wanted her to follow. She rose to her knees.

Without opening his eyes, Redbeard reached behind him and held her thigh. "Where you going?"

Tammy's eyes widened but they never left Crow's excited face. "I have to pee."

The biker rolled over without a word.

Standing as one, Crow led her toward the arroyo. They stopped short of the parked bikes and he drew her close, breathing her familiar musk that made him feel weak in the knees. "Let's get out of here."

She pulled back, glancing toward the camp. "How'd you find me?"

"I'll tell you when we're gone." He pointed toward the bright glow of the desert sunrise.

She planted her feet and stopped again. "Crow! We can't. They'll follow us."

"That's all taken care of."

"How?"

"You're asking too many damn questions, and keep your voice down!"

Still, she refused to move. "We can't!"

"Of course we can. I've found you. We can get away."

She twisted her arm, yanking free. "You're going to get killed. I've seen these guys leave half a dozen people out in the desert. Most of them are on drugs and they're mean as snakes. Crow, they don't think anything of beating or killing anyone. I can't go."

Shocked, he stood silent for several long moments. "What? Why?"

A twig snapped somewhere beyond the brittlebushes to his left and Redbeard stepped around the thick screen, fumbling with his zipper. "You had a good idea, baby."

He still hadn't seen Crow. Tammy sucked in a startled breath and the man reacted by turning his head toward the sound. Without a wasted motion, Crow dug in with his foot and swung Ned's sap.

Instead of catching Redbeard on the side of the head, the leather-covered chunk of lead exploded the biker's cheek. The blow knocked him back into the bushes and he landed in a crackle of breaking branches. It would have probably killed an ordinary man, but this guy was tough as a boot.

He came up with a roar, thrashing and kicking his way out of the brush. Crow danced sideways when the Demon Rattler swung a haymaker. He saw it coming and dodged the blow at the last minute, responding with a quick snap of his wrist and catching Redbeard on the ear. He roared from the pain and drove in swinging.

Tactics like that work in the close quarters of a bar fight, but Crow had more than enough room to move. Knowing he needed to finish the guy before the whole camp joined in, he dodged and snapped two lefts into Redbeard's already bloody face and then swung the sap again. It missed and Crow danced back.

Redbeard still hadn't landed a blow, but Crow knew it was only a matter of time before he did.

The fight caught someone's attention in camp. "Hey! You two knock that shit off! We're trying to sleep."

Other voices rose in response, asking what happening.

For the moment, those shaking sleep from their heads thought it was a dispute between two gang members, but it wouldn't take long to realize what was happening, especially when they recognized the man in the sleeveless jacket.

An outsider wearing the gang's colors was a death sentence.

It didn't take long.

"Hey! Who are you?"

Chapter Eighty-six

A gunshot echoed across the desert, but it came from the wrong direction. "Careful, Red. He don't fight fair."

Stunned at Tammy's comment, Crow took his eyes off the biker. It was enough for Red to connect with a roundhouse blow. Crow's head snapped to the side and he staggered, momentarily stunned. He had a sudden urge to vomit, but his sense of self-preservation kicked in and he stutter-stepped back out of reach.

From his peripheral vision, Crow saw others step into view. The cover of darkness was gone, and it was only a matter of minutes, if not seconds, before someone realized what was happening in the early morning light.

Redbeard had learned his lesson, and with the arrival of the others, he knew everything was on his side. Instead of charging in like a bull, he stalked Crow. It was too slow, much too slow, eating up valuable time as Crow retreated. "You're not going?"

Tammy paused for a moment, studying the men appearing like apparitions.

She nodded, and Crow realized the indecisive and untrustworthy woman he'd desperately loved since high school would come after all. He threw his head up. "Shoot!"

A pistol cracked again and the bullet snapped overhead, but it came from the wrong direction. An entirely *different* direction from where Rocky should have been.

Experienced fighters, the bikers either hit the ground or melted back toward camp, going for their own guns. Another round cracked through the air above them, and then a third clipped through the brittlebushes.

Two more gunshots crackled from near the row of Harleys and Crow knew those rounds came from the pistol Rocky carried.

At the sound of gunfire, Red paused long enough for Crow to deliver a massive kick to the groin. No matter how tough, a direct kick there will take the fire out of any man. Doubling over, Redbeard gasped. Crow swung the sap against the top of his head and Redbeard fell sideways, completely out. Crow held out his hand. Tammy hesitated for only a moment, then grabbed it and they ran.

A Demon Rattler rounded a cholla and landed on one knee. He threw a pistol up and the gun roared. Fire burned in Crow's side. He snapped a shot in return that threw sand into the man's face causing him to flinch, the next round going wild.

Fire erupted from one of the nearby bikes. The startling dull whump of an exploding gas tank robbed the man's attention and he paused long enough for Crow to thumb the hammer back. He shot again. The kneeling Rattler fell sideways with a gasp.

Another bike whoofed alight. More shouts and curses came from the camp. Gunshots popped like firecrackers in the morning air. A series of methodical shots came from beside the bikes as Rocky returned the favor. Black smoke rose in two columns, then three, then four as the bikes erupted into flame in quick succession.

Rocky had given up on putting sand in the tanks and with all stealth gone, he lit the rest.

The deep crump of a shotgun came from near the rock house, the same direction as the first shots, and a dark figure charged. Crow drew the second revolver from his waistband and snapped off a round that missed.

"Don't shoot *me!*"

Recognizing James' voice, Crow threw two more shots to each side. Bikers jumped and ducked. Gunfire came from several directions, eliciting shouts and screams from both sides of the camp as the missed rounds struck unintended targets. James stumbled and landed hard on his stomach. Crow thought he was hit, but James rolled to his knees, held the trigger back on the shotgun as he pumped the forepiece as fast as he could. The wall of pellets discouraged return fire from one side, but scattered flashes told they were shooting back from the other.

James scurried away from the melee like a crab, using both knees and one hand. Bullets whizzed overhead. Targets flashed between the bushes as bikers dodged for cover and position.

Punctuated by pistol shots, the bikes continued to cook off one after the other. Kneeling behind the flames, Rocky thumbed fresh shells into the pistol and rose to shoot again. One man fell, but the bikers were slowly organizing themselves. Pouring lead in Rocky's direction, they moved forward as he retreated back toward the arroyo.

Crow fired with a pistol in each hand, backing away and shielding Tammy with his body. She screamed and pulled at his shirt, urging him to turn and run. James finally regained his feet and charged past the retreating couple. Crow's revolvers clicked dry and he spun to follow.

There was no time to find an easy way down into the wash. Tammy led the way, still gripping Crow's shirt. She leaped over the edge, pulling Crow off balance. She caught the sloping side over halfway down and managed to maintain her balance with great leaps to the bottom. Crow landed wrong and tumbled, losing the grip on one pistol.

He rolled to the bottom in a spray of rocks and sand as more rounds blasted from Rocky's position. On the camp side of the arroyo, a steady count of deep, methodical gunshots echoed across the desert as if someone were taking target practice.

James found footing over the arroyo's edge, giving him a protected position to shoot. Exposed only from the chest up, he rested one elbow on the ground and pumped rounds at anything that moved. Bodies fell, possibly from the impact of the #4 buck he was throwing in the bikers' direction, or they were ducking—he didn't know. Most of the bikers' return fire whizzed overhead, but occasional close shots threw sand into his face and eyes. When the last empty shotgun shell rattled to the ground, James drew a .38 from Ned's holster and threw six shots at the scattered muzzle flashes.

Below, Crow found his feet as Tammy hauled him up. Seventy-five yards away, Rocky slipped over the side and stumbled to the bottom of the wash. Taking advantage in the brief lull, he ran for the safe side.

James quit shooting and all was silent. He took that opportunity to leap down the crumbling side and landed hard. Regaining his feet, he saw the other three racing across the open space. Shouts filled the air and ineffective shots snapped overhead without finding flesh. James ran, and in seconds, all four were scrambling to the top.

More bikes whoofed to light and flames rose into the still air, sending thick columns of black smoke that mixed and stretched skyward. When he reached the top of the arroyo, James realized he was far behind the other three. He reloaded both weapons and resumed the uniform pattern of gunfire to keep their heads down until both ran dry.

He wiped tears from his eyes and ran.

Chapter Eighty-seven

Still shaken, Sheriff Davis and Cody leaned against the game warden's truck as the Oklahoma lawmen handled the details of the shooting between the rain showers.

Cody lit a dry smoke from the pocket of his slicker and blew a long stream from his nose, watching them carry the wounded woman from the shot-up cabin.

The game warden, Ricky Garfield, was already on his way to the nearest hospital. A deputy directed the second funeral home ambulance as the driver backed through the melee to the cabin's little porch. "Back, back. Stop."

The driver hit the brakes too hard and the tires slid a couple of inches on the wet pine needles, piling up the straw and leaving two inches of cleared sand. Seeing the short skid, Cody's head swirled with a feeling of *déjà vu*.

Thinking it was the result of stress and too many smokes, he ground out the butt and studied the propane tank sitting in a clearing only feet from where he stood. The stationary object spun in his mind and he waited, thinking it was lucky one of the wild rounds during the shootout hadn't hit the tank. He drew a deep breath and sighed, crossed his arms, and watched something skitter through long grass growing up around the tank. A mouse darted across a clear space and disappeared into another clump.

There was something about those ambulance tires. He studied them again, but kept coming back to the sand cleared of pine needles.

"You all right, Cody?" Big John joined him.

"Yeah, swimmy-headed's all."

"You ain't hurt, are you?"

"No. I'm fine."

A cat darted across the clearing toward the propane tank, launched itself through the grass and came out with the mouse. It made Cody think of the cat that had given him a split second of warning before Marty ran out of Melva's house.

The tires popped into his mind. Tires on the broken down truck sitting that long should have been low at least, and then he realized what had been nagging at him. There was a slight indention *behind* the truck tires where the grass wasn't growing.

Some of that grass there was yellow, protected from the sun.

Cody jerked up straight. "John, that truck's been moved."

"What?" He scanned the area. "Which one?"

"Melva's truck. That wore-out old truck sitting beside the fence in front of her house. It'd been moved."

"So?"

"When you move a truck or a car that's been sitting in the same place for a long time and try to put it back in exactly the same place, you'll miss. You always do. It's impossible to park right where it was, especially in the dark."

"What are you saying?"

"The truck runs. It don't look like it, but it runs."

John's face broke into a grin. "Somebody drove that truck and used it to run Leland Hale down on the highway."

"Sure did. I bet if we check the fender on the opposite side, it's liable to have a dent in it." He mentally kicked himself. "I didn't pay it no mind, because it looked like it hadn't run in years."

"Which one of 'em do you think did it, Marty or John T.?"

"Could have been Freddy, but we'll find out. We're done here. Let's go talk to Marty and see what he says."

Chapter Eighty-eight

Crow dodged a creosote bush, nearly yanking Tammy off her feet. "You need to go faster!"

They ran like bandits through the desert. Halfway to Ned's car, the throaty sound of a Harley rumbled in the distance.

"Missed one." Rocky loped easily beside Crow and Tammy. Another bike roared to life. "Two. They're probably the ones under that cover. Didn't get that far."

Sucking air, James followed at a distance. "Slow up some!"

Needing to cross the deep arroyo, the bikes had to turn west before they could circle around and cut the fleeing trio's trail. It was only a matter of minutes before they caught up. If they were riding double, at least four armed and angry gang members were on their way.

Crow reached the Bel Air first and yanked the door open, startling Cale who was soaking a rag with water from a small plastic bucket they'd taken from the motel. He'd been bathing Ned's face with ice water while they were gone, the only thing he could think of to cool the old constable's dangerous fever. "Get the hell out of the way, kid!"

Wide-eyed, Cale dropped the rag and slid to the middle of the bench seat.

In the backseat, Ned jerked upright. Glassy-eyed, he had difficulty getting his bearings and came within a hair of shooting the strange woman who jerked the back door open. She hesitated, staring down the muzzle of Ned's 32.20. He lowered it and pulled his feet into the wheel well on his side. "Get in."

Rocky straddled his bike and hit the kick start. The engine refused to cooperate. He glanced over his shoulder and saw James fifty yards away, followed by *three* plumes of dust. He put all his weight onto the starter and pushed again. This time the engine roared to life. He gave Crow a thumbs-up.

Dropping the shifter into gear, Crow growled through gritted teeth. "C'mon! C'mon!"

The distance closed as James raced as hard as his legs could pump. He circled a thick clump of cactus and didn't see a twisted piece of wood nearly buried in the sand. It tripped him as effectively as if he'd been lassoed. He hit the ground hard, nearly losing his grip on the shotgun.

A third Harley appeared and they split into three prongs. James rolled and came up on one knee. The passengers riding on the back threw round after round through the desert brush and cactus with crisp snaps. A rolling thunder of shots came from the backseat of the car, causing the riders to veer. James threw the twelve-gauge shotgun to his shoulder and swung the muzzle past a bike like leading a rabbit running through the brush back home. The pattern had plenty of time to spread before it arrived, spraying the two bikers with over two dozen .24 caliber pellets.

The driver shrieked and threw up his hands. They slammed into a particularly tall silver cholla cactus. It exploded around them, covering both men in lush branches full of long thorns.

Ignoring the screaming men, James snapped another shot at a second bike, but had no idea if it connected. Taking out the nearest bike, though, gave him the time he needed to reach the car. He rose and sprinted with a second wind, arriving only seconds ahead of the growling Harleys. He threw the shotgun into the open window, nearly knocking Cale in the head. The Bel Air was already moving as he opened the door and jumped inside, falling onto both the gun and the kid. The door slammed from the momentum as Rocky led the way.

Ned fired six times in the direction of the Harleys and pulled his arm back inside the open window. Holding the empty smoking revolver, he collapsed.

Crow stomped the accelerator, throwing a cloud of sand and dirt into the air. The bikes separated, splitting around the cloud, and when they could see, the Bel Air was already speeding away. Crow followed their tracks back to the dirt road and leaving a billowing cloud of dust, they flew toward the highway, winding around the natural obstacles that left twin ruts resembling a sidewinder's tail.

The Rattlers realized where they were heading and tried an intersecting angle to cut them off, but two people on a Harley riding like hell across the desert was a disaster. The lead bike struck a large rock. It flipped in an explosion of sand and rocks, throwing two bodies onto the hard ground. Neither moved after they stopped rolling.

The other bike angled toward the Bel Air in an attempt to cut them off. The man riding on the back raised a pistol. The bullet whizzed overhead. He tried again as the bike bounced, this time shooting behind the fleeing car.

Reaching the highway, Rocky dropped one foot and slid onto the pavement. Making sure the Chevrolet was out of danger, he twisted the throttle and shot away.

Crow took the turn in a long, dusty slide, fishtailing for a moment on the hardtop before regaining control.

The Harley's driver stopped. The Demon Rattler on the back stepped off and emptied his revolver in their direction, but none of the shots came close.

In the rearview mirror, Crow saw Griz straddling the black Harley. He held up his middle finger as Crow punched the big V-8 and the engine roared.

Chapter Eighty-nine

The Lamar County Courthouse didn't have interrogation rooms, so Marty Smallwood slouched on one side of a long rectangular table in an empty office opposite Sheriff Cody Parker. Arms crossed, John Washington waited.

Cody tapped a finger on the file folder in front of him. "You're lucky, in a way."

"How's that?"

"Anna's gonna make it."

"I didn't shoot her."

"We have proof that you did."

"No, you don't. I wasn't there."

"Where?"

"Wherever you say I shot her."

"Didn't say she was shot."

The room was silent for a moment.

"It was you and John T."

"I wasn't with him."

"You guys set up an ambush."

"Go arrest John T. It wasn't me."

"We have him and you won't like what we found out."

"He said I did it?"

Cody raised an eyebrow.

"He's lying."

"I think the whole thing is gonna rest on your shoulders. I

wonder how they're gonna do it. Deputy Washington, do you think they'll charge him with everything at once?"

"You never know how a judge will think. I heard they're not going to pin anything on John T. right now. It's all gonna fall on Marty here."

"Bullshit!"

"Nope, it's true." Cody answered Marty's outburst with a soft voice. "They won't prosecute Freddy, because he turned state's evidence. Deputy Washington says John T.'s out of the running." He spoke over his shoulder. "You think it's for rattin' this idiot out?"

Big John shrugged.

"So that leaves you holding the bag."

"I'm not taking the fall for none of it."

"Then you better give me something that'll make the judge happy. The more you cooperate, the more lenient he'll be when it comes to sentencing."

Marty frowned at the table and tried to change the subject. "How's my mama? She okay?"

"She's fine." Cody had an idea for the mama's boy. "She's in a cell upstairs."

"You ought not have her in jail. She didn't do nothing."

"I think aiding and abetting a fugitive is something. She let you stay in the house and lied when I asked her. She'll do time for that, too."

"You leave my mama alone!" Marty's eyes welled.

"She's talking pretty good herself, ain't she, John?"

Deputy Washington nodded and fished a toothpick from his shirt pocket. "I was surprised."

"Yep, your goose is cooked. I realized what happened with the truck. That was a pretty good trick, but there was one small mistake. It wasn't parked back in the exact same spot."

Surprise showed on Marty's face. "She told you?"

Cody was on the question in a heartbeat. "She sure did. Women think different than men, and you know how she is."

Marty nodded. "Yeah, I know how she is, but I never thought she'd do me this way."

"It's what I told you, Marty. She's cooperating so the judge will go easy on her." He took a chance. "She don't care about anybody but herself. She said it was you."

Marty's head snapped up. "*Me*?"

"That's what she said. They're all turning on you, Marty."

Cody opened his mouth, but then realized he might say the wrong thing. Instead, he waited.

It was a staring game that didn't last long.

"All right. You'll tell the judge I cooperated?"

"Sure will."

"I'm not carryin' the water for all of 'em."

The room was silent. Outside the frosted glass door, a woman laughed. It was an odd sound in a room full of unanswered questions and sounded a little like Melva's nervous giggle. Marty tilted his head, listening.

A change came over his face, thinking his mother was nearby. "Tell her to come in here."

"No."

Silence.

Marty's eyes flashed at another faint giggle. "She had it with Leland."

"Who did?"

"Mama. She gets these headaches, you know? She keeps one most of the time and Leland kept getting on her nerves. She told me this for the truth. They had an argument and he left a-walking because she hid his truck keys and wouldn't tell him where they were."

"The keys to the truck by the fence?"

"Naw, *his* pickup in the barn. The one he uses all the time. The othern'n is my old one. I drove it until I got that job working on the lake. Made enough money to get the Dodge."

John uncrossed his arms and moved to the end of the table to better see Cody's face while Marty talked.

"So you did her a favor and ran your step-daddy down, knowing we wouldn't pay attention to one with grass all growed up around it?"

Furrowing his brow, Marty worked on what Cody was saying. "Why, no. That ain't it at all. I didn't do no such of a thing. I thought you said Mama told you what happened."

Cody's face remained impassive.

"Wait, she told you that *I* run over Leland?"

Once again, Cody went with it. "Didn't you?"

"Hell no. I had to clean it up, just like I cleaned up after John T."

Totally confused, Cody caught John's eye. Not knowing what Marty was leading to, Cody followed blindly. "It's all on John T.?"

Marty laced his fingers, as if praying. "I didn't do it all. I might have been there, but John T.'s lying too if he said it was me down there. The first one was an accident with that damned hair trigger on that cheap-assed .38. He shot the second one, too, when him and John T. got to fighting."

Cody followed the him down the second rabbit hole. "You're talking about the two men in the lake. Was Freddy in on that one, too?"

Marty licked his lips but didn't make eye contact. "He helped."

The two lawmen studied Marty. "Did he?"

"He was there."

"He gave us a full confession about that night in the bottom."

"Figures."

"Did one of 'em run Leland down, too?"

Marty shrugged "Ask *her*."

Cody was ready to pull out his hair.

Disgusted, he stood. "All right. I've had enough of this." He opened the file and plucked out several sheets of lined paper and slid them across to Marty. He handed him a short pencil. "Write down what you told us. When you're finished, I'll get this typed up and you'll sign it. I imagine it'll make things easier on you, but I'm not sure I really care one way or another, now. We'll talk about Leland later. You don't have to use big words, either."

He and John left while Marty Smallwood began to write his confession about the murder of two Dallas businessmen, very slowly, with his tongue sticking out.

Chapter Ninety

Crow half expected to get pulled over in Barstow, and that might have happened if he'd been driving, but James insisted on that duty and the only police officer they passed was writing a ticket. Interested in the busty blonde behind the wheel of the new Ford convertible, he didn't see road grimy Bel Air cruise past. With James driving, Tammy on the opposite side and Cale in the middle, his bruised face covered by a cap pulled low, they were the epitome of every other family of tourists traveling Route 66.

Except for one difference. They were in shock, riding in silence for over three hours, all the while expecting to be pulled over at any minute, or to see a herd of motorcycles appear in their rearview mirror.

As the state line receded into the distance and they entered Arizona, the tension broke and Crow slapped James' shoulder. "We made it! Good job!"

Instead of answering, James ground his teeth watching Rocky and his motorcycle disappear over a rise. Ned dozed in the backseat, racked by chills, his face gray as a cold winter sky.

Crow kissed Tammy. "You're safe now."

She smiled out the window. "Where are we going?"

"Back to Oklahoma."

Before she could answer, James put his hand on her shoulder. "Did you see my daughter, Pepper?"

She shrugged, disinterested. "I don't know."

"Fourteen years old. Dark hair. She has a mouth on her."

"Lots of girls came through. Some rode for a while, some stayed and partied. Some came to get high and hang out with the guys, until they realized how rough they are."

"But Cale says they took her in Flagstaff."

Tammy's eyes flicked to the teenager between them. He was silent, staring straight ahead. "They didn't take anyone in Flagstaff."

That statement alone was enough for James to pull off on the side of the highway. Dust blew past as he threw his elbow over the seat back. "Were you with them?"

"Yes."

"Cale says he got in a fight on the street and they took her."

"They aren't that stupid. I know they've sold people before, but they're usually Mexicans and they don't steal them in broad daylight. Griz got in a fight, sure. Was that you that broke his nose?"

Cale stared at the highway. "I was scared when they stopped me and Pepper."

She laughed. "I didn't recognize you, but they didn't pick anyone up. A street fight is a good way to call the law down on you, so we haul-assed out of town. You busted him a good one, though."

"I didn't break his nose."

"Who did?"

"Pepper kicked him." The admission seemed to take some of the weight off Cale's shoulders and he was visibly relieved.

Tammy and Crow laughed, an explosion of relief. Tammy picked a strand of black hair out of her mouth. "She about kicked his head off his shoulders."

For the umpteenth time, James asked the question. "Where *is she?"*

"There never was a Pepper with us."

"That all was for naught, then."

Crow slapped his shoulder. "I couldn't have found Tammy without y'all. It wasn't for nothing."

James choked, swallowed, and shook his head. The lines on the highway were a blur. He blinked his eyes clear. "My daughter is still missing."

Ned finally moved and raised his head. "I believe I need a doctor pretty quick, Mama."

Tammy twisted around and felt his forehead. "He's burning up."

Cale dipped a washrag into the last of the water and mopped Ned's face, worried sick about the old man, and deep down inside afraid he was responsible for his condition.

James wanted to stay there until he got an answer, but he pulled back onto the highway instead and aimed the Chevy's nose toward Kingman, Arizona. The Scenic Hi-Way U.S. 66 placemat they'd picked up from a café long ago in Tucumcari showed that the only things on the crooked road between Barstow and Kingman were tee-tiny towns full of BBQ joints, coffee shops, and motels.

Ned didn't need a sandwich, or coffee, or a bed. He needed a doctor.

Chapter Ninety-one

Cody and John waited in the hallway for Marty to finish writing his confession. Hat tilted back on his head, Cody lipped a Camel from the wrinkled pack and lit it with his Zippo. "What in hell was that all about in there?"

"I don't know. He knows a lot more about there goings on than he's letting on."

"Yeah, and I want to know what it is."

"Why'n't you ask him, then?"

"Because he'll clam up. I wanted to get his confession down, and then we'll talk about Leland."

"You think he ran him down?"

"Might have. Somebody drove that old truck into Leland, and I'm wondering if it was Freddy or John T. Freddy, most likely, because he thinks so much of his mama."

LaNette, Cody's secretary stuck her head out the door and gave him the same giggle they'd heard from behind the closed door. "I thought I heard you out here. Cody, phone."

"I'll call them back."

"It's a deputy sheriff down in Harris County. He's really wanting Anna, and it's not my place to tell him what happened. He says he has some information she wanted him to find. He thinks it's important enough to tell you if she's not here."

Leaving John outside the door, Cody went into his office. He punched the blinking light on the phone. "Sheriff Parker."

"Howdy, sheriff. This is Burt Stevens down in Houston. I got a call from Anna requesting some information. Your secretary says she won't be back for a while, but she wouldn't tell me why, and it's too important to wait."

Taking a deep breath, Cody told him about the ambush, and condition. "She's a lot better today, and the doctor here says she's gonna pull through."

"That's a damn shame. I'll pass the word to the boys around here. They'll take up a collection and send it your way to help pay her medical bills."

"She'll appreciate it, and we will too. We're doing the same thing."

"'Course you are. Now, here's the information she asked for. She called about one deceased, Leland Hale. Said she's trying to track something down that's bothering her, but I couldn't find out a thing about the man, other than he lives in your county and paid his taxes on time. Sounded like a good man."

"He was."

"After that, I checked on the other two names she gave me. Melva Hale and Marty Smallwood. Marty came up clean."

Cody chuckled. "He might have been, but he's here in my jail right now, writing a confession for the murder of two men, and maybe for Leland Hale if we can convince him to confess."

"Well, I'll be damned. Ain't that something. From nothing to a murderer. The apple don't fall far from the tree. Now, you got something else on your hands you need to know about."

"And that is?"

"Melva Hale."

"She's here too."

"You're kidding."

"Nope. We have her in custody for hiding Marty and getting in the way while I was trying to arrest him."

"Well, keep her there. She's the worst of the bunch."

"That old woman?"

"She's been wanted for a long time, under a different name.

Listen to this. I ran down information that led me to New Boston. That's not far from y'all, is it?"

"Hour and a half as the crow flies, couple of hours on the highway."

"Well, she moved around quite a bit when she was younger. Melva's from Pea Valley, Arkansas. She's had six husbands all together, that I know of, and half a dozen kids. Two daughters died of food poisoning when they were…" A paper rattled "… six and eight. They suspected her of killing them, but they'd been buried for so long when the laws got around to questioning her, it was too late."

Cody recalled their conversation. "Did her old man take a baby and leave?"

"Sure did. Henry Clay's somewhere in Kansas, and I haven't been able to run him down yet, but I will. When her two sisters died under strange circumstances not long after, the sheriff up there got suspicious and went out to talk to her about it. They say she went crazy, carrying on so that they had to put her in a home in Little Rock for a while. Son, they let that woman out and she went right back up there. She wasn't back a week and Henry Clay's mama was found dead, drowned in a cistern. They started asking Melva a lot of questions and she cleared out one night and no one ever heard of where she went."

"I can't believe that old woman is a murderer."

"She disappeared until Marty was born in Texarkana. I reckon that's the one you got locked up there. She might have changed her name during that time, but who knows. So in the long run, I have her under suspicion of murdering two children, her two sisters, maybe even her mother and a mother-in-law."

"Well, I'll be damned. I might have her for the murder of a baby, too, and she's already in my jail. Send all that up here to me, but I'm gonna have a talk with her."

"I'm bringing it personal. I need to see that woman for myself, and I want to see Anna, too. I'll bring her money with me tomorrow."

They said goodbye. Thinking, Cody hung up and called the largest insurance company in Chisum, William Carroll Insurance. The secretary put him right through to Alvin Jones. Cody explained as briefly as possible why he was calling. "What I need to know is if Melva Hale had an insurance policy on Leland."

"I have it right here on my desk. Your deputy Anna Sloan asked the same thing a day or so ago. Mrs. Hale has a hundred thousand-dollar policy on Leland. We haven't paid off as of yet, of course. It's too early."

"That's what I needed. Put a hold on it until you hear back from me."

"Will do, Sheriff."

His next call was to the sheriff in New Boston. After another lengthy explanation, Cody got to the point. "Did you have any unexplained deaths in your area that included a woman named Melva?"

"What was her last name?"

"Depends. This old gal said 'I do' more times than you can shake a stick at. The best name I have here is Leland Hale."

"Oh, I know who you're talking about. That was Melva Winneford. She lived with Eugene Florentine for a while, and yeah, there were rumors that when Eugene died of heart failure, she might have had something to do with it."

"What makes you say that?"

"Eugene was strong as a horse and then one day he started going downhill fast. The doctor here at the time, he's dead now, suspected some kind of poisoning, but the family wouldn't let him do an autopsy. Melva got Eugene in the ground quick. Not even a decent casket. Buried him a box made out of wooden orange crates. Said she didn't have the money for anything else. Well, she come into some not long after that and moved off."

Stunned at the revelation, Cody stared out the window at the gray skies that finally showed signs of thinning. "Thanks, Sheriff. I'll get back to you soon."

"You bet. Let me know what you find out."

Chapter Ninety-two

James wasn't sure they were going to find the one-story hospital in Kingman before they lost Ned. It was a long drive across the desert. They had to stop half a dozen times for the old constable to be sick. By the time they pulled up at the emergency room doors, he was waxy and ghost pale.

Cale jumped out before the car was completely stopped and dashed inside. A ragged, underfed Indian woman suddenly appeared beside the car, reeking of armpit and whiskey. "My name is Betty, and he needs a blessing."

Crow started to hold her back, and then recognized the dim eyes of a lost healer. "Go ahead, Mother."

He stepped away as she reached through the open door and rested her palm on Ned's chest. Closing her eyes, she began to pray in what Crow took to be Navajo.

"*Diyin ayóí át' éii.*"

Ned's eyes opened and he squinted at the woman. "Tom? Tom Bell?"

"His feet, my feet, restore."

"Tom, we need you."

"His limbs, my limbs, restore."

"We thought you was dead."

She repeated the lines in Navajo. "His body, my body, restore. His mind, my mind, restore. His voice, my voice, restore."

"Tom, we need to find Pepper."

"With pollen beautiful in his voice, with pollen beautiful in my voice."

"She's what? Pepper's found?"

Betty shook her head and clenched her eyes. "It is finished in beauty. It is finished in beauty. In the house of every light. From the story made of evening light. On the trail of evening light."

Ned relaxed, and for the first time in hours, he was peaceful. For a moment James thought he was dead, and then he saw Ned's eyes flutter. "Good, Tom. We owe you again."

"*Diyin ayóí át'éii.*"

A young nurse appeared. "Is Betty bothering you?"

"No. Funny name for an Indian, though." James had never heard Navajo, but he liked the rhythm.

"Don't know why. Mine's Linda."

"What's she saying?"

"It's the Navajo healing prayer. Betty drifted this way from the Navajo rez a year or so ago. Said she needed to be here to meet someone."

An older nurse arrived and cut Linda off. "Linda, what are you waiting for? You men get him out of there now. Get that old drunk out of the way."

Crow pushed past Betty, interrupting her prayers and grabbed Ned's feet as James took him under the arms. They pulled him out of the backseat, limp as a dishrag.

Two more nurses rushed through the doors with a gurney. "What's the matter with him?"

"I don't know. Keeps saying it's his stomach. He got shot there a few months back."

The older nurse, Harriett, pointed. "Why is he wearing a gun?"

"He's a lawman."

"Well, we don't need it in here. Take it with his badge." She saw Cale's black eyes. "What happened to *him*?"

James plucked the revolver from the holster as the nurse ripped Ned's shirt when she yanked the badge off. "Got crossways with some guys tougher than he was."

"I'm fine." Cale unconsciously touched his face. "I've been taking care of Mr. Ned. Is he going to be all right?"

Harriet studied the boy for another long moment and her expression softened. "I bet you did a good job. C'mon on in and we'll take care of him together."

Betty stepped forward and rubbed Ned's forehead with her thumb, singing softly. "*Hodiyin tł'ééʼgo soʼ bee dáʼdinídíingo, Áko Yisdá'iiníiłkii biʼdizhchí.*"

"Move!" Irritated, Harriet shoved between and elbowed Betty out of the way. "Let's go!"

In seconds, they disappeared into the hospital. James pitched the pistol into the seat beside the shotgun that still rode muzzle down in the floorboard. Without a word, he followed them inside. Taking a long moment to consider Crow and Tammy, Cale went inside, too. He wasn't as worried about Ned as he had been, but he still wanted to keep an eye on him.

Crow watched Betty, her arm outstretched, releasing something invisible into the breeze.

Linda hesitated, remembering her childhood on the nearby Hualapai Reservation. "She's a healer. She prayed for him. He'll be all right."

"I knew someone like her, once. What was that last part? She was singing it, and it sounded familiar."

Linda smiled, revealing a set of deep dimples. "It was 'O Holy Night.'"

"The Christmas carol?"

"Yep. Gotta go." She disappeared into the hospital.

The rumble of a Harley filled the nearby parking lot as Rocky rolled to a stop. He killed the engine and joined them. "The old man dead?"

Brow furrowed, Crow pondered the closed door. "He was still alive when they rolled him inside."

"Well, we've done our due. What now?"

Tammy shrugged. "We don't have a car, unless you want to take that one." She pointed at the Bel Air.

Crow shook his head, realizing for the first time how strange he felt without his long hair. "Nope. They've been through enough. Rocky, how far is the bus station?"

"It ain't a station, it's a stop. You can barely see it down there."

"Then we'll walk. What about you?"

He shrugged. "I've had enough of California and Arizona. I'll head back the way we came, to Vegas, and check that place out."

Crow grinned. "You're going to see Mel Torme, aren't you?"

His secret pleasure revealed, Rocky nodded. "How about y'all?"

Tammy brightened. "Florida."

"Florida!" Crow crossed his arms. "What in hell for?"

"I want to see a white sand beach." She made a pouty face. "Please, baby? Take me to the beach."

"How do you think we're gonna pay for that?"

She pulled a wad of bills from a jean pocket. She counted them as they watched. "Six one hundred-dollar bills."

Crow stood hipshot and stared at the cash. "How you come to have that?"

"There's a lot of money in LSD. I kept it for Red because he'd spend it all on liquor and grass."

"He didn't know you very well, did he?"

"I'm glad you got there, now. I'd had enough of bikes and the desert, too."

"You're not leaving me again, are you baby?"

"No. I'm here to stay."

Crow hugged Rocky. "Thanks, Brother. Call Mama and check in so I'll know where to find you."

"You do the same."

Without a backward glance, Crow twined his fingers with Tammy's and they left to catch the next bus.

Rocky watched them for a moment, then twisted the key behind his leg and put his boot on the starter. The engine rumbled to life on the first push and he sat there, idling, wondering when Crow's girlfriend would leave him again for the next man, or the next adventure. It wouldn't be long, that's for sure.

Crow had been chasing after her since high school. He never could get it through his head that she was no good. Rocky knew the next time she left and Crow called, he'd quit what he was doing and go.

That's what brothers do.

Betty watched them go with one last prayer. *"Akóó níláahdi naních'į́į́dii bii' hodéezyéél."*

Go find peace.

She walked the opposite direction, singing "O Holy Night," in Navajo.

Chapter Ninety-three

"Pepper!"

Pepper heard Ida Belle's shout from the parking lot. Norma Faye had the key, and they knew which room Pepper was in, but Ida Belle couldn't stand it. She ran from the motel office, flashing past the ice machine to Room 1.

The owner of the motel put Pepper there to keep her as close as possible. He'd called the Flagstaff Police Department despite Norma Faye's arguments, long before they arrived. The officers dropped by to speak with the manager, then Pepper. They found her in front of the TV, full and content as far as they could tell. After a long discussion outside her door, they decided it would be all right for her to spend one night in the room since her mother was on the way, as long as the manager kept an eye on her.

Relieved that she'd been found, the chief sent a patrol car to drop off snacks and teen magazines for Pepper. The car cruised through the horseshoe-shaped motel more than once that night, to make sure everything was quiet.

Still full from breakfast, she was stretched out in the middle of the bed, unconsciously rubbing the feather in her hair and watching "The Guiding Light," or what her mama called "stories" on television. She was bored with it, but there was nothing else to do while she waited. She shot off the bed when she heard her name.

"Hallelujah!" Ida Belle rushed into the room, nearly knocking her daughter down. Weeping and shouting, she checked her daughter for injuries. "Are you all right?"

"I'm fine."

Ida Belle grabbed her shoulders, giving her a shake. "I could kill you."

"I know." Pepper smiled at Norma Faye over her mother's shoulders.

Ida Belle held her at arm's length. "Let me see you. Blow."

"What?"

"Blow."

"What for?"

"This room smells like cigarette smoke. Have you been smoking?"

Norma Faye spoke under her breath. "Oh, Lord. Ida Belle, all motel rooms smell like this."

"Well, smokin's a sin."

"Mama. I haven't been smoking. I've been laying here, watching TV."

"Open your eyes wide."

"Now what?"

"Did you take anything while you were gone? Some of that LSD?" She gave Pepper a shake. "I could pull your head off."

Norma Faye snickered, and Pepper joined her.

"What's so funny, you two?"

Norma Faye hugged them both. "It's all right. She's fine. We have her now. Honey, have you heard anything about Cale?"

"Not a word. Are Daddy and Grandpa coming? Y'all said they were here."

"We haven't heard from them, but I'll call back home in a little while."

Ida Belle regarded the room and the sparse Indian decorations, the wagon wheel headboard, and the one chair beside a round table under a drop light. "Well, this is nice. It even has refrigerated air."

"Can we leave now?" Pepper dropped to the bed.

"Not yet. We're gonna say here a day or so until we hear from your daddy." She sat beside Pepper and patted her leg. "Praise the Lord. I feel so much better now."

Norma Faye took the chair by the window and watched a family load their car. "Well, I told Miss Becky I'd call when we got here and had Pepper with us. Then you know what I think we should do while we wait to hear about James and Grandpa?"

"What?"

"I saw some of the cutest places on the way in from the airport. Why don't we poke around a few of these trading posts and museums to pass the time?"

Pepper forgot who she was with. "Well, shit."

"Pepper!"

Chapter Ninety-four

The jail was completely empty, except for Melva. Cody figured the rain took the aggravation out of people, and they stayed home till the skies cleared. That was all right with him, because it had been way too busy for his taste.

He stopped in front of the cell. She was reading a romance magazine from a stack someone had brought her. "Melva?"

She glanced up. "Can I leave now?"

"No. I think you're gonna be here for a long while. I know about you, from the time you were born in Pea Valley to New Boston. I know about your marriages and your kids. I know how people died. I know about the insurance policy you have on Leland that you aren't going to collect on. You killed him, didn't you Melva? He was walking to Ike's house because you wouldn't give him the keys and you ran him over with Marty's old truck. No one would suspect it, parked right back where it was, but you missed your mark and I saw where it had been moved."

She giggled and shrugged her shoulders. "I don't drive."

"Yes, you do. You don't have a license, and no one ever saw you drive, but you know how. What happened? The poison wasn't working fast enough so you had to run him down?"

Her eyes flashed, and he knew he was right.

He left and sent Deputy White to check the house and barn for arsenic.

He came back three hours later with two bottles and several jars of home-canned jellies and stewed prunes full of the stuff, as was Leland himself.

He was too tough to die from it.

Four hours later, in the same room where her son confessed to his participation in the murders of two men, a sociopath named Melva Hale stuck her tongue out and wrote of how she'd killed men, women, and babies because they annoyed her.

Chapter Ninety-five

I tell you what, a lot of things popped around here at the same time. The phone rang with all kinds of good news, after we heard some bad news first.

Uncle James called to tell us that Grandpa was in the hospital in Kingman. The doctor explained to Miss Becky the infection in there was one of the worst things that could have happened and it nearly killed him. They had to do some emergency surgery on his bullet wound and got it stopped, but barely, by using that thick white penicillin that hurt so bad when they gave it to me in a shot. They gave him gallons of the stuff, the way they talked.

Uncle Cody bought Miss Becky a plane ticket, and she flew out there to meet Uncle James, Norma Faye, and Aunt Ida Belle in Flagstaff, then they drove on out to see to Grandpa. Everybody, including that fartknocker Cale Westlake, got a trip out West but me and Uncle Cody. Even though I did the right thing all around, I had to stay with him at night after I got home from school.

It wasn't fair.

Grandpa took a while to get better, but after a week, they let him come home. He still had drains in him, though, and once he was back, he kept having to take even more penicillin for a long time.

The first week of December was cold, and Sunday dinner was more like Thanksgiving. The house was full with folks laughing and talking. When Miss Becky called everyone to eat, I saw two more plates set at the corners of the table with cane-bottom chairs pulled up there. They were for me and Pepper. That's when I knew things had changed and the adults didn't think of us as little kids anymore.

We sat down at our places and Grandpa was filling his plate with mashed potatoes and peas. Though his stomach was better, the doctors still had him on soft foods for a while, but I could tell it was aggravating him, because he dearly loved Miss Becky's fried chicken.

Uncle Cody took a chicken leg off the platter. "Anna'll be back to work after Christmas."

Grandpa salted his potatoes. "She's the best thing you've done since you took the sheriff's job."

Everyone laughed and Uncle Cody passed the beans. "Oh, like solving the murder of two strangers here in town, and getting convictions on Melva Hale for all those murders through the years."

"I believe Anna had a hand in most of that, and Top," Grandpa said. I felt myself blushing, but appreciated his acknowledgement that I'd done the right thing.

"I can't believe that crazy old woman confessed to killing a bunch of people, and even her own grandbaby that she said was born dead." Norma Faye came around with the tea pitcher.

"They said Leland would have died anyway, without being run over, because his body had enough arsenic in it to kill a normal person." Grandpa picked a biscuit apart. "Her problem was she got impatient, and that's what finally caught up with her."

"Well, Marty'll be in prison for life. Like mother, like son."

Miss Becky and Aunt Ida Belle kept checking on Pepper like she was gonna slip out a window and be gone again. I couldn't stand it anymore and figured as long as I was an adult at the table, or almost an adult, anyways, I could start my own conversation. "Hey Pepper, so how was your trip?"

We hadn't much talked about her running away. I figured at first she'd talk about it, but she didn't have much to say.

Everyone at the table got quiet and I wondered if I'd made a mistake. She shrugged and locked her fingers together over her empty plate. "Living on the road wasn't much fun. We hitched quite a bit, but we walked a lot, too."

The silence after that stretched for a while, and I figured the old folks at the table were thinking way too hard.

"Did you get enough to eat?"

"We were lucky, we had Cale's money for a while." She stopped, remembering where the money came from, so she plowed on ahead to get out of that particular row. "But a lot of the kids had to panhandle, or beg for food, if they couldn't find anything out behind the restaurants. We did better, but we were still hungry most of the time."

"What'd you think of it?" I cut my eyes toward Miss Becky, realizing she was nudging the conversation toward the catch pen she favored.

Pepper saw the chute Miss Becky was herding her toward, but wouldn't have any of it. "The worst part is all that free love crap. I had to slap some jaws to get those guys to leave me alone."

Aunt Ida Belle covered her mouth in shock, but Uncle Cody threw his head back and laughed. "Atta girl! Keep 'em at a distance."

Miss Becky wouldn't quit. "What did you learn?"

All those strong-willed women were after the answers they needed, and so I backed out to listen.

Pepper gave up and gave them what they wanted. I think she was wanting to tell them how she felt, and that the whole thing had been a mistake. It was just the opening she needed. "While I was gone, I realized that things are about the same no matter where you go." She ran a thumb up and down her sweating tea glass. "You know, this place isn't as bad as I thought, in some ways. Most everybody here at least tries to take care of one another."

"Folks should be that way everywhere," Miss Becky said, satisfied by what she heard.

"Well, it kicked in with Cale." Grandpa dipped a spoonful of beans. "I've never seen such a change in a person. He's cut his hair and took a job up at the old folks home in Chisum. They say he's doing a good job there, taking care of them that's worst off. I hear he's started working at the hospital some, too. Says he wants to make a doctor when he's grown."

"Praise the Lord." Miss Becky held a hand skyward.

They were getting close to following a different trail, but I wanted some answers to things that I didn't understand. "It was a good thing you left, though." Pepper raised her eyebrows at me. "John T. was looking for you, and if you hadn't gone, he might have done something bad."

Aunt Ida Belle pursed her mouth. "We don't need to talk about that."

"Top's right." Uncle Cody gave me a wink. "John T. was up to no good. He was the worst of the bunch, and I don't doubt he'd have hurt Pepper. It's good that she got out of the line of fire for a while until we figured it all out. I hate for any man to die, but that one was a rabid dog, and there's only one thing to do with them. You put 'em down. Like Ned says, some folks just need killin'."

"Those others will do their time in jail." Grandpa was ready to eat, but all the talk had us stalled for a minute. "Marty's just like his mama, and I believe he did a lot more meanness than we'll ever know. Freddy, though, is another thing altogether. He'll be all right when he gets out of Huntsville, and he'll get a job where he won't have to talk much. "

"Bless his heart." Miss Becky finally quit fiddling around and sat down.

"Ned told us not all the folks y'all ran into was our kind of people." Aunt Ida Belle remembered what Grandpa told us about his search for Pepper. "There was the young boy in Dallas that had something to do with women...."

"That'd be a pimp," Uncle Cody said, grinning.

"Well, I won't speak such words, but from everything I heard, I believe I'll stay right here where I know people."

"Some of the ones you know, you can't trust." Uncle Cody glanced out the window, as if someone were coming up the drive to give us bad news.

Miss Becky finally took her seat. "Grandpa said the only light he saw while they were gone was the Indian woman who prayed for him in the backseat of the car."

You couldn't convince Grandpa it was an Indian woman, though. He swore up and down that it was Tom Bell who met them at the hospital to say a prayer. We all knew Mr. Tom was gone, but he said that right after they talked, he got easy and everything came together. Once he was in the emergency room, Uncle James called home to tell Miss Becky and he found out that Aunt Ida Belle and Norma Faye were with Pepper and only two hours away in a Flagstaff motel.

Miss Becky reached out and stroked Pepper's long hair. "Honey, the world is full of dark places, but the light is here, in *this* place, with us. We're thankful that you're home."

I saw that the conversation drifted away from what I wanted to know about Pepper's trip, but that's how adult conversations go. "You think that Crow feller will ever show up?"

Grandpa shook his head. "He's a drifter, a travelin' man."

"He was a liar, a thief, and as sorry as the day is long."

"Ida Belle, you weren't there." Uncle James motioned for her to be quiet. "You weren't there. Crow didn't do right by us, but at the same time, he got us close to Pepper and in a roundabout way, saved Dad."

I'd heard bits and pieces of what happened in the desert, but they didn't talk about it much when us kids were around.

"Crow was sent to us," Grandpa said. "I believe in a way that this family has a guardian angel watching over us, and sometimes that angel nudges people in our direction to do what needs doin'."

I noticed Grandpa's ice-blue eyes were moist and everyone got quiet around the table. "Crow was meant to be there at just the right time. What he did wasn't right, but it wasn't completely wrong, neither. We'd have helped him find that gal of his, if it had been around here under different circumstances. He used us, but if you look at it, we were using him to find Pepper, so there ain't no fault. Now, bow your heads."

Grandpa cleared his throat for the blessing, but Pepper interrupted. "Grandpa? Can I do it?"

Miss Becky smiled. "Why sure, hon."

We bowed our heads.

"Dear Lord, thank you for this family...."

After that, I didn't pay much attention to what Pepper said, because it was the same one we all used. I was kinda glad, because it gave me more time to think about what was going on in my own head about her being home again...and that was the best part.

But I couldn't get my new job off my mind, the one Uncle Cody got for me, taking care of Doc Daingerfield's stupid monkey until he came back from Dallas, after Christmas.